KT-548-902

Canadian **Dani Collins** knew in high school that she wanted to write romance for a living. Twenty-five years later, after marrying her high school sweetheart, having two kids with him, working at several generic office jobs and submitting countless manuscripts, she got The Call. Her first Mills & Boon novel won the Reviewers' Choice Award for Best First in Series from *RT Book Reviews*. She now works in her own office, writing romance.

USA TODAY bestselling, RITA®-nominated, and critically acclaimed author **Caitlin Crews** has written more than 100 books and counting. She has a Master's and a PhD in English Literature, thinks everyone should read more category romance, and is always available to discuss her beloved alpha heroes. Just ask. She lives in the Pacific Northwest with her comic book artist husband, she is always planning her next trip, and she will never, ever, read all the books in her 'to-be-read' pile. Thank goodness.

ACC. No: 05208359

Also by Dani Collins

Innocent in the Sheikh's Palace
What the Greek's Wife Needs
Her Impossible Baby Bombshell

Signed, Sealed…Seduced collection

Ways to Ruin a Royal Reputation

The Secret Sisters miniseries

Married for One Reason Only

Also by Caitlin Crews

Chosen for His Desert Throne

Royal Christmas Weddings miniseries

Christmas in the King's Bed
His Scandalous Christmas Princess

Rich, Ruthless & Greek miniseries

The Secret That Can't Be Hidden
Her Deal with the Greek Devil

Discover more at millsandboon.co.uk.

MANHATTAN'S MOST SCANDALOUS REUNION

DANI COLLINS

THE SICILIAN'S FORGOTTEN WIFE

CAITLIN CREWS

MILLS & BOON

All rights reserved including the right of reproduction
in whole or in part in any form. This edition is published
by arrangement with Harlequin Books S.A.

This is a work of fiction. Names, characters, places, locations
and incidents are purely fictional and bear no relationship to
any real life individuals, living or dead, or to any actual places,
business establishments, locations, events or incidents.
Any resemblance is entirely coincidental.

This book is sold subject to the condition that it shall not,
by way of trade or otherwise, be lent, resold, hired out
or otherwise circulated without the prior consent of the publisher
in any form of binding or cover other than that in which it is published
and without a similar condition including this condition
being imposed on the subsequent purchaser.

® and TM are trademarks owned and used by the trademark owner
and/or its licensee. Trademarks marked with ® are registered with the
United Kingdom Patent Office and/or the Office for Harmonisation
in the Internal Market and in other countries.

First Published in Great Britain 2021
by Mills & Boon, an imprint of HarperCollins*Publishers* Ltd,
1 London Bridge Street, London, SE1 9GF

www.harpercollins.co.uk

HarperCollins*Publishers*
1st Floor, Watermarque Building,
Ringsend Road, Dublin 4, Ireland

Manhattan's Most Scandalous Reunion © 2021 Dani Collins

The Sicilian's Forgotten Wife © 2021 Caitlin Crews

ISBN: 978-0-263-28259-7

08/21

MIX
Paper from
responsible sources
FSC® C007454

This book is produced from independently certified FSC™ paper
to ensure responsible forest management.
For more information visit www.harpercollins.co.uk/green.

Printed and bound in Spain
by CPI, Barcelona

MANHATTAN'S MOST SCANDALOUS REUNION

DANI COLLINS

MILLS & BOON

To Doug,
who graciously accepts the burden
of being married to a writer.
I love you.

CHAPTER ONE

NINA MENENDEZ WAS having a garbage day on top of a painful month in what was starting to look like a horrendous year. She'd didn't need a pesky man with a camera getting in her face, accusing her of being someone she wasn't.

"Oriel! Hey, Oriel."

Especially not that woman.

Nina's heart lurched in one direction while she veered in another, trying to hurry away from the Manhattan hotel where she'd tanked an interview with a British film star in town for a talk show. Nina didn't even want to go into costume design. Did she? She didn't know anymore. She didn't know who she was or what she wanted. Everything was wrong in her world. She might as well go to the garden and eat worms.

If she only *had* a garden. At the rate she was going, worms were all she could afford.

"Oriel. Why are you here? Where is your husband?" The photographer skipped alongside her, maniacally snapping his camera in her face.

Paparazzi hung around the entrance to swanky hotels like that hoping to ambush the celebrities who stayed there. In her case, she'd been trying to get on with an indie project that the star was producing for herself in

London. It wasn't a big budget, and Nina had only been granted an appointment thanks to a friend pulling strings, but she'd said all the wrong things and was beating herself up over what felt like self-sabotage.

"Are you working again?"

Well, that was just mean, wasn't it? She almost used her subway language, but kept walking, ignoring him.

The photographer kept after her and some of his colleagues did, too. They nipped like hyenas with baiting questions as they tried to get her attention.

"Why aren't you in India?"

"Is it true you're pregnant?"

"Look." She had to stop at the corner to wait for a car to turn in front of her. "I know who Oriel Cuvier is, but I've never met her. I just happen to look a little bit like her." Freakishly very much like her, but Nina was trying really hard not to think about that.

Being accosted and mistaken *as* her wasn't helping. Why had she thought coming back to New York was a good idea? Oh, right, to find out *why* she looked so much like a stranger.

"Who are you then?" one demanded, following her into the next block.

"Nobody. Go home and compare our photos."

That's what Nina had done after a friend from work— back when she had *had* a job—had remarked on how much she resembled the French model. That had been eons ago, when Nina had arrived in New York for the first time, bright-eyed and full of dreams. The photo of Oriel Cuvier on a runway had been making the rounds in fashion circles for the professionally tattered and much-lauded gown she had been modeling.

Nina had found their similarities unnerving, but other events had soon consumed her.

Now, after licking her wounds in Albuquerque for three months, she'd scrambled to get back here for that stupid interview, and it was the worst possible timing.

Oriel's star had already been rising, but Nina had nursed vague hopes of crossing paths with her. As she had arrived, however, Oriel had slipped out of the city, emerging in India, where she promptly began to dominate international headlines.

Oriel Cuvier was the previously unknown daughter of a Bollywood screen queen, and photographers were positively rabid to catch a photo of her.

"Her hair is different," Nina pointed out, mostly to shut them up. Thanks to Nina's sister's love of tints, Nina had streaks of pinkish red in her otherwise very similar near-black hair. Of course, the streaks were hidden by the half bun she wore. She'd been trying to look professional for her job interview. Maybe that had been her mistake. Maybe they had wanted someone with flair.

Maybe she should quit worrying what others thought of her and be herself. Who was she, though? Ignoring the twist of anxiety that went through her, she kept talking.

"Her mouth is different, too." The model's wealthy parents had been able to afford braces. Nina had a slight overbite. Hopefully, the photographers wouldn't look beyond that, because the shape of their full lips matched perfectly.

"Her profile says she's five-eleven. I'm five-nine." And three-quarters. Basically five-ten. Today, however, she was so dispirited she was probably five-three. "I'm not her."

"Who are you then? Talk to us. Are you related to her?"

"Why are you still bothering me?" She walked faster, annoyed, and also growing alarmed. She was a twenty-five-year-old woman being swarmed by a half-dozen men. The bustling people they passed averted their gazes, signaling they didn't want to get involved.

"Tell us why you're not in India. Oriel!" One of the men grabbed her arm.

Nina's self-defense training kicked in. She spun and jammed the heel of her palm into his nose.

The impact reverberated from her wrist to her elbow, all the way to her shoulder. A jarring rush of adrenaline poured through her chest like fire. She bounced back on light feet while her bag fell off her shoulder and swayed on her arm, knocking against her knee.

The man swore and bent, blood from his nose painting the sidewalk in bright blotches. The rest of the men fanned out, jeering and swinging their camera lenses between the injured man, who was straightening with a look of retribution in his eyes, and whatever terror was written into Nina's expression.

Dear God, they were everywhere. She was surrounded. Her airway tightened and her wild gaze swerved every direction, seeking a path of escape.

A blue-and-silver awning struck her eyes. She had walked in this direction unconsciously on purpose because, deep down, she was a masochist.

Normally, she would have stayed on this side of the street and glared upward as she walked by, but in her agitation, she darted straight for the entrance, not computing that she was running into traffic.

A car squealed its brakes and stopped on a dime right before it would have struck her. The driver laid on the horn, then honked again as the horde of cameramen chased her, all of them batting and bumping into the car in their haste to get around it.

Nina brushed past the startled doorman and ran inside, straight to the security desk where Amir sat today.

"I'm sorry. Please, can I stand here a few minutes while I figure out what to do? They won't leave me alone."

She was quivering with reaction, breathless and barely able to speak. She looked back to see the doorman holding out his arms while he ordered the men, "Back off! No entry."

Amir frowned at her, then at the disruption outside. One of the men evaded the doorman and pressed his camera lens to the window, clicking and flashing through the glass.

Amir picked up his phone and dialed.

Was he calling the police? Nina's scrambled brain tried to decide whether she should involve them.

"It's Amir, sir. Ms. Menendez is here in the lobby."

"What?" she whispered. "I didn't come here to see *him*."

Her stomach began to churn. She held her breath in dread-filled anticipation.

"Yes, I understand, sir. But she seems upset."

Her heart stalled out. How humiliating. After seducing her and leading her on, Reve had dumped her when she had asked if he wanted to meet her father. Three months later, he didn't even want to see her.

She covered her face, turning her back to the windows so she had a shred of privacy while she tried to think of where she could go or who she might call. The few friends she'd made in New York had fallen away when she'd been fired and moved in with Reve. And the friend who'd gotten her today's interview lived in London. The one who was loaning her his studio was backpacking in Australia.

She didn't know what to do. She was upset by more

than the fact those men had chased her. It was everything that had happened lately. Her ears were rushing with the sound of her galloping pulse. Her life was falling apart at the seams, but she couldn't crawl home this time. Where *was* home? *Who was she?*

"Miss…" Amir's voice was loud enough to make her jerk her head up. His frown told her he'd had to repeat himself to get her attention. She saw he had opened the doors for Reve's private elevator.

"Mr. Weston will see you. Would you like me to come with you? You seem unsteady."

She stared into the elevator, longing to see Reve even though she knew he only pretended to rescue damsels. Deep down, he was more of a dragon who lured them in and ate them.

Still, she could hear the doorman arguing with the men outside. She had to leave the lobby so they would disperse. She desperately needed to be transported out of her entire overturned, mixed-up life, and, God knows, Reve's world was the furthest thing from her own.

Her feet moved her into the elevator, and she instantly flashed back to what seemed like a million years ago but was really only three months ago. She had felt on top of the world then. Staying in a penthouse apartment over-looking Central Park had a way of doing that to a person.

She had stood right here every day, convinced she was in love and barreling toward happily-ever-after. Rather than work for someone else, she had begun to sew her own collection. She had anticipated that, by the end of summer, she would have enough for her own show at fashion week. Just a small thing that was more like a gallery showing, but it would gain her exposure, help her network and maybe glean her a few orders from bou-tiques. She'd flounced about in her own creations, each one set off with handbags and shoes and bangles that Reve had paid for.

She'd left it all when she'd walked out, sickened that she had let him buy her for the price of soutache and organza, Microtex needles and glass-headed pins.

Oh, how the mighty had fallen. Today she wore a simple maxi-dress she'd made from fabrics leftover from her college days. The knot of hair behind her crown had begun to fray while her natural waves had picked up the summer humidity, and flyaway strands were sticking to her face and shoulders.

She had hoped this look would project that she was casually chic, approachable and open to collaboration. Unfortunately, her portfolio said she hadn't worked since last year and never in costume design. She wasn't going anywhere and had nowhere else to go.

Being so self-pitying wasn't her usual MO, but even her reflection had ceased to feel like it was hers. Not when another woman had claim to it. Not when defeat dragged at the corners of her mouth and her eyes were hollow from weeks of sleepless nights. The dusting of makeup she'd put on this morning stood out starkly on a complexion that was a pallid version of her natural golden tan.

The elevator stopped and the doors opened, startling her again.

For one second, she had forgotten what had sent her rushing into Reve's building. She had to quell a compulsion to hurry into the belly of the penthouse in search of him the way she used to, calling his name.

Oh, what she wouldn't give to throw herself into him and feel his strong arms close around her. To let him kiss the hell out of her and take her to bed before barely three words had passed between them. The outside world had always ceased to matter when they were lost in passion.

That was all in the past. And as much as she would love to hide from reality, she had learned that it eventually had to be confronted.

She stepped tentatively into the foyer with its gold-veined marble and a round table holding a floral arrangement that was replaced every three days.

"Nina." He appeared abruptly from the hallway to the bedrooms.

The mere sound of his voice awakened her blood. The sight of him fed a thirst she had vainly tried to ignore since she had left.

He wore crisp, dark gray trousers and his feet were bare. He was shrugging on a blue-and-white-striped shirt over his muscled chest and flat abs. There was a faint glow beneath his winter-in-Florida tan and a sheen upon it. His dark hair was damp and messy.

Even amid her confusion of shock and fear and dread, she was taken aback by how ruggedly handsome he was. The uncontrollable attraction she'd felt from her first glimpse of him burst to life inside her, starved for that hint of curl in his dark brown hair, his steely blue eyes, his square jaw and his impervious air of assurance.

It felt so good to see him again that a smile began to tingle in her cheeks and pull at her mouth before a painful realization struck like a jagged spear of lightning, cleaving her apart and leaving her soul nothing but an acrid whiff of its former self.

"You're with someone." She knew how he looked when he was climbing out of bed after lovemaking. *Like this.*

Her knees went weak. She was so nauseated by despair, she lowered herself onto the upholstered bench by the elevator and leaned forward, trying to keep herself from fainting.

This was what a mental breakdown felt like. In her head, she had known he would move on. Confronting it like this was the final straw, though. She was flattened. Destroyed. She couldn't face him. She had to go, but her legs refused to work.

"I'm alone," Reve said in a clipped voice. "I was showering after my workout when Amir called. But I am on my way out."

That sounded like a warning. *Don't get comfortable.*

She lifted her head and, despite the standoffish wall that seemed to form a barrier between them, his gaze searched hers. Maybe, if she hadn't been at the very end of her rope, she might have thought there was a wary tension deep inside that look.

"Why are you here?" He scanned her thoroughly from her disheveled hair to her open-toed sandals, and whatever he saw made his brows slam together, thunderstruck. "Are you pregnant?"

"What?" She sat up so fast she bumped her head on the wall behind her and had to rub the hurt away. "*No. Gawd*, that's all I would need right now."

Only a complete fool would mourn the fact she had no lifetime reminder of her gullibility in getting involved with him. Then she must be a fool, because not being accidentally pregnant by him had made her very blue.

"Why do you think I'm pregnant?" Her dress was loose because it was midday and the hottest June on record, but she hadn't gained any weight. She was one of those annoying people with a high metabolism and had been told her whole life she could be a model or a basketball player. The second one had always been discounted about five seconds after she fumbled the ball and chased it, kicking it away in the process.

"You look like you're going to faint. Are you ill?" He had instantly gone deep inside himself in the infuriating way he had, becoming impossible to read.

"I'm fine." She really wasn't.

"Then why are you here? For your things?" He looked to each of his cuffs as he buttoned them, all business. "I texted to ask what you wanted me to do with it."

She had blocked him. She had feared if she started talking to him, she would fall right back under his spell. Which she was in danger of doing right now. *Help me, Reve. Save me. Love me.*

"This was a mistake—" She rose abruptly, and the blood rushed from her head. She set a hand on the wall as she swayed dizzily.

Reve quickly stepped forward to catch at her.

She just as quickly pulled away, brushing his hands off her. She was pretty sure she would dissolve into tears if he touched her. In her haste, she staggered into the bench, dislodging it and causing its feet to screech on the marble.

It was classic clumsy, reflexive Nina, but her panicked reaction had shocked him. She saw his eyes flash with outraged astonishment, then a shadow of stunned hurt.

He quickly blinked it away and took a few steps back, holding up his hands.

"You're totally safe here, Nina." Now his voice was grave and reassuring and nonthreatening enough to make her all wobbly inside.

She was acting hysterical. She *was* hysterical. It was taking everything for her to hold back the tears swelling in her throat.

"I just need somewhere to collect my thoughts," she mumbled, feeling foolish and messy and horribly gauche.

Was this why he hadn't wanted a future with her? Her whole family found her disorganized and overly sensitive and somewhat oblivious.

It was true. She often didn't have a single clue despite what might be staring her in the face. She led with her heart and saw only what she wanted to see. That's how she'd missed the fact she wasn't actually related to any of her relations. That's how she'd mistaken a wealthy man's desire for a mistress as love at first sight.

"Do you want to come sit down?" He waved toward the living room.

She moved into the familiar space of his penthouse with its vaulted ceiling and wall of windows looking onto the terrace. As she sank into her favorite corner of the overstuffed sectional, the one that faced the fireplace, she pulled the cushion from behind her back and hugged it.

"Would you like something? Coffee? Tea? A drink?" He was keeping his distance, which made her feel again like she was being melodramatic.

It was his influence making her act this way, she wanted to say. When she was with him, he sharpened her reactions to everything. The sun shone brighter, food tasted better. Orgasms became otherworldly.

"No," she murmured, biting her lip to distract herself from how much she had missed him.

It's okay to love someone who doesn't return your feelings, her sister had said when Nina had crawled home, a failure on all fronts. *You still got to feel it. Love is never wasted.*

Easy for her to say, married to her high school sweetheart and still deeply in love.

"Do you want me to call the police?" Reve's carefully neutral tone was unnerving. He was an assertive man who always knew what he wanted. When he had an opinion, he voiced it. If he thought a certain action should be taken, he took it.

Treating her as though she was made of spun sugar was making her unravel even faster.

"I haven't been attacked," she mumbled.

"There's blood on your bag. And your hand." His voice wasn't quite steady. His shoulders were a tense line.

She realized he was boiling with rage beneath that clenched jaw. She looked to the floor where she'd dropped her shoulder bag. One of the sagging ropes that formed the handle held a streak of red. The heel of her palm also had blood on it.

Wonderful. Now she had to scrounge up the energy to go to the powder room.

"I shouldn't have barged in on you like this." She rubbed her thumb on the stain. "I was at a job interview a few blocks over. Paparazzi chased me when I came out of the hotel. One grabbed me and I punched him in the nose."

"Because you and I were involved?" Reve's frown was instantly thunderous. He hated sensational publicity. *Hated* it.

He picked up his phone, not waiting for her to clarify before he spoke to someone she presumed was Amir. "Get the names of the men outside. Let them know charges of assault will be forthcoming." He ended the call.

"Against me?" she asked with a thin laugh. "*I* hit *him*."

"Good." He moved to the wet bar and soaked a cloth under the tap. "We've all wanted to do it."

"*Not* good. I feel awful about it."

He gave the cloth a hard twist to wring it out and brought it to her. "We're all entitled to defend ourselves. I guess those classes your sister dragged you to paid off."

He remembered her telling him that? She'd mentioned

it the first time he'd offered to drive her home so she wouldn't have to take the subway. The classes had been the only way her sister would allow her to leave for New York alone.

"Thank you." Nina accepted the cloth and wiped her hands clean. "But it wasn't about you."

How strange to acknowledge that when her life had been revolving around him from the moment she had met him on New Year's Eve. She'd been at the party as an assistant to her former employer, Kelly Bex, one of New York's top designers. Kelly had wanted to snare Reve's attention for herself, not that Nina had realized it. Seriously, she was *so* clueless.

"Be nice to him," Kelly had said. So Nina had made a point of introducing herself, saying something that had made him laugh. She hadn't realized he was a self-made bazillionaire who had gotten his start selling used car parts and was now a driving force—pun intended—in autonomous vehicles.

They'd chatted for a half hour and, rather than going home with Kelly, Reve had taken Nina's number, asking her to dinner the next evening. Nina had mentioned it to Kelly at work the next day, innocent as a spring lamb, asking if there was anything Kelly wanted Nina to bring up with him.

While Reve had seduced Nina that night, Kelly had browsed recipes for cooking and eating the hearts of her enemies. It wasn't until Nina was holding a cardboard box of her things on the street a few days later that she'd realized she'd been fired in direct retaliation for her budding affair with Reve. Her roommate at the time had also been an employee of Kelly's, so Nina had lost her sublet, too.

Reve was a much faster study. He'd understood the dynamic straight away but hadn't been particularly remorseful. However, since Nina had had no job and no home, he'd taken her in and offered to make reparations by supporting her career aspirations. She had let him act like a superhero because she had thought he believed in her work and wanted her to succeed.

He had wanted her in his bed. That was all. That was the happily-never-after to that story.

Even after she'd figured it out and tried to move on, he had affected her life. He'd left her so hollowed out she'd abandoned her dreams and scurried back to Albuquerque, where she had struggled to even look for work. She had lived with her father and swept hair in her sister's salon. When she did go on interviews, she failed to land jobs because she was walking around with such an angry look on her face.

Not today, though. Weirdly, this thing with Oriel Cuvier wasn't about him. At least, it hadn't been until she had run in here and drawn him into it.

Oh, heck. He was going to kill her when he realized that.

Reve took the cloth and threw it all the way across the room, where it landed in the sink with a dull thud.

"Why are they chasing you, then?" He dropped into the armchair that faced her. "Some other man you're seeing?"

She could have barked out a wild laugh at that. What did he think? That she had walked out on him for turning her into a paid escort so she could take up with another man in exactly the same capacity? As if she could even think about other men after him. Even as she sat here, she was thinking, *Why couldn't you have loved me just a little?*

She gave herself a mental shake and said facetiously, "Yes. Duke Rhodes." Oriel Cuvier had been at a premiere in Cannes with the actor six weeks ago. That's what had started Nina down this rocky path of self-discovery. "Haven't you seen our photos?"

"The has-been from those 'Frantic and Fuming' action movies?" He grimaced. "He's too old for you."

"I'm being sarcastic," she said with exasperation. "You really haven't seen them?"

"You blocked me, Nina," he said in a tone that was falsely pleasant. "How could I see any of the photos you post?"

Wasn't it supposed to feel satisfying when the object of your block realized it? She just felt petty and obvious. Now he knew how much he'd hurt her.

"They're not my photos. They're on the entertainment sites."

"I don't look at that garbage." His face hardened with genuine anger. "But if they're chasing you because of him, why the hell would you lead those vultures to *me*?"

CHAPTER TWO

"I DIDN'T! I was across the street and they surrounded me. I panicked and ran to what was familiar." She hugged the pillow she was still holding. "I didn't expect Amir to call you." Her chin trembled. "I just wanted to catch my breath."

Reve had been born skeptical. The life he'd led had honed his cynicism to a razor-sharp edge. The first time Nina had spoken to him, he'd seen her angle. She'd been cutting in line ahead of her own employer, a shark of a woman named Kelly Bex, to get to him.

That put Nina on his own level of ruthless buccaneering—not devoid of a conscience, but willing to leap on an opportunity when it presented itself in a bespoke suit with a Patek Philippe wristwatch and a gold credit card made from actual gold.

He respected that. Plus, she was pretty as hell. Mesmerizing with her silky, shiny hair and her expressive brows and her delicate oval face. She was curious and interesting and made him laugh, so he'd let her run her game. Why not? He liked to play as hard as worked.

He'd thought he was embarking on an affair with a like-minded partner, but their relationship hadn't gone the way he'd expected. Nina possessed an artistic temperament. She was naturally passionate and sensitive and effusive. She challenged his assumptions, and pushed up against him and *excited* him. Sparks had constantly been flying, especially in the bedroom. They were an A-hazard combustible combination, and his body refused to forget it.

The lust she provoked in him had been her ticket into this penthouse. He'd known he was being a fool. Emotions were a tool for manipulating a reaction. He sat in marketing meetings all the time where they discussed how to stir up envy and turn it into a luxury car purchase, but he'd still allowed her to enthrall him.

When she had stormed out because he had declined to eat dinner with her father, he'd seen it as a tantrum intended to bring him to heel. He'd balked—hard—expecting her to come back once she cooled off, but she hadn't.

Her social feeds had reassured him she was alive and spending time with her father, and then three days later he'd seen a "good to be home" post. The phone he'd bought her turned up at the desk downstairs, and he discovered she had blocked him from every aspect of her life.

That abrupt cutting of ties had thrust him into a fractured moment of fearing he had genuinely hurt her. Dread had leaned a sharp elbow into his integrity. He wasn't the most moral of men, but he didn't *harm* people. He didn't use them up and throw them away.

He didn't need them, either, but he felt her absence more keenly than he'd expected. It still put a sick knot in his gut recalling how discarded he'd felt for those few dark minutes.

Then he'd remembered that she'd left her precious sewing machine. This whole charade was a taunt. She had wanted him to chase her, but he refused. He'd sat back and waited, knowing she would turn up when she was ready, and here she was.

The part where she was claiming to have been chased here by paparazzi was an odd way to save face. Definitely *not* the quickest way into his good graces, but he knew how nightmarish those scrums could be and she seemed genuinely distressed. There was a haunted look around her eyes. Tension pulled at the corners of her mouth. Her cheekbones stood out as though she'd lost a few pounds. She was naturally slender and tall, but she had never struck him as fragile.

His heart sat crooked in his chest as he realized she hadn't smiled once yet. In fact, she looked like a rabbit run to ground.

"Are you sure they didn't hurt you?" he asked with gruff concern.

He was still twitching with adrenaline from noticing the blood on her hand. For a few seconds, he'd gone to a very violent place. He'd always been a scrapper, but today, imagining someone had hurt her so badly she was terrified of him, he had known he could kill.

It was sobering. And a stark reminder that she brought more tumult into his life than was comfortable. In fact, he was sitting here filtering through a thousand reactions when he ought to have already dismissed her from his life and left for his engagement.

"I'm fine." She was rubbing her thumb into the heel of her palm. "I might have a bruise later, but I'm just…" She heaved a sigh that contained a metric ton of despair. "Tired."

That he believed. The way she stared sightlessly at the fireplace, her mouth pouty with desolation, bothered him. He didn't like seeing her like this, trampled and sad. It slipped past the armor he was donning and sank like an ice pick in his gut.

He fought softening toward her while she blinked slowly once, twice, then drew a breath and shot him a tight, brave, flat-lipped stretch of her lips that was evidently supposed to be a smile. She set aside the pillow.

"You're right. I shouldn't have come to you."

His lungs tightened in a very visceral reaction. Why not him?

This was her strange power over him, though. She said and did things that tugged reactions from him with a barbed hook. He didn't want to be the sort of man who could be led by his emotions. It left him open to all sorts of strikes.

He clenched his jaw against any declarations of concern or offers to help and stood.

She rose and shouldered her bag, tugging her hair free from the strap, making him want to reacquaint himself with how satin-cool those wavy tendrils were and how warm and smooth her skin was.

He jerked his gaze away. "I'll take you out through the underground parking and drop you wherever you're staying." It was the decent thing to do. That was the only reason he offered.

"A subway station is fine, thanks."

"I'll take you home," he insisted. "Your things are in storage downstairs. It will only take a minute to have them load—"

"No." She hit him with a look that accused him of hate crimes. "Why do you still have it? Sell it. Give it away. Throw it away. I don't care, but it's not mine." She disappeared into the powder room and slammed the door.

And there was the flare of temper that lit his own,

making him want to bang on the door and demand she explain herself.

No. He wouldn't let her manipulate him again.

He went down the hall to finish dressing, determined to end their association once and for all. Determined to ignore the gravel that sat heavy in his stomach as he did.

"Do you need a few more minutes?" Reve asked stiffly as she joined him in the elevator. He'd put on a tie and jacket and looked fantastic, the bastard.

Nina looked and felt like the crumpled tissues in her hand. She was as tired of crying as she was of everything else, but why had he thrown her shattered dreams in her face like that? Why?

"I'm fine." She felt his gaze on the side of her face, intense enough to leave a radiation burn.

His car was waiting by the elevator when it opened. He moved to open the back door himself and she slid in, slouching down even though the windows were tinted.

He came in beside her and gave her a disgruntled look, then flicked his gaze to their surroundings as though checking for cameramen.

"Where are you staying?" he asked.

"Lower East Side."

"Where?"

"A friend's studio. His lease runs out at the end of the month and he's in Australia. He said I could use it. The price was right." She spoke with indifference, as though she wasn't dreading going back there. "Drop me at whichever subway station is along the way," she told the driver, adding to Reve, "I don't want to keep you from…whoever you're seeing."

She flicked her gaze to his razor-sharp lapels, trying not to contemplate who he'd dressed to see.

"It's a lobbying fundraiser," he said.

"Oh, well, you know I'd love nothing better than to keep you from giving crooked politicians your money. Take me home, then," she said facetiously.

"Sorry to disappoint, but I've already paid for the tickets. Lower East Side," Reve said to the driver, and closed the privacy screen.

"I was being sarcastic. The subway is fine."

He put up a finger as he dialed his phone and brought it to his ear.

She looked out the window. The word *tickets*—plural—had stuck like a blade in her stomach. The knife twisted as she heard a woman's voice answer his call.

"I'm running late," Reve said. "I'll meet you there."

Nina did her best to transport herself out of body while the woman promised to "tell Daddy" and said, "See you soon."

"Dating a politician's daughter is not the way to stay out of the spotlight," she remarked pithily when he ended his call.

"It's cocktails on the lawn. I don't *make* the rules, you know. I simply play them to my advantage."

"Sounds like you're playing *her*." She used the voice of experience.

"She called me to say that if I bought the very overpriced tickets, she would join me to make introductions." He dropped his phone into the inside pocket of his jacket. "That's how the system works, and that's how I have a chance to swing things into better practices than the ones you hate. I recently succeeded in getting emissions regulations tightened, so you're welcome. Breathe easier."

"Don't act like that was about the planet. You're only trying to make the field more even for your hydrogen fuel cells."

"Air quality still wins."

True. And she wasn't swiping at him for chasing political influence. She was jealous. That was the ugly bottom line.

They drove several blocks in silence, the commuter traffic heavy but not awful.

"Why are *you* in the spotlight?" he asked in a tone shaded with skepticism. "You never said."

"It's a long and b—" She'd started to say *boring*, but it was tragic and painful and confusing and life changing. Potentially more so, if she pursued it, but she didn't think she had a choice. Not if she was being chased through the streets demanding answers she didn't have.

She dug into her bag, found her phone and then pulled up the photo of Oriel from Cannes.

Reve gave her screen the quickest, most cursory glance. His mouth twisted with faint disgust. "So you *are* seeing him."

"Read the caption."

He took her phone and stared longer. Frowned. "Oriel Cuvier?" He flicked his gaze to her face and back to the photo. "That's you."

"Nope." She reached for the phone. "She's a French model. Runway work, but also underwear and swimsuit ads. She recently landed one of the top brands for sunglasses. When I first came to New York, someone pointed out a photo of her and said we looked alike. I didn't think much of it. We all look like someone, right?"

"Your dad was in the air force, wasn't he?"

"Funny you should mention that, but don't malign the fidelity of a man you refused to meet. Especially because if you had, you would know he's white. What are the chances he would have two daughters with such dark coloring? If you say he must have a type, I will poke you in the eye."

He held up a placating hand. "What's *your* theory then?"

She looked at the phone, loathe to go to that other image because it made her seriously question her sanity. Her stomach had been nothing but acid since she'd seen it. She gathered herself and flicked, then handed her phone across, not glancing at the two photos that had been juxtaposed by the press in India. They showed a mother and daughter, both in their midtwenties.

"That's why Oriel Cuvier is making headlines right now," Nina said to the window. "She was adopted by a French couple and raised in France, but she recently learned her birth mother was Lakshmi Dalal, a Bollywood star who died about twenty years ago."

Reve scrolled to read the article beneath.

Nina dug into her bag for the keys to the building so she wouldn't have to look at him. Was he thinking she was pitiful? Reaching for a connection that was laughably beyond her? Soft in the head?

He didn't swear or give any indication of his reaction.

When she dared glance in his direction, he was watching her.

"Are *you* adopted?"

"No." Her throat closed, making the word more of a squeak. The pressure in her chest became nearly unbearable. Her eyes grew so hot she had to clench them to prevent the tears from leaking out.

"So this is a coincidence?" he scoffed. "A quirk of genetics?"

"Must be." She snatched back her phone, so abruptly it bordered on rude, and threw it into her bag. "Now all these stupid reporters think I'm her. I'll have to go back to Albuquerque so they'll leave me alone except I *can't*." She leaned to rap on the glass and then pushed the button to lower the screen. "Make a right at the light, please. I'm eight blocks up, but let me off wherever you can."

"I'm not letting you off here." Reve glowered as they rolled into a street full of stained awnings over pawnshops and moneylenders. There were homeless people sprawled with their belongings on the sidewalk. A woman in a short skirt paced alongside their slowing car and leaned suggestively, trying to catch Reve's attention.

"It's daylight. I'll be fine. I'm in the middle of the next block," she told the driver, pointing at a very dodgy building that had half its windows boarded up.

Reve swore and curtly ordered the driver, "Let us out here and drive around the block." He turned back to her and added, "I'll walk you in."

"Why?"

He ignored her and stepped out of the car after her, taking hold of her elbow as they crossed the street and walked the remaining block. He sent alert glances in both directions and subtly placed himself between her and the man blocking the entrance to the building.

"Spare change?" the man asked.

Reve handed him a few dollars, and his grip tightened on Nina's elbow as they moved into the darkened entranceway at the top of the steps.

"Why the hell are you staying in a place like this?" The simmering rage was back in his tone.

"I told you. It was free." She tried the key, but the building's front door had been broken in since she'd left this morning. It swung inward as she touched it.

"You're smarter than this, Nina."

"It's not that bad," she lied, secretly relieved that he was following her up the two flights of stairs. She unlocked the door to the studio and they entered what was admittedly a dim, squalid room of peeling paint and hard-used furniture. "See? Perfectly fine."

"Why is the window nailed shut?"

"My friend was robbed a few weeks ago, but it's safe now, right? No one can get in."

"It's a firetrap," he said grimly. "Get your things. You're not staying here."

"It's for a couple of nights. It's *fine*."

"There's a full bag of garbage right here." He pointed. "You know that attracts rats, right?"

"That's actually my suitcase. I bagged it to keep the cockroaches out."

He gave her the most condescending look in the history of condescending looks.

"So you're already packed," he said with muted fury. "Good."

"I'm not staying with you," she insisted.

"Well, you're not staying here, so tell me which hotel you want to go to."

"It's been so nice seeing you again, Reve. I can't imagine why I told you to go to hell and walked out on you."

"Yeah, I'm awash in warm fuzzies myself. Do you have more than this?"

"I don't have money for a hotel! And don't you dare tell me you'll pay for it. I already owe you thousands, and I feel sick about it every single day. So no, Reve. *No*."

"What are you talking about?" he muttered crisply. "I have never expected—" His phone pinged. "That's probably my driver telling me he's losing the hubcaps." He glanced at his phone and his expression turned to concrete. Accusation flashed into his eyes.

She fell back a step. "What?"

"My publicist is texting," he said through his teeth.

"Asking if I want to make a statement about my relationship with Oriel Cuvier, since she was seen coming into my building. There's speculation we're involved. So, yes, Nina. You will come home with me. You are going to tell me *exactly* what is going on, and we're going to find a way to keep my name out of it."

CHAPTER THREE

REVE DIDN'T BOTHER unknotting the garbage bag. He tore it open and left it on the floor, plucking her cheap red suitcase out of it.

"Get whatever houseplant you're supposed to keep alive and let's go." He was breathing through his mouth so the musty smell of this place wouldn't drag him into all of his worst memories.

Nina clenched her fists and tightened her mouth with stubbornness.

"I'm serious, Nina. I was used for publicity once before. *Once.* Never again. So you're coming with me and we're going to put a lid on this."

"Oh—" She whirled into the bathroom and came out with a yellow toiletry bag in one hand, a damp bra and underwear in her other. She shoved everything into her shoulder bag, picked up the romance novel off the coffee table and pulled a charger from the wall. She pulled a pink denim jacket off a hook and shrugged it on over her dress.

Minutes later they were back in the town car. Reve texted his publicist that he would be in touch with a statement shortly.

Then he texted his "date," telling her he wouldn't make it. Nina was right: a politician's daughter was under way too much scrutiny for his tastes. He hadn't planned to take things beyond drinks, but he texted that he would have his people call her people, not so subtly relaying a message that he had no interest in a more intimate connection.

"Why involve me?" He clicked off his phone. "If you want to capitalize on this look-alike thing, that's your business. There was no reason to bring me into it."

She was slouched in her seat, hugging herself, face forward, chin set at a belligerent angle. "I told you what happened. If you don't want to believe me, that's your choice."

"You running back into my life the day reporters start harassing you is just a huge coincidence? That's what you want me to believe?" Did she think he was born yesterday?

Her hand was crushing her denim sleeve. She made a noise of annoyed defeat.

"Okay, I walked by your building on purpose. I wasn't planning to come in. I didn't even know whether you were home."

"Then why come by at all?"

"It's called closure, Reve. I was supposed to get the job I wanted. I was going to mentally flip you the bird and fly to London to get on with my life."

"How'd that go?" he asked facetiously, aware of a gritty sensation in his middle as he imagined that plan playing out. He wouldn't have known she was right outside his door. It shouldn't bother him, but it did. "I didn't realize you were holding such a grudge. Is that what all of this is? Retribution for the way things ended between us?"

"What? No. Oh, my God." She sat up and glared at him. "I am sorry that your old girlfriend made a sex tape of you without your permission and posted it online. I didn't do that to you." She flopped back into her seat. "I would love it if you would stop blaming me for it."

"I don't," he growled, stung that she would even bring it up. The humility of it never went away, no matter how well his lawyer's takedown notices worked at keeping it from being shared. The exposure without consent was bad enough. The *you have nothing to be ashamed of* snickers turned the knife, but the worst was his own stupidity.

Reve closed his fist on his knee, hating that video for existing and hating himself even more for being gullible enough to think himself in love when it had been made.

"You don't trust me, Reve. You never have."

"I don't trust anyone," he shot back. "You're not special."

"Oh, I'm well aware of that," she said with a laugh that was a jagged scrape of sound. "She broke you. You're afraid to reveal a single thing about yourself that might be used against you. Here's news, though. We all get hurt. You're not special, either."

He drew in a breath that burned his nostrils.

This was something he couldn't stand about Nina. She had this way of turning things around on him, forcing him to self-examine. He hated it. He wasn't broken. He wasn't a psychopath. He was a law-abiding citizen who was considerate enough to let an old flame take refuge in his home. He'd walked her into that dive of an apartment and refused to let her stay there, hadn't he? He was capable of basic human compassion.

He wasn't *broken*.

"I take calculated risks, not stupid ones." That made him smart. His entire fortune was built on careful gambles. He made exactly as many bets as he expected would pay out. "So tell me what your game is and I'll decide if I'm willing to play."

"I'm not even good at games," Nina said with exasperation. "You're giving me way too much credit if you think I could put together some elaborate scheme against you. I can't win a hand of Go Fish against my niece. It's a family joke how obtuse I am. *All of this* is because of how slow I am to see the obvious." She turned her face to the window.

Her hand came up to her cheek, and he thought she might be wiping under her eye.

His heart twisted in his chest.

The car darkened as they came into the underground lot beneath his building. It stopped by the elevator and the driver came around to open Nina's door, then moved to the trunk to get her suitcase. Nina sat there unmoving, even when Reve came around to look at her through the open door.

"Are you going to be stubborn about this?"

"No. But I'm only coming up because I'm too exhausted to figure something else out. I haven't slept since I got here Sunday."

"Why not?"

"You saw the place. I was petrified."

He swore and held out a hand, helping her from the car.

She swayed slightly and he realized exactly how strung out she was. He wanted to draw her into himself, support her. Hell, he wanted to *hold* her.

Since when was he Mr. Affection? Since never. Touching during sex was great, but that's where cuddling and fondling belonged.

He made sure she was steady, then turned to punch in his code. The driver set her case inside the elevator and asked if there would be anything else.

"We'll have dinner from Antonio's," he decided.

"I'll cook," Nina said in a dull voice.

"You just told me you're tired."

"Would you *please* let me earn my keep this much at least?" Her tone shot up to a strident pitch.

"Fine," he muttered, and dismissed his driver.

They rode upward in thick silence.

He hadn't realized how often she had cooked until she was gone and he'd been stuck eating takeout again. Nina was damned good at throwing a meal together and had seemed to like doing it, but he'd always thought it was her way of playing house, pushing him toward domesticity and reliance on her. He wondered now if it had been her way of contributing.

I owe you thousands and feel sick about it every day...

A teetering sensation rocked behind his sternum. "You know I don't expect you to pay me back for—"

"Don't start that fight, Reve." The doors opened into his foyer and she shoved her suitcase out of the elevator. "I'll burn your dinner, and maybe the entire building to the ground."

Nina banged through the cupboards, taking a quick inventory and deciding she could manage some rice and peas and empanadillas.

She was tired, but there was something very soothing in making one of Abuela's standby dishes. It grounded her when she was otherwise completely adrift.

Reve appeared when she was wrist deep in dough. He had changed from his suit into tailored Bermuda shorts and a polo shirt. He looked casual, but tension radiated off him.

He had brought a bottle of red wine, which he opened, pouring two glasses and setting one within her reach.

"Thanks." She set the dough in the refrigerator and washed her hands before she sipped. It hadn't even breathed properly yet, but a small explosion of currants and black cherry and pepper hit her taste buds.

She had missed drinking wine that cost more than a pair of shoelaces. She had missed a lot of things, especially this little ritual of theirs.

Reve lowered onto one of the stools at the island the way he often had when she'd cooked. Invariably, they would have already made love and were mellow and pleased to get a little loose over a bottle of wine, bantering and squabbling over the nonsense of everyday life.

Tonight, there was a cloud of animosity rolling off him. A sense that whatever she said would be weighed and measured and examined for signs of deception.

She moved to start the rice, saying, "I was born in Luxembourg. Did I ever tell you that?"

"That's a long way from Albuquerque." He screened his thoughts with his spiky lashes. "Close to Germany. Isn't there an airbase there?"

It was almost laughable how much quicker he was than she could ever hope to be.

She nodded. "Dad was stationed there and my m-mother—" This was the part that was really, really hard.

"Nina." He set down his glass, speaking in the quietest, most careful tone she'd ever heard him use. "If this is going places you don't want to go, you don't have to tell me."

"No, it's fine." She didn't want to imagine what he thought she was saying. "You're actually the only person I *can* tell. Maybe the best person, because you have no emotional investment. You're so cynical and blunt, you'll recommend a psych evaluation, which is probably what I need."

She turned away to get everything simmering on the gas flames and turned back to see him staring holes into her back.

"What?"

"Nothing." He blinked and whatever impression she'd had was gone. "Continue."

"This is how the story was always told to me." She began to chop peppers. "Our mother was feeling cooped up in the tiny flat they had near the base. She wanted to take my brother and sister to a cuckoo clock factory for a day trip, but they got lost. She accidentally crossed into Luxembourg and stopped at a café to ask for directions. She collapsed with an aneurysm."

He swore softly.

"Yeah." She flattened her lips. "The people in the café didn't know that's what happened, but she was super pregnant—a couple of weeks from being due. There was a private clinic nearby, one of those places for Europe's elite to dry out or get plastic surgery on the down-low. She was rushed there for treatment. My sister has this vivid memory of sitting in the café holding my brother's hand, terrified and confused. A man brought them cheese and crackers and hot chocolate. He asked where they were from. He was trying to find out how to get hold of Dad, I guess, because Dad showed up a while later. He took them to the clinic, where they got the bad news that Mom was gone. They were all crying until a nurse brought me out and put me in Dad's arms. Then they all stopped crying and smiled."

Nina had to take a drink to keep her throat from closing. Her chest was scoured with emotion, her eyes hot. "I've always felt loved because of that part of the story. Always."

A muscle in Reve's cheek twitched, and his gaze dropped into his glass.

He had never told her much about his childhood. He played his cards close to his chest, never spoke fondly of a brother or sister or a father or mother. He never, ever spoke about love.

"Your father didn't ask for blood samples or anything?" He was a man of facts and computation, and had a natural skepticism of any information presented to him. *He* would never take on faith that the baby placed in his arms was his own.

"Dad was completely distraught. We shipped home and Abuela moved in with us. Dad was absent a lot until he was discharged, but he was home permanently by the time I was going to school. I graduated, saved for college, got my degree, then came here to work." She shrugged. "It was all pretty normal."

"Until you learned there was a model who looked just like you."

"Yes, but then I met you and didn't think about much else." She tossed him a flat smile before she turned away to check everything on the stove. He had consumed her. Had he realized that?

"Do you believe you were sent home with the wrong family?" he asked quietly.

"No," she said without hesitation. "They are the most loving people in the world. I'm very lucky to have them." Her eyes welled, and she had to use the back of her wrist to clear her vision.

"You know what I mean."

"I do." She brought the dough from the fridge and floured the surface of the counter. "People used to ask me if I was adopted. It upset me, but Abuela said I took after her sister. She told me that was why I struggled in school, that it was a family thing to have dyslexia. She didn't use that word, but that's what she meant."

"I didn't know that about you."

"It doesn't matter." It did. It mattered a lot. It had impacted her self-esteem, but she had developed strategies to pass her assignments and graduate. Her fine arts degree majoring in fashion was one of her proudest achievements.

She had gone through life wondering why her brother and sister found basic things like reading and math so much easier than she did, though. It had set her apart from them, and now she felt like a complete idiot for not seeing she'd been different in a far more profound way.

"I never had any reason to question whether my family was related to me by blood, not until I offered to have my sister's baby."

He paused in reaching for the bottle to top up his glass. "What do you mean you 'offered to have'?"

"Carry it. As a surrogate." She found one of the wide-mouthed glasses she liked to use to cut circles in the dough.

"Why the hell would you do that?" His eyes flashed with astounded disbelief.

"She's my sister." It was all the reason she needed. "She and her husband have had fertility struggles for years. That's one of the reasons I went home. Dad told me over dinner that Angela had miscarried again. She was heartbroken."

"You never told me that about her."

"Because it's none of your business. I'm only telling you now because it's relevant." She filled a few pockets of dough and sealed them, then set them into the frying pan to begin cooking while she filled the rest.

"They've talked about using a surrogate on and off,

but aside from the cost, it's a really personal thing. I offered once before, but I was still in college. Angela said it would be too disruptive to my education. She was so heartbroken this time, I was desperate to help. And I wanted to do something that would make me feel like my life had some sort of meaning or purpose."

"Nina." There was admonishment in his tone, but a man like him must know there was a huge difference between pursuing a goal and achieving it.

She crumpled up the scraps of dough and rolled it out again, leaning in hard.

"Surrogacy sounds simple, but it's a big undertaking. Most agencies won't let you do it until you've had a successful pregnancy of your own. Some people do it in private arrangements, and my doctor wasn't exactly encouraging about our doing that, but he was willing to at least screen me—"

"Blood tests," Reve said with dawning understanding.

"Yes. He sat me down with the results and said it wasn't uncommon for siblings to have different blood types, depending how your body puts your parents' chromosomes together, but I was enough of an outlier that he suggested I have a chat with my dad."

"Did you?"

"*No.* I told Angela I was anemic—which is true. I'm taking iron now." She gulped a mouthful of wine and turned the empanadillas in the pan. "Then I took one of those ancestry tests. I wanted to prove the doctor wrong."

"But?"

She released a shaky sigh. "My brother did one a few years ago when his wife didn't know what else to get him for Christmas. My results should have been in the same ballpark as his, right? If we both come from a Puerto Rican mom and a white American father? Marco's report said he was Spanish with some African and Taíno, which is the indigenous people in the Caribbean. Plus English and German, which lines up with where Dad's family is from."

"And yours?"

She felt a great pressure in her breastbone. "Some English. Mostly South Asian and Scandinavian."

"Scandinavian?" Reve snorted and searched her features as if looking for the evidence of Nordic blood.

She shrugged and emptied her glass in one gulp, then pushed it toward the bottle.

He refilled it. "Have you tried contacting the clinic?"

"The building has changed hands more than once. It's a spa resort now."

She checked the rice and turned it off, then prepared a couple of plates. She left a fresh batch of empanadillas frying in the pan as she took a stool next to Reve.

"The connection to Oriel wasn't on my radar when I got my results. I mean, there were photos of her with Duke Rhodes in the magazines at my sister's salon—What's wrong?"

Reve was staring at the plate she'd set in front of him.

"Nothing," he mumbled, seeming almost self-conscious. "It smells good." He shoveled a forkful of rice into his mouth and took a small breath around it because it was hot, but he didn't cool it with wine. He chewed and swallowed. "It's good. Thanks. Keep talking."

He proceeded to eat as though he hadn't been fed in a week.

She filtered her words carefully as she said them aloud for the first time.

"I wasn't thinking, *I wonder if she's my sister.* Not until her story broke about being Lakshmi's daughter. Then I read that she was born in Luxembourg the day before me. My time of birth is fourteen minutes after midnight."

He snapped a look at her. Then he finished chewing, swallowed and asked, "Have you reached out to her?"

"You're supposed to tell me I'm out of my mind, Reve!" She made herself eat because otherwise she'd have that bottle of wine for dinner. "You're supposed to say, *Save that imagination for the sewing room.* Say, *There's an obvious explanation*, then tell me what it is," she pleaded.

"It is obvious. She's your twin."

"Would you *stop*?"

CHAPTER FOUR

REVE CLEANED HIS plate in record time and rose to help himself to more even though he was already full. He turned the empanadillas over in the frying pan and then leaned on the counter, eating rice while he waited for them to finish browning.

God, this was good. He had never understood people who got nostalgic for certain foods. Eating was better than going hungry, so he ate what was put in front of him, but as the familiar aromas had gathered amid the sizzle and pop of the pan, a nameless tension inside him had eased. His mouth had watered.

Nina's story was not her usual animated discussion of buttons and weave and where hemline trends were headed, though. She looked miserable as she chased a pea and gathered a few grains of rice with the tines of her fork.

"This is why you were so upset when you got here," he realized. "It wasn't because the reporters were chasing you. It was because you couldn't outrun the truth."

She lifted her lashes and sent him a morose glare, soft mouth falling down at the corners.

"Suppose you are twins," he speculated. "Were you split up through incompetence or was it deliberate?"

"I came to New York with a half-baked plan to find

out. I thought Oriel was here. Or that I would get that
job—any job, but hopefully that one," she said with a
curl of her lip. "I thought if I could get myself stationed
in London, I could do some footwork from there. Take
a train when I had time off, see if I could find someone
who had worked at the clinic. I mean, I could send a few
emails from here to… I don't know. The spa? Or see if I
could find the doctor who delivered me. But if mistakes
were made, no one is going to admit it. Not to someone
whose life was changed because of it."

"They'll lawyer up and clam up."

"Exactly. If I go to Oriel, she's liable to do the same.
Imagine how many people are coming to her with bogus
claims right now, trying to get their hands on Lakshmi's
fortune."

"Those people aren't wearing her face. You have an
edge, Nina. One look at you and she will do a test to prove
exactly what you already suspect."

"Then what?" she challenged with agitation. "Then
I have to tell my family that the child they thought survived *didn't.* Is their baby out there somewhere? Living
with strangers? I don't *know* Lakshmi gave birth to me,
but if I go public with any of this I'll have to hire a bodyguard, because people will chase me down the street for
the rest of my life."

She poked at her food again, head hanging over her
plate.

He took out the cooked empanadillas and turned off
the stove. "What are you going to do then?"

"I don't know. Tell me what to do because all the options I see are terrible."

"Tell your father," he said plainly, not bothering to
cushion his words. "Prepare him for the fact that I'm
going to tell people it was you, not Oriel, who came here

today. Once he sees the photos, he's liable to have the same thoughts you do. You want to be ahead of that."

"Do I?"

"Why wouldn't you?"

The anguish and vulnerability in her expression made the hairs stand up on his arms. He unconsciously braced himself, expecting pain for some reason yet not understanding what kind or from where.

"What if he doesn't want me when he realizes I'm not his?" Her voice was so thin and vulnerable, it arrowed into his chest and left the space there cold and cavernous.

"Do you really think he wouldn't?" It was a stupid question. His own father hadn't cared if he'd lived or died.

"How would you react if you found out twenty-five years after the fact that you'd been raising a child who wasn't yours?" The anguish in her eyes was more than he could bear.

He had never planned to raise any children. If his own father was anything to go by, nurturing didn't come naturally to his kind, and so Reve had made the decision long ago not to perpetuate feral, junkyard hounds like himself or force anyone else's children to live with one.

Although, for those seconds in the foyer earlier, when it had struck him that she might be pregnant, his entire view had changed. For one flashing second, he'd seen a completely different future for himself, which had died a quick death when he heard, *That's all I would need.*

Obviously, Nina wouldn't be happy to be carrying his child, and why that left a hollow sensation in his chest was a mystery.

He brushed all of that out of his mind. Nina was begging for him to tell her that calling her dad would turn out fine. The brutal fact was that he was far too cynical to believe it. Based on what he knew of people, there was a very real chance her family could reject her.

And he instinctively knew that would break her. Whatever ulterior motives Nina might have where he was concerned, one thing had always been indisputable. She loved her family. She'd always had complete confidence that they loved her, and now that confidence was shaken.

She pushed her plate away abruptly and stood, her jaw set with decision, before turning toward the living room.

"Nina." He set down his plate and made sure everything was turned off before he followed her.

She was on the sofa with her phone in her shaking hand, instructing, "Text Dad. Do you have time for a call?"

There was a quaver of dread in her voice. Her phone whooshed and her anxious gaze came up to meet his.

Reve was ruled by logic. If you had a question, you asked it. If you had a goal, you found the quickest route to attain it and chased it until you got there. His head told him this was the right thing to do, but a hot lump formed behind his breastbone. What if he'd steered her straight off a cliff of some kind?

Her phone pinged and she gave a couple of quick voice commands.

How had he not noticed how often she used voice commands? He had, of course, but he hadn't understood the significance.

The robotic AI voice read aloud, "Dad. On a date. Will call when I'm home."

She slid her phone onto the coffee table and fell onto her side on the cushions, scowling hard enough a fire should have spontaneously burst forth in the hearth.

"Can you hold off for a few hours on making a statement?" she asked tersely. "I'll clean the kitchen in a few minutes. I just need to think."

"Of course." He went back to the kitchen long enough to put the leftovers into the refrigerator and fetch their wine.

When he set her glass on the coffee table, he saw she was asleep. The creases of tension had finally melted from her face, but dark circles were still smudged beneath her eyes. He wondered exactly how long she'd been living with all of these secrets and doubts, because that sort of exhaustion came from more than a few nights in a flophouse apartment.

When he realized he was staring and had his own brow pulled into a tense wrinkle of consternation, he drew a blanket from inside the ottoman and draped it over her.

Then he sat and picked up his tablet, calling up this twin of hers. He quickly landed on photos of Oriel in bikinis and sexy lingerie.

It was like seeing Nina in the bedroom and made him hot, but not in a titillating way. He was affronted on her behalf. This wasn't her, but it could be. This woman's figure was a little bit thinner—not much, but he knew Nina's curves intimately enough that the difference was obvious to him. Oriel had a polished gleam to her that contrasted with Nina's natural and very casual beauty, and Oriel posed in ways that accentuated her sexuality. Nina was far less overt.

These photos irritated him. Nina was modest at heart. She was passionate and sensual and uninhibited when she got into sex, but that was something she expressed in private. She wasn't one to flaunt excess cleavage, or flash her legs, or flirt and draw attention to herself.

The clear boundary around their sexual lives was one of the things he'd liked most about her. It was why he'd been comfortable letting her stay in his home. She didn't engage in shock talk or gossip about bedroom escapades.

Even so, from the moment she'd left, he'd been waiting for her to show her true colors, expecting her to exploit their relationship in some glaring tell-all fashion.

She hadn't.

Obviously, there was still time, but she wasn't racing to capitalize on the riches and notoriety of her likely association to Lakshmi and Oriel, either.

That left him with an uneasy suspicion he had pigeonholed her, failing to see past his own black-and-white judgments.

He absently played the backs of his fingers against the stubble under his chin as his mind strayed to the night she'd walked out, the move he'd convinced himself was purely a manipulation tactic on her part.

He never let himself replay their argument. When he recalled that night, he always stopped at the good part. They'd had sex when he got home after being away a couple of nights. Their lovemaking had turned into a hedonistic indulgence of their senses. He'd been drunk on her, kissing and suckling everywhere, caressing and licking at her most responsive flesh until she had been a quaking mass of lust.

She was incredible when she was like that, eyes glazed, lips swollen, body twisting without inhibition. Her voice got sexy as hell when she was that turned-on, and she knew it turned him on to hear it. She had told him what she wanted in the bluntest way, and he still got hard recalling it.

When she was aroused to that degree, he could unleash his own restraint. He'd slipped his arms under her legs so she'd been completely open to him. She'd reached to the headboard to brace herself, breasts jiggling under the power of his thrusts. The slap of their flesh and her animalistic moans had been raw and hot and wild.

Holding back to wait for her had been heaven and hell, but her tension had finally snapped in a rush of magnificent, glorious release. Her body had shuddered and her sheath had milked at his shaft. He had lost it. The orgasm that rocked him had been the most exquisitely sharp and sustained climax of his life. He still felt a dull ache thinking of it today.

Who remembered something like that? He'd probably had a hundred orgasms since, but he remembered vividly how hard he had come that evening—maybe because he replayed that evening nearly every time he was in the shower, he thought ironically.

He always stopped with that moment of culmination, though, not wanting to recollect the way she had wiggled his foot a millennium later, waking him from his sex-induced doze.

"I thought you would join me." She had worn only a towel. Her hair was in a clip, damp around her hairline, her face clean and fresh. "Are you going to shower before we go?"

"Where?" Maybe if he hadn't been drunk on endorphins and dopamine, he would have been thinking more clearly and handled things better, but his head had been full of cotton, his limbs made of lead.

"Dinner." She went into the closet and came out to throw a dress on the foot of the bed. "With my dad."

"Oh. No. I'm not going."

She had laughed, then realized he was serious and frowned with confusion. "I told you two weeks ago that he would be here to take me for a belated birthday celebration. That's why we waited until tonight, so you would be home and could come. You made the reservation."

"Yeah, they have my credit card. Go wild." He had curled his arm under his pillow, always happy to watch her move around wearing only a towel. "The car is yours, too."

"But—" She disappeared into the closet and came back wearing her bra and underwear. They were a lacy, spring green that made her skin glow like dark honey. "I don't understand. Did something come up?"

"No."

"Then why aren't you coming?" She leaned around the bathroom door to hang her towel. "Don't you want to meet him? He wants to meet you."

"I'm sure he does," he'd said drily. "But I know what meeting the family means and that's not where this relationship is going, so what's the point?" He had thought that went without saying.

Nina had come back into the bedroom to stare at him with a wide-eyed, ingenuous look. She was a master at this projection of artlessness. She'd worn the same look when she'd told him she had been fired, as though the news had arrived from left field.

He'd known from the outset that her boss was after him. He'd had no interest in the other woman and plenty in Nina. Since he was partially responsible for Nina's job loss and they were already sleeping together, he had said she could use his spare bedroom as a studio. He had no friends or family who came to visit so it was wasted space.

He had used those words when he offered it, so he couldn't understand how she might have read more into why he was letting her stay with him, but she'd stood there looking as though she'd been sucker punched.

"Where *is* this relationship going?" she had persisted. "Or not going, I should say."

He'd got his back up. Guilt had crept in—unwarranted.

He didn't lead women on, but he had sensed her affront. In response, his own defense mechanisms had locked into place.

"Why does it have to go anywhere? We're both comfortable."

"*Are* we?" Her face had darkened and her hands had knotted into fists.

"Oh, I think you're very comfortable, Nina." He'd sat up to find his underwear and pulled them on. "Why are you acting like this? I told you on day one that I wouldn't let anyone manipulate me ever again."

"How am I manipulating you?" The doe eyes again, as though he was roaring down a country lane straight at her and she didn't understand what was happening.

"You're not. Because I'm not stupid enough to let you. I gave you what you wanted." He flicked a hand toward her studio down the hall. "That's more than I've given any other woman, but that's as far as this goes. Outrage over the lack of wedding bells is completely misplaced."

"First of all, it's *dinner*." Her voice had begun to shake with anger. "I didn't expect any skywritten proposals. But, wow, I thought you respected my work. I thought—" She had hurried to dress, stepping into the jeans she'd been wearing earlier and yanked on a pullover. Her hair had come loose from its clip and she'd flung the butterfly hinge across the room.

"Of *course*, I respect your work." Had he rolled his eyes a tiny bit? Yes. Because she was always so sensitive about it. She had talent by the truckload as far as he could tell, but she had zero confidence in herself. Fake it till you make it was his motto while she seemed to be nurturing a hard case of impostor syndrome.

She had sent him the most scorchingly bitter look he'd ever received from anyone. It had stung deep inside where he had believed he was well-guarded and impervious.

"For God's sake, Nina. I've bought you everything you need. What does that say about my belief in your potential?"

"So much," she choked out as she grabbed her phone from the top of the dresser and threw it into her day bag. She had flung the bag over her shoulder and hurried down the hall.

"We'll talk about it later, then?" he'd called facetiously.

She had spun around in the hall to face him. Her eyes had been glistening with angry tears. "No one has ever made me feel as stupid as you have tonight. Goodbye, Reve."

She hadn't come back. He'd check her social channels and seen she was with her father so he presumed she was staying at the hotel with him, and next thing he knew, she was in Albuquerque and had blocked him.

The penthouse had felt hollow and quiet after she was gone. He resented that she had conditioned him to expect someone to be waiting for him and, out of sheer aggravation, had had her things boxed up. He'd had his assistant track down her father's address, but at the last minute Reve had balked at shipping it to her.

She would come back for it. Designing clothes in New York was her dream. She'd put hours and hours of work into each piece.

Sell it. Give it away. Throw it away. I don't care, but it's not mine.

She didn't really mean that. She couldn't. If she did, it meant that she really hadn't intended to see him today.

His heart teetered at that thought, and he quickly steadied it. Her turning up here was one more act in a play. He wasn't being a misogynist thinking this was nothing but mind games and manipulations. Men did it too. Everyone did.

But he kept hearing her say, *You're actually the only person I can tell. Maybe the best person, because you have no emotional investment.*

No emotional investment. That was certainly the goal, but hearing it stated like a blunt fact, without any taunting inflection, made him sound like a sociopath.

He felt things. He just didn't allow those feelings to control him or allow him to be controlled by someone else.

She really believed he felt nothing, though. She had only come into his neighborhood to flip him off because she was still angry at how stupid he had made her feel.

It made him sick to think she'd felt belittled by him.

How had he not clued in to her trouble with reading? She almost always dictated her texts. When she did type one out, she used a lot of emojis. She had invariably asked him to order for her when they went for dinner, or listened to the specials rather than read the menu. She spent very little time on social media or browsing headlines, but she loved audio books and podcasts.

He'd thought she liked to listen because her hands were always busy. He hadn't realized she had had to work twice as hard as everyone else to master the basics. He'd grown up in poverty of all sorts, but he'd had a mind that grasped concepts quickly and he often took that for granted.

He had also taken for granted that Nina was as jaded and pragmatic as he was. He *wanted* her to be like him. That's how simple, harmless affairs remained simple and harmless.

He looked at her, so innocent and defenseless in her slumber. No one could get through life with their heart pinned on their sleeve the way she seemed to.

Don't fall for it, he warned himself.

Her phone burbled.

Nina snapped awake with a gasp and a disoriented look around.

When her gaze snagged on him, a glimmer of wonder touched her expression. A smile began to dawn.

A sensation he couldn't describe bloomed in his chest, but before it could take hold, memory seemed to steal all the light from her eyes. Her expression darkened the way a cloud blocked the sun. Whatever flame of possibility had sparked to life in her was doused and buried.

She swung her feet to the floor and picked up her phone. "It's my dad."

For one beat, there was only another burble from her phone while she stared expectantly at him.

"What?"

Nina abruptly rose and walked down the hall, swiping the phone to speaker as she went. "Hi, Dad."

"Hi, button, what's up?" Then, with sharp concern, "Where are you?"

"Reve's." Her voice was fading, but he heard the heavy sheepishness in his name.

"Nina." The older man's voice rang with fatalism. *"Why?"*

Reve didn't hear her reply. She shut herself into the spare bedroom while he sat there thinking, *Ouch.* Dad certainly didn't want to meet him *now*, did he?

That's when it struck him why Nina had looked at him so strangely a minute ago. He had always left the room when her family called. Always. She had expected him to walk away today. When he hadn't, she had.

He didn't know why that felt like such a knee to the groin, but it sure did.

* * *

Nina turned her face up to the spray of the shower, washing away tears as they leaked from her closed lashes.

"Nina?" Reve walked into the bathroom without knocking.

"Reve! I'm in the shower." *Obviously.* The walls of the cubicle were fogged and they used to shower together pretty much every day, but that wasn't who they were anymore. She crossed her arms over herself, feeling naked in more than just a physical way.

"Are you crying?" He closed the door and stood there as a blurry bulk, arms crossed.

"Yes." She regretted ever telling him she preferred to cry in the tub or shower. It was starting to freak her out how much he'd taken in and remembered about her when their last conversation had convinced her she was nothing to him. "Can you leave me to it?"

"Look, I'm sorry he's turning his back on you. I wish I had some good advice on how to handle that, but most people are garbage and this is why I don't let people close to me. I'm not *broken*. I just hate expecting better from people only to be disappointed when they let me down."

Dear Lord, that sounded like a tragic way to live. And this was how she'd tricked herself into thinking he needed her. A man with such a big cloud hanging over him needed sunshine peeking through.

"He's not turning his back on me. He was perfectly sweet. He already *knew*."

"And never told you?" He sounded outraged. "What an ass. No wonder you're upset."

"I'm *relieved*." Did he understand anything about how human beings worked? "I'll tell you what he said in a minute. Can you go? Please?"

He made a grumbling noise and left.

She finished up, combed out her wet hair and walked into the bedroom wearing only a towel.

Reve was in the chair, legs straight, ankles crossed. He was turning a small abstract sculpture in his hands.

She came up short, asking with exasperation, "What are you doing in here?"

"Do you have pink in your hair?" His hands stilled as he studied her. "It's cute."

"I'll tell my sister you like it. Could you wait in the living room?"

"This isn't new to me." He waved at her.

"That was basically my dad's reaction," she said ironically as she secured her towel. "Is my suitcase still by the door?"

"I brought those." He pointed at the foot of the bed.

She looked at the familiar ice-blue silk boxers and matching T-shirt. Her brightly colored kimono was there, too. She had made the set for herself and had worn them every morning when she had risen naked from his bed.

She touched the cool, sleek fabric. "Why do you still have these?"

"They were in the drawer. I never got around to sending them to storage with the rest." He shrugged off any significance.

"Has anyone else worn them?"

"*No*. Why would you ask that?" His mouth warped in insult.

"Well, I don't know, do I?" She gave a defensive shrug. "Thank you." She had slept in her pajamas on her friend's decrepit sofa the last few nights and would rather burn them than wear them again.

She took the shorts and top into the bathroom and left the door cracked as she changed behind it, talking as she did.

"I was almost a year old when Dad found out. He was running out of time to claim a life insurance benefit on—" She peered around the door. "I hate to say she wasn't my mother even though I never met her and she didn't give birth to me."

"'Kay." He was tossing the sculpture between his hands.

His gaze flickered to her bare legs as she came back into the bedroom, touching her ankles just long enough to pull warmth into all of her exposed skin, and then he met her gaze without remorse. In fact, there was a flickering flame of appreciation in his gaze.

She did her best to ignore it, but she was hideously conscious of the fact she was braless in silk and her nipples were hardening to press against the light-as-cobwebs fabric.

She shrugged on the kimono and tied it closed, her lower back tingling with the sense he was watching her every move.

"The insurance company called Dad to clarify because the copy of the death certificate he'd submitted didn't match the one they had requested from the government in Luxembourg. The government one had a box ticked that indicated his wife was pregnant at her time of death. They said that usually means she hadn't delivered. Dad had only seen her for a few seconds, just long enough to identify her because he had three kids right outside the door, one of them a newborn, the other two completely traumatized. The clinic took care of cremation, and the doctor called him with the autopsy results a few months later. Dad never saw the actual report, though. He told the insurance company he definitely had a baby, but by then I was starting to look not so much like them." She turned and waved at the door. "Can we—?"

She couldn't stay in such an intimate place while she told him all these intimate things.

He shrugged and rose, all of his masculine energy swirling around her, making her aware of their thin, loose clothing, and his height and strength and lazy regard.

She swallowed and picked up her phone before she led him to the living room, where her glass of wine sat on the coffee table.

She picked it up and wandered out to the terrace. The concrete still held the day's heat, and the setting sun turned the surrounding buildings to rose gold.

Reve joined her a moment later, having detoured for the bottle and his own glass.

"He was starting to have suspicions?" he prompted as he topped her up.

"Thanks," she murmured absently. "Yes. He didn't want to believe he'd brought home a stranger's baby, but had a paternity test done and discovered he had."

"Did he tell the clinic?" His focus on her was intense.

She'd always found Reve's full attention to be thrilling and disconcerting. It made her feel as though she was the only thing that mattered in the world.

Don't read into it, she warned herself, looking away. It had taken weeks to fully grasp that he'd only been using her for sex. He wasn't the charming, concerned protector that she had cast him to be.

"He left a few messages, but no one got back to him." She moved to the half wall that formed the rail of the terrace. Below her, shadows were collecting in Central Park. "Dad didn't want to rock too many boats, though. He told Abuela. He thought she deserved to know since she was raising her daughter's children while he was still flying for the air force. They were both afraid I'd be taken away if they revealed what had happened. Children get deported, too."

He grimaced an acknowledgment as he joined her.

"The little that Dad remembered about the clinic was that they handled discreet services for celebrities. He presumed I had been given up voluntarily by someone who couldn't keep me. He didn't want me to end up in some orphanage in Europe, forcing them to grieve another loss. He said Abuela said her daughter had made sure they had a baby to help them cope with losing her. She said I'd already brought her so much comfort and love that she couldn't bear to give me up."

Nina had to bite her lips to steady them. Abuela had been the only mother Nina had ever known. She had loved her with everything in her and missed her every single day.

Reve didn't say anything.

She glanced to find him watching her with intense concentration, but as she met his gaze, he turned his to the horizon and gave a light snort.

"You're such a product of the material world," she said with affront. "There are things that can never be seen or measured or proven, you know. If you believe they're real, they are. I thought it was a lovely thought that I was brought to them through her daughter's spirit."

"It is," he allowed. "And it's true I don't believe in ghosts or cosmic fate, but it was wrong of him to keep it from you. You shouldn't have found out like this."

"It's a really painful topic for him." Her father had cried openly as they had revisited the grim loss, breaking her heart. "He said the time never seemed right to bring it up, and he never wanted me to feel anything but his. He was pretty freaked-out that I might have a twin." She chuckled softly into her glass.

"What about the rest of your family?"

She sobered. "He's asking my brother to meet him at my sister's. He'll text as soon as he's spoken to them." She hoped they took the news as well as her father had. "You can make whatever statement you want after that." A searing sensation went from the base of her throat to the pit of her stomach. "And I'll get out of your hair."

CHAPTER FIVE

SHE REALLY HADN'T come here to pick up where they'd left off.

Reve wet his arid throat with wine, absorbing that.

"Where will you go?" he asked. "Back to Albuquerque?"

"Not if, um…" She swirled her wine and licked her lips. "Dad's going to call one of his air force buddies who became a commercial pilot. He keeps a flat in Frankfurt and has offered it to Dad in the past. Dad said he'd ask if I can use it. I feel so light now I've told him. Like I can *think*. Thank you for pushing me to call him."

She gave him the smile he'd been missing, the one that lit her up as though she had swallowed pure sunshine. She beamed it at him so hard his chest stung with the force of it.

"That's it, then? You'll leave in the next day or two?" He had the bizarre sensation of a bandage being peeled very slowly from his chest, taking one hair at a time and a layer of skin with it, but it was happening on the inside of his rib cage.

"Depending on flights, yes. I'm still eligible to fly military, but it's space available. I don't want to hang around here like bait for the photographers, so I might have to book commercial. And I have to look into whether I can work once I'm there," she said with a distracted frown. "I'm sure a bar or club would hire me for cash. At least I brought my passport. That interview was good for something," she said with another overbright smile.

He could already see ten things wrong with her plan, but her phone pinged with a text.

She moved across to peer down at where she'd left it faceup on a side table next to the settee. Whatever photo appeared on the screen made her shoot him an uneasy look.

"My brother." She tucked her hands into her neck as though her phone was a coiled snake she was being forced to pick up.

Chewing the corner of her mouth, she cautiously let one finger dart out to tap the screen. The AI voice read, "Marco. I love you, sis. Tell me what you need."

"Oh." Nina moved her hands to stack them over her heart. She glanced at Reve with eyes like exploding stars. Her mouth was a wobbly line. "Isn't he the best?"

Her phone pinged again. She tapped.

"Angela," the AI voice read. "I always knew you were special. Get a hotel on me. You don't have to stay with him. Call as soon as you're there. I want to hear everything."

"What have you been telling them about me?" Reve asked with offense.

Nina didn't meet his gaze as she picked up the phone and voice texted to both of them, "I love you both. I'll call as soon as I've figured out my next steps."

"You're not going to a hotel," Reve said when she lowered her phone. "The paparazzi will find you and we still have things to talk about."

"The press release? Say whatever you want, but it would be better if I wasn't here when you issue it, don't you think?" She polished her screen on her hip, then set her phone back on the table.

When she glanced at him, there was a deep vulnerability in her expression. Only a heartless bully would throw such a lamb to the wolves.

"We'll circle back to the press release. You know you don't have to go to Europe, right? I looked up Oriel while you were sleeping. Her new husband is a VP at TecSec. He'll want my business." The global security company had been on his radar for a while as an alternative to the one he was using. "I can make a call right now. He'll pick up."

"You don't want to be involved," she reminded, rolling her wine in the bowl of her glass. "I'm not sure *I* want to be involved. I mean, I do. I want to know if Oriel is my sister. I definitely want to meet her if she is, but…" She took a deep breath and slowly let it out. "I'm not ready to reveal myself. Oriel seems fine with the attention she's getting, but today's taste of it makes it seem pretty awful."

"It is. But you won't stay anonymous walking around with her face."

"There's nothing I can do about that, is there?" She paced down the length of the terrace and turned back, brows tugged into a wrinkle of consternation. "The problem is, I have questions that can't be answered by meeting her. She was legally adopted, but I was given to my father in a way that seems…opportunistic. As though someone was trying to hide me. That's weird, right? I'm not imagining it?"

He'd been thinking that, too. "It suggests criminal activity, yes." Which concerned him.

Her mouth tightened. "I keep thinking that right now is my only chance to poke around for answers, before whoever did this realizes I know who I am and starts to cover their tracks."

"Okay, but you can't go jabbing hornet nests without knowing what you're up against."

"I don't have *time* to take a more cautious approach." She pointed at her face. "This is a ticking clock."

"Hire someone," he threw out. "Tell your family to keep their mouths shut, lock down your social media and lie low. That buys you a little more time off the radar while you wait for a report."

"I don't know first thing about hiring a private investigator let alone have the money to pay for one. I certainly can't sit and watch game shows in a hotel room while they try to get answers to questions I've barely articulated."

"I'll pay for it." He shrugged that off.

"No, thank you," Nina bit out, cheekbones darkening with temper.

"Which brings us to something else we need to discuss." Ire prickled at him as he noted her hackles were rising. "Where did you get the idea you owe me for the things I bought you?"

"I already told you where I stand on this. You bought it. You own it." She walked past him and went inside, snapping the door back into place.

"For God's sake, Nina," he said as he followed her. "What are we even talking about? A few yards of silk and a few pairs of shoes?"

She flung around to face him, pronouncing spitefully, "Twenty-nine thousand, four hundred and seventy-eight dollars and sixty-eight cents. That might not be much to you, but it's a lot to me."

That took him aback. "You kept track of how much you spent?"

"Of course I did! I was always going to pay you back once I established myself."

"So why haven't you?" he asked with exasperation.

She jerked her head back.

"I mean, why haven't you continued trying to establish yourself? Put on a show. Get some orders. Find a factory to produce it. What the hell are you waiting for?"

"Oh, it's just that easy, is it?" Her face was crimson, her eyes wearing the glossy sheen of venomous fury she'd worn when she'd walked out on him. She looked to her phone, which was still outside, then her bag on the floor.

It made his stomach clench, but he kept pushing.

"All I did was underwrite your ambitions. Stand here and explain to me why that was such a crime."

"I may be thick, Reve, but even I know that sex work is a crime! Buying *and* selling. Thanks for implicating me in that because I wasn't aware that's why I was here." She chucked back the last of her wine and clanked her glass onto the bar top.

"How the hell do you make that leap? *How?*" he demanded, astounded.

"Oh, were you *in love* with me?" Her sarcasm held a rawness that scored deep into him. "Was that why you asked me to live with you? Because I *thought* you were. That's why *I* was here. I thought I was in love with you, Reve. Then I found out I was here to keep your bed warm. 'We're comfortable,'" she mocked. "'Why does it have to go anywhere?'"

Thought. He leaned back on his heels, sternum vibrating under the force of her anger and sense of betrayal.

He wouldn't have believed her if she had claimed to have actually been in love. Love was like the spirit that had guided her into her grandmother's tender arms—a nice thought, but mostly existing through acts of deliberate self-delusion.

He was starting to see that Nina was prone to that, though. She was a romantic, which made him the sort of person who took advantage of that, and he didn't like that view of himself one bit.

"I thought you wanted me to help you." He tried for a reasonable tone.

"And I thought you were helping me because you believed in me as an artist." She blinked fast. Even from across the room, he could tell her lashes were wet and matted. "You didn't care about my work, though. You wanted sex on tap."

"Not true. If all I wanted was a warm body in my bed, Kelly Bex would have been here. I want *you*, Nina." He pointed at her.

She took a step back.

Because he'd spoken in the present tense.

He ran his tongue over his teeth. He hadn't meant to reveal that, but yeah, his craving for her was circling him like a school of sharks. He kept batting his urges away because she was going through some stuff, but for one second he let her see it. He *wished* what he felt for her was the sort of base attraction any woman could satisfy. It wasn't. It had to be her.

Her expression twisted in confusion and she crossed her arms defensively.

"I wanted you to succeed," he insisted. "Maybe I don't know the fine points about fashion and trends, but I knew how hard you were working to have a voice in that world, how passionate you were about every stitch and pleat. Your sketches alone were enough to show me you had talent. Hell, Nina. I believe in you more than you believe in yourself."

"That is the most arrogant thing you have ever said in your life." Her arms shot straight down at her sides. "Which is saying a *lot*."

"Your dream was *right there*." He waved toward the hall. "And you walked away from it. You're still trying to walk away. That has nothing to do with me. If you want it, it's there. Quit making excuses and make it happen. But you're too afraid to pull the trigger. Aren't you?"

"What do you know about it? You think it's easy to put yourself out there?" Her arm flailed and she knocked her glass flying into the bar sink with a tinkle of broken glass. She made an infuriated noise, barely glancing at the damage. "It's not just ego, you know. Not for me." She smacked a hand onto her chest. "I've always had to do everything twice. Once my way, then I had to reverse engineer it so I could prove I knew how to do it the 'right' way." She made air quotes with her fingers. "Then Kelly picked apart everything I made."

So she could steal Nina's ideas. He'd watched her hurt and confusion as she saw her modified designs appear under Kelly's name.

"I've never understood why you let her get away with that."

"It was my first job in this industry! I thought I was *learning*." She touched her brow. "I thought I wasn't good enough yet and she was mentoring me, making me better."

Yet. That word encapsulated Nina's hopefulness and conviction in her ability to succeed, but where had her faith in herself gone?

"I was giving you a chance to do it your way, Nina."

"Because you wanted to have sex with me," she accused.

"Because I liked seeing you happy. What a jerk to want

to put a smile on your face," he scoffed. "But even if I was doing it as a transaction, *so what*? Why would that matter if you were getting what you wanted?"

"Don't be gross!"

"I'm not being gross. I'm asking how badly you want that dream? Not bad enough to do whatever it takes to get it."

"Because I'm not like that," she cried.

"Like what? Ruthless? I am." He moved to pick up the cordless house phone. "If you don't want all those boxes of clothes you made, fine. I'll call Kelly, tell her to get them out of my storage locker."

"Oh, you just try it, you bastard. I'll—" She stormed right up on him, glowing with incendiary fury.

His heart nearly exploded in reaction to the threat rolling off her even as another part of him gloried in how magnificent she was.

"You'll what?" he invited, heart galloping. "Fight for it?"

"Yes, damn you, I will." She grabbed the phone out of his hand and blindly threw it.

It hit the coffee table, where it bounced and skittered to the floor, possibly breaking into pieces.

He didn't look. Their gazes were locked, and all of his senses were drinking her in. Her loose hair with its shocks of pink, fine strands lifting as if electrified. Her pupils were exploded so there was only a glow of dark gold around them. She breathed in uneven pants.

He could feel his teeth showing as he smiled in atavistic glee. He was hard, so freaking hard for her in an instant. His blood had become hundred-proof alcohol, sharp and hot in his arteries, searing through his system and making his head swim. All his logic and calculations of risk and brain cells melted into the simmering pool of testosterone he was drowning in.

"Are we doing this?" He barely recognized his voice it was so guttural and raw.

"Yes." She grabbed his head and dragged his mouth to hers, lifting her mouth to meet him.

His arms went around her, and he tried… He honestly tried not to ravage her. Her fists knotted in his hair, and the pain made him realize he was squeezing her with all his strength, but she wouldn't let him lift his head. Her teeth raked his lips and he knew they would both have bruises after. Maybe she would even break his skin, but he'd be damned if he would protest her kissing him as if she wanted to bite his lips from his face.

He ran his hands down to her ass and squeezed, bracing his feet in a signal that was so well practiced between them he didn't even think of what he was doing until her weight landed against him. Her breasts mashed into his chest as he absorbed the force with a single staggered step back.

Her arms looped behind his neck, and her legs wrapped tight around his waist. His muscles strained as he held her tight and kissed her again. Plundered. Swept his tongue into the hot, wine-flavored cavern of her mouth and sucked her tongue into his.

He wanted to take her to the sofa, the floor, against the wall. They were both making noises like animals landing prey after weeks of starvation.

He *was* starved. He'd been suffering deprivation since she had left, and he was furious with her for it. Did she think any woman would be good enough after he'd had her? No one had even tempted him.

Holding her tight, he strode into his bedroom.

* * *

Nina had forgotten—or blocked out—how good it felt to be held by him. How his strong arms made her feel as though he wanted to meld them into a single being.

The friction as he walked stimulated her in primitive ways. Their mouths met, tasted and tangled and pillaged. She knew she was making carnal noises. So was he. She could hardly breathe, but she didn't want to give up one second of having her mouth sealed to his. She started to feel herself being pulled away and scrabbled her hands against the hard cords of muscles across the tops of his shoulders, hanging on.

The mattress hit her back and his weight came down between her legs, knees pushing behind her thighs to shove her higher onto the mattress. He yanked her kimono open, his hands busy between them as he fought with her belt. She drove her hands into his hair, dragging him back to kissing the hell out of her.

He did, and then swept his mouth to her throat. She felt the sting of him planting a hickey against her skin and let a jagged, encouraging cry scrape from her throat. She arched and his touch slid under her top, up to her breast.

The sensation of his hot palm claiming the swell was so acute she lifted her hips and bit through the shoulder seam of his shirt just hard enough to express the intensity gripping her.

They were both being rough and greedy. She was, anyway, but she *needed* this. She needed to see his gaze come up blind with lust. When she moved her hands under his shirt, skating her fingertips over his hard abs and up to his tight nipples, she couldn't get enough of the light scour of hair against her palms. She drank in the sight of him closing his eyes and smiled as she felt him shake under her touch.

He rocked onto his elbow and pushed her top up, baring her stomach as he slid down to open his mouth across her belly, taking soft, wet bites. He kissed his way up to the underside of her breast, pushing her top up to expose her, causing heat to swirl through her and lewd craving to pulse between her legs.

Their clothes kept getting in the way, but she didn't want to stop to undress and he didn't seem to want that, either. He captured her nipple and gave a strong, wet pull, drawing another keening cry from her. She wrapped her arms around his head and held him there, tortured by the delirious pleasure he was bestowing on her.

As he moved to her other breast, his hand went under her back, slid into her silk shorts at her tailbone and started to push them off. As they went down her thighs, so did he, his mouth kissing wetly down and down as though called there.

"Reve," she gasped, trying to pull her ankle free of the silk.

He used two fingers to part her folds, the way he'd always done, and set his mouth to her bared flesh. He paused—one breath, two—waiting for her to catch up to the intense heat and acute sensations. Waiting for her to want the circle of his tongue. Waiting for her to get over her moment of shyness and relax into this caress.

As she shivered and instinctually lifted her hips, spearing her hand into his hair, inviting him, he settled in to pleasure her with his clever tongue.

It was everything she remembered and more. Sharp streaks of pleasure went down the insides of her thighs. Tension coiled in her belly. It was so good, so good, but not enough.

"I want—" She tried to roll to the nightstand.

He rose and reached.

"And the stuff."

He handed her the lube and stood on his knees over her, pushing his shorts down only far enough to bare his erection so he could roll on a condom.

She spread cool gel across latex and he stole a dollop, touching her shoulder in a signal to lie back. He worked the slippery coolness into her and it nearly made her cry. She had missed his touch so much. She had missed the way they knew each other's bodies and spoke without words. He knew exactly how to press and tease and make her gasp with pleasure.

It had been so painful to lose that a latent sob throbbed from her throat.

"Hurt?" He started to withdraw his touch.

"No. I want you in me so *much*." She beckoned him to cover her again. She guided him herself, closing her eyes as she lined him up.

She wasn't completely ready. There was a pinch as he pressed for entrance. It made her shiver but, oh, it felt good to have him filling her, so thick and hot and hard.

He was swearing, eyes glazed. She could feel him shaking with an effort to hold himself in control.

"Don't be gentle." She let her nails bite into his buttocks, then drew her knees up to his rib cage. "I'm really so close."

With a groan, he kissed her open mouth with his own, lascivious and proprietary. Then he began to move with firm thrusts, watching her through slitted eyes.

She was so aroused, so ravenous for his powerful body moving in hers, she met his thrusts with lifts of her hips, encouraging him to let go. It was raw and gratifying and made her breaths shorten.

Her grip on him tightened. He increased his tempo. The sensations redoubled, and she slipped into a place of pure pleasure that seemed to have no peak, only more and more hot joy as all of her awareness narrowed to that point of potential inside her. She tensed, reaching. "Don't stop. Harder. *Please…*"

She shattered. All of her exploded into a thousand pieces while he roared and pinned his bucking hips to hers. His iron-hard arms caged her tight while he groaned into her neck and pulsed deep within her.

CHAPTER SIX

AFTER AN EON, when she floated in a space devoid of thought, Nina realized she needed a full breath. She touched his shoulder.

Reve dragged in his own breath, as though preparing himself for supreme effort, then carefully withdrew. In the same motion, he rolled to grab the box of tissues, offering it to her, exactly as he had always done.

Still dazed, Nina took two and used them while he removed the condom. He took the tissues from her and dropped them into the bedside wastebasket with the condom. He lay back beside her with a heavy sigh. He pulled his shorts into place before tugging his shirt down over them.

Her shorts were still on the floor somewhere. She closed the kimono and stayed beside him, stunned by what had just happened. It had been good, *so* good. Fast and…necessary? Probably not. Inevitable, she supposed.

Her own exhale was weighted with despair.

His head turned on the mattress. They were both still crooked on the bed.

"Made it longer than I expected." She looked to the clock as an excuse to turn her face away. "Almost six hours."

"And may have set a land speed record." His humor was as thin as hers, the edges brittle.

She pressed the back of her head into the mattress and looked at the familiar ceiling, trying not to cry. Why hadn't it been awful? Why didn't she feel dirty so she could hate him and hate herself and leave without ever looking back?

Instead, she felt as she always had, as though he knew her in ways she didn't even know herself. As though, together, they were greater than the sum of their parts.

It was just sex, though. Really, really good sex, but sex all the same.

"Do you want to stay here?" he asked. "Instead of a hotel?"

"Here?" She pointed at the mattress. She should have seen that coming. "No," she pronounced disdainfully.

"In the apartment," he clarified with equal condescension.

"Why would you even offer? Don't turn this into more than it was." Good advice for herself. She sat up and scooted to the edge of the bed.

"What was it?"

The spiteful thing to say would be, *Why does it have to be anything?*

"I don't know." She folded her arms across her middle, where an empty ache reached from the bottom of her stomach to the top of her heart. "I'd love to say stress relief, but I think I needed to feel like that again, to remind myself there was a reason I fell for you. We were really good for a little while and there's no shame in enjoying that. Is there?"

She peeked over her shoulder at him.

His gaze was flinty, his face shuttered and hard.

"So this was closure?" His lip curled.

Her lungs were filled with powdered glass. She looked forward again, unutterably sad. "Yes."

"Fine."

The word knocked the stuffing out of her, leaving her so bereft her whole body went numb.

He sat up beside her. "But that means dealing with your things."

"I told you—" She dug her heels into the rail of the bed, propped her elbows on her thighs and held her palms over her eyes.

"I believe you were threatening my life if I disposed of it without your input?" he reminded in a falsely friendly tone.

"Don't give it to her. Anyone but her," she begged, still hiding behind her hands.

"Who then?"

"I don't know," she moaned. "No one wants a cardboard box full of some unknown designer's blood, sweat and tears. I'll ship it home to Dad, I guess."

"Quit being such a coward."

She dropped her hands and glared at him.

His brows went up to a pithy angle. "Yes, that's what I called you."

"Oh, okay. I'll just throw together a show, then. Getting media attention won't be any problem! But I'll forever wonder if any success I have is mine or because of the stranger I happen to resemble, won't I?"

He stared down at her for so long she started to shrink under the weight of his penetrating gaze.

"That really bothers you, doesn't it?" he said with a baffled snort. "Most people would use every advantage to get what they want." He shook his head as though it didn't make sense to him.

"I told you, I'm not like that."

"I'm starting to believe that. I also think you're using it as an excuse not to try."

"Reve!" She stood up, angry and hurt, sweeping her hand out in helpless confusion. "Look at my life right now. I don't have time to reboot my failed career. Even if I tried to put together a show, it wouldn't be how I had planned it. The themes would be all wrong. My entire sense of self has changed. I don't know who I am anymore."

Even as frustrated tears burned behind her eyes, another part of her latched on to her own words. Maybe that could be the message. Any collection would be a snapshot of her life, not all of it. Sometimes things happened, forcing a detour. If a goal was important enough, you came back and picked up the pieces and tried a new approach...

Concepts began to swirl in her imagination. She was warming to it, playing with it.

"I know that look. You're thinking about it," he said smugly.

"So?" She tightened the belt of her kimono and began to pace. "I still don't have time. I don't have money." She threw up a hand at him. "Don't."

"I *will* offer to underwrite it and I'll tell you why." He rose, hair mussed, clothing wrinkled, and sexy as hell with his powerful muscles and stern jaw. "I refuse to let you boot this down the road or cobble it together on a shoestring and say you tried. I'll hire someone to do it right, pay for the show and take eighty percent of net profit in lieu of you paying me back for any of it."

"That's ridiculous."

"Seventy-five."

"I'm not arguing the percentage! Take eighty percent of zero. See if I care."

He swore under his breath. "I might get twelve dollars. I might get twelve million. That's called investing."

She shook her head and walked toward the window. "Don't."

"Don't what? Believe in you more than you believe in yourself?"

She stopped and spun and huffed an annoyed noise at the way he kept throwing that in her face.

"You only need one order for one piece, Nina. If it's big enough, I could make tenfold what I've invested in you so far."

"You always talk like these things are easy. Get a grip on the real world, Reve! Even if I did get an order, I would have to source the fabrics and find a factory. Get it made, get it here. At a profit. It's not *one thing*."

"So I wouldn't get my money tomorrow. That's also called investing. I know how to get a business off the ground, Nina—in the real world," he snarled. "I've had to do it many times. You need capital to set up shop and put a supply chain in place. That's what I'm offering you."

"I need to figure out who I *am*."

"You're not a fashion designer? An artist? That always seemed to be at the core of your identity."

It was, but... "Why are you pushing me like this? Do you want my stuff out of your storage locker that badly?"

"I want it out from between us," he said forcefully, pointing at the stretch of floor that separated them.

He seemed as startled by those vehement words as she was. He stood straighter and glanced away, jaw clenched.

"Why?" she asked helplessly. "Because of that?" She pointed at the bed.

"No." He pulled a wrinkle from the bedspread and then dropped the lube back in the drawer. He kept his back to her. "No one gave me a leg up or looked out for me in any way. That's all I want to do, Nina. Maybe I wasn't the best *boyfriend*." He drawled the word as if it was too puerile a label for what he'd been to her. It was. "Maybe I looked on your being here as a convenient arrangement, not…" His fingers tapped on the night table as he seemed to search for words. "Not a relationship with a future, but I do care what happens to you."

He turned. His expression was difficult to interpret. He was too self-confident to be defensive. Guarded, maybe?

She swallowed, but the scoured feeling behind her breastbone remained. She had spent months backpedaling through their relationship, taking all of his small kindnesses and thoughtful gestures and reframing them as quid pro quos for sex. Despite the very good sex they'd just had, he didn't owe her anything, not even a night's sleep in a comfortable bed. There was no reason for him to keep after her this way beyond the reason he was giving—that he wanted to support her aspirations.

Maybe he always had.

Her eyes grew hot with unshed tears. She bit her lips to keep them from trembling.

"I don't think you should fly off to Germany by yourself to hunt down potential criminals," he said, squeezing the back of his neck. "At least let me hire someone to go in for a discreet recon. Stay here while you figure out flights and make a plan. My security is watertight. You can organize a show while you're here."

"And you would give me all this support why?" she asked with a husky laugh of disbelief. "So we can part as friends?"

"We'd be business partners," he corrected.

"You *want* that?"

"Why not?"

"Because it's impossible! I'll wind up in bed with you." She waved at the bed as proof. "And you don't want the sort of future that I want."

"Which is what? Marriage? Children?"

"Yes," she said firmly, though it felt like a very far-off, abstract goal right now. It had always been in her realm of expectation that her life would include making a family with a man she loved, but as she sank down into the overstuffed chair in the corner, she wondered what the new Nina would want once she came out the other side.

It struck her that these were her final moments as Nina Menendez, the woman she'd always known herself to be. Soon she would be Oriel Cuvier's sister or Lakshmi Dalal's daughter. Everything would be different.

Reve was offering her the gift of being herself a little longer.

Damn him, he shouldn't be making this into such a difficult decision. She had sworn to her family that she wasn't coming back to New York to see him. He was bad for her. So bad that she had just slept with him. Obviously, she couldn't be trusted around him.

On the other hand, she didn't want to rush into the unknown, turning over rocks at random. She needed a plan. She wasn't actually that good in new places, sometimes confusing her directions. And the signposts would be in different languages, which would be even harder for her to read than English. Her father couldn't afford private investigators, but she saw the sense in hiring one.

"I would want to know how much you spend," she said cautiously. "One way or another, I want to pay you back for—"

"I'll make some calls." He walked out before she could say anything more.

Reve was a man of action. Moving, shaking, tearing down and rebuilding gave him the illusion he had control over his life. Back when he'd had little to no say over what happened to him, he'd achieved small triumphs in bashing rusted nuts from a wheel so he could get at the brake parts or by puzzling out how the water pump was installed so he could remove it.

As long as he'd worked toward a goal of some kind, he hadn't been standing still in the run-down shack that had held an alcoholic father and an empty refrigerator. At the very least, staying busy had allowed him to forget his empty stomach for a while.

He issued his statement that he'd never met Oriel Cuvier and began making calls for Nina's show. As he did, he realized this was an ironic version of his long-held coping strategy—he was trying to forget her desire for "closure" by providing it for her.

It made for an itchy, irritable sensation within him, but he got the ball rolling. Otherwise, he would sink into reliving their flurry of lovemaking.

Then the memory arrived anyway, running over him like a mile-long train and, *damn*, that had felt good. He was embarrassed by how little finesse he'd shown, but she'd matched every greedy caress and every scorching kiss. It had been exciting as hell and over far too quickly. He wanted to say, *Let's try that again. Take it slow. Do it right*.

Do what right?

Don't turn this into more than it was.

Her dismissal of their lovemaking had been jarringly close to what he had said. *Why does it have to go anywhere?* That had sent her running back to Albuquerque.

Guilt crept into his consciousness like fleas under his shirt, itching and biting and driving him to prove something to her. Prove what? That he really did want her to succeed with her dream? He did, but it went deeper than that.

He hadn't realized how many inner hurdles, along with the external ones, she'd had to overcome. He knew something about not feeling good enough. It ate at him to know she was still struggling with that. That he'd contributed to it by believing she was as driven by self-interest as everyone else in his sphere.

He was still skeptical that anyone could be *that* honest and empathetic and warm, but he couldn't deny that she was in a very vulnerable position. Thinking of the hyenas of the press getting hold of her caused an overwhelming protectiveness to rise up in him.

It killed him to see the defeat in her eyes. The uncertainty. He was compelled to do something to build her up, to help her get back the joy she'd felt in her work. He felt good taking these steps on her behalf, as though it forged something between them. Not an obligation, but a connection. One that wouldn't break the minute she walked out again.

He clenched a fist, disturbed by how much the thought of her leaving filled him with dread. *Loneliness.*

He brushed the childish emotion aside. Solitude meant autonomy, that's why he preferred it. He wasn't trying to cling. He was trying to be a decent person. If helping her kept her under his roof a few days, fine. At least he got some home cooking out of it.

By the middle of the next morning, Reve was showing her a two-thousand-square-foot loft in Chelsea that made Nina have to pick her jaw up off the hardwood floor. The row of windows that ran the length of the narrow space provided amazing light. It was perfect!

A man named Andre, who organized fashion shows

for some of the top designers, signed an NDA before he met them there. He smiled warmly when he saw Nina.

"Oriel! I wondered who the mystery designer was. It's so good to see you again." He walked forward, trying to embrace her.

"I'm, um, Nina Menendez." She pushed her hand between them, offering to shake.

He fell back on his heel and dipped his chin as though she was pulling his leg.

"Really," Nina assured him. "I'm not her. I believe she's currently with her husband in India."

"You look *exactly* like her." His confused gaze went to the pink streaks in her hair and her deliberately bare face and dressed-down jeans and T-shirt.

"I've heard that before." Nina shrugged as if it was a mild nuisance that meant nothing. "It's one of the reasons I'm keeping such a low profile. I don't want to be seen as trading on our resemblance. I want my work to stand on its own."

"Of course."

Reve left to finalize the lease agreement. After thirty minutes of discussion with Andre, Nina was confident they were on the same page creatively. By that afternoon, Andre's well-versed team had arrived and Nina was unpacking her work from the boxes. There would be no models and catwalk, but along with a set designer and lighting technician, Andre planned to bring in a photographer, a digital marketing expert and a communications specialist to ensure maximum exposure.

The costs were adding up so fast they made Nina hyperventilate. The rent alone was twenty-five hundred a day, which Reve shrugged off.

"I paid more for that garden party I didn't attend."

She searched his expression, still having trouble believing he was willing to gamble this sort of money on her, but from things he'd said about past deals, some in the hundreds of millions, this was small potatoes.

Even so, she couldn't stand the idea of failing and causing him to take a loss. She worked sixteen-hour days, lingering long after Andre and his crew had left, adding finishing touches so her show would be ready by the end of the week. She probably would have slept there if Reve hadn't been in his car when it arrived every night at ten, texting her that dinner was waiting and he was hungry.

She also probably would have slept with him if he'd invited her to his bed, but he didn't. She ought to be glad for that, she supposed, but she was a little hurt that he was suddenly treating her like a professional acquaintance.

That's not how she was thinking of him. Despite her exhaustion, she lay awake every night, longing to go down the hall and lose herself in their special brand of passion.

When she did fall asleep, she woke abruptly to anxious thoughts—worries about whether the investigator was learning anything and whether she'd be okay at the loaned flat in Germany.

She worried about how she would say goodbye to Reve again. It had been a lot easier when she had been angry and hurt.

"Why are you up so early?" He came into the kitchen wearing only pajama bottoms and a night's worth of stubble. His voice held morning rasp that was intimate enough to awaken her erogenous zones, even as his morning erection was subsiding against the loose fabric of his pants.

She moved to the coffeemaker to hide the fact she'd noticed, but her cheeks were stinging and her voice was strained. "Early bird avoids the paparazzi. I asked your driver last night if he minded. He said it was fine."

"Anything before seven a.m. is double time. Of course, he doesn't mind," he said drily.

"Oh. Shoot." She faltered in rinsing out her travel mug. "I'll add it to my expenses."

"Don't worry about it." He moved to the cupboard and took out bread for the toaster.

They were back-to-back, and she was so aware of him that all the cells in her body seemed to align like magnets finding north. She could have stood there forever, basking in this closeness.

She swallowed and picked up the tea towel to dry her mug. "I didn't mean to wake you."

"I wanted to talk to you. I need to go to Europe."

"Today?" A zing of loss jolted through her, rooting her feet to the floor. She wasn't ready to say goodbye.

"Soon. There's a company I want to acquire." Dishes rattled as he set out a plate and a butter knife. "We already have some capability for making car parts with 3D printers, but this German outfit is taking it to the next level."

"Oh." With a shaky hand, she poured the espresso she'd made for herself into a mug for him. When she caught his eye, she found him watching her.

Her pulse leaped in reaction, and her gaze took an involuntary inventory of his wide shoulders and relaxed biceps, the muscled pecs with small dark nipples and his sectioned abs.

"I can be out of your hair anytime. Dad heard back from his friend. He's leaving his key with his neighbor. Dad wasn't able to get me on a flight, but I've looked at what's available. I just have to pick one and book it."

"I'm not kicking you out." Reve sent her a disgruntled scowl and yanked open the refrigerator. "I'm saying I could take you with me. When were you thinking of leaving?"

Her inner Reve-addict jumped on that suggestion, particularly as lust was trying to take hold in her, but she made herself say, "That's not necessary. You're doing too much already."

"It's nothing. I'm going anyway. I usually stay at my apartment in Paris. You can stay with me, same as we have been here."

Platonically?

Her sister had been alarmed when she learned Nina was staying with Reve. And that they'd had sex.

Nina, it's fine if you forgive him. It's fine if you believe he never meant to mislead you. But your eyes are open now. Don't let him hurt you again. Where are you two going if you start up again? You have a right to ask those questions.

Angela was right, but Reve didn't seem to be taking anything for granted. She almost wished he would pressure her into an affair so she could succumb, then blame him for her own weakness.

"I might get recognized in Paris," she pointed out.

"You might get recognized anywhere. That's why my apartment is a good option. It's more secure than some pilot's walk-up in Frankfurt."

"How long is the train from Paris to Luxembourg?"

"Three or four hours." The toast popped and he turned to butter it.

She screwed fresh grounds into place in the espresso machine. "Could we leave Friday?"

"*This* Friday? The day your show opens? Don't you want to be there?"

"Gawd, no."

"Why not?" He frowned at her.

"Fear." She curled her lip in disgust at herself.

"Chicken," he chided, then offered her the plate with the buttered toast. "Eat. I suspect you've been skipping lunch. Would you trust Andre to break everything down?"

"Yes. Maybe. I don't know what to think of him anymore." She took one slice. "He said something that freaked me out."

"What?" Reve clacked the plate onto the island and the second piece of toast nearly slid off it. His demeanor had gone from morning lazy to protective Neanderthal so quickly she could hardly swallow the bite of toast in her mouth.

"It wasn't anything mean." She cleared her throat, then turned to finish making her coffee one-handed. "It was actually encouraging, but I'm terrified he's deluding both of us. He said he would cover the cost of leaving the show up an extra week if I gave him the green cocktail dress. I told him about my deal with you and that I would ask."

She sent Reve a sideways look as she set the machine to gurgling and hissing.

His brow furrowed. "Can you alter that dress to fit him? He's a pretty big guy."

"He wants it as an investment." This was the part that sounded like a delusion. "He thinks in a year, once my work has had a chance to circulate and build momentum, an original piece by Nina Menendez will go for, um…" She could hardly say it. "Five figures."

"Is that a fact." Reve leaned his hips on the counter and folded his arms. "If I had known that, I might have kept it in my storage locker."

"Ha ha." She rolled her eyes.

"I'm not joking." He cocked his head. "Does he know about your connection to Oriel?"

"*No.* He probably suspects, but he genuinely likes the dress. He's been super honest with me about all of my work. If he thinks I played it too safe or missed an opportunity to elevate a piece, he says so, but he doesn't want me to change anything. He says it shows my evolution. He uses words like 'inspiring' and 'exciting.' I can't *bear* to see his face when he discovers no one else likes any of it." She was having flashbacks to Kelly's tight smiles and bitchy nitpicking after a fellow seamstress had gushed over something Nina had made. "Being across the Atlantic when the doors open sounds ideal."

"You big, giant chicken," he accused, but his tone was gentle and the curl of his mouth held affection.

That smile put the sweetest joy in her heart, an expansive feeling that made her feel shy and emotive and happy.

His gaze touched her mouth and sexual tension crackled.

He swallowed and picked up his coffee. "If you change your mind and want to stay, let me know. Tell him I'll call to work out something for the dress."

She nodded, releasing a low breath, disappointed.

Reve had been working long hours to keep his mind—and hands—off Nina. Every evening, after he'd gone home and worked out to the point of physical failure, he'd gone to collect her, texting from the street so she could slip in beside him undetected.

She always sagged with weariness, which helped him keep from making a pass, but he didn't like seeing her push herself so hard. He knew how much this meant to her, though, and that she was trying to keep her mind off what would happen once she went to Europe.

Reve had hoped his investigator would turn up more, saving her from going to Luxembourg herself, but the village had been overrun with reporters when Oriel's story broke. Apparently, the locals were being very tight-lipped. The man had at least located a property that was still in the family of the doctor who had delivered Nina.

Reve had taken a small liberty with that information, still concerned with what would happen to Nina once her story broke. He couldn't leave her to fend for herself, not when he had the resources and experience to buffer her from the worst of the attention.

At the same time, he knew he was setting up himself—and her—for a rehash of his unsavory past if he let himself become part of her story. It disturbed him how much he was leaving himself exposed and why. He'd been blinded by sexual infatuation the first time with her and, yes, he still was. Despite working his body to quivering fatigue every day, he woke in the night so hard for her his whole body ached. Knowing she was just down the hall was pure torture, but there was a primitive, possessive part of him that liked having her close even if he couldn't touch her. Plus, he knew no other man was touching her.

Ah, jealousy. The most manipulative emotion of all. He fairly groaned aloud as he realized how susceptible he'd become to it.

Did she realize how much power that gave her over him? She would, he thought with a dour look at the champagne he'd picked up on his way to collect her. He was practically advertising it.

But he was here now, literally turning into the block where the showroom was located. It was Thursday, and Nina had texted that the photographer was coming at seven and she would be ready to leave after that. Reve had purposely arrived at six thirty.

He went inside for the first time since the day he'd leased the space, and could hear Nina and Andre bantering good-naturedly as he neared the cloakroom at the top of the stairs.

"See Now, Buy Now is everything that is wrong with today's world, not just fashion," Andre bemoaned. "It's the *manufacture* of trends. There's nothing organic or artistic about it. Why even bother— Oh, hello." Andre stopped dialing the switch that controlled the dimming of a track light. He poked his head into the showroom. "Nina, the most dashing man has turned up with champagne and only two glasses. I think that means one of us is supposed to take a walk."

"What? Reve!" Nina appeared with a flushed smile that struck the backs of his eyes like sunshine, but she used her body to forestall his entering the showroom, which prickled his old, suspicious instincts.

From here, all he could see was a table set up in front of a window. On it was an ornate business card holder that looked like an antique from a French chateau, a cup of pens and a single rose in a silver vase.

"Text me when the photographer gets here. I'll come back and close up after him," Andre said as he put on a tailored green jacket.

Nina thanked him for all his help and they embraced, kissing each other's cheeks.

As Andre stepped back, he said to Reve in a falsely pleasant tone, "If you spill one drop of that in my showroom, I will hunt you down and kill you with my bare hands."

Reve thumbed the cork so it popped loudly and fell to the floor. Only a wisp of condensation emerged from the neck.

"So long as we understand each other." Andre smirked and trotted down the stairs.

"This is a nice surprise. Thank you." Nina smiled nervously as he handed her a glass crackling with a head of bubbles.

"I thought I'd come see—" He stopped short of saying *what I've paid for.* "How it all came together."

They touched glasses and sipped, but she didn't move from the doorway. Her eyes grew wide and anxious. Panic-stricken.

"What's wrong? I've seen all of it before."

"Not like this."

"Like what?" She drove him a little crazy sometimes, being this emotionally attached to what? His opinion? "I'll be kind, Nina."

"I don't want you to be kind," she said, instantly cross. "I want you to be honest. I just don't know if I can handle it." She drained her champagne in a couple of swallows and set the glass on the shelf next to the bottle. "He's serious about no food or drink in there."

Reve seared his own throat with the cool, sizzling Salon Le Mesnil Brut and set his glass beside hers.

She jerkily waved him in ahead of her, then trailed behind him as he entered the long room. Tall tables and a couple of benches had been set up on the side of the room with the windows, probably to provide a space for buyers to sit and make notes or calls. The blinds on the windows were down, the showroom lit with lights that angled and pooled to guide focus.

The clothes were arranged down the inside wall and told a story that felt familiar to him since Reve recognized so many of the pieces. Still, it was a story he hadn't fully understood until now.

The first few outfits were pinned to cloth-covered

squares that hung on the walls. Sketches were pinned alongside them, showing how the pieces had first been conceived. Each was pretty and well constructed. The lines were straight, the buttons were scrupulously spaced. They were undoubtedly good quality and classic—and very safe. There was an innocence to them. A hesitation.

As he ambled along, however, the sketches and outfits grew more daring. Brighter colors mingled with contrasting textures. Here, the clothing was draped over chairs and displayed on hangers that created an impression the pieces had begun to breathe and find life.

He remembered Nina being the same as she gained confidence in what she was trying to say and do. Her growing excitement had been evident in the way she had begun to stray from strict symmetry and played with adding a bracelet or sewing on a spangled pin.

Now he stood among mannequins in polished ensembles fit for high-powered boardrooms and elite social events. There was a white pantsuit with a wide-brimmed hat, the green cocktail dress with its gold chain belt and spiked heels. A yellow top with a sharply pointed collar was accented by a long-strapped purse and sexy sunglasses. A frozen wrist was cocked to hold a jacket and a marble leg kicked out the slit of a cheeky ruby skirt.

Standing among these pieces felt as though he was at a party, one where everyone was having the time of their life.

The fun then ended abruptly.

A gown of silver and blue sat upon a dress form with sequins only partially applied to its neckline. The waist gaped because it was attached by dozens of pins, not stitches. One sleeve of the gown hung lifeless from the sewing machine beside it.

On the floor, among spilled sequins and scattered pins,

a pair of designer shoes looked as though they'd been kicked off as the owner fled like Cinderella from her ball.

It was jarring, but even more so was the empty space that followed. A beam of light emphasized the emptiness. It shouldn't have felt like such a blow to the heart, but it was. He was responsible for that absence of work. Guilt settled as a bitter taste in the back of his throat. Loss. He had hurt her with his callousness that day. Hurt her so badly she had stopped doing what she loved and run away from her dream.

He had to close his eyes to absorb the pain that enveloped him.

He kept wanting to paint her actions with ulterior motives, but that was his own defense mechanism. The truth was this was who she was—a sensitive, emotive artist who only wanted to add beauty to the world. She was so raw and honest she had put her entire soul on display for the world to see.

She had shown it to him, and he hadn't appreciated what a privilege that was. It scared him that she was this open, it really did. Did she not realize how badly she could be hurt?

Bad enough she could walk away and tell him to *burn* all of this.

His nostrils stung as he drew in a breath. He wanted to take her into his arms, pour himself around her so nothing could touch her, but when he opened his eyes, he was looking at the dress she'd worn the day she'd come running back into his life.

It was a simple blue thing hung on a clear torso suspended from the ceiling—no head or accessories. It seemed to drift in midair like an apparition and was symbolic of her lost self, he supposed, with a hollow ring in his heart. The sense of something unfinished or unfound left a coil of deep longing inside him. It made him want to help her discover the rest of herself because he couldn't bear how insubstantial and adrift this suggested she was. As though she was only a shell of the woman she used to be, untethered.

The blue fabric was light enough to show the small bloodstain she must have brushed onto it that day. Despite that, and despite the fact it wasn't fancy or glamorous, he saw the small details that made it unmistakably part of the collection. Part of *her*, still alive and showing through. The skirt had a sophisticated flare that eschewed restrictions. There were crisscrossed straps at the back that had been hidden by her hair. They suggested a quiet defiance of convention, almost like graffiti that claimed, *I was here*.

Beyond that dress was a table piled with bolts of silk and linen and velvet in an array of colors. Ribbons and lace fell in coils from the top of it like ribbons off an unopened present. A pair of scissors sat atop a sketchbook open to a blank page.

Reve backed onto a bench and sat down, blowing out a low breath as though he'd been through something intense. His elbows went onto his knees and he rubbed his jaw before letting his gaze flicker back over the display.

"Is it too on the nose?" Nina asked with dread.

"Shh," he murmured, and absently took her hand.

He drew her to sit beside him, and his thumb played across her knuckles as his gaze slowly retraced the journey from the door to the unused fabrics. Finally he swiveled his attention to her, and the fierce light in his gaze made her heart pound in her chest.

"I don't know how to take this." She drew her hand from his and tangled her fingers over the unsteady sensation in her middle. "Are you appalled that you've thrown your money away? It's okay. Just say it."

"Nina," he breathed. "This is what you want." He pointed at the bench. "To knock people onto their ass." He spoke in a tone that was stunned—moved, even.

Her insides squirmed harder and her eyes grew damp.

"You're just being nice," she dismissed, pushing her hands between her knees and anxiously looking over what she feared was a vanity project.

"Stop it." He rose and pointed back to the beginning, his tone sharpening. *"Look* at what you've done. You *made* this." His arm swept the whole collection. "And you know what? I'm *proud* that I had something to do with it. *That* pisses me off," he said, pointing to the empty space. "Don't let anyone have that kind of power over you. *Especially me.*"

Too late, she thought, her heart squeezing as she watched how he ran his hand over his jaw, his gaze agonized as he stared into the dust motes dancing beneath the empty spotlight.

"I hate that I had anything to do with you losing even one minute of pursuing your dream, but the rest? If you want to run yourself down, you're going to have to find someone else to listen to it because no, Nina. This is better than I expected and I expected a *lot.*"

"Well, don't make me *cry,*" she wailed. Although she had wanted his approval, his admiration, hearing it was too much to handle. It made her vision blur as tears soaked her lashes.

"You're crying because you're tired, you silly woman."

She was tired, but this was about him and how much it meant to her. When he caught her by the wrists and tugged her into his arms, she went there gratefully, still trembling in reaction.

"I didn't realize, Nina." His breath tickled against her hair, and his voice wasn't quite steady. "I didn't realize you have no filter or shield, that what you show the world and what you showed me, is actually *you*. That's too much. You know that, don't you?"

His hand clenched in her hair behind her neck. He drew back to search her eyes.

"It's who I was," she acknowledged, glancing at the floating dress. "And I had to say goodbye to her."

She'd been coming to terms with that all week. She would always have a home with her family, but the life she'd had with them in Albuquerque would never be the same. New York was no longer a place of promise where her dreams were yet to be realized. Even the artist who had imagined these pieces and turned them into reality was gone. She had felt it as she reacquainted herself with them. She still yearned to design and create, but she already knew her future work would be different. Her priorities had shifted. *She* had.

Even her visions of what she might have had with Reve were gone. Oh, she hoped they could continue this—affectionate embraces and a thread of trust—but she knew now that this was all they ever would have. At best, they were business partners with a past—hopefully friends—but they weren't lovers…and they would never be soul mates.

"Thank you," she said. "For not throwing this away. For giving me the means to make it in the first place, and for nudging me into taking this chance. No matter what happens with it, I'm grateful."

He cupped the side of her face, his thumb moving restlessly against her cheek as he searched her eyes. He started to dip his head and then stopped himself. His mouth pulled down at one side in self-deprecation.

She wanted that kiss. Yearned for it. She went onto her tiptoes and he met her halfway.

They clashed like storm waves to a shore, forceful and beautiful and thrilling. It was the most painful kiss of her life and the most tender. Her dream was all around her, in large part thanks to him. She poured her heart into their kiss, trying to convey what it meant to her to tell her story. What *he* meant to her.

His breath hissed and his hands moved over her with strength, but in a way that cherished, making her feel precious and needed and safe even as her soul was bared for all to see.

Just as passion started to flare, as they canted their heads to deepen the seal of their lips, a distant bell sounded.

Reve jerked his head up and his arms tightened protectively around her.

"It's the photographer," she said, pulling away to press the back of her hand to her buzzing lips. "For the… things." Her brain couldn't find words.

Footsteps paused in the cloakroom, probably as the champagne was spotted.

"Um, hello? It's Munir. Andre said I should come around this time to get the final shots."

"Come in, Munir," Nina called. "We were just leaving. I'll text Andre to come back."

CHAPTER SEVEN

THE PLANE WAS long and narrow and pointed like a pencil. It had bladed wings attached to its sides and a booster rocket as an eraser.

Nina had spent January through March living Reve's life. Staying in his secure building with its daily housekeeping and obscenely gorgeous views had already been a lifestyle far beyond her middle-class experience. He had often spoken very casually of other extravagant things, like his house in Hawaii or his yacht in Florida, so she ought to have been prepared for this.

There was a big jump between hearing him mention a supersonic jet, however, and walking into one where he was greeted with warm familiarity.

"Mr. Weston, it's nice to have you aboard." The uniformed staff placed their luggage in the stateroom located in the tail. Glancing in, Nina saw it held a king bed amid built-in furniture in glossy mahogany. The curtains were open, showing the private airfield, but the hostess touched a button that opened a skylight, allowing morning sun to pour onto the bed.

They moved into a sitting area that held a half-dozen recliners and a couple of sectionals. Everything swiveled into different configurations to allow for private conversations or conferring as a group. Tables emerged from various wall pockets for dining and holding a laptop.

Before she sat down, Nina unabashedly peeked into the galley. There was a wine fridge and something baking that smelled like fresh croissants.

She settled in a recliner that faced Reve's, and glanced behind him at the screen showing the weather and their flight plan. She was completely intimidated.

After their kiss at the showroom last night, she'd cooked dinner, wondering if something more would happen between them. The way he'd reacted after viewing her collection had been so…

Well, she didn't know what she'd seen or heard in him except that she felt as though he had finally seen her exactly as she was. There was little triumph or comfort in it, though. Especially when he skirted talking about any of it when they arrived back to the privacy of the penthouse. He knew how much he had meant to her and how deeply he'd hurt her, but he only brought up innocuous topics like how she planned to travel to Luxembourg.

Confused, she had wound up making calls to her family, bringing them up to speed on her plans. Reve had been talking to Australia when her long hours of work had caught up to her and she'd fallen into bed.

It was just a kiss, she kept telling herself. Same as she kept saying, *It was just sex*.

It was just Reve. He had this effect on her. He made her want and yearn and rationalize and wish and hope for impossible things to come true. He made her like him and laugh and want to spend every moment of her life in his presence.

But he had never wanted those sorts of roots and family ties, and she didn't understand why.

They took off, leaving a small bang behind them.

"That was it?" she asked.

"The boom? Yes. This technology has come a long way. The original was banned for overland travel because the booms were damaging buildings. They were also fuel hogs. You'll be happy to hear, we use biofuel and have a near-zero carbon emission."

This was a funny old argument they loved to dig their heels into. He called her a tree hugger who starved so she could make clothes that only rich people could buy. She called him an elite industrialist who was out of touch with the way common people really lived, even as he made off-brand car parts so blue-collar workers could save a few bucks.

They were both right *and* wrong, but she still bit.

"I imagine you're happy, too, since you live on the same planet as I do." She played with the touch screen that came out of her armrest, glancing through the various entertainment options. "This spaceship is overkill, isn't it? I mean, we're not transporting a kidney, are we?" She pretended to look under her seat for one. "Why do you need to be able to get to Paris in three-and-a-half hours?"

"Time is the new luxury, haven't you heard?" He nodded at the air hostess to serve them breakfast. "And I like to surround myself with the very best. That's why you're in my life."

"Ha ha." She looked away, a tiny bit hurt that he would mock her like that.

The hostess efficiently made a table appear from the wall and flicked a tablecloth across it. Moments later, she brought fresh pastries with coffee and took their orders.

Nina noticed Reve was watching her as his thumb and finger rubbed pensively against the handle of his coffee mug.

"I bought this jet because I can. There was a time when I couldn't afford a baloney sandwich, even though my father somehow always had enough for a bottle. That sort of thing leaves you hungry for the rest of your life. It makes you reluctant to apologize for acquiring nice things when you can afford to buy them."

While she had known he hadn't had much growing up, she hadn't realized it was that bad. She bit her lip with contrition. "Why did you never tell me that before?"

"So you could see me as noble because I was once poor?"

"So I could understand you better."

"What's to understand? I want to eat and be warm and dry, same as everyone. I want those needs to be met consistently."

"But you don't believe they will be. Is that what you're saying?" A stark, tragic truth dawned on her. "Deep down, you're always worried that this—" she waved at the extremely high standard of living on display "—is temporary."

"Nothing in life is permanent," he said with conviction. "But yes. That's why I have a dozen fail-safes. Property here, extra cash there. I'm like a dog burying bones in the yard." He was being very self-deprecating, and it made her ache to hear it.

For her whole life, she had always taken for granted that if her life fell apart, she could fall back on her family. In fact, she *had*. When she had walked out on Reve, she'd cried in her father's hotel room. She'd been home a few days later, sleeping in her old bed, pouring her heart out to her sister, who had helped her get back on her feet.

The one time she had worried her family wouldn't be there for her had been this recent crisis. Fearing she might lose them had been the darkest, most terrifying time of her life.

She tried to imagine a whole childhood of being that isolated and unsupported. Her throat closed on a lump.

"You don't believe people are constant, either. Do you?" she realized.

"They're not." He used his lobster fork to draw meat from the bright orange tail that had been butterflied and broiled. It sat amid deviled eggs and blanched beans decorated with capers and olives and mushrooms. "Even when people don't betray you on the way out the door, they still leave."

"Like me?" she asked in a thin voice.

"You. My PA left a couple of months ago. She worked for me for four years and I never once made her cry. I asked. She made six figures and had two months of paid vacation every year. She said it was the best job she'd ever had, but she was getting married and wanted to start a family. Now I'm training Melvin." He lifted a shoulder, conveying his lack of enthusiasm. "He's fine, but I've learned my lesson and won't get attached."

Nina broke the yolk on her poached egg so it oozed across the lox stacked with asparagus and tomato on toasted crostini. "Will you tell me what happened with *her*?"

"Her? Oh. *Her*." His mouth twisted. "It's all online. I was involved with a sex advice blogger who filmed us during an intimate moment without my knowledge. She also posted it to her site without my permission."

Nina had the feeling his lawyer had crafted that statement because it sounded word for word how he'd described it the first night they'd had dinner. *I like to get this out of the way*, he'd said. *So you understand why I am so adamant about not allowing people to use me for their personal gain.*

Since it had never been her intention to do so, and he had clearly not wanted to talk more about it, she'd pushed the whole thing to the back of her mind. He must have thought she hadn't appreciated how truly devastating it must have been.

"Would you tell me how you got together?" She was treading very carefully. "What led her to think that would be okay?"

He kept his gaze on his plate as he chewed and swallowed, then chased it with a gulp of orange juice. Just when she thought he was going to ignore her question, he spoke.

"We got together because I was twenty-two and she was a very sexually experienced twenty-nine. I was getting press for closing in on my first million. She had her blog and was determined to make her first million by thirty. She said she wanted to achieve it in her own way, without a man helping her. How ironic is *that*?"

He spoke with droll amusement but glowered into the middle distance.

"Was she angry with you?"

"Not at all. She was on a kick of trying to normalize older women sleeping with younger men. She was already writing posts about our sex life, and I didn't care because she was only using my first name. I didn't know about the video until I got a call from a reporter. I told her to take it down. She said I should enjoy the publicity and left it up. To be fair, I did benefit from it. And the publicity around the court case."

"Did she think that justified it? What happened when you went to the police?"

"They said it was her word against mine. By the time we went to court, she was claiming she'd done it to expose the lack of teeth in revenge porn laws. She came to court armed with a hundred instances where men had done something similar to women and had their cases dismissed. There was no way for her to lose at that point. Either she would become a martyr, suffering a heftier punishment than any man ever had, or our case would be dismissed like all the rest. Either way, her website was making hundreds of thousands in advertising. She made her million by thirty with months to spare," he said with false admiration.

"What happened? Was she found guilty or...?"

"She paid a fine of five hundred dollars and did thirty days of community service."

"Are you serious?"

"The laws *are* inadequate," he said with a fatalistic shrug, though she could tell he was still simmering with rage beneath his laissez-faire attitude.

"What about civil damages?"

"We settled out of court." He dipped another morsel of lobster into his melted butter. "There was no win for me in publicly flogging someone who was being lauded as a social activist for revealing a flaw in the system. I just wanted out of the spotlight. She had already received a pile of donations for her legal fund, so I had her roll it into a nonprofit that pays the fees for other victims pursuing justice for similar crimes. She is not allowed to speak my name, and whenever our tape is regurgitated into the blogosphere, I bill her for the takedown expenses."

"You must hate her so much." Nina did. She had never before wanted to cause another person harm, but she sure did now.

His expression darkened. "I'm angry with myself for allowing it to happen."

"Reve. That's called victim blaming. She did that *to* you. You didn't provoke or invite it."

"Nina." He mocked her tone of intervention. "A person like you, who has every reason to believe in others, is not to blame when someone takes your sincerely offered trust and crushes it under their heel. I already knew people could be rotten to the core. I failed to protect myself because I thought we had something."

"You loved her?" Oh, that was a dagger to the heart. Her fingers went numb. She set down her cutlery with a clatter so she wouldn't drop it.

"I don't know what I thought I felt." His cheek ticked and he didn't meet her gaze. "Whatever it was, she betrayed it in a very public and humiliating way."

She nodded jerkily. No wonder he hated paparazzi so much. She contemplated why she was going to Europe and how much attention she might garner.

"There's still time to distance yourself from me, you know. Before my identity comes out and things blow up."

"I know," he said gravely. "I will."

His quiet assertion caused her throat to close up. As she coughed and tried to recover, she realized breakfast was over for her.

Reve had offered up his heart to another woman, and she had essentially sold it to the highest bidder. Nina had no idea how to help him get past that. Why would he want to? It would mean leaving himself open to another betrayal like the one he'd already suffered. His inner walls had been forged in fire and she understood why he fought so hard to keep them in place.

Reve's phone buzzed. He pulled it out, glanced at it and said contemplatively, "Humph…" Then he set the phone facedown.

It buzzed again. Then again.

He picked it up to read the screen.

"Is something wrong?"

"Not at all." His mouth pushed sideways in something that bordered on smugness.

He started to put it down, but it buzzed again.

"Something about your deal in Berlin?"

"No," he said mildly, but when his gaze met hers, there was a light in his eyes that was pure, wicked enjoyment.

Her heart shrank, then exploded with alarm.

"You did *not* tell Andre to text you." She had expressly told the man she would be in touch if and when she wanted to know how things were going. Otherwise, he should maintain radio silence.

"I plead the Fifth." Reve set the phone facedown again and went back to eating, grinning around his fork.

She stared at his phone, not realizing she was holding her breath until it buzzed again. She gasped for air and looked at Reve.

He lifted his brows.

"Oh, for heaven's sake! *Tell me.* No, don't. Wait. Do I want to know?"

"It's not that big a deal," he said with a hitch of his shoulder, but he was shaking with quiet laughter. "You've had a bid on the unfinished gown, as is, with the sewing machine and shoes. It's from one of Andre's colleagues who designs window displays for upscale boutiques in Asia." He reached for his phone and read, "'He set a reserve bid of twenty-five thousand dollars and has recommended a couple more buyers fly in to view the rest of your collection.'"

"No! That's…" She started to pick up her glass of orange juice but didn't trust herself. She pointed and asked the air hostess, "Can you put a little vodka in this for me, please?"

"He also has an order for the pantsuit." Reve flicked at his screen. "Only two hundred, but he's certain that will go up."

"Make it a double." She smiled heroically at the woman.

"There's been a *very* friendly tweet from *Vogue* after their sneak peek. They're teasing a full column to be posted later today. The photos are also gaining momentum on social media."

"Please stop." She set her elbows on either side of her plate, her head so dizzy she had to brace it in her hands.

"Wait." He frowned as he read. "Nina." His voice was somewhere between awe and affection. "I was already proud as hell of you, but this…?" He licked his lips, smiling with relish as he read aloud, "'Kelly Bex has requested an appointment. Per Nina's instructions, I explained that Ms. Bex has been critical of this designer's work in the past and so the designer felt there was no value in Ms. Bex attending.' *Ruthless.*"

"It's true," she said with a defensive shrug, then bit her lip. "But I also asked myself what you would do and decided she could kick rocks."

He touched his chest. "I feel like my little girl is all grown-up."

They both dissolved into laughter. The dampness in her eyes wasn't humor, though. It was more poignant than that. This was the man she'd fallen for, the one she had imagined making a life with. The closer they grew, however, the clearer the gaps between them became.

There's still time to distance yourself.

I will.

She didn't blame him for that.

But it still broke her heart.

"I've always wanted to come to Paris, and I can't explore it!" Nina lamented, her face pressed to the car window as the Eiffel Tower appeared on the far side of the Seine.

"I've booked us a private dinner cruise so you can see some of it."

"You don't have to do that." She sat back.

"It's done." He brushed it aside. "We both have to eat. I never take time to enjoy the city when I'm here." And he wanted to make the most of the little time they had.

There's still time to distance yourself.

He became perversely annoyed every time she said something like that. He could take care of himself. She was the one he was worried about, thinking she could put on a pair of sunglasses and wander around like Sherlock Holmes looking for clues.

They left the river and headed into the Eighth Arrondissement.

"That's Oriel's building," he said as they approached it. He recognized it from the street view online. "The yellow one."

Nina sat up, alert. "She's not there. She's in Mumbai. They had dinner with her husband's sister last night—which you would know if you went anywhere near a gossip site." She swung her head around to flash him a teasing smile. "Their photos are everywhere."

She leaned to look upward against the window as they passed the building.

"Oh, shoot." She quickly slouched into her seat again. "I think there was a photographer waiting for her on the stoop. He jumped to his feet when he saw me." She craned to look out the rear window. "He might be following us. I'm really sorry."

He shrugged. "We're catching the train in the morning."

"To Luxembourg? You're coming with me?"

"I am." He might not read gossip sites, but he had devoted some time to reading up on Oriel. The model was being mobbed everywhere she went.

That sort of attention might be bearable if there was a visible endpoint, the way interest died down after a court case was settled. Oriel was expecting, though. Each detail of her pregnancy was being picked apart and, if history was anything to go by, the world had an endless appetite for celebrity babies. There was also speculation that Lakshmi's manager had forced her to give up her baby, and the mystery of Oriel's biological father had yet to be solved.

Given all of that, Lakshmi's story was destined to make headlines forever. Once Nina came forward, the publicity would explode exponentially.

Reve had no desire to be in the middle of that, not only because he loathed the idea of his own scandal being dredged up. He was never happy when that happened, but he'd learned to live with it. No, he was dreading his history smearing Nina. She had enough to deal with.

He couldn't bring himself to let her face all of this alone, though. Better to help her fly under the radar a little longer and enjoy her last few days of anonymity.

His driver turned onto Avenue Montaigne and stopped outside his building. They hurried inside before any scooters caught up and, moments later, entered a space that seamlessly mixed old-world authenticity with modern expectations. The attic space above his unit had been opened to the main floor, creating high ceilings and skylights that allowed light to pour down to the living space on the main floor.

A wine and a charcuterie board awaited them. Nina ignored the pinwheel of meats, cheeses, fruit, crackers, nuts and olives, instead swinging wide the doors to the narrow terrace that ran the length of the apartment. She plucked a sprig from an herb plant in the pot and rubbed it between her palms, inhaling the fragrance before sighing as she looked out at the cityscape.

"I'm starting to think it would be worth the notoriety

if it meant I could walk into the boutiques I've dreamed of seeing my whole life," she said with a wistful sigh.

"Come." He took her hand and tugged her back into the apartment.

He felt the jolt go through her. It sent a spark of electricity straight into his groin.

He was leading her toward a bedroom for other reasons, but the way her lips parted and her expression grew soft and receptive nearly fried all of his best intentions.

"It might take you some time to dress for dinner." His voice wasn't quite even. "You should get started picking out your clothes."

"Why? If it's a private cruise, I can go like this, can't—? Oh, *Reve.*"

She stepped into the spare bedroom where the bed had been removed and racks brought in from a dozen of the most exclusive haute couture designers. Not the dominant names exported worldwide, but the up-and-comers who had moved to Paris from Tokyo, Seoul, Saint Petersburg and São Paulo.

She sagged into him as though confronting something too monumental to face. Her fist closed on his shirtfront while she stared and stared.

"What have you done? That's seven figures. Easily."

"I don't expect you to keep *all* of them."

The look on her face was worth every penny if she did, though. Her mouth trembled and her eyes gleamed. There was awe and excitement, anticipation and reverence.

It disappeared as she turned her face into the crook of his neck, hugging him so hard she shook with it.

Reve had never had Christmas as a child. As an adult, he went through the motions of bonuses and corporate gifts because it was expected, not because he really understood the celebration. It sounded a lot like doing someone else's shopping and then lying about it. Santa was, at best, a manipulation tactic. At worst, he was a cruelty against less fortunate children who were striving to be "good" for a promise that wouldn't manifest.

This was it, though. This was Christmas—giving someone something they had always wanted. Taking Nina by surprise and witnessing pure joy on her face was filling his chest with a swell of pride and pleasure and a sense that they now shared something deeply personal and precious.

He could hardly breathe as he prompted her to go into the room. "Don't you want to meet your new friends?"

She was still shaking. She was *crying*.

His heart lurched.

"Nina. I thought you would like this."

"I do. I'm so excited I can't bear it." She drew back and pushed the heel of her shaking hand across her cheek. "But I don't want to lose myself in that because..." She looked up at him and her chin trembled. She wiped another track of tears from her other cheek. "Because it takes away from my time with you. I want to be with you, Reve. Like, *with* you. I know it's not forever, but for what little time we have."

She played with the button on his shirt, and his libido resounded like a struck gong, singing *yes!*

Then a harder, crueler sensation pierced into his stomach.

"That's not what this is, Nina." He dropped his arms from around her and stepped back. "I'm not trying to bribe you into sleeping with me."

CHAPTER EIGHT

"THAT'S NOT WHAT I think." She caught his hand as he started to move away. "Not anymore. But you've done *so much* for me—"

"I'm not interested in being paid back for any of that," he said coldly.

"That's not what I'm trying to do!" She let go of his hand and they glared at each other.

She folded her arms and looked at the clothes.

"You did nice things for me before, and I thought it meant you cared, really cared. And I built that into all these big assumptions based on what I'd always imagined I would have when I found the right man. When I realized… When I realized you didn't love me, I thought all of those things you'd done were—"

"I know what you thought," he said through his teeth. His profile was hard as hammered iron.

"I hated myself for being so blind, for wasting my time, *myself*, with someone so shallow."

She heard his sharp inhale.

"But that's not what you are," she hurried to say, taking a step toward him. "And I realize now why you don't have the same expectations I do. I respect that. You're still a good person."

He snorted. "No, I'm not. And the more I learn about

you, the more I realize what a bastard I was for getting involved with you. I didn't mean to lead you on, but I did. If anything, this is me trying to buy your good opinion." He waved at the clothes.

"It's working."

He swore under his breath and rejected that with a jerk of his head.

"It's true," she insisted. "I needed to know that I wasn't completely blind, Reve. That you really are generous and protective and thoughtful and have a core of integrity. I needed to know the man I fell for wasn't a mirage."

"But I *am*," he assured her.

"No, you're not." She set her hand on the front of his shirt and let her fingernails slip between the buttons so her touch sat against his warm skin.

"Don't." He caught her wrist.

Beneath his tense expression she saw a flash of something that might have been stark need.

"Don't do this," he said in a roughened voice that might have been an order or a plea. "Because I will take you to bed and I will hurt you again. Not because I want to, but because I can't be the man you want. It wouldn't be fair to you."

"Really, Reve? Talk to me about how fair life is." Her voice creaked. The things he'd told her on the plane were still sitting inside her, jagged as broken glass. "Life is *never* as simple as we want it to be. Even a dream as common as marriage and family is harder to achieve that it sounds. Look at my dad, losing the love of his life far too young. My sister, unable to carry the baby she desperately wants."

"Exactly why I won't risk falling in love! I don't want to expect good things and have them turn bad."

"I don't expect you to fall in love. I don't expect anything from you if we have sex." She dipped her head against his chest. "I shouldn't have expected anything before."

His hands came to her shoulders as if to push her away, yet there was no force in them. They rested there while tension gripped him.

She lifted her gaze to his hungry, indecisive expression.

Slowly she let her body lean into his. Tiny detonations began going off inside her as his warmth seeped through their clothing, past her skin and into her blood. Her throat and breasts and belly and thighs grew hot. She touched her mouth under his chin.

His chest expanded and his hands shifted up her back.

"I am only a man, you know." His voice reverberated against her lips where she touched them next to his Adam's apple. "And this is all I've been thinking about."

"Me, too."

He choked a laugh, already dropping his head, sealing their mouths together.

The intensity of sensation that went through her might have alarmed her if his strong arms hadn't closed around her, grounding her. Promising to keep her safe.

She curled her arms around his neck and conveyed that he should kiss her harder, but he skated his mouth across her cheek to her ear and whispered, "Slowly."

His lips nibbled around the shell of her ear, his breath tickling until the hair on her scalp and arms stood up. Her knees softened and she gasped, "I don't think I can wait."

"You will have to, though, won't you?" His tongue dabbled at her earlobe. "Because I will not squander this time, Nina. Not one second of it."

What had she unleashed? A beast. A possessive, patient, tender, sensual beast. His arms tightening, his mouth went to her throat, and her nipples stung where they pressed against his chest.

"Reve." She roamed her hands over his flexing shoulders, standing on tiptoe and tilting her head so he could bite softly at the tendon where her neck joined her shoulder. He was hard. She could feel him against her mound. She was excited, but she wanted to savor this, too. She brought his mouth back to hers, and they shared a long, lazy, powerful kiss that became her entire existence.

When she drew back, she blinked with incomprehension, surprised to find herself here, with him, in Paris.

Lust shone from between his tangled lashes. He turned her and walked with himself glued to her back, ambling slowly and kissing her neck as he guided her into the master bedroom.

"I've always liked this dress on you," he said, sliding his hands over the brushed jersey against her stomach.

"Why? Because it's soft?" The wrap dress was comfortable and the mauve color flattering to her skin tone. She'd put it on for travel thinking if she *was* spotted, at least she would be wearing one of her own designs.

"Because it's sexy as hell. Short and flirty." His hand traced along the belt to fiddle with the tails of the bow that draped her hip and then followed to where the skirt flap overlapped. "You think I haven't been staring at your legs all day?"

"These old things? They barely run."

"Hmm. Funny." She felt his smile against her nape.

The floor in the bedroom was parquet wood in a basket weave pattern. She lifted her gaze to a fireplace that looked through to a bathtub. There was a painting above it in silver and blue abstract ribbons. The massive bed was made up with white and gray bedding, and a translucent white curtain covered the pair of doors onto the terrace.

"This is beautiful." Romantic. Like a dream. A perfect fantasy, which was all this was.

He said, "I can't see anything but you," and she was okay with fantasy.

She sent him a look over her shoulder.

He kissed her smile away, then said, "Before I get too distracted…" He went to the night table, withdrew a box of condoms from the drawer and turned it to find the expiration date. "Still good." He left them next to the lamp.

She had noticed he'd used one the other day, and even though a small pang of hurt had struck, she admonished herself that *she* had left *him*.

"What's wrong?" He came across and stilled the hands she was wringing, forcing her to lift her gaze to his.

"Nothing."

"Nina. We can't do this if we're not going to be honest with each other."

"It's fine that you've been with other people," she blurted. "I didn't expect any different."

"I haven't been with anyone." His head went back. "I used a condom the other day because I thought you might have been with someone. Maybe that boyfriend you left when you came to New York?"

"He's married now."

She wasn't sure of the wave of stiff emotion encasing him, but she thought it might be defensiveness. Did he think it said something about how important she'd been to him that he hadn't found anyone else?

Don't, Nina. She needed to keep this in perspective.

She brushed away deeper yearnings and offered a saucy smile. "Put those straight back in the drawer."

One side of his mouth pulled. "You think you're in charge here? Think again."

She grew tight all over, anticipation overwhelming

her. She wanted him to drag her dress apart and ravage her, but he only picked up the tail of her braid where it dangled in front of her shoulder.

"I've been staring at this all day, too. Thinking about taking it apart." He removed the elastic from the end. His gaze came up to crash into hers. "Thinking about taking you apart."

Excited tension rose in her throat. If she were another animal, it might have been a purr or a growl.

He took his time, the rogue, working his fingers into her braid to free it, turning her so he could follow it when it turned into a French braid that started above her opposite ear. He paused a few times to set maddening kisses against her neck.

"I like the pink." He turned her to face him and combed his fingers into her hair. "I want to feel you run this all over my naked skin."

"Oh, you think you're in charge?"

"I do." He made one careful revolution of the hand still tangled in her hair. Now he had her trapped with a tighter grip. "I think you're at my mercy." He touched his mouth to her lips, barely leaving a burning spark of static before he set a peck on her nose and a tender kiss on her brow. Another grazed her cheekbone, then the corner of her mouth, then the base of her throat.

He roamed his free hand all over her, waking her body to his touch. She did the same, rediscovering the muscled strength beneath his crisp shirt and tailored trousers.

When she felt the belt of her dress tugged open, she held her breath. A cool rush of air wafted across her abdomen and upper thighs as he opened the dress. His hot hand crept inside, sliding across her waist and around to her lower back, drawing her half-naked body into his clothed one. The cool metal of his belt buckle branded her stomach.

"Reve." She curled one hand under his arm to rest on his shoulder blade, her other around his neck.

"Why have I never taken you dancing, Nina?" His hand went to her tailbone, but he left the other in her hair. He opened his hot mouth against her neck as he gently swayed them against one another.

Her mind nearly exploded, she was accosted by so many sensations. Her hands moved on him, trying to ground herself in his solidness, but her eyes nearly rolled into the back of her head as he continued placing seductive kisses across her collarbone and under her chin.

When he kissed her again, the tenderness was still there, but the heat had arrived. The *need*.

But even as she drank up his deep, ravenous kisses and sucked flagrantly on his bottom lip, sinking ever deeper into the greedy underworld of lust, she was overwhelmed with a tremendous need to *give*.

His hand slid down to her bottom, palming her cheek through lace and silk, and she moved in time with his petting, seeking more of his fondling while also pressing into the hardness behind his fly. When she would have dipped her mouth into his throat, the sharp tug against her scalp reminded her he still had a fistful of her hair.

They looked at each other with dazed eyes. He released her, causing her to wince a little as he untangled his fingers, but he smoothed his hand over her hair in apology and wordlessly drew her back into their kiss.

Now they blatantly tangled their tongues and clung to each other, and her only thought was that she didn't know how she had lived without him. Without this. She wanted to stand on his feet and climb inside him. Have nothing between them but the perspiration he brought forth onto her skin.

He drew back enough to brush her dress off her shoulders, his gaze reverent as he looked down on her breasts. She opened the front closure of her bra herself, peeling back the cups in offering, reveling in the growling noise that sounded in his throat as he cupped her breasts, firmly and slowly, massaging as he went back to kissing her, then finding her nipples and giving gentle pinches that struck twin shots of electric gold straight to her loins.

A sob escaped her and she gave a light scrape of her nails through his shirt against his shoulders, telling him how torturous this was.

When he let her breathe, she gasped, "I can't stand. I'm too weak."

"I'll hold you up." He wrapped his arms around her, his hands going to her bottom again, sliding inside her panties and squeezing the taut globes.

She stood on tiptoe, barefoot because she'd kicked off her sandals when she entered the apartment. She clung to him and felt all of her inhibitions slipping away. Everything in her became *want*. His.

She rubbed him through his pants and felt his whole body go taut. "Do you want my mouth here?"

"Yes." His breath hissed through his teeth as she continued caressing him. "Your hands, your mouth. I want to suck your nipples until you're ready to come. I want to feel your thighs squeezing my ears when you do."

She was nearly there now, her panties so damp he must feel it where he was reaching his long finger from the back of her thigh toward her hot core.

"What are you waiting for?" She sucked the side of his neck, wanting to mark him. Wishing she had the right to call him hers for all time.

His muscles gathered and he twisted, pressing her toward the bed. She sat and opened her knees, hooking her hands in his belt to draw him closer. It was the playful push-pull they'd always had. The small oversteps of familiarity formed a link of trust that grew stronger with each passionate encounter.

As she began to unbuckle him, however, it struck her this might be one of the last times she made love with him. It made her clumsy as she worked to open his fly and push his pants off his hips.

She exposed his thick, straining erection, and his hands on her shoulders gave a restrained clench while she breathed out a shaken breath upon him. His abdomen hollowed and she kissed the tense muscles there. Then she tasted and caressed and swallowed him into her mouth, applying delicate suction so his hands moved to her head and he shook.

His breaths were the sound of metal on gravel, uneven and loud enough to fill the room. His buttocks were hard. She tested them with the sharp dig of her fingernails and wanted to finish him like this. Leave a memory in him that would live eternally, but he dragged himself free of the draw of her lips and clenched his fist around his shaft, visibly straining to keep control of himself.

"My turn." He set splayed fingertips on her chest and nudged her to fall backward onto the mattress, then leaned over her to kiss her.

He ravaged her mouth the way she'd been aching for him to do. The way that said she was his entire world right now, the only thing that mattered to him. His bare chest was against hers, the fine hairs just rough enough when she twisted to create delicious friction. His steely thighs were planted between her twitching legs. His hot sex teased her through the wet silk of her panties.

She ran her hands under the edges of his open shirt, caressing his damp back, and pushed the shirt off his shoulders. He lifted long enough to throw it away, then gathered her breasts again, murmuring, "So pretty."

His mouth went to her collarbone, her breastbone, the upper swell of her chest and the turgid nipple of one breast. He tortured the other with a soft pinch, keeping it up as she wriggled and dove her hands into his hair and tried to speak past the swirl of intense pleasure that gripped her.

He shifted and his blunt tip pressed against her, teasingly blocked by wet silk.

"Move it," she gasped, trying to grapple the placket aside.

"I want all of you." He went to his knees, as aware as she was that their time was short. That they couldn't hold anything back at this point because there wouldn't be a next time.

That thought had her giving herself over to him, letting him kiss and lick at the insides of her thighs and steal her panties.

His bared teeth were too feral to be called a smile as he easily arranged her how he wanted her, with her thighs draped over his upper arms. His breath wafted against her curls.

"Hello, lovely." He parted her and swept his tongue along her folds, slowly tightening the coil of need in her abdomen with ruthless languor.

When she gasped, "I want you inside me," and tugged at his hair, he slid a finger inside her and continued lapping and loving and driving her ever closer to sheer madness. She trembled with need, moaning with loss as he removed his finger. Two came back, and he delicately worked them in and out of her as he swirled and sucked.

Her last vestige of self-consciousness disappeared and

she became pure instinct. She pressed him to increase his tempo and lifted her hips into the press of his mouth. Then she gave herself up to the wild wave that threw her into the abyss.

She might have screamed. She didn't know.

This. Reve needed nothing in life beyond Nina exactly like this, utterly weak with passion. He kicked off his pants and shifted her into the middle of the bed, then settled over her. His swollen tip felt as though he would split his skin, but he soothed the ache by anointing himself against her slippery, pulsing folds.

She made a soft, receptive noise and her knee came up, her calf slipping across his back with invitation.

He slid in and went blind at the sensation—hot and soft and blissfully wet. She was the only woman he had ever been truly naked with, which wasn't the only reason this was so intensely pleasurable. It was the surrender in her soft body beneath his, the welcome in her sigh against his ear. The heaviness in her eyelids and the caress of her fingertips against his spine reduced the world to just this. Them. Joined.

He had forgotten how profound this was, and his heart shook in warning.

He might have withdrawn then, but the slightest friction on his impatient flesh sizzled his brain and caused her to hum with renewed arousal. He felt a quake of pleasure go through her and he was lost.

His only thought then was to hold back while he waited for her to catch up to him. He made himself lie still with his heartbeat buried inside her. When he whispered how good she felt around him, she shivered and tightened her clasp on his flesh.

He caressed her shoulders and arms and thighs and

bottom, sliding his touch to where they were joined, and delicately drew another hum of awareness from her. He contorted so he could suckle her nipples and feel the lovely tension gather in her.

When she opened her eyes and he saw the haze of passion clouding her pretty brown eyes, he rolled her to straddle him.

This was the woman who had haunted him for months. She sat tall and ran her hands over herself, watching him with a seductive smile as she touched where she held him captive.

He ground his teeth and cupped her breasts, lifting his hips because he was unable to help himself.

Her pupils seemed to explode. She caught his wrists and began to lift and roll as she rode him. Every breath was a harsh sob that accompanied the impact of their flesh. He moved his hands to her hips, guiding her so they were in perfect sync.

Her sobs grew more anxious as she closed in on the finish. His throat burned with the ragged noises he was making, striving to hang on, to get there, to arrive at exactly the same moment—

She froze, and her mouth hung open to release a silent scream.

All his senses disappeared. He was torn from this world for long seconds before he was thrown back with such a slam of pleasure, it was nearly pain. He gripped her hips, trying to meld them into one as he bucked with jolts of sheer ecstasy.

He knew at a distance that he was losing something of himself. Something he would never get back. But in these sharp, endless, euphoric seconds, he didn't give one tiny damn.

She could have all of him. He was already hers.

CHAPTER NINE

"FOR A FOUR-HOUR train trip?" Nina looked around the extravagant stateroom that was their private car. "This looks like something from the Orient Express." She trailed her fingertips along the beveled edge of the cherrywood dining table, wondering what he must have paid to have this car added since she doubted this route typically had sleeper cars.

"I tried to book a helicopter. You said no." He hung his jacket in the closet.

"Because I thought I would be traveling alone and would buy the ticket myself." When he'd asked her in New York how she wanted to travel to Luxembourg, she had thought he was making conversation, trying to avoid talking about their kiss at the showroom. "I wanted to go by train so I could watch the scenery." She peeked through the closed drapes.

"We'll open them once we get going. At least in here, we don't have to see anyone, not even the conductor. Unless there's something we don't have." He glanced in the well-stocked refrigerator and checked the labels on the wine in the racks. "Hungry?"

"We just had breakfast." She glanced around the jut of a separation wall. The top of it was clouded by etched glass, and the bottom was cherrywood paneling that matched the rest of the room. There was a very plush-looking double bed tucked behind it.

"We could go back to bed," she suggested.

They had been doing little else other than making love since last night. Dinner on the Seine had been canceled, and they'd made do with the charcuterie board for dinner. They had wound up fooling around on a dining room chair and then having sex on the sofa. They'd dozed there, then had a bath together—along with a couple of orgasms. Sometime after midnight, they'd woken and come together in a wordless fog of simply needing to be joined.

They'd both risen achy and sore this morning, agreeing that it had to stop. But they'd showered together and landed on the sheets soaking wet, groaning each other's names as they drove each other to another lofty pinnacle.

It was the best possible madness, and also a type of hoarding for the cold winter they were both avoiding any mention of.

"You're not going to see much from the bed," Reve chided, his eyelids already drooping with the drug of lust.

Nina lifted her chin. "Depends what I want to see, doesn't it? For instance, I have had it with that tie." She pointed. "Get rid of it."

"I pity the conductor," he said as he loosened the red silk with its subtle paisley pattern. "Having to go home to his wife and tell her he found a couple today who had literally screwed themselves to death."

"We all die of something. Pick your poison."

He barked a laugh. "You. It has to be you." He tackled her in a handful of steps, tumbling her onto the bed beneath him.

This immersion in each other was pure denial of reality, as well as deliriously exquisite.

Also, it turned out to be exactly what they needed. They conked out immediately after climaxing and jerked awake when a bell sounded. A voice announced, "Arriving at your destination in fifteen minutes."

"Is this one of those hibernation capsules, and we've traveled through space and time?" She rose to dress, her brain barely functioning. "I am definitely not going to earn the fashion designer's secret handshake if they see the way I treat my new clothes."

She shook out her chiffon culottes—an old standby that a Tokyo designer had given a chic makeover. They hugged her waist and hips then fell in loose, flirty pleats to accentuate her calves and ankles. Her muslin blouse by a Vancouver designer was a deceptively simple peasant style that had its own billowy grace.

When she'd gone through her things from Reve's storage, she'd found and reclaimed her lace-up retro-looking saddle shoes. They'd served her well on the endless sidewalk commutes of New York so she'd brought them for what she expected would be a lot of footwork in the tiny village near Mondorf-les-Bains.

The spa town had sprung up around the discovery of a hot spring back in the eighteen hundreds, but a smaller, more exclusive "retreat" had been built among the neighboring vineyards a hundred years later. It hadn't had thermal waters, but it did have top doctors charging top dollar for discreet services.

As the train slowed, she glanced up from fixing her hair to see Reve watching her with a sober expression as he knotted his tie. Each rock of the carriage was a slow tick of their time winding down. They both felt it.

"Don't look like that." He came over to squeeze her shoulder and kiss the top of her head. "Nothing in life stays the same."

He was right, but it still put a lump in her throat.

She donned sunglasses and a hat, but if there had been any interest in Oriel's connection to Luxembourg, it was long over. No one seemed to give them a second glance as they disembarked. A young man waited with a key fob and directed them to a sedan outside the train station.

Reve programmed their destination into the navigation system, and within minutes they were traveling east toward the German border, leaving the city for softly rolling hills and picturesque villages.

"Was there no border check when your mother came through?" Reve asked as the Moselle River came into view. "Did she realize she was leaving Germany?"

"It was already a very low-key system. She stopped to ask the border guard where they could eat while she figured out how to get back to where they were going. He suggested the café where she wound up collapsing."

"The investigator said there were private houses in the area that were a cottage industry—pun intended. They provided discreet accommodation for the celebs who used the clinic, but he wasn't able to find which one Lakshmi stayed at. Most of them are still operating, serving the wine tour crowd."

"Is that where we're staying?"

"Actually, he found a vineyard owned by the family of the doctor who signed your birth certificate. I had to pay triple to get another reservation bumped, but I'm hoping to succeed where the investigator failed. Get some answers."

"That's a lot of money for them to take one look at me and refuse to say anything without a lawyer present." Her stomach was nothing but snakes and butterflies as the car ate up the miles.

"We'll see."

"Are you enjoying this?" she asked, narrowing her eyes in suspicion.

"A little." He side-eyed her. "It's a puzzle. I'm curious. And I want you to have answers." He reached to squeeze her hand.

That sounded a little like he was emotionally invested, but she didn't tease him over it. She let the sparks of possibility dance in her, even though she knew it was an indulgence she couldn't afford.

A short while later, they stepped from the car in front of a villa surrounded by rows upon rows of grapevines. A dog wagged itself nearly to pieces as it waddled up to them.

A middle-aged woman came out of a stone cottage nearby. She was wiping her hands on a tea towel. Her smile fell away into shock.

"When they said a high-profile couple from New York insisted on staying here, I didn't realize…" The woman gave Reve a confused look, perhaps expecting Oriel's Indian husband, before mustering a fresh smile for them both. "I'm Farrah. Let me show you into the house. My husband, Charles, will bring your luggage if you'd like to give me the key to the car."

"Reve Weston. And—"

"I know who you are." Farrah flipped her tea towel onto her shoulder.

Reve left it at that and said, "We're hoping to speak to the doctor's family. Are you…?"

"No relation." Farrah shook her head. "Charles and I arrived ten years ago. Answered an ad. The family needed someone to run things because the doctor had passed away and he was the one with the passion for the vineyard."

"Dr. Wagner?" Nina cocked her head. "The one who worked at the clinic?"

"That's what I was told. Like I say, before our time,

but I understand he came from Austria every week or so and had all sorts of famous clients." Farrah opened the door into the villa. "His family still lives in Austria. I run this as a vacation rental. Charles manages the vineyard."

Inside, the house was bright and well maintained if slightly dated. It had a beautiful terrace with expansive views of the vineyard and the silver river below.

Charles came in with their luggage and Reve asked him to leave it by the door. He took back the key and they drove straight into the village. The investigator hadn't had much luck at the café, but Reve went in while Nina stayed in the car, sunglasses on like an undercover cop on stakeout.

Reve came back with pastries and the news. "The owner will ask his father if he remembers a pregnant American woman collapsing twenty-five years ago, but the old man's memory is failing. We shouldn't expect too much. I left him my card."

"Humph."

They tried the small medical clinic that serviced the village. The receptionist had no desire to tell anyone the names of any retired medical professionals living in the area. Then they drove to the spa, which was swarming with tourists and didn't inspire Nina to believe there was much they could learn there, either.

They returned to the vineyard and took a walk to stretch their legs and breathe the warm, earth-flavored air, but she was feeling very disheartened.

"It was a waste of time to come all this way, wasn't it?" Not to mention the cost to him.

"You wanted to know what you could find. Now you do. Did you expect it all to become crystal clear the second we arrived?"

"Kind of," she said glumly.

"Come here." He drew her into his embrace.

It felt so natural to be with him like this, leaning on him and lifting her mouth for the kiss he lingered over. How could this be anything other than the way they were meant to be?

"Where do we go from here?" she asked with a forlorn pang in her throat.

"I'll call Oriel's husband if you want." His hands roamed her back, but his touch didn't soothe the prickles of anguish gathering within her.

"I can do that." She drew back. "And once I do... Where do *we* go?"

He dragged in a pained breath, and he gripped her arms briefly before setting her away from him. "This is what I was trying to avoid," he muttered.

"I *know*. And I'm not blaming you or trying to pressure you into anything, but I don't want to say goodbye, Reve. I..." She clutched at her elbows, feeling hollow inside. "I feel safe with you."

He swore under his breath and ran his hand through his hair. "I don't. I feel as though I'm losing every part of myself when I'm with you, and that's terrifying."

His words set fire to her chest.

Whatever anguish came into her face made him wince and turned away.

"I can't be like you. Open and trusting."

"Because of her." She meant the woman who had posted his sex tape.

"Her, my father, my aunt. Anytime I've let myself believe in others they have always let me down."

"What happened with your aunt?"

"Nothing," he said flatly, his profile sharp as chipped granite. He squinted as he looked to the past, and his voice grew raspy. "She turned up looking just like the photo I had of my mother. I remember this shred of hope coming awake inside me. I thought, *Now things will get better*." His face contorted with helpless anger. "But she looked around and asked my father, 'How can you live like this?' and left me there."

His bitterness was so tangible she tasted it on her own tongue. She felt his crushing disappointment as a profound weight on her chest.

"And then I left," she said with anguish, hating herself for doing that to him.

"What were you going to stay for?" he asked with self-disgust. "*I* broke what we had. You're right about that. I *am* broken."

"Reve, don't." She started toward him, but he stiffened in rejection and she halted. "You're not. I never should have said that. I was being cruel because I was hurt."

"It's still true. I'll never be able to give you what you want, Nina. I could go through the motions. Marry you and give you kids, but you want more than a couple of boxes ticked. You want things inside me that just aren't there."

"I don't know what I want anymore," she cried, unable to imagine finding happiness with someone else when the price was him.

"You do." He rounded on her. "You want the kind of love you've always known. I won't let you compromise yourself and settle for less because we happen to be good in bed."

His voice was so harsh and final that her mouth began to quiver. She couldn't stand here and start bawling like a child.

"I'm going to run a bath," she choked, and hurried inside.

CHAPTER TEN

HER VISION WAS so blurred by the onset of tears that she tripped over their suitcases, still in the foyer.

She cursed loudly and bitterly as she went down. The floor jarred her palm and her knee crashed onto the stone tiles. For a brief second, she sat there stunned by the lightning-sharp agony of her fall as it outshone the despair overwhelming her.

Reve lurched in behind her. "What happened? Are you okay?" He swore when he saw her trying to pick herself up amid their tumbled bags. "That's my fault. I told him to leave them there."

"Don't worry about it."

When he tried to help her, she recoiled, unable to let him touch her right now. She would fall apart for sure.

A grim silence formed around him as he picked up both their bags and started up the stairs.

She followed to the master bedroom, afraid to so much as thank him because she was on the brink of a breakdown.

Before she had properly taken in the luxurious room in cream and moss tones, Reve slipped around her and walked out—with his own case in his hand.

Reve. His name stayed locked in her throat, hot and sharp. He wouldn't even sleep with her.

Biting her lip, she took slow, deliberate breaths, telling herself she would wait until she was in the tub, but agony was gushing upward within her, filling her with greater and greater swathes of misery. She was sniffling and gasping, going through the motions of opening the taps and waiting for the water to warm, trying not to hate herself for being honest with him. She only wished—

Reve walked in.

"Do you ever knock?" she cried, and swiped guiltily at her wet cheeks. Through her dejection, a streak of hope flashed to life.

His hard expression became even more severe. He moved around her to turn off the water. "I have to show you something."

His voice was grim, and her blood went cold in her veins.

Dread became a heavy boulder atop the emotions that were sitting under the surface of her control. Leaving the drip of the tap behind, she followed him from the master bedroom to the end of the upper hall. His suitcase stood outside the door of a spare bedroom as far from the master as possible.

Okay, I get it. You regret ever meeting me.

He pointed into the room. "Look."

She peered through the open doorway. It wasn't a bedroom. It was a den with a sofa that she imagined pulled out into a bed. There were floor-to-ceiling shelves stuffed with books and board games and DVDs. In one corner sat a wooden desk with a globe and an old-fashioned-looking landline telephone. On the other wall, a television sat on a credenza. A gaming console was hooked up to it, and the controllers were on the coffee table.

"What?" She moved to glance out the window. It was

the uphill view of the vineyard, pretty but nothing she hadn't seen already.

"Look." He followed her in and lifted the crocheted tablecloth that served as a doily on the credenza. "Twelve drawers. What do you want to bet these little cardholders once held labels that went A/B, C/D, E/F...?"

"Oh, my God." She began yanking at the pulls, running the alphabet as she did. "K/L— They're all locked."

"It's full, though." He grabbed an end, and the tendons in his neck and arms strained as he tried to lift it. He gave it a push, but it was solid as a rock. "They haven't painted behind it. This has been here for years."

"You don't think it holds the doctor's records. Not *here*. Not *still*."

"Why not? Say you're a doctor traveling from Austria to treat private patients. Where would you store their records?"

"At the clinic."

"Until they're discharged, sure. After that, it's risky to leave them there with staff and other patients coming and going. No sense dragging them back and forth to Austria. Maybe you get a couple of your burliest laborers to drag this behemoth up to your home office and store them here. When you die, no one bothers to clean it out because it's locked and this is just a spare room where the kids play video games."

"Where's the key? On a keychain in Austria?" She moved to the desk and started rummaging through the drawers, finding only crayons and coloring books.

"Is there a letter opener?" Reve ran his hand around the edges of the credenza, then lifted the doily to expose the lock mechanism. "This will take about five seconds to pop."

"We can't break in."

"What's the difference between that and unlocking it with a key?"

"Good point. We should contact the family and ask for permission to search it. Otherwise, we might invade the privacy of living and dead celebrities." She stared at the cabinet with equal measures of temptation and regret.

"That's exactly why I think it still holds the doctor's records. It's a solid asset for a family to hold on to."

"Reve! That is by far the most cynical thing you have ever said. We don't know anything about this family. Do you really think they would keep something like this as an insurance policy? So they could bribe a dead doctor's patients if they ran out of money?"

"*Yes.* Nina—" He stared at her as he gave his head a bemused shake. "The more I realize how naive you really are, the more I realize how badly I took advantage of you. This entire property is a laundry for the doctor's side hustle with celebrity patients. Do you not see that?"

"You don't know that. You're just guessing." As she said it, she felt the sting of truth. They were here because her birth had been covered up by this doctor. It stood to reason that more than one crime had been committed over the years. She folded her arms, saying defensively, "I like to give people the benefit of the doubt."

"Me, for instance. I always thought you were blowing smoke when you complimented me, being sweet so I'd let you stay in my home. Turns out you're actually that innocent and charming. I'm not."

"What are you doing?" Nina asked as Reve moved into the hall to open his suitcase.

"Criming." He found his nail clippers and clicked the file open like a jackknife. He would never be the kind of man she wanted or deserved, but at least he could help her unlock the secrets of her past. "If you prefer not to be implicated, I suggest you leave."

He tried to slide the file into the mechanism and discovered it was seized from lack of use. Might need oil, so he crouched to see if he could slide the file along the crack and release the mechanism that way.

"How do you know how to do that?"

"Do you really want to know?"

She was still hugging herself, her shoulders hunched. "Yes."

His chest felt constricted by coils of thick rope that were sliding and burning across his naked skin.

I don't know what I want anymore.

She didn't want him. He knew that much. She only thought she did because he'd hidden the worst of himself from her. It was time she understood why it was best they stop their involvement and part for good.

"I used to break into cars."

"For money?"

"Kind of. I learned to do it at the junkyard where I grew up, so I could strip parts and sell them to local shops. Then a couple of men from those shops started asking me to break into cars on the street. They would say it was their uncle's car or it belonged to a customer. When I was picked up by the police, I realized I was being used to take the initial risk. They stole them once the car was open. That's when I learned that innocent people get used so it's best to keep my eyes open."

"How old were you?" she asked with astonishment.

"Eleven." The nail file wasn't strong enough to jimmy the latch. He went back to his bag for his lip balm and lubricated the file, returning to work on picking the lock. "While I was at middle school, I realized I could use the library computer to set up websites and sell parts that way."

"That's how you got started as an auto parts dealer."

"That's what my PR prints in my bio, yeah." He wiggled the file in the lock, trying to work the waxiness of the lip balm against the pins so they'd move. "But stripping parts is sweaty, time-consuming work, and shipping them is a pain in the ass. I realized I could simply become a broker, match seller with buyer and take a cut of the transaction. Fill the site full of ads and make money that way, too."

"I'm impressed that you thought to do that so young, but it doesn't sound bad. Agents are allowed to take a cut for a service they offer."

"The parts were hot, Nina. That sort of agent is called a *fence*."

"Oh." Her eyes widened.

So naive. He had always thought that was an act, and now he saw how real her trust was. It made him sick that he had walked all over her, soaking up her softness and passion as if he had a right to it. That's why this had to stop. He knew how mismatched they were and, he was realizing, she wasn't tough enough to protect herself. Not against him. He had to do that for her.

"Are you still, um…?" Her brows were squiggled with perplexity as she tried to figure out if she had been sleeping with an active criminal all this time.

"I mostly stick to the rules these days, but that's how I know a laundry when I see one. When my dad died, I was sixteen. I closed my site and used the money I'd made to buy a run-down repair shop in Detroit. If anyone asked, I said my inheritance paid for it, but my father hadn't owned the land we squatted on. I left town owing for his cremation. I'm actually not much of a mechanic, but I knew how to get good parts for cheap, and that was most of my business."

"Were the parts still hot?"

"Mostly aftermarket knockoffs unless it was a special case. I knew better than to push my luck." He swore as the file started to turn, then stopped and needed more coaxing and wiggling. "Do you understand how embarrassed I am that this is taking so long?"

"You're out of practice," she said gently. "You haven't done it in a long time."

And there was the forgiving, accepting purity in her voice that was like a drug to him. It made a pang resound in his chest.

"It doesn't change the fact that I'm doing it, Nina."

He was still a street punk deep down. A sex tape stud who had benefited from the very notoriety he'd resented. His profits had tripled while he'd been making headlines and, much as he'd felt cheapened by the scandal, he'd also capitalized on it. He'd fought to get the tape taken down, but there'd been a part of him that figured he deserved that grim chapter of his life because of the kind of person he was.

Nina's phone buzzed in her pocket. She glanced at it. "My sister. She'll want to know how things are going." She walked toward the door. "Do you want me to get a butter knife?"

"No." He wouldn't corrupt her any more than he already had.

Angela told Nina there was a photo of Nina and Reve gaining traction online. Back when she'd been living with Reve, they'd gone for dinner and had been caught behind a tourist taking a selfie. Now the grainy image was being blown up in every possible way.

"All the headlines are saying it's Oriel," Angela said with concern. "Even my clients are starting to talk about

how much you look like her. I don't know how long I can
pretend it's all a coincidence."

"I know. I'm sorry. This feels like a bomb going off
in slow motion," Nina said, distressed at the thought of
Reve being freshly linked to Oriel.

She didn't tell Angela what Reve was doing right
now—or that Reve had basically broken up with her.
Again. She finished the call and went into the bathroom
to set a cool cloth over her eyes, trying to keep from tearing up with despair.

You want the kind of love you've always known.

She did. And she wanted that love *with him.* She was
falling in love with him all over again—this time far
more deeply because she knew him more intimately. He
could throw his checkered past at her all he wanted, and
it didn't change the fact that he'd been playing human
shield since she had run into his penthouse ten days ago.
He could say he was only betting on a horse with his investment in her work, but he had removed any obstacles
between her and her long-held dream.

She *was* prepared to compromise those things she had
always wanted because a greater want was taking its
place inside her: Reve. She wanted Reve in her life.

*I won't let you settle for less because we happen to
be good in bed.*

Was that all it was for him?

Did it matter what he felt? He'd been through a lot
at the hands of others. He had told her no one had ever
looked out for him. The last thing she wanted was to be
as callous about consequences to him as everyone else
seemed to have been. She knew he was trying to protect her from himself, but maybe she had to protect him
from herself, too.

With gritty eyes and the deepest ache in her heart,

she went back to the office and found him at the desk, files stacked before him. He had his laptop open and was using his phone to photograph documents. Drawers in the credenza were half-open.

Her heart leaped. "You got in?"

"Yes, but everything is in German."

"Oh. Of course." She moved to the sofa and dropped to sit, pretty much defeated by the weight of stress and problems surrounding her.

"I'm converting it to English through a translation app."

"Oh?" She perked up. "Have you learned anything?"

"That stolen evidence is not admissible in court—or so my lawyer tells me. He absolutely, positively advises I do not make copies of anything I have found on these premises without the express permission of the owners. I told him to draft a request for permission, which I will forward to them the minute I'm done here."

She gave a halfhearted laugh, struck by the sheer absurdity of this situation, then asked, "Do you want help?"

"I've got a system going. But listen, from what I've read so far..." He turned another page, clicked his phone over it. He glanced at the image, tapped, then looked to his laptop, where he tapped a few keys. "I don't want to make any decisions for you that should be yours, but this has to be shared with the Dalal family. Your family got screwed, Nina. *You* did."

That wasn't news, yet her mouth began to tremble. "How?"

A click, a tap, a sharp glance.

"Take a minute to be sure. This will be difficult to hear."

"I need to know, Reve. Tell me."

Reve hesitated one more second, then tapped his laptop and read aloud, "'Female presenting at twenty weeks.' Lakshmi, when she first arrived," he clarified. "'Midwife suggests possible multiple pregnancy. Scan for confirmation declined.'"

"Declined by who?"

"Lakshmi's manager, Gouresh Bakshi. He was running interference." Reve tapped a few more keys. "She had sixteen weekly visits from the midwife, then, 'Twin girls delivered on either side of midnight. Maternal distress, a transfusion...' She doesn't regain consciousness for a couple of days. While she was out it says, 'Baby Monday placed as arranged.' You should see Lakshmi's signature on the documents." He ruffled through the pages. "I'm no expert, but it's a man's handwriting."

"Of course it is. She was unconscious! Is that really what they called us?" It was a good thing she was sitting down. She felt sick.

Reve's expression softened. "I'm afraid so." He tapped a file. "In this one, it says Baby Tuesday was placed with an American family. There's also a confirmation for a wire transfer for a revoltingly high payment with a note that labels it 'discretionary.' The banking info ties into the other payments from Bakshi for Lakshmi's care."

"Oh, my God." Nina buried her face in her hands.

"I know. Nina, I'm sorry." He rose and came to crouch before her, taking her cold hands.

"Who does something so awful to a woman who is so vulnerable and—"

"You were all vulnerable. He did that to all three of you."

"He just gave us away like p-puppies."

Reve shifted onto the couch and drew her into his lap. Nina should have been cried out, but these tears were different. They were for Lakshmi and Oriel and herself. She was breaking into agonized pieces as she imagined her birth mother awakening and learning her babies were gone, gone, gone.

"I feel so *robbed.*"

"You were." He was rubbing her back, setting kisses on her hair. "You all were." He held her in strong, safe arms while she completely fell apart.

She wept until her eyes swelled shut and her whole body ached with grief.

"Nina."

Reve's raspy voice and the feel of his hand rubbing her arm dragged her awake.

She blinked eyes that felt like sandpaper and found herself in the den. Morning sunlight was beaming through the window. She had a blanket over her, a pillow tucked under her head.

"What—?"

"Farrah's making breakfast. There's a woman downstairs who wants to meet you."

"Oriel?" Her heart leaped into her mouth. She sat up so fast Reve had to lean back to avoid her forehead crashing into his unshaved chin.

"No. But I got a message from my doorman in Paris. Oriel came looking for you there."

Her head throbbed, and she couldn't hear anything but the blood in her ears. She was disoriented. Her heart was seesawing in her chest. She grasped at Reve's arm and he steadied her, but there was a stiffness to his touch, as though he was holding her off. The remoteness in his expression caused her unsteady heart to plummet into freefall.

Don't, she wanted to cry, as everything came rushing back to her. Still, she couldn't keep leaning on him. It wasn't fair to either of them.

She drew her hands into her lap and tried to catch up to what he was saying.

"How did she know—?"

"There's a photo of us online that people are saying is her. She must have tracked you to being with me."

"Oh, I forgot," she sighed. "Angela told me about that photo. I meant to tell you, but…" She looked to the credenza. All the drawers were safely closed, the tablecloth in place, and all the files were gone from the desk.

"I've booked a helicopter to take us to Paris as soon as we've eaten."

She noticed he was still wearing yesterday's clothes. "Have you slept?"

"No. Do you want come downstairs? This woman is married to the man who owns the café."

"Oh. Yes. Okay." She staggered down the hall to the master bedroom and made herself presentable.

When she came down, Reve was sipping a coffee at the windows. Farrah was gone and a woman of about fifty was on the sofa. There was a cup of coffee steaming on the table in front of her, but she had her hands clutched anxiously over her purse.

The air was so thick with tension it could have been sliced and fried.

The woman stood when Nina appeared. She searched Nina's face as Nina offered a faint smile. "Hello."

"I'm sorry to come here uninvited. I'm Inga Klein." She offered her hand. "Your, um…" She looked to Reve. "Your friend left his card with my husband yesterday and said you were staying here. My husband thought he was a reporter. I've just explained that my father-in-law has

dementia. He doesn't have any information that would
be helpful."

"I see." Nina looked to Reve, unsure if she should offer
her real name. "I'm, um…"

"The other one," Inga said with a sad nod of wonder.
"You're not Oriel Cuvier. I've been following her story
very closely. As soon as my husband showed me the card
last night, I knew you weren't her. You're the other one.
Aren't you?"

"You know?" Nina felt Reve's hand take hold of her
arm and ease her toward the sofa. Her knees felt like jelly.

"I didn't *know*." Inga sank back into her seat. "It was
a suspicion that has haunted me for years." Her gaze
pleaded for understanding. "I was fifteen when I got a
job as a maid, cleaning cottages for the rich people being
treated at the clinic. It was impressed upon me that I
could never talk about anything I heard or saw."

Inga nervously clicked the clasp on her purse.

"I saw a lot of strange things. Eventually the Indian
couple were just one more odd memory I locked away, but
I've always wondered what happened to her. You look just
like I remember her." She sent an unsteady smile, then
looked down again, growing somber. "They claimed to
be married, but they fought constantly. Not in English. I
only guessed that it was about her pregnancy. She cried
when he wasn't around."

She clicked open her purse and darted her hand into
it, bringing out a folded sheet of paper with scorched
edges. She offered it.

"She wrote letters and threw them into the fire when
he got home. I don't know why I took this one. It has always tortured my conscience that I did, but once I had
it, I couldn't bring myself to get rid of it. I think it's to
your father."

Nina accepted it but was too upset to make head or tail of it.

"We can read it in a minute." Reve gave her shoulder a bolstering squeeze. "Is there anything else you can tell us?"

"Only that I came to work one day and he said she'd gone into labor the night before. He said I should pack their things because they would leave from the clinic as soon as she was discharged. He went out and I don't think he knew I was still there when he got back because I overheard him on the phone. He was speaking English and asked for Dr. Wagner. He asked if the woman who came in from the café had survived. Then he said, 'That's what we can do with the other one. Give it to her family. Tell them it was hers.' He said, 'Name your price.'"

Tears of remorse stood in Inga's eyes.

"I'm very sorry. My English wasn't very good. I thought I misunderstood. I was concerned about the mother, but no one connected to the clinic would tell me anything. When Oriel Cuvier began making headlines, I dug out the letter to see if there was a clue I'd missed. I've been trying to decide what to do with it. May I leave it with you?"

"Of course. Thank you," Nina said in a daze.

They thanked Inga and took her information, then Reve read the letter to Nina. The sentences were cut off by the burned sections of pages, but it sounded as though her biological father had had a son who was sick and Lakshmi had understood his need to be there for the boy.

"'...and when it's time he insists I must give it up...'" Reve continued. "She's referring to Bakshi, I imagine."

"'It...'" Nina repeated, latching on to the word. "Not *them*. She didn't know she was having twins."

"Doesn't sound like it. The last line is '…know what else to do. I wish you were here to…'"

"She sounds so tortured—and also as if she loved him." Her heart wrenched and twisted with bittersweet consolation. As she looked at the man *she* wanted and couldn't have, she knew exactly how her mother had felt. Torn, helpless and devastated.

Reve slept through the helicopter flight to Paris and only noticed how quiet and withdrawn Nina was as they drove into the city.

"Okay?" He tried to still the fingers she was liable to twist right off her hands.

"Hmm? Oh. Yes. You didn't have to come with me," she murmured. "This is when we said we would part ways," she reminded him with somber tension across her cheekbones. "I *need* to see her, Reve. I can't put it off any longer."

Her eyes said, *Even for you.*

"I know." He'd had a lot of time to think last night while she'd slept and he'd copied records. The more he realized what she was up against, the less he was able to leave her to it. He was confident the family of Lakshmi Dalal would pursue justice, but the only reason Oriel was so well protected was because her adoptive parents were wealthy and was married to a VP of TecSec. Reve would like to believe they would help Nina navigate all of this, but he didn't know that. He couldn't walk away until he was sure Nina would be safe.

"I want to meet her with you. See how she reacts."

"You know I'm too freaked-out to be brave, right?" She reached across and closed her clammy hand over his. "I know I should be saying I can do this alone, but…"

"I won't let you." He sandwiched her trembling fingers between his warm palms and directed the driver to Oriel's building. As they approached, they saw a throng of paparazzi lingering around the entrance.

"Looks like she's home," Reve said. "Do you want to go in? Or call her from my place?"

"In." She nodded convulsively.

They waited in the car while the driver went to the door.

As the driver rang the bell, the photographers began sniffing at the car's tinted windows, trying to see inside. A man in a dark suit appeared. A bodyguard, if Reve had to guess. He took Reve's card from the driver and glanced toward their car, nodding. He held the building's entrance door open while the driver came back.

Nina's hand tightened in Reve's right before the car door opened.

They stepped out and the paparazzi went wild.

CHAPTER ELEVEN

THE PHOTOGRAPHERS MUST have been baffled as to how Oriel had left the building without them knowing. Now she was with Reve?

Reve had glued her to his side with an arm that nearly cut off Nina's ability to breathe. He walked so fast her feet barely touched the ground, whisking her through the downpour of questions in French, Hindi and English.

"Oriel! Did you leave your husband? What is your relationship with Mr. Weston?"

Reve elbowed one of them who got too close, and then they were inside the building. The din faded as the bodyguard firmly shut the door and directed them up the stairs.

When Reve released her, Nina still couldn't breathe. She glanced at him in weak apology for putting him through the media storm and hurried up the stairs on shaking knees. The man who'd let them in brought her to a door guarded by another man. He knocked for her.

She blindly reached for Reve's hand. Her vision was getting fuzzy around the edges. Her heart was all she heard as she waited. *Thump, thump, thump.*

The door opened.

The woman who stood on the other side was a version of herself that was more polished, a tiny bit taller, with a face that was a smidgen softer. If Reve's hand hadn't been crushing hers, Nina would have felt completely untethered to reality, as though she occupied two timelines and was committing the mortal sin of disrupting the space-time continuum.

Someone said something. Her ears were rushing with her hammering pulse. Her eyes were glossing and blinking in time with her reflection's. Her throat was dry, the air in her lungs growing thin. Weirdly, amid all that sensory confusion, the butterflies in her stomach settled into placid stillness, as though they were coming to rest after migrating across a continent.

It's been so long.

She didn't know if the voice was in her head or Oriel's as Oriel moved in the same split second Nina did. They stepped into a hug, and the most incredible sense of homecoming swamped her.

You're back, the voice in her head said. She was hugging a person she had no memory of knowing, but it was good and right and all she could think was, *I missed you*.

The piercing whistle of a teakettle startled the women apart.

Reve said, "You two sit down. I'll get that." He pressed them into the flat and closed the door.

He needed a minute. Reading about the cold and calculating way Nina had been separated from her mother and sister had filled him with outrage, yet he hadn't expected to feel this moved by her reunion with Oriel. He wanted Nina to be happy so it made sense that *seeing* her happy would please him, but this was exponentially more than that. His eyes were wet, and he didn't feel as though his sternum could withstand the pressure behind it as he went to silence the kettle.

He listened as he made coffee, though the women seemed too overcome to speak. They still hadn't spoken by the time he brought out two cups.

Oriel looked like a 3D copy of Nina. Like a wax figure in a museum. She was pregnant, he recalled, but it wasn't obvious.

Reve had the weirdest thought, though. This was how Nina would look if she was expecting—glowing with happiness.

A jagged truth tugged on his conscience. *You can't cheat her of that.*

"Do we need introductions?" Reve gave Nina's shoulder a squeeze to remind her he was here if she needed him. "I'm Reve. This is Nina."

"Oriel. Forgive me, I'm still in shock from learning about my birth mother. I had no idea I had a twin." She spoke in Nina's voice with a French accent, and Reve instantly liked her for it. Well, that and for the radiant smile she'd put on Nina's face.

"I'm sorry I wasn't here when you went to Reve's to find me," Nina said. "We were in Luxembourg, trying to find answers about…well, everything. I didn't actually know my parents weren't my birth parents. How could I have a secret twin?"

"Did you find anyone from the clinic?"

"No, but we found medical records on our delivery and…" Nina explained about Inga as she dug up the letter.

Oriel set her hand over her heart. "She kept it all this time?" She carefully unfolded the paper.

While Oriel read, Nina picked up Reve's hand from her shoulder and pressed her damp cheek to the back of his knuckles. It was a gesture of gratitude. Perhaps she was only trying to include him in her special moment. A few short months ago, he wouldn't have allowed himself to be drawn into anything this emotionally charged. As it was, he felt privileged to be part of this with her.

"This is so sad. My heart is absolutely broken for her," Oriel murmured, tears standing in her eyes.

"Mine, too." Nina then told her the rest, how Lakshmi hadn't been allowed to hold her babies or learn she'd had twins.

The sisters' anguish was palpable as they hugged it out, and Reve had to step away to a window and swallow back the lump that rose in his throat.

Behind him, they moved on to the deeper mystery of where they'd each gone after their birth, beginning to share and laugh in bemusement. Reve didn't listen to the words so much as the pleasing sound of Nina's voice in stereo. He didn't know how he was going to give her up, but his head was pounding with the knowledge that he had to. He cared for her more than he'd imagined he could care for anyone. It was a double-edged sword. The more he cared, the more he wanted to protect her from anyone who could harm her—himself included.

An abrupt knock cut off his rumination and the women's conversation.

Reve moved to open the door and confronted a man wearing the most hostile, contemptuous, death wish of a lip curl Reve had ever seen on anyone. Ever. And he'd seen a few in his lifetime.

"Ah," Reve said with false magnanimity. "The husband."

"Vijay!" Oriel leaped to her feet.

Nina rose and, even though she'd seen dozens of photos of Vijay Sahir with his wife, she was a little bowled over by how movie-star sexy he was. He crossed to kiss his wife's cheek.

Nina was envious of that, the simplicity of being in love and greeting each other with a kiss.

Oriel introduced Nina as her sister, and Vijay shook her hand graciously enough despite a noticeable hostility in his demeanor. He didn't shake hands with Reve.

"We don't know I'm her twin," Nina clarified, thinking he must be suspicious of her claim. "It's what the birth records we found would suggest, though."

"And anyone with eyes," Reve said laconically. She heard the edge of steel in his tone, as if he was offended Vijay might have doubts about her.

Had he forgotten that, as recently as yesterday, he'd been telling her what venal souls most people possessed? Vijay was allowed to be skeptical.

"I imagine Lakshmi's family has been inundated with people claiming to be her daughter. I'm happy to do a DNA test," she assured Vijay.

"Seems redundant, but I've already connected with our lab," Vijay said. "I'll arrange it shortly. I need to speak with my wife first." He looked at Oriel, and the air between them crackled with enough sexual tension that Nina immediately felt like an interloper.

"You should check in with your family, Nina. Warn them that things are about to get very chaotic," Reve said.

"Oh. Vijay will arrange protection for you." Oriel looked to her husband.

"Already in the works," he assured her.

"I can protect her," Reve said in a tone that sounded both offended and territorial.

"Do you think I'm going to let anything happen to my wife's sister?" Vijay moved aside with Reve to exchange cards.

"Shall we meet for dinner?" Nina invited, anxious not to lose another minute with her twin.

"Of course. I just need a few minutes…" Oriel sent Vijay a conflicted look, then put Nina's number into her phone and promised to text.

Minutes later, Vijay's bodyguard helped Nina and Reve slip out a side door and into their car undetected.

"I feel like we were rude, leaving so abruptly," Nina said, her head still spinning.

"Did you not see the way he was looking at me?" Reve's voice dripped with ironic amusement. "He blamed me for the photos that made it look like his wife was having an affair. I suspect that's why she came to Paris alone and was so surprised he turned up."

"Why would he be mad at you for that? It was my fault."

"He can't be mad at you. It would be like yelling at his wife while trying to apologize to her. He kicked us out so they could kiss and make up."

"Oh." They arrived at his building and darted in before any enterprising photographers caught them.

In the elevator, she asked curiously, "*Would* you have an affair with her?"

"I never sleep with married women," he dismissed firmly. "You?"

"Have I slept with a married woman? My sister. And my brother's cat preferred to sleep with me, which made him furious. Does that count as cheating?"

"Sure does. Home-wrecker."

They both laughed and his smile lingered. "You're happy. It looks good on you."

She was happy because she was still with him and they were bantering like the things they'd said yesterday hadn't happened.

As if they both suddenly recalled the conversation, they sobered. He stared at the doors, which conveniently opened.

"As I said at Oriel's, you should call your family, tell them what to expect," he said as he let her into the penthouse.

Nina waited until he had shut the door to ask, "What *should* I expect? Are we saying goodbye for good now? It's okay if we are. I just—" she cleared the gathering thickness from her throat and almost dropped her phone as she drew it from her bag "—need to find a hotel."

"You're not going to a hotel," he said gruffly. "You still need my help, Nina. Tell your family you're safe and let them know I'll arrange security for them. I've already made preliminary calls. I'll have my people draft a statement, but we won't release it until we've coordinated with Oriel's people. Ask your family to sit tight for a little longer."

"How am I supposed to afford all that? Do *not* say you'll pay for it," she warned.

"I will pay for it. I protect what's important to me," he said implacably.

"Reve." She wanted to stamp her foot and also hug him with all her might. He was the most infuriating, endearing man she'd ever met. "I can't keep leaning on you. Not when—" The tendons in her throat flexed. "I don't want to lose your respect. Not after I've worked so hard to earn it."

"Bloody hell, Nina." He paced a few feet, then shoved his hand through his hair with uncharacteristic agitation. "You don't have anyone on your side. Not anyone who knows how to survive the mess you're in the way I do."

"I have Oriel." Was she being presumptuous? They seemed to have an immediate connection, but maybe that perception was only on her side.

"You literally met her an hour ago. She has a husband

and an unborn baby and her own family to protect. You can't be her top priority. Let *me* lead you through this."

"I can't do that to you, Reve." It killed her to say it, to provoke the darkness blooming in his expression as she rebuffed him. "It's everything you hate. You'll start to hate *me*."

"I can take care of myself," he dismissed with a wave of his hand. "It's you I worry about."

"And I'm worrying about you! Reve, what are we doing?" she cried, struck by the absurdity of it all. "We obviously care about one another. Why are we putting all these…things between us?"

"I'm simply trying to help a—" He cut himself off, his mouth tightening.

"What? Business partner? Is that what I am to you?"

Ironically, she had been terrified of this moment when she left the old Nina behind and became this new woman. Oriel's sister. Lakshmi's daughter. She hadn't known what to expect, only that her life would change. She would know more about herself and some of that would be difficult. It was.

But as she let go of her old self, and the layers of hurt and existential angst she had been using as self-protection, she saw herself more clearly than she ever had.

She was still Nina. She had loved Reve before and she still did. Her love for him had been beating under her skin with her pulse all along, and she couldn't keep it in any longer.

"Reve, *I love you*."

"Don't." He closed his eyes.

His rejection stung like a million ant bites. A wound opened in her chest, but she understood him so much better now.

"Don't say it? Or don't feel it? Because I can't control it."

"Don't feel it. I'm not worth your love," Reve said, each word scoring into her. "That's for people like your family. People who know how to love you back."

"It's okay if you don't love me back," she said. Her throat was tight with agony because, yes, deep down she longed for him to love her back. "I don't want you to say words you don't mean. You were right when you said I wouldn't want to marry and have children just to tick those boxes, but I'm realizing I would rather leave them unticked than give up the man I love."

He withdrew more firmly, his hands clenching into fists as though he was enduring some kind of intense pain.

"I won't force you to accept my love, either," she said with quiet dignity. "Love isn't supposed to be transactional. I'm not saying it to get something from you. I'm offering it freely. Here is my heart. Pick it up or not. That's your choice."

He still wasn't looking at her. The veins in his arms stood out as he inhaled deeply and released a long breath.

"I am so afraid of hurting you again, Nina. Now I don't see how I can avoid it." His expression was anguished. Tortured. "I want to stay and protect you, but I don't want to lead you on. I don't want you to believe…" He pinched the bridge of his nose. "To think that I'm going to become more than I am."

A skip of hope pulsed through her.

"You're enough, Reve. You are. Could we…?" She stepped closer. "Could we agree to take it day by day and see how far we get?"

His expression contorted with conflict, but as she slowly approached, his arm shifted so his hand settled on her hip.

"This is why you're so damned dangerous to me," he

said in voice thick with fatalism. "All I can think about is how I don't want to make you cry—"

She threw her arms around him.

Maybe I do love her, Reve thought as Nina sealed her mouth against his.

Whatever this feeling was, it was big and unwieldly. He was still trying to figure out how to grasp and hold on to it, and the trying made him feel clumsy and expansive and raw. He couldn't fudge something like that, though. His worst nightmare would be for her to look at him with disillusionment and betrayal again.

It made him take things very carefully as she led him to the bedroom. He undressed slowly, giving her time to be sure, before they slid naked into his bed. There he settled his mouth over hers with aching gentleness, trying to convey the need in him to protect her. Cherish her. Celebrate her.

When he looked into her eyes, he saw so many emotions he was certain he was physically falling through air. His throat thickened and his chest hurt. Every emotion filled him, then. Regrets and awe, conflicts and need, the heat of lust and the sweeter, softer glow that wanted her to know how incredibly precious she was to him.

A sting hit behind his closed eyelids. Joy. It burned his chest in a painful bliss as he swept his hands over her skin, wanting to gather and caress, worship and incite all of her.

She did the same to him and it was exquisite. She touched him with reverence even as she did all the things she knew drove him mad with pleasure. He couldn't help the broken groan that left his throat or the possessive growl that resounded in his chest.

He claimed every inch of her, too, caressing her with

a delicate saw of his fingertip until she was shaking with need. Then he settled over her and slowly pressed into her, both of them sighing as they were finally where they needed to be. Together. One.

They stayed like that a long, long time, moving in small, savoring strokes, holding fast to each other until their bodies betrayed them and demanded more power, greater depth. They were basic elements then, creating heat and friction and, aligning perfectly, they melded into something new and gleaming and indelible.

Nina shivered and clenched beneath him. Reve's voice tore.

The waves of culmination soared over and through them, holding them at the brink of heaven for eternity, bathing them in its glorious light before slowly releasing them to drift gently back to earth.

With a sigh, Nina relaxed beneath him.

After a time, Reve gathered himself to withdraw, but she pressed him to stay inside her, whispering, "Not yet."

He shifted and they fell asleep still joined.

The next hours were a roller coaster of emotions, but Nina was at peace with it. She had Reve. Maybe they weren't committed for a lifetime, but they were united for now and that was enough.

Oriel and Vijay turned up looking like honeymooners. They could barely keep their hands off one another, which had Reve sending Nina a told-you-so look behind Oriel's back.

She bit back a smirk, then sobered when Vijay began rhyming off the security he was putting in place.

"That seems like a lot." Nina was daunted. "Is it really necessary?"

"Vijay is extra cautious. I'm afraid you've acquired

more than a twin," Oriel teased. "You also get an over-protective brother."

"I already have one of those!" Nina said, pretending to be disgruntled before she added cheekily, "I guess there's no such thing as too many?"

"That's what I was thinking about sassy little sisters." Vijay winked as he stepped away to talk press releases with Reve. Nina grinned. She liked him.

Nina and Oriel sat to have their cheeks swabbed by a nurse who would personally courier their samples to a private lab. She said they would have the results by morning. "But, honestly?" the nurse continued. "This seems like a lot of money and trouble to state the obvious."

They were all thinking that even before Nina and Oriel discovered they were alike in ways beyond the physical. They laughed at the same things and disliked the same foods, and Oriel went into raptures when she saw the pop-up boutique Reve had installed in the spare room.

"Vijay," Oriel called from the doorway. "I'm throwing you over for Reve!"

"Reve already has one of you," Reve called back drily. "But I'm given to understand one can't have too many?"

Oriel snickered, then asked Nina, "How long have you two been together? I only ask because Vijay thought I had something going with Reve when your photo turned up." She began to comb through the racks. "I'm surprised there weren't more. Reve is very well-known in New York. We might have found each other sooner if I'd seen you with him."

"Reve hates the spotlight. He avoids photographers as much as possible." Nina didn't explain why.

Oriel's gaze flashed up and softened with compassion. "He won't enjoy the attention in India. I don't know how to prepare you."

After hearing the security measures, apprehension was sitting like heartburn in Nina's chest. She tried not to think of it and chatted fashion with Oriel, eventually showing her a couple of her own pieces from her luggage. Oriel gasped with delight.

"These are beautiful. You should make my maternity clothes." Then she joked, "We should start a label like those other twins who had a house here in Paris."

"The Sauveterres? Are you being serious? Because I'm so on board I'm riding all the way to the station."

"I was kidding, but…" Oriel cocked her head, considering. "Design isn't my strong suit. That would definitely be on you. I would excel at networking, though. I know a *lot* of people. Plus, I'm in India full-time. I could source textile and garment factories."

"I'd want it to be the fair wage kind," Nina said. "No exploitation."

"Agreed. Ethical from soil to shop. Prove to the industry it can be done. Are *you* being serious? Because I've been stressing about giving up modeling. I love this idea so much." Oriel excitedly locked her hand around Nina's wrist. "You're coming to Mumbai, yes? We'll hammer out our business plan while you're there."

Nina laughed at the idea of her dearest-held dream coming to fruition so easily—and with the perfect person.

She hadn't fully processed that she would go to Mumbai, or that she had other blood relations besides Oriel, but one video chat with Lakshmi's brother, Uncle Jalil, and she longed to meet him. He already felt like family.

Jalil wept openly, deeply upset at the way his sister and her daughters had been treated. "Bring all the papers. I already have a lawyer working on this. Whatever settlement we win will go to Lakshmi's estate," he told them. "Oriel has been resisting accepting that, but you two are entitled to it. I want you to have it."

"I'm just happy to know where I came from," Nina told Oriel when they ended the call. "I don't want to offend him by refusing, but I really don't want her money."

"Same, but he's adamant. I suggested we use some of it to make a biopic on her life."

"Oh, I love that idea."

They sat down with the men then, eating grapes and cheese and crab croquettes while they finalized the press release.

"Do we bother waiting for the DNA results?" Vijay asked, glancing toward the terrace. "I think we're losing our chance to stay ahead of the story."

Photographers had been gathering outside in greater numbers since Oriel and Vijay had arrived.

Nina looked to Reve. It meant putting him under a microscope as well as herself.

"It's your decision." He squeezed her hand.

"It feels like the nuclear codes," she said with a pang, thinking it was the first test of this tentative future they had agreed to try. She glanced at Oriel. "Do you want to run for shelter before all hell breaks loose?"

"Hell is already loose in my life," Oriel said wryly. "Honestly? I want to stand on that terrace and show the world I have a sister." Her eyes grew bright with happy tears, her smile wide and unsteady. "But you should do this however it suits you best." Her glance flickered to Reve as if she read Nina's concern there. "*I* know I have a sister. That's the most important part for me."

Nina knew then that she really did have a sister in Oriel. The truth was that she was equally excited to tell the world she had a twin.

Whether her sudden fame would destroy what she had

with Reve was a question that could only be answered by letting the secret out. It wasn't a secret they could keep forever anyway.

She gave a jerky nod. "Let's do it."

CHAPTER TWELVE

NINA'S APPEARANCE ON the terrace last night with Oriel had set Paris on fire. The news traveled around the world within hours. Despite the downpour in Mumbai when they landed, even bigger crowds were gathered at the airport and outside the building where Oriel and Vijay lived. The roar when they paused to wave before hurrying out of the rain and into the high-rise rang in Nina's ears as they stepped into the elevator.

"It's a lot, I know," Oriel said with a small wince of empathy, leaning into Vijay.

"Settle in and rest," Vijay suggested, looping his arm around his wife. "Jalil and my sister will join us for dinner, but we'll put off talking about interviews and appearances until tomorrow or the next day."

"I think the baby needs to nap," Oriel said with a sleepy blink up at him.

"Then baby should." Vijay settled his hand on her belly, seeming completely enamored with her.

Nina's heart pinched and she glanced away, but her gaze was snagged by Reve's intense one. She looked down guiltily. She couldn't help it that she was envious, and wished he hadn't noticed. It put a lot of pressure on him that she didn't mean.

The pair stayed in the elevator while she and Reve

departed two floors below her sister's penthouse into a very swanky apartment with a living space that opened onto a covered terrace overlooking the sea.

Nina immediately went to stand at the rail. Rain gusted toward them, but she only grinned at the storm waves and heavy gray skies.

"Doesn't it smell good?" She drank in the sweet, earthy, salt-scented air.

"It does, but—" Reve nodded at someone pointing a camera toward them from the beach twenty stories below. He drew her back into the apartment. "Can you imagine bringing a child into this sort of fishbowl?"

She bit the corner of her lip, debating how to react.

"Oriel's mother is a renowned opera singer so she's used to being the daughter of someone famous. She seems comfortable with the attention, but they weren't planning to have a baby this soon." In a private confidence between sisters, Oriel had confessed that she and Vijay had married because Oriel fell unexpectedly pregnant. Nina kept it to herself.

"Accidents happen," she said with a defensive shrug. "I'll try not to have any and certainly wouldn't deliberately let it happen, but you should probably consider that it could."

He walked into the kitchen and her heart sank. She followed and found him glowering. Her stomach cramped.

"Look, if you're not comfortable with that risk…" She couldn't finish the sentence. She hated how tentative this was! Without any firm promises between them, every little thing felt as though it could defeat them.

"I don't like this kitchen. We need to remove that wall and put in an island so you can cook without me getting in your way."

"Really?" she said, perplexed.

"Am I being sexist? I thought you liked to cook."

"Sure, but that sounds very... I mean, I can't afford this place."

"The show has done well, and I have every confidence you and Oriel will quickly become a force to be reckoned with in the fashion industry. At some point, you absolutely will be able to afford this, but I'll buy it. That way we'll have somewhere to stay when we visit."

Her stomach swooped. "I thought we were taking this day by day. Did you hear what I just said about accidents?"

"Yes. And if I'm not comfortable with that risk, I can wear condoms as an extra precaution. I probably won't, unless you want me to."

"Really?" A bubble of optimism rose to press painfully behind her breastbone.

"Really. Let's go see if we like the bedroom."

The next days were challenging and busy, but Reve couldn't resent the demands and privacy difficulties when Nina was positively incandescent.

And while he still loathed the intrusion of paparazzi, he discovered what a disservice he'd done to her and himself in the past, when he had refused to meet her family. He had thought it would feel like an overstep to allow strangers into his personal life, but spending time with Nina while she got to know Oriel allowed him to see parts of her she had never revealed before. At night, she decompressed, confiding in him the complicated feelings she had about all of this. It formed tiny threads that meshed them closer together.

He enjoyed coaching her and Oriel on their business plan for the fashion house idea, too. Nina's confidence in her worth as an artist grew by the day, making him so proud he was in danger of becoming insufferable. Vijay's sister wanted in on their fashion label idea even though she was already busy with the security work she did with Vijay, and soon Reve was sent to do "boy things" with Vijay and Jalil. He enjoyed their company, too.

With the evidence Reve had found, Jalil was commencing formal legal action against Lakshmi's manager. Suing the clinic was much trickier since the business had been dissolved two decades ago and the doctor who'd colluded with Bakshi was dead. Still, they were going to try. In fact, Reve had just left Nina with Oriel and Jalil at the lawyer's office and was killing time by wandering down the block.

Restlessness chased him. He was ignoring his own business by lingering here with her, but he didn't want to leave, even though he knew she would be okay. Jalil was footing the bill on the legal proceedings and security. Everyone had welcomed Nina with open arms. She was regaining her sense of self and making decisions about her future. She didn't really need him.

Which wasn't as comforting a thought as it ought to be. If she didn't need him, why was he here? Because she loved him and he didn't want to hurt her by rejecting that love?

That was true, but he was also starting to realize that he needed her. He had already tasted life without her voice and touch and laughter. It was empty and meaningless if he didn't have their playful bickering or quiet moments of sincerity.

From the moment she had stumbled back into his life, he'd been thinking he should pry her out of it, and he hadn't once found the strength. He still didn't think he was right for her, but their soft promise of "wait and see" wasn't enough for him. He saw the commitment between

Vijay and Oriel and knew Nina wanted that. Love, marriage, children… It still felt very foreign to him. Impossible to achieve.

Yet, every time he saw Vijay touch Oriel's belly, curiosity rose in him. He wanted to ask him, *What is that like? How does it feel? How do you know you'll be a good father?*

He looked at his ghostly reflection in a shop window and was struck by how much he looked like a younger version of his father. Had there been a time when that man had loved him, before he'd lost the woman he loved and gave himself up to a bottle of grief?

Could this man reflected back at him be a good father after that example had been set for him? Despite Reve's mind riffling through all the ways he would make a terrible parent, a resounding truth rose above the noise. Nina wouldn't let him fail. She would help him be better. *He knew that.*

A swell of possibility rose in him.

"Sir, would you like to come in? Can I show you one of those rings?"

Reve focused his gaze and realized he was standing outside a jewelry store.

"You still need to go to Berlin, don't you?" Nina asked Reve the next morning.

They'd had a late night. She and Oriel had been interviewed on a television show, which had been surreal, but seemed to result in a wave of public outrage for what had been done to Lakshmi and support for them. Reve had been quiet and distracted, and she wasn't sure if it was because of the attention or because he was growing tired of playing second fiddle to her needs.

"I have business in New York that needs to be addressed sooner than later. Why? How long were you thinking of staying here?"

"Forever?" she said on a wistful sigh and flopped onto the sofa. "I love it here, but I feel very far away from my family. I also haven't even started the work I need to do with Andre. I have to fill those orders so my investor doesn't send his goon squad after me." She reached her toe out to nudge him in the thigh.

"You're saying that having a twin isn't as convenient as it sounds?" He caught her ankle and sat to swing her feet into his lap. "Isn't it like having a clone? Can't you be in two places at once now?"

"Turns out, no. Family is many things, but convenient is rarely one of them." She shifted to straddle his lap, so in love with him she thought she might die of it. "Even so, you can never have too much."

She faltered slightly as she realized how that might sound.

"Nina, it's okay that you say what's on your mind and in your heart." He tucked her hair behind her ear and looked at her in a way that sent a spear of hope straight into her chest. "That's how I know I can trust you."

"Do you trust me? Because sometimes I worry it's not the publicity that will drive you away," she confessed softly. "I worry it's the moments when I get excited about Oriel's baby or I do something else that makes you think I need what she has. I only need you." She cupped his stubbled cheeks. "I promise you that."

"It seems impossible that I could ever be enough." He searched her eyes pensively. "I keep thinking that I need to do more."

When she started to shake her head, he tightened his hands on her hips, forestalling her from saying anything.

"I can't ask you to leave places where you have roots

and family and people who love you to follow me around the world. Not unless I give you a good reason to."

She wanted to ask, *Such as...?* She had stopped breathing, and her eyes teared up.

Ask me to marry you, she silently pleaded, pulse rushing in her ears. If he was her family, she would go wherever he wanted to take her, convenient or not.

He swallowed and started to reach into his shirt pocket.

Her heart stuttered and soared with anticipation.

His phone rang in the opposite pocket. He swore, glanced at her sheepishly and made a face of annoyance as he drew it out and looked at the screen.

His features froze with concentration. Hardened. When he clicked it off, his expression was grave.

"I have to leave." He spoke quietly and with a finality that landed on her like a meteorite.

Her limbs became cold and unwieldly, too weak and heavy to fight him as he moved her off his lap and rose.

"Right *now*? Why? I'll go with you." Panic edged into her voice as she scrambled to her feet.

"No. Spend time with your family. Tell them..." His expression tightened. "Tell them I'm sorry."

Dread slid down her back in cold fingers. Nina scanned his features, growing more and more distressed. Maybe she and Reve hadn't made any promises for a future, but she had thought she would have more warning if he decided to leave.

"What happened?" She looked at the phone he'd tucked away.

"The smear campaign has begun."

"On *me*? By who? Lakshmi's manager?"

"On *me*. There's nothing Bakshi can say to discredit *you*, is there? You're an innocent victim. He'll only look worse if he comes after you. Better to say your accusations against him are being prompted by a man who lacks morals. One who makes up any story for money."

"Oh, Reve, no. I am *so* sorry." She took a faltering step toward him, but he was already putting up a hand to hold her off.

"It was bound to happen, Nina." He was speaking in a tone she hadn't heard in a long while, the one that said nothing could touch him. Except it could. She heard through that aloof tone to the pain it disguised. "He'll soon discover he has started a fight he doesn't want with a ruthless bastard who stops at nothing. But my past, and the dirty fight we'll have, cannot be your problem. So here we are. This time we really will end it."

"No." Pain began to seep like poison through her veins and arteries and nerve endings, growing too intense to bear. "Reve, I don't care what he says about you. I *love* who you are. Everything about you."

"Nina." His voice was gentle, as though he was holding something fragile and trying to release it into a breeze. "It's not just you I'm protecting." He nodded to the ceiling and Oriel and Vijay, two floors up. "They'll all suffer if I allow myself to be used as a weapon. If I leave, he has nothing against any of you. You don't need me anymore. You'll be fine."

"No, I won't! I do need you. We belong together. *You know that*. You were just about to ask me to marry you, weren't you?" she demanded, pushing the strained words through her tight throat.

He looked away and a muscle clenched in his jaw. "You don't want to be married to this. I've always known that, and you would have seen it, too, if you had really wanted to. When you do, you'll thank me for making the hard choice that you refused to."

"That's bull. You're being a coward."

His head jerked back as if she'd punched him.

"I'm doing what has to be done." He walked into the bedroom where he threw a few necessities into a bag, gave her one last look of agonized regret and then left.

She didn't go to the shower. She was too devastated for tears. She sat on the sofa in a paralysis of loss, unable to form a thought through the pulsing pain that enclosed her.

Eventually, she became aware that her jagged breaths were the only thing she could hear in the otherwise profound silence. She had never felt more abandoned in her life.

But she wasn't alone, she realized dimly, and ran in a blind hurry up to Oriel's apartment, banging urgently on the door.

"Nina? Are you okay?" Oriel let her in, alarmed.

"No! Something happened." The words stumbled against the sobs that were stacked like uneven blocks in her throat. "Gouresh Bakshi is dragging up Reve's past to discredit me and harm Jalil's case. Reve *left*. And I don't know how I'm going to bear it."

"Oh, Nina." Oriel's arms came around her.

Nina clung to her sister and heard Vijay swear vehemently.

"That can only mean one thing," he said.

He sounded so grim that Nina was pulled from her anguished need to weep and lifted her head. "What?"

"I'm next."

Reve's jet had gone back into service after dropping them here in Mumbai. It would meet him in Dubai, and a conventional executive jet had been chartered to get him there. He was stuck in a private lounge, waiting for it to make its way onto the tarmac.

Would he start drinking, he wondered? He tried not to use alcohol as a coping mechanism, but he really didn't know how he would survive leaving Nina. He had to protect her, though. Had to.

Because he loved her. He must. There was no other explanation for this feeling—it was as though a part of him had been amputated. He could hardly breathe.

Although he wanted to berate himself for letting it happen, he hadn't had much choice in the matter, either. Not from the first moment she had approached him at that New Year's Eve shindig, saying with the wide-eyed blink of an ingenue, *Your performance of boredom is extraordinary.*

He had never been bored again. Not while she was around. Now, all he could think was that his life would become a wasteland again. Meaningless.

Ironically, by leaving her, he was trying to be the sort of man who deserved her. He was trying not to hurt her by hurting her. It was the most untenable position to be in, but he understood now. Love wasn't a selfish thing you used to make others do things. It was something that drove your own actions on another's behalf. It was complete selflessness. The sacrifice of your own happiness for their betterment.

Why was he forcing loss on her, though?

His phone pinged again. He'd been ignoring it. His PR people were becoming aware that his reputation was being attacked. They were reaching out for guidance and, furious as he was by Bakshi's efforts, another part of Reve couldn't care less. If he couldn't have Nina, what was the point in fighting? Let Bakshi do his worst. He'd rather be dead.

Someone was trying to video call. He gave in and pulled his phone from his pocket, but missed it. Vijay.

He wasn't in the mood for whatever rebukes Vijay wanted to spit at him. Reve's past was stinking up all of their lives, he knew that. That's why he was leaving—to mitigate the damage.

It bothered him that he was losing Vijay's respect, though. Friendships of any kind had always eluded him, but he and Vijay had fallen into a comfortable camaraderie. This whole experience of watching Nina meld with her sister's world had drawn Reve into believing he was part of that thing she was forming. The f-word. *Family.*

He wasn't meant to have such a thing, though. He was alone and always would be.

His phone was still faceup, so he saw the text from Vijay as it arrived.

You tool. Do you think you're the only one with dirt in his past? We're both under attack. If you care about Nina at all, you'll come back and fight with us.

"Sir?" A woman appeared beside him. "I can show you to your plane now."

"Why is this man intent on destroying my family?" Jalil lamented. He sat between Nina and Oriel, one of their hands in each of his. Vijay's sister, Kiran, was clattering away on her laptop, and Vijay was in the loft, issuing sharp orders in Hindi into his phone.

Jalil's lawyer continued issuing advice over video chat.

Nina shouldn't have tuned it out, but she was one raw, exposed nerve, throbbing with agony. Empty. It was all she could do to reassure Jalil that she didn't blame him for Reve leaving. It wasn't his fault that Gouresh Bakshi was lashing out.

The truth was that she and Reve had always been

unsustainable. She had wanted to believe her love was strong enough to carry their relationship, but she realized that the mightiest bridge did nothing if the man she extended it to didn't trust it enough to come across. Although he could say he was leaving to protect her, deep down, he was protecting himself.

He trusted her, but not *enough*. And that destroyed her. She didn't know how she would survive losing him this time, she really didn't.

Their discussions were disrupted by a sharp knock on the door.

They all went silent and looked at it.

Vijay came to the rail of the loft. "No one should be able to get up the elevator."

"Maybe it's—" Oriel glanced hesitantly at Nina.

"Should we guess? Or look?" Kiran rolled her wheelchair across the room and turned the latch. As she pulled the door open, she said, "It's about time you came back. Oh. You've brought a friend. Hello."

She rolled back far enough to let Reve in. He was accompanied by a blond, white man, tall and thin like a marathon runner, maybe in his early thirties.

Nina barely noticed the other man. She slapped her hand over a heart that had begun to pound. Her vision blurred as hot tears arrived in her eyes. *He came back*.

"Pascal Hansen," Reve said with a nod, his gaze not leaving hers. "He was arguing with the doorman in the lobby when I came though, trying to get them to call up and tell you he was here."

"I haven't had any luck with leaving messages," Pascal said, rubbing his hands on the seams of his jeans. "I, um—goodness!" He looked between Oriel and Nina. His bemused smile revealed a small overbite very similar to Nina's.

She started to feel dizzy and clutched Jalil's hand even harder.

"I found a letter in my father's things when he passed five years ago," Pascal said. "I knew he'd had an affair when I was young and that I had a sister in India, but… I guess I have two?"

"You should get some rest," Reve said when he finally got Nina back to their apartment. She looked more emotionally drained and subdued than he'd ever seen her—which was saying something, considering she'd been riding one crisis after another for weeks.

He hoped the resolution they'd arrived at today would finally put the worst of that behind her. Through the afternoon and evening, everyone had been on calls with lawyers, putting pressure on Gouresh Bakshi from all sides.

Reve had spared nothing in his threats to sue the man into oblivion for defamation. Vijay had made similar threats. There was an element of bluff in both of them since they each had a muddy past, but the cost of defending himself was an expense Bakshi hadn't wanted to take on.

Pascal's letter from Lakshmi to his father had secured Bakshi's final surrender. Lakshmi had laid out everything—how the affair she'd had with Pascal's father, a Norwegian academic, had resulted in a pregnancy. How she'd been pressured into having the baby far from home and forced by Bakshi to give it up.

He said our baby would never be accepted because she was mixed race, so I chose a French couple who were also mixed race. I was told the

*wife was an accomplished singer and the husband
a scholar, like you.*

*I didn't get to hold her or even see her. She was
gone when I awoke. Perhaps that was for the best,
because I don't think I could have released her if
I'd held her.*

*I will hate him for the rest of my life, though.
There doesn't seem any point in living if I don't
have you or our child.*

Once those sentiments were conveyed through the
lawyers, word came back that Bakshi would make a settlement that included all the rights to Lakshmi's movies.
It was a reclaiming of Lakshmi that meant more to all of
them than any financial gain.

Pascal had a wife and children to get back to so he
was returning to Norway, but he promised to bring his
family to meet his half sisters very soon.

Nina called her family, and they were thrilled to hear
she had a half brother and even more thrilled to hear that
once this final announcement was made, things should
finally calm down a little.

"Nina?" Reve followed her into the kitchen.

"I want some tea," she murmured.

"I can make it. Go sit down."

She set the kettle aside without filling it.

"How long are you back for?" she asked in a choked
voice. "Because I can't keep doing this."

"Nina, I was trying to protect you."

"You're doing a terrible job!" she accused, flinging
herself around to face him. "Life has run me over again
and again and you haven't stopped any of it. You *can't*,
Reve. Do you realize that? I mean, I don't want to sound
ungrateful for all the things you've provided me." She

sniffed and briefly covered her face as she gathered her composure. She lifted her face. "In some ways you've held off the speeding train while I untangled myself from the tracks. I'm grateful for that, but the only thing I have really wanted from you in all of this is *you*. Your presence next to me. And you *left*."

He pinched the bridge of his nose and moved out of the kitchen, but still feeling claustrophobic as he reached the dimly lit living room with the terrace doors blackened by night.

He saw Nina's reflection in the one and glanced over his shoulder to see her leaning her shoulder on the wall, arms crossed. The corners of her mouth were pulled down with despair.

"I was going to ask you to marry me," he admitted, and felt the sting of her flinch. "But how the hell does that go? *I love you, Nina. Here are all of my worst behaviors making headlines. Please marry that?*" he mocked.

"Okay. I will."

"Don't." He looked to the ceiling. "I will take you at your word, and I will lock you down for the rest of our lives because I cannot take being apart from you. Not again. Not ever."

"Okay." He sensed her coming toward him and felt her arms come around his waist, but kept his gaze on the ceiling, afraid she would see how wet his eyes were.

"Don't forgive me that easily. I know I was a jerk for leaving. I was so…" His arms closed convulsively around her. "I was so *happy*, beginning to see a future with you. It felt too good to be true, and it was. Gone like a candle being blown out."

"*You* blew it out. You didn't trust *us*. It's not gone, Reve. It's right here."

"I don't know how to believe this will last, though."

"You just do. That's how this works. You trust my love is there and believe in it and feel it inside you. That's how I feel. I know you love me. I do."

He did let her see into his eyes then, wanting her to know that his love for her was so big inside him, he didn't know how to contain it.

She dragged in an emotive breath and set her hand against his face, her eyes filling with tears. "Oh, Reve."

"I love you, Nina. Will you marry me?"

"Yes," she said with a trembling smile.

He wanted to kiss her, but he couldn't see. He scraped the heel of his hand across his wet lashes, then patted his pocket and withdrew the ring. His heart hammered. He kept the ring in his closed fist a final second.

She closed her hands over his fist, keeping his fingers folded over it. "You know I only want a future with you, right? A ring isn't necessary." She kissed his knuckles.

"It is to me. I want the whole world to know we're committed to one another. There's a wedding band that goes with this, and I'll wear one, too. I picked it because it looked like it wouldn't catch when you're working. You can exchange it if you want to." He opened his hand and watched her closely.

"Oh, my God, Reve." Her eyes bulged, and she brought both hands to her mouth as she took in the square emerald set flat and framed by multiple diamonds adorning the wide band.

"You like it?"

"I *love* it, but…" She saw a shadow come into his eyes. "No 'but,'" she corrected gently. "I was going to say that you have to stop being so generous, but no. You're perfect exactly as you are. I love *you*."

Perfect seemed a stretch, but she placed her trembling fingers on his palm, allowing him to thread the ring onto her finger. It caused the most profound feeling within him, as if he was truly joining himself to her in a way that went beyond the physical, material world.

They were both blinking wet eyes as he brought her knuckles to his lips and kissed her hand. "Be mine always?"

"Always," she promised.

When he drew her close and kissed her, he felt the joyous light of her spill through him, filling him with all those hopes and dreams she had for them. It was thrilling. The possibilities before them were so endless he could hardly catch his breath.

They married in Albuquerque with her "American" family in attendance. While Oriel couldn't fly because she was nearing her due date, she was very understanding about not being included.

"It should be about you and Reve, not you and me," Oriel said, wryly acknowledging that they always became the center of attention when they went anywhere together. "Besides, my mother is planning a wedding reception for Vijay and me for next summer. You and I can celebrate each other's marriages then."

Any initial coolness over the way Reve had broken Nina's heart was quickly forgotten by her family when they saw how doting he was. Also, as a wedding present, Reve got her sister fast-tracked and financed for one of the top family planning clinics in the country.

When Angela tried to demure, he asked, "What's the point in having all this money if I can't do nice things for Nina and the people she cares about?"

"I see how confusing he is," Angela confided when she put the final touches on Nina's hair. "It feels like he's buying my good opinion, but also I'm a little bit in love with him for doing something so magnanimous."

It was as though Reve had never had people to spend money on before, and now he was determined to spoil rotten everyone close to her. Nina's father didn't know it yet, but Reve had paid off his mortgage. Her brother, the real estate agent, was also about to earn a stinking great commission from the house Reve intended to buy so they would have a home to stay in when they visited.

Nina's father walked her down the aisle. They were all very weepy for the people who couldn't be there, but when she arrived to place her hands in Reve's, her joy was absolute.

He nearly crushed her hands as he spoke his vows and gave the ring on his finger an extra push to secure it in place, ensuring she knew he was hers. Always.

They didn't honeymoon, both too busy with work, but they settled into the New York penthouse with a pleasant sense it was their primary home. Nina and Oriel were making progress on their plans to open a fashion house. Nina found the perfect studio space and was beginning to equip and staff it while coordinating production contacts in India with Oriel.

In fact, she was so busy, her husband was the one who noticed she'd forgotten something very important.

"Nina, do you know what day it is?" he asked, coming into the kitchen where she was making their morning coffee. He wore only his pajama pants.

"Tuesday."

"It's Wednesday, but I was looking for the eye drops and, according to this, you think it's Sunday." He held out the blister pack that she kept in the cabinet over the bathroom sink.

"No!" She snatched it from him and stared in horror. "I *always* remember."

"Except we wound up staying at the hotel on Saturday night after the gala and didn't come home until afternoon. Then you were up early Monday for that meeting, and Tuesday morning you were talking to Oriel while you got ready for work."

"I…" She wanted to say she would have noticed this morning, but they'd had sex before rising and she had honestly completely forgotten. "I didn't do this on purpose."

"I know." He gave her a perplexed frown. "I just thought you should know."

"Okay, but if I miss this many, I'm supposed to throw the package away." She swallowed. "And we should use condoms for a few weeks until…"

The coffeemaker hissed behind her. She gave it a distracted look.

"Until we…um…" She swallowed again. "Until we know whether there's anything else to, um, worry about."

"I'm not worried."

"No, Reve. Do you realize what I'm saying? I'm not *protected.*"

"Oh, my God, Nina. Yes. I know where babies come from." He chuckled. "Would you please stop having a panic attack?" He caught her hips to draw her close. "Honestly, this is a conversation I didn't know how to have, but ever since Angela said their surrogate was pregnant, I've been thinking about asking you when you want us to start a family."

"Oh." She pretty much melted into a puddle. "Short answer? From the day I met you." She stroked her fingertips along the fine hairs against his breastbone. "I've always known I wanted you to be the father of my children."

"Yeah?" His smile was a slow dawn of self-conscious pleasure. "Well, let's hope we just got lucky, then."

"Oh, I'm already lucky," she assured him, lifting her smiling mouth for his smiling kiss. "I'm the luckiest woman alive."

"And I'm the luckiest man. But just in case…" He tilted his head toward the bedroom. "Should we improve our odds?"

"Oh, yes. Absolutely we should do that."

They did.

EPILOGUE

Three years later...

"DADDY!" MARTI—SHORT for Marta, which was Nina's grandmother's name—came running at him the minute he entered Nina's studio above the showroom for the Lakshmi label.

Reve caught up his two-year-old and closed his eyes in a moment of deep gratitude as her small arms went tight around his neck, constricting his breathing and filling him with the most incredible sense of wealth.

"Look." She showed him her bandaged finger.

"Did you find one of Mommy's pins?" No matter how vigilant Nina was, here or at home, their daughter was a magnet for finding them. She never put them in her mouth, always bringing them to the nearest adult, but had pricked herself more than once.

"She found Mommy's scissors," Nina said, her expression appalled. She moved in a slow, heavily pregnant gait, cute as hell when she was all round like this. "I left them there—" She pointed to her worktable, well above what Marti could reach. "She pulled over that chair and stacked those books on it so she could reach. Because she heard me telling Auntie that we would have to cut the order off at ten thousand. So obviously, I needed the scissors."

"Mmm…helpful girl." He kissed Marti's cheek, proud even when he was daunted by what a resourceful and determined little sprite they had created. "You're supposed to work at your own table when you visit the studio," he reminded, and set her in the corner that was fenced in with a countertop over shelves where her baskets of toys and books were stored.

She couldn't crawl under it, but immediately stepped on the books she'd left stacked on the floor. She was over it and free in record time.

"That's what I'm up against when the nanny drops her off now," Nina said with a bemused chuckle. "I don't know whether to be proud or frustrated."

"I had the same dilemma when she turned off the power bar under my desk. IT loved me when I dragged them in and that's all it turned out to be."

"No one in the history of having children said it was easy," she said with a rueful shake of her head. She absently moved his hand on her belly so he could feel their second baby moving. "I wouldn't have it any other way, though. This is exactly the life I wanted. Messy and confusing and so full of love I can hardly stand it. Thank you." She looked up at him with the smile that wrapped him up in so much love, his heart could hardly bear the force of it. His knees went weak.

"It's the life I didn't know I *could* have. Thank *you*." He loved her back with everything in him and bent his head to kiss her, wanting her to know it, but he kept one eye on—

Marti bent and immediately came toddling over. "Here, Mommy." She held up a pin.

"Ah. Thank you, baby. Should we go home with Daddy?"

Marti nodded and held up her arms to Reve.

Home. Reve loved that word. They had several, but whichever abode they were in was home so long as he was with his family.

And three weeks later, when he returned to the penthouse with Nina and their son, it was even better.

* * * * *

THE SICILIAN'S
FORGOTTEN WIFE

CAITLIN CREWS

MILLS & BOON

CHAPTER ONE

JOSSELYN CHRISTIE DID not expect to enjoy her wedding day.

It wasn't that kind of wedding. She wasn't that kind of bride—the sort who had dreamed her whole life of a white dress, a battalion of attendants, and a ceremony filled with personal details and love—which was just as well, because there was an appropriate dress, but no battalion. And the ceremony had been about the solemnity of marriage itself, not the couple getting married. A necessity as the couple hardly knew each other.

Josselyn understood it wouldn't be a modern marriage, either, bristling with romance and mushy public declarations. Enjoyment really wasn't on the menu.

But she had hoped for some degree of civility from the groom.

Her reception was in full swing in the ballroom. Old money Philadelphia milled genteelly around the ballroom in all their usual glory, here in her father's house on the historic Christie estate, considered one of the most elegant addresses in Pennsylvania. And therefore, by definition, in the whole of America.

Just ask anyone here, Josselyn thought, as close to amused as she'd been in months.

The money on display in this ballroom tonight was so ancient that those who had inherited it didn't call themselves Old Philadelphians. They preferred *proper* Philadelphians, or *perennial* Philadelphians, depending on the audience. But one thing they could all agree upon was that they were the direct—and in some cases, indirect—descendants of the first families of Ye Olde Pennsylvania colony. They felt, almost universally, that their bloodlines made them personally responsible for settling the state of Pennsylvania—and by inference, therefore, these United States.

If she listened closely, Josselyn was sure she could hear some of the snootier guests murmuring the so-called Philadelphia Rosary just under the sound of the band, that old rhyme of worthy Pennsylvania family names.

Morris, Norris, Rush and Chew...
Drinker, Dallas, Coxe and Pugh...

The Christies had Whartons on one side and Penny-packers on the other. Their money was old, their blood blue, and Josselyn supposed she should always have known that she was destined for a future precisely like the one she was embarking upon tonight. She should not have imagined that, somehow, she would be saved from sacrificing herself to her family name like all the blue-blooded brides before her.

"You look pensive, my dear," came a familiar voice from beside her, startling Josselyn out of her gloomy thoughts. Thoughts of bloodlines and sacrifice did not inspire the average bride to beam about her reception, apparently. But she smiled almost instantly anyway, the usual rush of affection taking her over.

Even today.

Especially today.

Because she loved her father to distraction. She would do anything for him, as this day proved. She smiled down at him now, remembering when he had seemed bigger and stronger than anything that might threaten her. Now the years had seemed to shrink the elderly Archibald Christie, but she could see the differences in him already. Now that he had settled his daughter's affairs as well as he could, in the best way he knew.

Because he believed that this marriage would keep Josselyn safe. And having lost her mother and brother, even if the accident was so long ago now, Josselyn had always understood that her safety was her father's primary concern.

Even at such a cost.

Her gaze moved of its own accord toward the towering, brooding figure across the ballroom, engaged in deep conversation with a collection of other billionaires—all hanging on his every word, naturally—but she forced her eyes back to her father. No good could possibly come of making herself more anxious. Worrying would not change what lay ahead of her.

"I think the beginning of any marriage requires some level of pensiveness," Josselyn said, but lightly. She slid her arm around her father's shoulders, trying not to notice that he felt more frail than he should have. Because noticing it only broke her heart anew. And her poor heart was in enough trouble today. "Some sober reflection, perhaps. Clearheadedness and calm in preparation for what is to come."

She could feel her father sigh a bit, next to her. They stood side by side, looking out over all the very best people who danced, drank, and cavorted beneath the gleaming lights. And who, Josselyn knew, would give not one thought to her again. Not one single thought.

Because this was the kind of wedding people attended for any number of reasons, but none of them having to do with celebrating love. And really, Josselyn had no one to blame but herself for imagining love would ever factor into her situation.

More fool her.

"I understand that this is not, perhaps, what you wanted," Archibald said in his usual tone, gruffness overlaid with seven decades of innate polish. "I may be an old fool, but I hope I'm not entirely delusional."

"Of course not, Papa," Josselyn murmured. Placating him, of course. She'd told herself a million times that she needed to stop doing it, because surely it was time she strode forth and claimed her own life. But no matter how many New Year's resolutions she made, she couldn't quite bring herself to stop.

That was what affection did. It made her act against her own interests, and she couldn't even say she'd minded too much until now.

Her father was many things, but easily placated was not among them. "You might think that I am a doddering idiot. I accept that. But I think, in time, you'll see that all of this is for the best."

"I understand," Josselyn said as calmly as she could. "If I didn't understand, I would never have agreed."

And that was the thing. She had agreed.

No matter how overwrought she might have felt when she'd walked down the aisle this afternoon, no one had forced her to do it. There had been no gun at her back, no threats, no direct pressure. Josselyn had taken her father's arm of her own free will and walked down that long aisle to her own doom.

Her father was drawn into conversation with an old family friend, but Josselyn stayed where she was. She smoothed her hands down the front of her exquisite gown, a near replica of the one her gorgeous mother had worn at her wedding. It had been Josselyn's great joy, if laced with the usual bitter sweetness, to hold on tight to that connection today. She ordered herself to breathe. To smile. Instead, against her will, her gaze was drawn back across the room to where *he* still stood, holding court in his typically unyielding fashion.

Cenzo Falcone, a man so widely feared and admired that his first name was usually enough to create commotion. *Cenzo*, they would whisper, then shudder, and no explanation was needed. Cenzo, descended through European royalty and considered Sicilian nobility, heir to crumbling castles across the globe and a fortune so vast it was said a man could not possibly spend it all in ten lifetimes.

Cenzo Falcone. Her husband.

God have mercy on her soul.

A passing waiter offered Josselyn a drink and she took it gratefully. She was tempted to neck it straight down, but she managed to control herself. Rendering herself insensate might be appealing—more than appealing, at the moment—but she doubted it would end well. Because the wedding and the reception were one thing, but the clock was ticking. And all too soon, Josselyn would have to leave this place.

With him.

As his wife.

She took a small sip of the sparkling wine and kept her gaze trained on the groom.

Her husband. Maybe if she kept calling him what he was, this whole thing would seem more real. Or less overwhelming. Because many people had husbands. They were thick on the ground. There was surely no need to find the term intimidating.

Maybe if she called him what he was, she would find her way to some kind of peace with her new role as his wife.

When she looked across the room at this man who had stood up before all these people—there at the head of the long aisle, unsmiling while tightly coiled power swirled all around him, his brutally sensual features a raw assault—her mouth went dry. When the wedding ceremony had been hours ago now.

It was something about those arresting eyes of his, copper and gold, as if he was making a mockery of all the robber barons who had made their fortunes here. Many of whose descendants were currently eating canapés and having a waltz across the ballroom floor.

Breathe, Josselyn ordered herself.

Their courtship, such as it was, had been conducted over the course of only two in-person meetings. The first meeting had occurred two years ago, in Northeast Harbor, Maine, where Josselyn's family had been summering for more than a hundred years. Josselyn had been acting as her father's social secretary since she'd graduated from Vassar four years before, and she had been spending the cool afternoon catching up on his correspondence in the blue and white sitting room where her mother had once sat and read to her.

And everything seemed divided into before and after that fateful meeting.

There was before, when she had been writing out notes by hand because her father prided himself on his old school, old world approach to things. *The secret to my success, my dear,* he would tell her jovially, when they both knew the real secret was having been born a Christie. And better still, the male heir.

Josselyn had been humming her favorite summer anthem beneath her breath, silly and bright. She had been thinking that the breeze coming in through the windows was lovely, but it was making her a bit cold, so she might run up in a moment to grab a light scarf. Her plans had involved a walk later. Possibly a sail, though her father didn't like it when she sailed out alone, so she rarely did it. It had been a Thursday, so her father's housekeeper was off and it would fall to Josselyn to prepare their supper later. She was planning on a cold soup with fresh vegetables from the garden.

Such a mundane, quiet summer's day in the middle of what she'd considered a happy little life. At least, Josselyn thought she'd been happy. It seemed to her she must have been, in those last, sweet moments before everything changed.

"Josselyn," her father had called from the parlor in the front part of the house. "Come meet our guest."

She could remember the suppressed excitement in

her father's voice and had stood quickly, frowning, because she hadn't expected any visitors that day. Her father's interests ran mainly to his golf game and his club when he was in Maine, and when he threw the odd dinner party—rarely more than a handful all summer—he had Josselyn plan them well in advance.

Still, there were longtime family friends and what seemed like half of Philadelphia's upper crust all around on the rocky, craggy island, some twenty miles from Bar Harbor. Any one of them might have stopped by.

Josselyn had tried in vain to smooth down her usually long and straight dark hair, gone thick, wispy, and frizzy with the sea air. She'd been thinking a little bit crossly that she shouldn't need to worry about her appearance with no advance warning, but knew she would have worn something more appropriate if she'd known she'd have to appear in the parlor today. Appropriate by her father's definition, that was, whose take on modesty seemed to have gotten stuck midway through the previous century.

Then she'd walked into the room and promptly forgotten her Bermuda shorts and soft chambray shirt, clothes better suited for, say, a spell in the garden where there would be dirt. Her father was seated in his usual chair, and she noted distractedly that he was beaming. But that wasn't the alarming part.

The alarming part was Cenzo Falcone, leaning up against the gentle old fireplace across the bright and happy room.

Dark and brooding and the end of everything.

She couldn't remember what he'd chosen to wear, though she had the vague impression of a suitable shirt and dark trousers. But all she'd really registered was *him*. All that power. All that unrelenting intensity of those curious eyes of his, as if they were ancient coins his ancestors might have traded in, off in lost kingdoms long ago. The impression of his chiseled male beauty, almost alien in its severity. The close-cropped dark hair, the nose of a Roman emperor, the sense that whole nations rose and fell on his wide shoulders.

The man would have been an affront to the senses in a city of glass and concrete. Somehow, there on the coast of Maine, he was more like a terrible outrage. A dark and knowing storm that had rendered her powerless at a glance.

Her ears had been ringing, her heart had taken up a terrible pounding in her chest, and Josselyn had felt simultaneously winded and wild. She'd wanted to run out of the house that had always been her refuge, as fast as she could until she hit the water. The moody Atlantic, where she could take her chances with the currents that might sweep her off, all the way to Iceland and beyond, if she was lucky.

Though at that moment, Cenzo's eyes heavy upon her for the first time, drowning had seemed like a pleasant alternative. And also redundant.

Josselyn had stayed where she was, rooted to the spot, while her father mouthed some pleasantries, conducted whatever he considered appropriate introductions that she hardly heard, and then made everything worse by quitting the room.

Leaving Josselyn all alone with this man who had looked at her like she had chosen this fate. And made it clear he did not think highly of her for the choice.

"I... I don't know what my father told you," Josselyn had said, haltingly.

"He has told me the bare minimum," Cenzo had replied.

It was the first time she'd heard his voice. Low, dangerous, and spiked with that accent that whispered to her of European capitals and Italy's rolling hills. He made her shiver. Made her break out in goose bumps.

Made her wish she had already started running.

"I don't know what that means."

"Then I will tell you." Cenzo stayed where he was at the other end of the room, dominating the old fireplace. It was impossible not to notice how tall he was. How he commanded this space that had been her family's for generations. As if it was his. As if she was his. As if this was no more to him than going through the motions. "Your father, who was in another life my own father's roommate at Yale, has made me an intriguing proposition. And I have accepted it."

"Proposition?" she had repeated, her heart hammering in her chest. When she'd already known. When this had been inevitable all along. It was a wonder only that her father had not married her off before now, and how had she convinced herself that he had let go of that notion? She'd known full well her father was not in the habit of letting go. Of anything.

"We will marry, you and I," Cenzo told her. There had been something cruel in his gaze. In the elegant brutality that she could see all over his features, no matter that it was tempered with that sensuality beneath it. She had the thought that a knife could be dulled, but it was no less a knife. "It is your father's wish and I have chosen to grant it."

"Before even meeting me?" Josselyn had asked, feeling as if she was being daring when surely it was a reasonable enough question.

But Cenzo had smiled, that was what she remembered chiefly from that first day. That smile. It was as if he'd carved it down the length of her spine with the dullest knife in his possession.

"Meeting you is but a formality, *cara*," he had said. "Our wedding, now I have agreed to it, is a foregone conclusion."

Josselyn, despite a lifetime of having the necessity for good manners at all costs pounded into her, had turned on her heel and run. Not into the sea, only off toward the woods, a choice she would have a lot of time to regret.

Over the next year, she had spent entirely too much time remembering Cenzo's laugh as she'd run, chasing her from the room. Following her into sleep. Disturbing her wherever she went.

But her father had not been swayed by any arguments. He hardly acknowledged them, much less any talk of laughter. He had chosen Cenzo Falcone for his only daughter and that was an end to it.

Josselyn had assured herself that this time, she might defy him. This time she would stand up to him, because surely—though he had spent years telling her of his plans to assure her safety even after he was gone, and what he expected her to do—he could not mean he truly expected her to marry a stranger.

But he did.

She had tried to comfort herself with the knowledge that while Cenzo was a stranger to *her*, their families had long been connected. Their fathers had been friends since university, and Archibald had spent time palling around with his friend and Cenzo's mother in places like giddy London and the South of France. Long before Archibald had married Josselyn's mother, then lost her. And before Cenzo's father had died, as well.

Archibald had told her these stories since she was a child. Surely, she thought that first year, the fact that she and the forbidding man she was to marry had both lost a parent should work in their favor. It should connect them, that enduring grief.

She'd convinced herself it would.

If she couldn't change her father's mind, it would.

A year later, she had met Cenzo once again.

This time, the occasion was their engagement party, to be held in a restaurant high in a Philadelphia skyscraper with views to die for and Michelin-starred food to tempt the well-heeled guests. Josselyn had not staged a protest, no matter how many times her friends offered to act as getaway drivers. She had been dressed and, she'd thought, prepared.

Her schemes to escape her fate had all ended in nothing, because her tragedy was that she understood her father. She knew why he wanted her to do this archaic thing. And she had never managed to mount a satisfactory rebellion because she cared too much about him to hurt him. It had been only the two of them for so long, and they were the only ones who knew what they'd lost. They were the only ones who still felt the ghosts of Mirabelle Byrd Christie and young Jack wherever they went.

Josselyn didn't have it in her to defy him. Not when all that was required of her was no more than had been asked of countless women through the centuries.

Including her own mother.

That was the argument that had worked the best. The one that had allayed a great many of her fears. Because Mirabelle had been nineteen when she'd become engaged to Archibald, twenty when she'd married him, and barely twenty-one when she'd had Jack. Her notably stern father, Bartholomew Byrd, had arranged the match himself. Mirabelle had famously sobbed on her wedding day and had locked herself in the bathroom of the fancy Philadelphia hotel that was the first stop on the couple's honeymoon later that night.

And yet despite such inauspicious beginnings, Josselyn's parents had fallen in love.

Trust me, her father had told Josselyn the morning of her engagement party. *All I want for you is what your mother and I had.*

And Josselyn had wanted that too. Really, she did, she'd decided. She'd taken care with her outfit, choosing a gown that she was certain could only please the implacable man she was to marry. Even if it did not, because men were nothing if not inscrutable, she felt confident it would look beautiful in all the society pages and her father would feel honored by her acquiescence. She had lectured herself, repeatedly, to remain openhearted. To trust in her father, as he'd asked, because surely he would never choose for her a man who was truly as harsh and inhuman as Cenzo seemed to be.

Remember, she had told herself, *you have that connection.*

She'd ordered herself to cast aside all the gossipy tidbits she'd collected about him over the past year. The many stunning and often famous ex-lovers, all of whom seemed broken when he finished with them. Broken, yet never spiteful, no matter how publicly he had tossed them aside. Josselyn knew too many things about him. A collection of details that together created an overwhelmingly ferocious mosaic and did nothing at all to calm her fears. Like his father before him, Cenzo had come to the States for his education, spending his formative years at Choate before going on to Yale. At Yale he had distinguished himself as a great intellect and excellent football player, then had gone on to Harvard Business School, where he parlayed a small fraction of his fortune into the beginnings of the multinational Fortune 500 company he had sold off five years back. For another fortune, and then some.

They claimed he'd done it simply to prove he could. That a man born with too many silver spoons to count had made his own.

Where Cenzo Falcone walked, the Italian papers liked to claim, the earth shook.

Josselyn had laughed at that in the privacy of her bedroom in her father's house. But she had not laughed when Cenzo had arrived that night to pick her up. For she was sure that she could feel the ground beneath her feet buckle when he strode inside.

He had studied her as if she was a bit of livestock on the auction block.

And despite herself, Josselyn had found that she

was biting her tongue, hoping that he did not find her wanting.

Cenzo had not spoken. He was a vision of rampant masculinity, somehow elegant and breathtakingly ruthless at once. His evening clothes only seemed to call attention to the width of his shoulders, the narrowness of his hips, and the wide swathe of muscled chest in between. Most men of Josselyn's acquaintance looked somehow antiseptic in evening clothes, but not so Cenzo. He seemed to burn bright where he stood. He was alarmingly raw and shockingly vital, so that it was hard to look at him directly.

She'd had the unnerving notion that though this man might pretend that he was civilized, though his blood ran hot with the dawn of too many civilizations to count, he was not.

He was not.

A notion that was only compounded when he, still silent, came to take her hand.

Josselyn had frozen still, even though his touch had made a new, insistent heat roar through her. But it was good that she hadn't leaped away at his touch, because he was not caressing her or making advances. He was not holding her hand. He was sliding a ring into place.

"The ring has been in my family for too many generations to count," he had informed her, his ancient eyes gleaming with a light she could not have begun to read, though it made her skin prickle. "It is always worn by the bride of the eldest Falcone son and heir."

As if she lived in a cave and had never heard of the Sicilian Sky.

Standing in her wedding reception, Josselyn looked

down at the famous deep blue diamond. It was a remarkable heirloom, passed down for centuries and possessed of its own myths. It had been stolen in the sixteenth century but recovered after much accusation and suffering. There had been duels to procure it, intrigue and backstabbing across generations. And it was no dainty, elegant ring. It looked like what it was. A twelve-carat stamp of ownership in the ornate setting it had enjoyed since the Industrial Revolution. The mark of the ferocious clan who had wrested power from almost every European government that had ever existed, yet had both lived and thrived.

It had fit Josselyn's finger perfectly.

Today, Cenzo had slid a deceptively simple band of gold onto her finger. His expression in the church had been grim. His eyes had glittered while his absurdly male jaw had been hard. His vows had fallen against her like threats.

But it was that band of gold that seemed to Josselyn to be made of concrete, even now. She looked down at her hand and it no longer looked like hers. Not with that blue diamond weighing down her hand. Not with that gold ring that declared her a wife.

His wife.

The music stopped playing and Josselyn looked up to see what was happening in this reception of hers. Only to find everyone looking at her with varying degrees of pity and speculation. She looked around to see Cenzo—her new husband, God help her—moving through the crowd that fell back to allow him through. Like a knife through butter.

Directly at her.

She told herself it was excitement. Hope. Even happiness. But the truth was that as he bore down upon her, a look of hard triumph on his face, Josselyn felt as if she was on the verge of a full-scale panic attack.

But she could not allow it, no matter how her heart pounded.

Pull yourself together, she ordered herself. She looked to the side, possibly in search of the nearest exit, but instead her gaze fell on her father. Archibald, beaming at what he saw before him. Filled with all the hope and happiness she couldn't feel herself.

Josselyn reminded herself, again, why it was she did this thing.

It was for the man who had raised her so gently in the wake of her mother's and brother's deaths. The man who had not fobbed her off to nannies or servants as she knew so many in his position would have.

The man who had dried her tears, who had held her and comforted her.

Now it was her turn. This was her chance to comfort him.

And so when Cenzo Falcone—the beautiful calamity she had married today and who might well be the end of her—stopped before her and extended his hand, Josselyn smiled. Brightly, as if this truly was the happiest day of her life.

Then she screwed up her courage and took it, letting him lead her away from all she'd ever known.

CHAPTER TWO

CENZO FALCONE BURNED.

And his wife's hand in his had not helped matters any.

Hours later, high above the Atlantic in one of his fleet of private jets, he sat in his office while his palm yet stung. He flexed it, scowling down at his own flesh when what he wanted was to storm down the length of the plane and find her. And make her account for her unexpected effect on him.

Josselyn had politely excused herself not long after they'd taken off, eyes demurely downcast—no doubt to hide her skepticism of this whole enterprise, and he could not have said he blamed her—and Cenzo had let her go.

Graciously. Magnanimously.

Because she might as well get used to the fact that she was his wife before he showed her what their marriage would entail.

That same old roaring thing in him stirred anew.

Cenzo called it his dragon. The beast that lived in him and had done since his father had taken his own life. The creature that roared and spouted fire, clawed and fought, and had led him here at last. To Archibald Christie and the one and only thing he held dear.

My daughter is my one true treasure, the old man had said when he'd had the temerity to contact Cenzo. When he had seemed wholly unaware of the damage his inattention had done when it mattered most. *I hope I can entrust her to your care.*

And Cenzo had known his duty as a Falcone—the last Falcone in his branch of the ancient family—from a very young age. Regardless of his feelings on the subject, he knew that he must marry. It was up to him to continue the bloodline. To make certain that the Falcone legacy did not end with him, nor get shunted off to one of the distant cousins his mother always called *those circling vultures* no matter how obsequious they were.

Still, he had always assumed that he would do that particular duty…later.

Much later.

But when Archibald Christie had made his astonishing offer, there was not one single part of Cenzo that could refuse it. Because it was immediately clear to him that there could be only one thing better than taking out his revenge on the old man who deserved whatever he got, and it was this.

He would destroy the daughter instead, and make Archibald live with *that* for the rest of his miserable life.

A task that he would have set himself to with the same intensity no matter the circumstances, but one that had taken on a different shape since the day he'd actually met the daughter in question. He had seen any number of pictures. Once he had agreed to come to Archibald in his remote summer retreat in deepest Maine, Cenzo had studied up on the girl. He wanted to know everything about her. He wanted to learn her inside and out.

Because the more he knew, the more he could use it against her.

And against her vile father.

He had seen from the pictures that she was lovely. Lovelier than the daughter of his enemy had any right to be, he had thought when he'd seen the first round of photographs. And far more attractive than those bloodless Americans usually were, always swanning around so enamored of their history when it amounted to very little in the grand scheme of things. Cenzo could trace his family to the Holy Roman Empire. What was anything American but a blink of an eye next to that?

What he had not been prepared for was the reality of his enemy's daughter, standing there looking like some kind of beach bum that day in Maine. Unstudied. Artless. He had expected her to vamp a bit. To make at least some attempt to flirt with him, for that was what women did when they found themselves alone with the great Cenzo Falcone.

Instead, Josselyn Christie had looked at him as if he defied understanding—and not in the way he usually did, by simple virtue of being himself—and had run.

It had troubled him all throughout the following year as he'd set about making his arrangements and, far more daunting, preparing his embittered mother to accept what must happen. He had pored through the reports his people delivered on Josselyn, looking for scandals. Anything to shift the balance, to make the daughter at least as compromised as her father, and best of all—to give him ammunition.

He did not care to ask himself why he, Cenzo Falcone, required *ammunition* to deal with a poor little heiress being sold into his keeping.

And in any case, there was nothing.

There was only the stain of her, seeped deep into his skin, surprising him at the strangest moments.

Then came their engagement party, when he had bestowed upon her the Sicilian Sky that he had only before then seen gracing his own mother's hand. The stone that had caused as much trouble as it ever had joy. More, perhaps. Such was the weight of history.

But what purpose is there in joy, his father had liked to say, *if it does not carry with it the weight of sorrow? You cannot have one without the other,* mio figlio. *They only make sense when they are fused together into one.*

His mother had always been the more severe of his parents, and rarely worried herself overmuch about the unlikely appearance of any joy. Though Cenzo knew that Françoise Falcone did not consider herself dour so much as realistic—and French.

And since her husband's death, the Widow Falcone had also felt that it was her sacred duty to protect the Falcone name—and interests—at any cost. She had not wished to hand over the ring to an upstart American, no matter what Cenzo planned to do with her.

The stone is worth a fortune or two, certainly, Françoise had said, back when it was valued for a mere fifty-five million euros. *But its true value is that others covet it. And the more they covet it, the shinier it seems. This has always been so. The myth of it makes it far more valuable than any mere piece of jewelry.*

And she had always made it clear that while not every woman had risen to the occasion of wearing such an iconic heirloom throughout its storied history, *she* did not intend to fall beneath its weight. Nor had she. She had still worn it years after Cenzo's father had died, spine straight and tall, her eyes forever trained on the glory of the Falcone name. And had required no little coaxing to relinquish it when Cenzo had asked, though she had claimed that had everything to do with its intended new recipient and nothing at all to do with the fact she'd grown to consider it truly hers.

The ring is only ever on loan, Maman, Cenzo had murmured. *It can never truly belong to anyone.*

She had shaken with the force of her distaste. *It is the chain of custody that I find objectionable. And perverse.*

He had not had to remind her that the ring was his by rights, and had been since his father had drawn his final breath. He had not needed to.

And he had resented how it looked on Josselyn's finger, how it caught a new light. He had more than resented it—he'd told himself he had actively disliked it. That it was *dislike* that had moved in him, forging a new path of fire.

What else could it have been?

But now he was suspended between the moon and the vast ocean below, and he was not a liar. Not even to himself. Not ever. He might have pretended there in the foyer of her father's house, because the ring on her finger had disconcerted him. He was too attuned to its history, perhaps. He was too aware of the things that tended to happen when the ring changed hands. Wars and ruin, horror and shame…though not in recent centuries.

He had lied and told himself that his reaction was nothing but distaste for the task before him, however necessary. But the engagement party had told him the truth. There had been dancing, because there was always dancing at these things no matter what year it was. Old formalities never died. And because it was expected, he had led his fiancée to the floor so that other wealthy people could gawp at them.

A public service, he had told himself, as none of the guests were the sort who liked to read the society pages to see things they believed they ought to have witnessed in person.

That night, Josselyn's dark hair had been glossy, caught up at the nape of her neck in something quietly elegant—complicated enough to suggest a bit of drama without actually committing to it. Her dress had been a revelation after the beach clothes he'd seen her in before. There was no disguising her figure in the gown she'd chosen, a sweep of red held at one shoulder by a clasp of sparkling jewels.

He had found himself unduly obsessed with the mark near her lips that should have made her flawed, to his mind. But instead it did the opposite. It was as if her one slight imperfection made everything else more perfect, not less.

And Cenzo did not wish to think of this woman as *perfect* in any regard. Everything in him had rebelled. He had ordered himself to walk away from her, there in the middle of their engagement party, surrounded by the sort of empty, overly fatuous society people he detested. No matter their country of origin.

But instead, he danced with her, because he was playing a long game. He had held her close, so close that he'd been able to identify the scent she wore—a whisper of something like citrus with deeper notes that reminded him of the sea.

They had not spoken. He'd had nothing to say. And Josselyn had looked at him as if he were part monster, part dream. Cenzo had told himself that she saw the dragon in him, that was all.

Maybe he only hoped she might.

And he had spent another year attempting to come to terms with the odd…complications he'd felt that night. The need in him, when he did not wish to feel such sensations where she was concerned. It made things easier that he wanted her, he could admit that, but he did not wish to want her to the extent he did.

It was sheer lust, if he was truthful. And it didn't make sense. His object had always been perfectly clear when it came to the Christies. When he had been younger, he'd focused more intently on Archibald as the obvious architect of his father's untimely end. But it had been clear to him, ever since that very first, astonishing call when Archibald had dared to suggest marriage, that the daughter was the better target.

Because what he did to Josselyn would hurt her, but it would kill her father—yet let him live with it.

Lusting for her seemed to fly in the face of all he intended to accomplish.

Accordingly he'd spent this last year digging even deeper into what made Josselyn Christie tick.

Like him, she had gone to an American East Coast boarding school. After she graduated, she and some friends had taken the summer to wander aimlessly through winter in Australia and New Zealand. In the fall, she had returned to follow her family's tradition, on the women's side, and started at Vassar. Cenzo had found no indication that she had been any more scandalous there than any other coed. The odd parties, a cringeworthy attempt at black box theater, a semester abroad in Italy. She had lived on campus all four years and had maintained the same group of close friends, all of whom had attended their wedding today.

After college, she had spent another summer traveling, this time in Europe. When she'd returned, she had moved back in to her childhood home, and as far as he could tell, had done nothing but serve the interests of her father ever since.

There were no deep, dark secrets to dig up. He would have found them. And in many ways, that was a good thing. Because it meant the focus could be entirely, deservedly, on Archibald's sins.

He thought now, staring out the window at the darkness beyond and the moon above, that he was going to take great pleasure in showing her exactly who her father really was.

"I will avenge you, Patri," he said quietly, using the same words he always used. The vow as much a part of him as his own bones. His own flesh. "I will make them pay."

Cenzo did not sleep, for he had waited far too long. A lifetime, it seemed, though he knew full well his father had only quit this life some fifteen years before.

Promise me, his mother had said before he had left to make this trip to America. His final trip, to collect his bride and bring her home at last. *Promise me that no matter what else happens, you will not forget who you are. What these people have done to you. To me. And most of all, to your father.*

How do you imagine I could ever forget? Cenzo had asked.

Françoise Falcone was not a happy woman. This was forever evident in her face, for all that she was very beautiful. There was always that sternness. That coldness. He liked to think it had been put there since they'd lost his father, but he knew that was not so. She had never been warm.

And still, the way she had looked at him then had chilled him.

Young women have their ways, she had told him, her tone dark. Her gaze had fixed on him as if he had already betrayed her. *Their wiles. It may be, my son, that you believe yourself to be the hunter when it is you who are the prey.*

Cenzo had laughed.

But then he had stood at the head of the church aisle and watched the woman who would become his wife move toward him, a vision in white. She had looked serene, her face a perfect oval, marred only by that beauty mark that was no flaw at all.

Her touch had warmed him, but he should not have cared about such things. About biology. He had held her hands in his, said the ancient words in English, and now he wore the ring that she had placed on his finger in her turn. He could not get used to it.

He looked at it now, gleaming in the light of the plane. He could not get used to any of this.

Cenzo did not wish to react to this woman. He wished only to use her for his own ends.

And he vowed, yet again, that would be so.

Because he was Cenzo Falcone. What he wanted was his, one way or another.

It was still dark outside as the plane began its descent into Sicily. He left his office, moving out into the common area of the jet, and was somehow unsurprised to find his bride already waiting there. He eyed her critically as he approached the sitting area, the jet's many hints of gold making her seem to gleam.

Once again, she was a new version of the woman he knew so many details about—yet still did not know at all.

Today she did not wear her wedding gown, of course. And as he registered that, Cenzo had a brief, horrifying pang of need. Sharp and alarming, because it wasn't the simple lust he had tried to come to terms with already. He understood that though he had never considered himself sentimental, he found himself wishing he might have taken the traditional role of removing that flowing white dress from her slender body. To see, after two years of wondering, if her breasts were as plush and high as they looked. Because, like it or not, he had spent a remarkable amount of time considering the flare of her hips and wondering how they would feel in his hands while he drove himself inside her.

Soon enough, he told himself. Soon enough.

He took the seat opposite Josselyn, letting his gaze fall where it would. She'd chosen to wear a deceptively

simple outfit to begin her life as his wife. A sweater,
a pair of jeans, low-heeled short boots. An outfit that
should have been unremarkable, but for the excellence
of the pieces she'd chosen. The drape of the fabric, the
heft, the rich camel leather of her boots—it all spoke of
understated elegance and impressive wealth. She wore
diamonds in her ears—small, yet of high quality. There
was a delicate chain around her neck, a faint glimpse of
gold, because she did not need to be flashy.

Especially not when she wore the Sicilian Sky on
her finger, elevating her sartorial choices to high art.

Cenzo told himself that he was gathering information, that was all, and there was no need for the immediate response in his sex. There had been the beach bum
he'd met first, her hair wild and her clothes soft with
age. He had imagined that version of her was the real
one, untutored and unaware that he had been coming to
call. As for their engagement party and their wedding,
he had assumed that stylists had intervened—because
the weddings of heiresses were not simple family affairs, and certainly not when he was involved. There
had been extensive press coverage. He had imagined
steps had been taken to tame her, to contain her, to make
her fit the expected mold.

But it seemed he'd been wrong.

And that sensation was so rare that it took Cenzo
some moments to place it. He was not often wrong. To
his knowledge, he had never been wrong, in point of
fact. But his bride—his *wife*—could have worn anything now that they were alone. And she had chosen a
rather well-armored, well-conceived look to face any
eventuality. Even if he'd been tempted to assume that

her choices had been made for her by the same army of stylists he'd imagined had handled her at events thus far, that wouldn't explain her hair. She had taken it down, washed it, and had to have styled it herself, for there was no staff on the plane. It looked perfect, like the rest of her.

Meaning this was her natural state. Or her preferred defense.

He was forced to admire it.

And then told himself that was as well, because it could only benefit him if it turned out that she was a worthy adversary.

In and out of the marital bed.

"You have not told me where we are headed," Josselyn said into the taut silence, sounding perfectly calm and at her ease. As if she often found herself flying off into the unknown, married to a stranger.

"I have not," he agreed.

And then he lounged there, letting the moment drag out.

All Josselyn did was blink. There was no other outward sign of reaction. He filed that away.

"I see. Do you intend to let me in on the secret? Or is it to be a surprise? I was told only to bring my passport."

Cenzo eyed her, still looking for flaws. "This feels a bit like a bait and switch. I don't recall you saying a single word to me before now unless prompted by a priest, and now it is as if you are made of demands. Is this what I can expect from my wife?"

She sat straighter and he realized that her posture, too, added to the overall sense of her elegance. Even without the Sicilian Sky on her hand, her poise alone would have shouted out that she was a woman to be reckoned with.

It really was such a shame that he could not simply admire her.

"There has been no opportunity for conversation until now." Josselyn's voice was as serene as she looked. Yet with a hint of steel beneath, which pleased him. "At our first meeting, I will admit, I felt overwhelmed by the decision you and my father had made. Appropriately, I think. We only met one other time before yesterday and as I recall, you spent most of our time alone engaged in a series of business calls."

"Is that a complaint?"

"Not even remotely." She smiled the same smile he'd seen her flash all over the place on two occasions now, all good manners and vast, unbridgeable distances. "I am only offering you an accounting of our interactions. From my perspective."

"It is all the same to me, *cara*. If you wish to fight. If you wish to make demands. If you fling yourself prostrate and attempt to impress me with a show of submissiveness. None of that will change what is to happen."

Her face brightened. She folded her hands before her and placed them on the little table that separated them, the huge stone on her finger making light bounce all around them. "Wonderful. There's an agenda. I can't wait to hear it."

Cenzo laughed. "Truly, you are like a lamb to the slaughter."

Her polite smile cooled, but only by a degree. "Surely there will be no need for slaughtering of any kind. This is a marriage, not an abattoir."

Josselyn waited, clearly offering him the opportunity to leap in and explain himself. He declined it.

"I think it might serve us both well if we lay out our expectations," she said after a moment. And while her smile did not dim, her voice sounded more…careful. "We're lucky, really. No need to be encumbered by romantic notions. No need to hope and pray that love wins the day. We can civilly decide, you and I, what our life together will be in a way that people in our generation rarely do. I find myself quite optimistic."

He only laughed. For longer, this time.

But his wife did not crumble. She kept that smile on her face and did not seem to tense so much as a stray muscle. It was impressive.

Or would have been, had he allowed himself to find her impressive.

Josselyn's gaze was level on his. "If you will not share what you wish to get out of our marriage, perhaps you might share the source of your amusement. Or is the aim to laugh mysteriously, and alone, for the rest of our days?"

Cenzo regarded her, doing nothing to wash away the laughter he was sure was still stamped all over his face. "Why do you suppose your father bartered you away in marriage to a stranger?"

He thought he saw emotion in her gaze, but she blinked it away. "You are not a stranger to him. Only to me."

"I suppose that is true, though he had not seen me since I was a boy. It was my late father that he knew."

And she could not know how those words cost him. When Archibald Christie had done so much more than simply *know* his father. But he kept his dragon in check. It wasn't time, yet, to let his fury take hold.

"In any case, it is not as if he chose you off the street," Josselyn said. "But he did choose you deliberately. And he did this because my father is of an old school. He believes that money and power are the only things that could possibly keep me safe in this world."

"You must agree with him, then. To have accepted this arrangement."

"It's funny," she said, though she wasn't laughing, "but I thought these were the sorts of conversations we should have had at any point over the past two years."

Cenzo lifted a careless shoulder. "We are having the conversation now."

"Whether I agree with him or not doesn't matter, because I decided—" and he was certain there was an emphasis on that word *decided* "—to acquiesce to his wishes for me."

"Convenient, then, that his wishes for you have made you one of the wealthiest women in the world. Overnight."

It was Josselyn's turn to shrug. Hers was delicate, yet no less dismissive. "As he has quite a bit of money and power himself, I expect my father looked around for one of the few men he believes has more."

"You make it sound like a fairy tale," Cenzo murmured. "The dutiful, obedient daughter who does as her father wishes no matter the cost. But I'm afraid, *cara*, that your father has made a terrible mistake."

Josselyn did not react. Which, he supposed, was itself a reaction. "What do you mean? What mistake?"

"I did not know if I would tell you this." He was enjoying himself, now. "Your father seemed to have no notion of what he'd done. It was perhaps unsurprising that you would not, either. I will confess that at first, I didn't believe it."

"I have absolutely no idea what you're talking about."

"And for some while I've thought it would be amusing to have you figure it out as we went." Cenzo smiled then and did nothing to make it more palatable. Less edgy or dark. "But you see, simply punishing you for your father's sins would not be enough."

"Punish me?" She shook her head, making her hair move. And he could smell the sea once more, sweet and crisp. Inviting, damn her. "Why on earth would I require punishment? Or my father, of all people? He has his flaws, like anyone, but he is a good man at heart."

"No." Cenzo bit out the word. "He is not."

Josselyn laughed then. "You must be joking. He's set in his ways, sure. He's a product of his generation. He has some very outdated ideas and believes too much in his own discernment, sometimes to his detriment. But he's not *evil*."

And he could not tell, in that moment, if he regretted going down this path. Perhaps he should have done as originally planned and let her parse it out over the coming month, assuming she had the faculties to do such a thing. He did not intend to give her much room or time to *think*. Maybe he should have kept her in suspense. That had been his intention.

But she was too perfect. She seemed less a tool to him now and more an actual opponent.

He had not been able to resist.

That was on him. But when it came to the terms of

what would happen between them, there could be no equivocation.

"You may feel a sense of daughterly obligation," Cenzo said, his voice low and his gaze a bright fury on hers. "I suppose that is to your credit. But it is misplaced."

"But you like my father," she protested, her eyes widening. "You spent time with him. He told me he'd thoroughly vetted you and furthermore, enjoyed the time he spent with you. He said that you reminded him of your father."

"The rantings of a guilty conscience and nothing more."

"Guilty?" Josselyn frowned at him. "Of what?"

"I'm glad you asked," Cenzo growled at her, and knew in that moment that this was the right course of action. Because it felt like a relief. "Your father might not have driven the car as it went over that cliff, but he killed my father all the same."

CHAPTER THREE

JOSSELYN FELT AS if Cenzo had driven the two of them over the side of a towering mountain. Some part of her, in a sudden rush of madness, almost wished that he had.

Because she'd spent her wedding night alone, and she had chosen to view that as consideration on his part. As a sign of respect. *He's giving you space*, she'd told herself. He might have been overwhelming and intense in every regard, but this marriage of theirs would be fine if it started that way. On such rational, reasonable footing. She'd assured herself of that, again and again.

She had curled up in a ball on the bed in her stateroom and had chanted that to herself as she tried to sleep. Over and over as the jet flew through the dark.

This marriage will be fine.

Finding herself confronted with the news that this marriage was not only not going to be fine, but that he had been *plotting revenge* all the while, was jarring.

More than jarring. Josselyn felt winded.

"I don't understand," she managed to say after a few moments. She was doing her best to present a calm, impenetrable surface, the way she'd learned long ago. It was the best way to handle excitable men who believed deeply that they were anything but. Normally her own serene facade made her feel better, but not today. It did nothing to keep her heart from catapulting itself against her ribs. Still, she refused to give in to the panic that rose inside her. "You worked out the details with my father yourself. Why would you do that if you thought that he was involved with what happened?"

Cenzo laughed, but it was a terrible sound. Mocking. Dark. It curled inside of her and made her bones feel cold. "Archibald Christie was not *involved* in what happened to my father. He *is* what happened to my father."

Josselyn wanted to leap to her feet. She wanted to put as much distance as possible between herself and this conversation. She wanted to escape…whatever this was.

But she was on a private jet. There was nowhere to go. And even the small protection of her stateroom wouldn't help her now, because they were landing. Even bouncing a little on the tarmac as if in tune with his laughter.

It took everything she had to stay put. To keep her panic from her face. She wasn't sure she succeeded.

"There were any number of ways I could have made your father pay," Cenzo told her as the plane taxied on a dark runway, with only a few lights in the distance to make it clear they weren't still in the air. He sounded as if he was *confiding* in her. And as if the act brought him great pleasure. "I chose the one calculated to hurt him the most."

"How lovely," Josselyn managed to say, through lips that felt frozen. She kept her gaze on him, though the cabin lights had gone dark. That did nothing to dim those ancient eyes of his, blazing straight at her. "Here

I thought that despite the archaic nature of our situation, we might be able to work together to come up with the kind of union that benefited us both. Since we both agreed to do this."

"There will be a great benefit, I assure you." Cenzo laughed again. He looked entirely at his ease. "But the benefit will be mine."

It took her a breath, maybe two, to realize through the tumult inside her that the plane itself had stopped. Cenzo did not move. He continued to lounge there across from her as if he was an ancient emperor preparing to order an execution. And it was as if everything inside Josselyn shivered to a humming sort of halt, waiting for that gesture that would decide her fate. Desperate for any hint of compassion in his gaze when there was none.

But the jet door was thrown open then, and Josselyn told herself it felt like a gift. Even if, somewhere beneath the relief, there was a part of her that almost resented the interruption. Because she wanted to *do* something. Make a stand. Refuse to exit the plane when Cenzo stood, then beckoned for her to precede him down the stairs with exaggerated courtesy. But she didn't see the point in a protest. Not now, when she didn't even know where they were.

Or perhaps you worry that he would simply bodily remove you himself, a voice inside her countered. *And what do you think you would do with his hands upon you?*

She repressed the shiver that notion caused. She repressed it so hard it almost hurt.

And either way, Josselyn walked down the stairs

herself, stepping out into a thick night. Once she made it down to the tarmac she paused, trying to figure out where they were. Her location seemed far more critical in that moment than...the peril shaped like a man who prowled down the stairs after her. The air was more sultry here. Back in Pennsylvania it had still been warm, but there were hints of the coming fall in the September mornings. Whispers in the wind at night. Here she could smell nothing of fall. There were flowers on the breeze, and a rich salt that told her she was near the sea. The very dark around her seemed secretive, whispering things she couldn't quite understand.

Josselyn accepted that she was being fanciful. And fanciful wasn't going to help her. Nothing was.

You married him, her trusty voice within condemned her.

As if she might have forgotten that part, with what passed for the Crown Jewels on her hand.

Not to mention the terrifying man who had given it to her.

Cenzo appeared beside her and gripped her elbow with a possessiveness that would have stolen her breath even if she wasn't already so...undone. And there was a moment, a breath, where he looked down upon her from his great height and Josselyn wondered if she might do as everything screamed in her to do, tear her elbow from his grasp, and run for it.

But that would be giving him what he wanted. She understood that implicitly. He wanted her reaction. He wanted some acknowledgment that whatever game he was playing here, it was working.

Josselyn decided she would rather die where she

stood than give it to him. So all she did was smile coolly, remaining as outwardly serene as she could.

Something she would continue to do unless and until it killed her.

Cenzo handed her into the front passenger seat of a rugged sort of SUV, then rounded the hood and swung into the driver's seat. Josselyn was surprised. She would have assumed his tastes ran to sports cars like crotch rockets, not hardy vehicles with four-wheel drive. He did not spare her a glance—another gift, she told herself stoutly—as he drove into the dark as if he knew it well.

Josselyn clutched at the handle beside her, not exactly shocked to discover that Cenzo Falcone drove too fast. As if his expectation was that the narrow road would arrange itself before him to best suit him. It irritated her that, as far as she could tell, it did.

She focused out the window, where his headlights picked up groves of almond trees, tangles of bougainvillea, and a rocky coastline that flirted with the sea.

"You've brought me home to Sicily," Josselyn said into the dark tension between them. "You could have just said so."

In the distance, the sky began to lighten. The first sign yet that the sun was soon to rise.

Maybe it was foolish that she clung to that notion as if it meant that there was hope.

"To Sicily, yes," Cenzo replied. Though he took his time with it. "But not home. I have something else in mind for you, *mia moglie*."

My wife. It was truly something how he made that sound like an insult.

"How wonderful," Josselyn said smoothly. "I can't wait."

And that same mocking laughter of his seemed to draw tight around her, like a noose.

He drove her down to a rocky cove, where a boat waited. He ushered her on board, and Josselyn supposed she ought to have been grateful that it wasn't a tiny little outboard motor, barely more than a skiff. It was a much larger, sturdier sort of fishing boat, with a cabin below and a deck to shield passengers from wind and waves. She stood as near to the bow as she could get without stepping back out into the early morning breeze. And she gripped her hands tight together to keep herself from screaming while Cenzo and his crew had what was clearly a riotously amusing conversation in Italian. All of them speaking far too quickly for her to pick up much more than a few words in the Italian she'd last used during her semester abroad in Rome.

Another set of headlights came down to the cove, and Josselyn watched as luggage was loaded onto the boat. Her luggage as well as a set of cases that she had last seen in Pennsylvania, and so knew belonged to Cenzo.

Another sign that boded ill, she had to think.

Once again, it was almost a relief when the boat set off, moving slowly from the cove and then picking up speed as it left the land behind.

"When will you tell me what it is you plan to do with me?" Josselyn asked when Cenzo came to stand beside her, though she kept her gaze trained on the dark waves and the ever-brightening sky. It was pinkening to the east, water and sky alike. "Or is the mystery part of your fun?"

She felt that impossible stare of his on the side of her face, but she did not look at him. Because she was certain that was what he wanted her to do. And hers might be a soft and pointless rebellion. Josselyn accepted that. But it was all she had at the moment, so she leaned into it.

"I'm not going to toss you overboard, if that is your fear." Cenzo, by contrast, continued to sound more and more amused.

"I'm delighted to hear it," Josselyn said crisply. "But there's a lot of room between being forced to walk the proverbial plank and the civil, polite marriage I thought we'd agreed to. You can see how a reasonable person might doubt your motives."

"When did we make such an agreement? You appear to have all manner of notions about this agreement you say we made when I cannot recall ever discussing the particulars of our marriage." He laughed. "Not with you, *cara.*"

She wanted, very badly, to tell him not to call her that. But suspected that whatever else he might choose to call her was worse than any ubiquitous endearment.

"I think you know that my father would never have agreed to anything that might hurt me. Like, for example, a revenge plot." She squeezed her fingers more tightly together as the boat bounced across the waves, and she liked that it wasn't comfortable to do that any longer. Not with that enormous ring cutting into her flesh. Because the discomfort grounded her, somehow. It made it matter less that she was on a boat somewhere in the Mediterranean with her brand-new husband and his *plots.* "I must assume that you misrepresented yourself."

"I did what was necessary."

She looked at him then, the precarious dawn seeming to call attention to the stark lines of his face. Cruel and yet still beautiful, even now that she knew better. "We are agreed, then. You're a liar."

A corner of his hard, sensual mouth kicked up. "You may call me whatever you wish, Josselyn. It will not change a thing."

"So what is it to be?" she demanded, with a grand sort of sweeping bravado she in no way felt. "Will you lock me away in some tower? Will I be put in jail for the supposed sins of my father? Or do you intend to abuse me yourself?"

Cenzo studied her face while around them, the world got brighter. His gaze did not.

He lifted a hand and Josselyn braced herself, everything in her spinning wildly. Did he truly plan to strike her? What would she *do*?

Was this really happening?

But he did not land any blow. He reached over and traced her cheekbone with a careless finger, moving it down after a lazy sort of sketch to find her beauty mark.

Just that odd little touch, then he dropped his hand.

And Josselyn felt the same great tumult she always did where he was concerned. Panic and longing, and that terrible heat.

Too much heat.

She was glad it was still dark enough that, if she was lucky, he would not see all the ways her body reacted to him. Josselyn wasn't sure she could bear the shame.

What had seemed hopeful yesterday—that attraction,

that fire, between a bride and groom who hardly knew each other—seemed like nothing but a betrayal now.

"I will not have to abuse you," he told her softly. Much too softly, when the look on his face was enigmatic. And made the blood in her veins seem to run hot and soft, like syrup. "For one thing, I have no taste for such things. I'm not a monster."

"Are you not?" she bit out, though her cheek still felt as if he had lit her on fire.

Again, a tug of his lips. "You might wish that I was a monster. That might bring you clarity, I suppose. But what I intend to be to you is far worse."

Deep inside her, Josselyn felt a kind of trembling. It wasn't fear. It was where the fear went, what it turned into. It was years of tamping down her feelings and putting herself last. Always so understanding of her father's needs, and his losses—far greater than hers. For it was true that she had lost her brother and her mother, but there was nothing worse than losing a child. And the love of one's life, all at once.

He had never made that argument. Josselyn had made it on his behalf.

She could hear her friends' voices in her ears, begging her to reconsider this marriage. Just as they had begged her over the years to gain some measure of independence from her father. To think of herself for a change. To build a life of her own.

But Josselyn had always taken comfort in the fact that her father cared for her. Truly he did. He was not vicious or cruel or even dismissive. He truly believed that what he was doing was the best for her, because he loved her. Just as she loved him. So she had held her tongue. She had let things go. She had never, ever showed him her true feelings about things unless her feelings aligned with his. What would be the point?

All of those choices bubbled up inside her now.

It was temper. And it was volcanic.

And she couldn't think of a better recipient than this man beside her. Her husband, whether she liked it or not.

"So far," she said, her voice harder than it had been in years—or possibly ever—"all you are to me is a duty to my father. And now, having acquitted that duty to the best of my abilities, this sounds like nothing but empty threats. Am I meant to be afraid that a man I care nothing about might harbor conspiracy theories? Why on earth would I care?"

Cenzo, apparently, did not realize that even so civilized a volcanic eruption from Josselyn was nothing less than a sea change. All he did was laugh again. "It seems you do have some fire within. I doubted it."

Temper kicked its way through her, making her think she might actually combust where she stood. "You do know that whatever it is you're planning, it cannot last, don't you? Whether you leave me on a raft in the middle of the sea, beat me black and blue, or merely lock me up somewhere, it will all end the same way. Sooner or later, my father will demand to see me. And then what will you do? Do you imagine that I will not tell him each and every indignity you make me suffer in the interim?"

"But that is the point," Cenzo said silkily. "I want you to tell him."

Josselyn felt her heart stutter a bit at that. The waves

grew choppy, so she had to reach out and hold on to keep from being rocked off her feet. She noticed that Cenzo did not hold on to anything, and she instantly felt as if she'd lost any higher ground she might have gained by proving herself weaker.

But she ignored all that and focused on him instead. "Or we could fast-forward to the part where I tell him you're a terrible person, then file for divorce. Why all the theatrics?"

"I had a great many conversations with your father," Cenzo told her, and if she wasn't mistaken he sounded something like…satisfied. Her belly twisted into a knot. "Once I understood that you would obey him, there was no need to repeat those conversations with you. And I feel confident that your father does not believe in divorce. I should warn you, Josselyn, that neither do I."

It was a bit late for warnings, she thought. "Maybe not. But he also doesn't believe that I should be harmed. I think you'll find that his number one object in life is to make certain that I am never, ever, hurt in any way."

"I will not be 'beating you black and blue,' as you put it," Cenzo replied, as if she was the one who had said something distasteful. "I do not have to resort to brute force. I will not have to take you apart, *cara*. You will do it for me."

The boat, having picked up speed on the choppy water, began to slow. And Josselyn was more grateful than she wanted to admit that there was an excuse to look away from him. So quickly that it took her a moment or two to take in the island before her.

Though *island* seemed an exaggeration. It was a small bit of land, really more of a barren rock, and the only thing upon it was an ancient castle that rose up from the sea. More than half of it in ruins.

"You can't be serious," she said, hardly realizing she spoke out loud.

"Welcome to the Castello dei Sospiri," Cenzo said from beside her, sounding triumphant. And something far darker than that. "You would call it the Castle of Sighs. It was built as a fortress many centuries ago to keep invaders at bay. But not long after the Normans came it was converted to its current purpose, which is to serve as a kind of retreat for members of my family."

"A retreat," Josselyn repeated, scowling up at the unwelcoming old rocks before her. "Really."

There were stairs hewn into stone, leading up from the water. A great many stairs marching up toward the ruins. At the waterline there was nothing like a beach. There were rocks and a kind of jetty, a forlorn-looking dinghy hauled above the high tide mark, and what looked like a very rudimentary sailboat.

Dawn was breaking, painting the sky with gold and pink, and even that failed to make the castle before her look anything but lonely. Isolated.

Dangerous, something in her whispered. As if she needed the reminder.

Cenzo gazed up at it as if it was Buckingham Palace. "It is many a Falcone over the centuries who has been sent to this castle to rethink. Redirect. Relearn some things, even."

Her heart kicked at her wildly. "What you're saying is that this is a prison."

"Precisely." He smiled down at her then, those arresting eyes of his all the more breathtaking with the sunrise in them. "The world as you know it does not exist here. There are no servants, no staff. No mobile phone service. No internet. All such things are back on the mainland. When this boat leaves us here, it will not return for a month."

"A month?" Josselyn repeated, her voice beginning to sound thready. She cleared her throat. "That doesn't sound safe. What if, to pick a possibility at random, you woke up one morning to find you'd been justly stabbed in your sleep?"

"How delightfully bloodthirsty, Josselyn," he murmured, and she got the sense that he approved. "This obviously will not occur, if only because I do not intend to give you access to any sharp blades. But there is, naturally, a radio for emergencies."

"I thought you were supposed to be the most powerful and important man alive," she said, desperately trying to make sense of her predicament. Why was he doing…whatever he was doing? And exactly how prison-like was this going to be? "How will you continue to convince the world that's the case if they can't access you for a month? I thought men like you couldn't go without business calls for more than fifteen minutes at a time. Surely you'll crumble to ash if you're not buying or selling something."

"For you, Josselyn, I have cleared my schedule." When she only stared back at him, nonplussed, he laughed again. "It is our honeymoon, is it not? And you are a beautiful woman. Surely it cannot surprise you that I have set aside the whole world that I might enjoy the spoils I have gone to such lengths to claim."

"Wait. Is this… Is this a sex thing?" She shook her

head, but she couldn't make sense of any of this. "You've got to be kidding me."

His laugh changed, then. It sounded like less of a weapon, and more like something real. And that wasn't any better.

Josselyn told herself that what slid down her spine, like a lick of naked flame, was fear. Or fury. Or both, fused together into a molten hot reaction that made her nipples tighten.

Because she refused to let it be anything else.

"I do not kid," he told her, almost gently. "Nothing will happen on this island unless you beg for it. Know that now. I told you I am not a monster, and I am not. I do not intend to take what will be so freely given."

Arrogant, she thought then, was really not a strong enough word to describe this man. It didn't come close to the reality that was Cenzo Falcone.

"If you really wanted me to give you anything," she managed to grit out from between her clenched teeth, as the boat docked on the small outthrust bit of jetty that looked like it was only available at low tide, "anything at all, you've played your hand all wrong."

"I can assure you that I only play to win." He moved then, and she found herself turning her body as if to follow him. As if her body simply *wanted* to follow him. As if he was a magnet and she was helpless before the pull of him. "I want you to know, at every moment, exactly what is happening to you."

"But I don't—"

And then his hand was on her face, his hard fingers gripping her chin.

Cenzo tilted her face to his and kissed her.

It was a bruising, punishing kiss that she was shocked to find packed that same punch. That same delirious heat flooded through her, and it was not fear. It was nothing at all like fear, and it pooled between her legs like a new pulse.

When he lifted his head, Cenzo did not release her chin. And she could see from the expression on his hard face he knew.

He knew.

"In a month's time, we will leave here," he told her, his voice a rasp that seemed to do the same things in her that his kiss had. "And you will be my slave. Not because I make it so in some show of strength, Josselyn. But because you will beg me for the role. In my bed, of course. But everywhere else, too, because that is how much you will want me."

"You're delusional," she gasped, as something in her roared.

Again, not in fear.

That was more alarming than anything he'd done or said. Josselyn shoved herself back from him, jerking her chin out of his grasp. And found herself chastened at once, because even though she managed to put space between them, she was far too aware that he'd let her go.

"I knew from the moment we met how this would go," Cenzo said, his gaze so intense it hurt. It actually hurt. "It is inevitable. You should have lost your innocence while you had the chance, Josselyn. For I will shatter it, hoard it, and make it my own. And you will thank me for the privilege."

"And this is…" It seemed as if her heart was literally in her throat, trying to pound its way out of her body.

"Do you truly believe that somehow, breaking me down in this fashion is revenge?"

"Josselyn. *Cara*. What is it your father wants for you most of all?" But he didn't wait for her to answer. His ancient eyes were aglow. His cruel face was too beautiful to bear. "He wants you safe and comforted, and so I promise you this. You will never know a moment's peace. Your life with me will be an agony. I will make you an addict for my touch, my gaze, the barest possibility of my approval. You will live for it. And you will never be happy. You will never feel safe. You will be nothing more than a junkie. Strung out on a man who will never love you back. Ever."

Then he took her hand in his, a parody of the kind of touch a bride might expect on the first day of her marriage. And he led her from the boat, onto that hateful rock, where the brooding old castle rose into the sky.

But Josselyn knew that her doom was not in those weathered rocks, rich with history and pain. It walked beside her, made of flesh and spite.

Because her tragedy was that despite everything he had said and done since he'd found her waiting for him on the plane, she already wanted him.

Meaning he had already won.

CHAPTER FOUR

BUT SHE DID not have to make it easy for him.

Josselyn jerked her hand away from Cenzo's once she was off the boat. She charged ahead of him along the jetty toward the narrow, endless stairs that climbed up from the rocky beach. And instead of standing about, politely offering to lend a hand as they began unloading the luggage so she could settle into her imprisonment in style, she did what she'd been wanting to do for what seemed like a lifetime now.

She ran. Up the stairs and away from the boat. Away from *him*.

His words seemed to chase her, blaring within her and snarling like demons at her heels.

The stairs wound around and around the outside of the castle, and she ordered herself to slow down when her breath deserted her. Before her heart clawed its way out. The climb was steep and his words only seemed to echo more loudly inside her, but as she slowed she noticed something else. This might be a rocky ruin of an island, but the view was stunning.

The Mediterranean Sea stretched out in all directions, an impossible blue. Josselyn assumed the land she saw in the distance, not quite over the horizon, was

Sicily. The morning was bright and though the breeze was cool, it felt as if it might warm as the day went on. If she'd found this place on a vacation of some kind, she thought she might have found it charming.

And what struck her then, as she accepted the beauty of even so desolate a place, was the quiet.

She couldn't think when she'd last been so utterly by herself. If she ignored the evil bridegroom issue—as she felt she needed to do or she would simply scream and leap from the stairs to dash herself on the rocks below, something that felt unduly dramatic—she could hear the sound of high-above birds. Waves below as they surged against the rocks. The breeze rushing through the very few trees and down from the heights.

It was stark and it was lonely, but that didn't make it any less beautiful.

Josselyn told herself she would hold on to that. Somehow.

And on she climbed.

The ruined part of the castle intrigued her, but she somehow doubted that the richest man alive planned to camp there, exposed to the elements, no matter what lesson he thought that might teach *her*. She passed the half-fallen walls and the stairs began to widen, eventually leading her up from the rubble to a kind of landing and an old stone gate.

She pushed her way through it and stopped short.

Because she'd expected nothing but stark ruins and crumbling stone, but the moment Josselyn stepped through the gate, she could see that this castle was not nearly as abandoned as it looked from below. Not the highest part of it. She now stood in the forecourt of a small keep, but on this side of the gate everything was… polished. It *gleamed*. She crossed over the stones, her boot heels beating out a cadence as she moved. And when she reached the other side, the great wooden doors that greeted her opened soundlessly and easily.

Inside, she found the same old stone walls but with new windows to let in the light. In the place of the dreary antiques or possibly prison cells she'd anticipated, she found open spaces, hints of modern steel, every furnishing clearly carefully chosen to make everything seem bright and new.

She was still trying to take that in when she heard the door open behind her, and whirled around to face Cenzo once again.

Her heart, having settled down, leaped into high gear again.

"I told you that you would not be harmed," Cenzo said. "I see that you did not entirely believe me. Perhaps you even wished that you might end up in the dungeons, all the better to martyr yourself."

"As a matter fact, I'm not a martyr at all."

"Are you not?"

He prowled inside, and suddenly the great hall that had felt airy and light to her moments before seemed to close in on top of her. It had something to do with the way he trained those hawk's eyes upon her, as if he was only waiting for the right moment to swoop in and eat her whole.

Her heart kicked at her and her belly twisted at that notion, but between her legs she was shamefully hot.

"I'm really not," she told him. "I didn't do as my father asked because it brought me some pleasure to sacrifice myself to his desires. Or to yours. I did it because I love him. And I understand him. I like that I can take care of him in this way after the lifetime he spent caring for me."

His smile was a mirthless blade. "You might as well not bother trying to convince me that your father is a good man, Josselyn. I know better."

"And will you tell me what sins my father committed against yours?" she demanded, taking a kind of refuge in the temper that kicked in her then. It was far better than the other, more worrying things she felt. Like attraction. Or the competing sense that she should not go about bringing up his lost father—and no matter that he seemed to have no qualm using that loss as a weapon. She knew that *she* would not react well if he threw her mother at her in this way. She hated that she felt shaky, deep inside, as she pushed on. "Surely if the crime requires this kind of punishment, I should at least know the details."

"In time, *cara*," Cenzo murmured, those eyes of his gleaming. "In time."

His men entered the hall then and did not pause in the great hall, seemingly knowing already precisely where they needed to go. Josselyn had the sudden notion that if she went now and ran full out, she could race down the stairs, take the boat, and leave them all here to rot.

But Cenzo only laughed, dark and low.

"You can try," he told her, as if he'd read her mind that easily. "But I will catch you before you make it to the gate. And I do not think you will appreciate my response."

Her lips tingled at that, reliving the crush of his hard

mouth to hers. She told herself she'd hated it, but it still took everything she had to keep from lifting her fingers to touch her lips, to see if they still felt like hers after he'd imprinted himself upon her.

The trouble was, she believed him. She believed that he would chase her and catch her, and more than that, she understood what he hadn't said. That it was not so much what he might do—but the simple fact that running like that would encourage him to put his hands on her body.

Josselyn might have been innocent, an accident that had somehow gone on for more years than she would have thought possible when it had never been a *plan* of hers or any kind of statement, but that didn't make her an idiot. Whatever she might want to call what happened when they touched, it was clearly combustible.

And given what he told her he intended to do with her, it was obviously in her best interest that she see to it they touched as little as possible.

She turned away from him then—away from her escape route—and followed his men. Or rather, the men carrying her luggage, hoping that at some point they would veer off from the others and settle her somewhere far away from their master.

But no such luck. She had a brief tour of lovely rooms clearly modernized with an eye toward bringing the sea and the sky inside, then she was led up into a high tower. Where all the men with all the luggage climbed all the winding stairs to the top until they reached the sprawling master suite.

And, naturally, Cenzo was standing there in the doorway when all the men retreated.

Blocking her exit, if she wasn't mistaken. Again.

"You can't really think that we're going to share a room, can you?" Josselyn crossed her arms, but mostly because she wanted to make sure that if she started shaking, he couldn't see it. "Do you actually imagine that there's any possibility we're just going to leap into bed together?"

"I would not be averse to it." He looked amused when she scowled. "But there are no other bedrooms here, I am afraid. I told you. The *castello* is a place for solitary reflection. There is only the one bed."

"Then I am very sorry that you will have to sleep on the hard stone floor somewhere," she said, with an admirable stab at a sweet tone. "I know you seem to think that I'll be writhing about on the floor in the throes of a sex addiction soon enough, but I'm happy to say that no such addiction currently exists. So if you'll excuse me, I need to freshen up after an overnight flight and a round of unwanted kisses and unhinged threats from my brand-new husband."

Josselyn expected him to argue, but instead, all he did was laugh again. That damnable laugh of his that made her shudder, then overheat. He sketched a deeply mocking bow, there in the doorway. And she couldn't believe it when he...turned and left. She actually ran to the door herself to make sure that he really was walking down the stone stairs, leaving only the sound of his footsteps behind as he went round the bend at each landing.

Was she happy he'd left her? Or did she feel something...more complicated?

She opted not to analyze that too closely. The first

thing she did was go back into the sprawling bedchamber and close the door behind her, not particularly surprised to find it had no lock. Then she pulled out her phone and checked to see if what he'd said was true. Sure enough, there was no cell phone service. No Wi-Fi. Though all around her the Mediterranean lolled about seductively on the other side of the windows, she found the quiet seemed a little more ominous, suddenly.

And the curses she muttered under her breath, then not so under her breath, didn't help any.

Still, Josselyn did what she could. She checked to see that the bathroom did, in fact, have a lock—and that was the only reason she drew herself a bath, then settled into it, trying to soak her equilibrium back.

And it worked well enough, because she was certainly calmer when she got out. She supposed that if she was to be locked away here for a month, it was a nice touch that the bath was fully outfitted, like a spa, so she could while away her terrible honeymoon with luxurious bath salts and a view.

Josselyn meant to march back downstairs the moment she was dressed, to confront Cenzo yet again, but instead she found herself drawn to a cozy chair that sat in one of the tower's sunny alcoves, offering her nothing but the sea and the sky. She curled up there, intending to gaze out for only a moment or so, but instead, nodded off to sleep.

And when she woke again, with a start, she could tell from the light outside that hours had passed.

Maybe it was a good thing. Maybe she could spend this month catching up on her sleep—because Lord knew, she had been plagued with sleepless nights ever since Cenzo Falcone had turned up in the family cottage in Maine that day.

She splashed cold water on her face, avoided her reflection in the glass, and then set off to see what, exactly, she was dealing with.

Josselyn told herself she was exploring, that was all. And that was what she did. First to see if what he'd told her was true. And she found that though there were other doors in the tower, they led to rooms…but not to other bedchambers. There was a small library. A sitting room. Something that she would have considered a yoga room if it had belonged to anyone else.

But no other bedrooms. And not even a sofa big enough to act like a bed in a pinch.

Down in the main part of the new castle, she accepted that she was looking for her husband only when she made no effort at all to run toward the door now that no one was guarding it.

Was he right, after all? Was this how it started? Was she to be drawn to him against her very will?

"Don't be ridiculous," she told herself sternly. "You're trying to salvage something from this situation, that's all. It's perfectly rational."

But she didn't feel particularly rational when she found him in the large kitchen. His intensity seemed to her like a living thing. Like a hand that reached out and caught her up, then held her in a fist.

Cenzo stood at a center island surrounded by steel and inviting tile, a rack of copper pans hanging above him, while he wielded what looked like a very, very sharp knife. She could see the old hearth on one side and could imagine that it had once been the center of the castle, but today it stood cold. And Cenzo appeared to be preparing food, which struck her as... Well, as nothing short of astonishing.

"I trust you slept well," he said, without looking up. In a mild tone that very nearly sounded friendly.

Something skittered around inside her at the idea that he'd looked in on her while she slept. She wanted it to be dismay, and she told herself it was, but it was too warm for that. Much too warm.

"I find it difficult to believe that you actually know how to cook," Josselyn said, maybe too severely. She tried to breathe through her *dismay*. "Surely in all your other many residences, you are besieged by servants ready and eager to meet your every need before it forms."

"I am." He was chopping up tomatoes and tossing them in a small pot before him. "But there are a few places I go where it is only me. And if I would like it to remain only me, that means I must take care of my own needs. The first time I attempted it, I cannot say the cooking was a success. So I hired a chef to teach me. Because it turns out that even on my own, I insist upon a certain standard."

Josselyn found herself clinging to the kitchen door. "Why are you telling me anecdotes about yourself?" She swallowed, not surprised to find her throat was dry. "Are you trying to lure me in with a false sense of camaraderie?"

Those predator's eyes met hers. "Yes."

She huffed out a breath. "Well. Points for honesty, I guess."

"I am not, as you have said, a liar, Josselyn. I did not

lie to your father. I merely did not correct him. These are not the same thing."

She drifted farther into the kitchen, feeling not unlike Persephone creeping into the underworld. Because there was a platter before him with what looked like cheese and bread, and her stomach rumbled. But she dared not take any. Wasn't that the rule? Eat something and you were doomed to stay in hell forever.

On the other hand, she was really hungry.

It helped that Cenzo did not appear to care overmuch what she did. He carried on fixing the meal before him, as if he was alone in the renovated kitchen. Josselyn crept closer and decided it would do her no good to ignore the physical realities of a situation.

You really do need your strength, she told herself piously.

And though she could feel Cenzo's gaze on her from time to time as she stood across from him, every time she glanced at him he appeared to be entirely engrossed in preparing a pasta dish.

Long before she was anywhere near satiated, he whisked the cheese and bread away. He carried the platter out through doors she'd thought were windows, leading her out to a wide terrace off the side of the kitchen. It seemed to hang there over the sea, nothing but the horizon in the distance and exultant bougainvillea closer in, clinging to the rail.

"Sit," he ordered her.

And he did not wait to see if she would obey; he simply strode off back into the kitchen.

To say that she had whiplash would be vastly understating the situation. Josselyn moved to the bright and fragrant rail, because despite the careening sort of feeling inside her, she couldn't keep herself from staring out at the sea. She didn't *want* to keep herself from it. The Mediterranean was deep blue and beckoning, and the ruckus inside her shifted into a kind of thrill. It was as if she couldn't tell what her body might do of its own accord, suddenly. It felt entirely possible that she might simply find herself leaping off the terrace. Hurling herself out into all that glorious blue.

And not because she was filled with the need to end herself. But because she thought that for a while there, she might actually fly.

She heard a sound behind her and turned to find Cenzo coming toward her again, this time bearing two plates of the pasta he'd made. And she couldn't help but notice that looking at him felt very much the same as looking down from this great height to the sea far below.

He set out the plates on the table, which was perfectly placed to take in the view, and took one of the seats. Then did nothing, save raise one brow.

And wait.

Josselyn didn't move. "I'm trying to fit in a homemade dinner with the list of threats you unspooled for me earlier. I didn't expect to be enslaved via food."

"It is the way to the heart, Josselyn. Surely you have heard this, even in the rustic wilds of your Pennsylvania."

It was a bit rich to call Pennsylvania rustic and wild when they were currently perched on the top of a big rock, with civilization far off beyond the horizon. And yet she drifted toward the table despite herself.

She told herself it was the pasta. "I think you're going to have to explain to me how and why you're pursuing this remarkably intimate bid for my destruction. Surely you could also put me under house arrest in one of your many properties and leave me to rot."

"But that would not give me what I want." Cenzo indicated the empty seat opposite him with a peremptory hand.

Josselyn should have ignored it. She should have made a stand, started how she meant to go on, and made it clear he couldn't treat her like this. But again, she was hungry and she doubted very much that he would stoop to poisoning her. And in any case, even if it was poisoned, and/or it kept her in his underworld forever, it smelled delicious.

She took her seat, glad that she'd kept her sweater on though the day looked sunny and warm. Maybe it was, but here up high where the castle pierced the sky, the sea breeze was constant.

"Mangia," Cenzo murmured, and then they each set to the task of eating.

And Josselyn was far too aware, of everything. Every possible sensation. She felt the wind play with her hair and toy with what little skin was exposed. She felt the sun, pleasingly warm but never hot, and far off she could hear the seabirds sharing songs with each other as they flew.

"This is delicious," she said. She couldn't help herself.

"It is Pasta alla Norma," he replied. "It is Catanian." His gaze swept to hers, then lowered. "That is, from farther down the coast."

The food he'd prepared was simple. Sicilian, apparently. And the flavors burst on her tongue, making her feel something like seduced.

Then again, maybe Josselyn was kidding herself. Maybe it had nothing to do with the food or the sea air or her admittedly scenic location. Maybe what she was truly aware of here was the man.

Cenzo had changed his clothing while she slept—and she didn't want to think about him doing such a thing in the same room where she'd slumbered on, unaware. It made her breath catch. Now he wore more casual dark trousers and a T-shirt that looked as if it might, very possibly, have been created specifically to glorify his form. He should have looked less dangerous out of the bespoke suits that she'd thought he lived in. But instead, the change did the opposite.

It had nothing to do with the clothes. There was no disguising that the brooding, elemental danger that exuded from him was as much a part of him as that old coin profile. His predator's gaze. That cruel mouth that made her hunger for another taste—

What she couldn't understand, she thought as she very carefully placed her utensils back on her plate, was how he'd known.

He could not possibly have anticipated that there would be any attraction on her part. Attraction was far too funny. It waxed or waned or failed to turn up at all, based entirely on the individuals involved. Their history, their needs, and simply how they were wired.

Yet he had sounded so sure that no matter who she might have been, he would have been able to elicit the same response in her.

"You're scowling at me," he pointed out.

"I want to circle back to my heroin addiction, such as it is."

"You might find that you wish for such sweet oblivion, when I'm done with you," he replied. Conversationally, which made it worse. It took a few moments to fully land, and then it seemed to sit on her.

She made herself sit up straighter. "I don't know what makes you think I find you remotely attractive. For all you know, I could be actively working to conceal my repulsion. Like bile in my throat."

Those copper and gold eyes gleamed. "You do not find me repulsive, Josselyn."

"You don't actually know that. I've had a great deal of practice concealing what I actually feel about anything. I'm very good at it."

Cenzo pushed his plate away and sat back in his chair. He looked like a man at ease, but she could feel the weight of his stare. "Let us say that I was in some doubt about your reaction to me, though I am not. It would not matter in any way. We are isolated here. And I will tell you this, *mia moglie*. I have found that where there is attention, attraction follows."

"You're either attracted to a person or you're not." She shrugged as if it was all out of her hands. "It's not mutable."

"Shall we test it?" He laughed when she shrank back. "I rather thought not."

Josselyn tried to look as if she indeed had bile in her throat instead of too much molten heat charging through her and settling low in her belly. "In case you wondered, I have found your kisses rather lacking. If a man of your much-vaunted prowess and certain narcissism takes notes on his performance."

She had the sense of his laughter, though all he did

was smile. "We were speaking in generalities, yes? The mythic possibility that I might encounter a woman who does not want me. I like a fairy story as much as the next person, but let us turn our attention instead to you, Josselyn."

Nothing about the way he was sitting or looking at her changed, yet she still felt as if that noose was around her neck again. And pulling tight.

Only she had never heard of a noose making a person burn like this, all the way through, until she had to fight off the urge to squirm in her seat.

Cenzo considered her for a moment. Maybe three. "You do know that one of the chief inducements your father offered me was your innocence, do you not?"

Josselyn felt her chin rise when what she wanted to do was scream at the violation of her privacy. "You've mentioned my innocence before. I hate to be the one to break this to you, but that ship sailed a long, long time ago."

"Did it?" Cenzo's eyes gleamed. "I think not."

"I couldn't give my virginity away quickly enough," Josselyn declared, lying through her teeth. "You went to boarding school. You must know what it was like. I don't believe any virgins were permitted to graduate from the hallowed halls of my high school."

"Your father seemed certain," Cenzo said. Also sounding certain.

Josselyn nearly laughed, because the absurdity of this conversation was too much. She was sitting in a half-ruined, half-renovated castle somewhere off the coast of Sicily, debating her virginity. Literally discussing it as if it was an estate sale item, like some former doyenne's silver. It was so absurd, in fact, that she couldn't muster up any of the numerous emotional reactions she suspected she was likely to have regarding it—but later. She counted herself lucky for that.

"I don't know how to break this to you," she told him, some of that near-laughter in her voice, "but my father is quite literally the last person on earth with whom I would ever discuss my sex life."

But Cenzo only smiled in that edgy, knowing way of his. "What I was going to say, *cara*, is that your father was very certain, yes. But I too live in the world. And am well aware that fathers are often the last to know what it is their daughters get up to. Yet any doubts I might have had were completely erased that afternoon in Maine."

Josselyn could still remember it all with such painful clarity. The shock of it, of him. Lounging there against an ancient fireplace, electric and impossible.

"Don't be ridiculous," she said now. "As I believe you've already pointed out, we didn't even speak."

"Words were unnecessary." He gave the impression of shrugging without quite doing so, though his gaze was even more intent. "Your eyes grew big. You stopped breathing. Then you turned red. Not, I think, the typical behavior of an experienced woman."

Josselyn had never felt her virginity like any kind of burden. She'd retained it through chance, not deliberation. It was difficult to have any kind of a social life when she spent most of her time in her father's company. And during her college years—and indeed throughout boarding school—when she'd been left to her own devices, she'd never really managed to understand how a person got from one place to the other. The flinging off of clothes had never seemed organic to her. Did one person start and the other follow? Did both parties agree to undress and then proceed from there in a kind of lockstep? It had always seemed fraught with tension and potential mishaps, so she couldn't even say that she'd avoided it. It was more the opportunity had never arisen.

She now wished that she'd spent more time applying herself to the issue.

But she only sniffed at Cenzo. "It's too bad that your Ivy League education failed to make it clear to you that a person's virginity is not, in fact, visible when they walk into a room."

"Generally speaking, no," he agreed. "But yours is."

That was horrifying to contemplate. "I'm not going to argue with you, Cenzo. It's pointless. Of the two people sitting here, I'm the only one who actually knows my sexual history."

A normal person might have looked abashed at that. But this was Cenzo Falcone. All he ever seemed to look was amused.

Josselyn forged on. "What I'd like to know is how, if you truly believe that I remained virginal all this time, you think that you can simply swan in and not only get me into bed but make me a slavering addict where you're concerned. You don't suffer from insecurity, do you?"

"I am a man who was taught since birth to know his consequence." Cenzo waved a hand. "My worth is not a mere concept to me, to be trotted out in sad self-help seminars. I know it to the decimal."

"I see. You intend to treat me like a bank balance. And that, you seem so confident, will render me so enslaved to you that it will break my father's heart from afar." Josselyn sat back in her chair and tried to look as unconcerned as he did. "This seems a bit far-fetched, I have to say."

"That is because you do not understand," he said, almost sounding warm. Inviting. If they had been discussing any other topic, she was sure she would have been confused. She would have imagined that somehow, this was nothing more than a domestic moment between a husband and wife.

Was that what he wanted her to think? Was it just another example of his mind games?

"I have studied your family," Cenzo told her, with perhaps too much portent in his words for her liking. "You were very young when your mother and brother died."

"I was ten." And it was funny how grief changed over time. She didn't feel the sharp edge of it any longer. She wouldn't like it if someone wielded it as a weapon, in temper, but she didn't mind when people brought up her family tragedy of their own volition. Because it was a simple fact that happened to be her personal history. Her mother and older brother had sailed out into Blue Hill Bay that summer's day and had never returned.

Nothing ever made that better. But then again, it wasn't as if anything could make it worse.

"There were those who expected your father to remarry, especially with a young daughter yet to raise. But he did not. He raised you himself, and as far as anyone is aware, never had the slightest interest in another woman."

"Their marriage was arranged, much as ours was," Josselyn said, nodding. "But the difference is, they quickly fell in love. I think my father has always felt that there is no possibility that he could ever hope that lightning might strike twice for him."

"How romantic." Cenzo did not sneer, but he certainly made it clear that he did not find that story romantic at all. "It has been nearly twenty years. It is clear to even the most casual observer that if your father is capable of loving anything at all, he loves you."

She laughed, more in shock than because she thought that was funny. "If he's capable? Let me assure you, he is. Of course he loves me. As I love him in return."

"So tender," Cenzo murmured, and this time, the sardonic inflection seemed to leave marks in her flesh. "But you see, that is exactly what I will use."

It shouldn't have felt like whiplash. She'd known he was playing games here. Still, she found herself winded once more.

And worse, molten hot straight through. Because apparently being more or less kidnapped and marooned on an island was the key to making her think about taking off her clothes. Who could have guessed?

"You speak so much of how you will use me," she managed to say. "Enslave me. Addict me. A lot of implied action and danger, I'd say. But when given the opportunity to show me how intimidated I should be by all your bluster, all you did was cook pasta and slice up some cheese."

"It's only the first day," Cenzo said, and smiled as if he was approachable. Or as if he wanted her to *think* he was approachable…if only for a moment. "But I want to be clear about the aim here. Your father is used to your attention. To being the center of your world. You think he is capable of love. I do not."

"Oh," she said mildly, "look at that. Another topic that I know more about than you."

He ignored her, lounging there as if daring the Sicilian sun to render itself prostrate before him too. "Either way, Josselyn, when I take all that you have to give he will be left with nothing. And you will be too far gone to care."

CHAPTER FIVE

Cenzo was enjoying himself.

Truly, this had all gone better than he could have imagined, and he had spent the past two years imagining it in every possible permutation. What she might say, what she might do. Having studied her extensively, he thought he'd been prepared.

But Josselyn defied study. And he hadn't been prepared for his response to her. He certainly couldn't have known that a simple conversation with this wife he had not wanted eclipsed any other form of entertainment in his memory.

He told himself that boded well for his plans and nothing more. For she was the quarry, not he.

And yet you seem to need reminders, a voice in him, sounding far too much like Françoise, commented acidly.

"I don't understand," Josselyn said, though he thought she lied. Her color was high again, though he would not share that with her. Not when it seemed such an excellent barometer of her reactions. Her dark eyes were glossy, her mouth militant. She stayed where she was, sitting perhaps too still after having eaten a meal he'd prepared with his own hands. He had intended to throw her off-balance. What he had not prepared for was how deeply such a thing would affect him in turn.

Because it turned out that he liked it. He liked that his wife should eat what he had made. He liked watching her eat. He liked talking to her, because he never knew what she might say when so many of the people he interacted with bored him silly. He liked too much of this—of her—particularly when it felt like the kind of intimacy he did not intend to allow.

But he assured himself that as time passed here, the effect these things would have on her would far outstrip any reaction of his own.

"Do you truly not understand?" he asked her. "Or is it that you imagine you can somehow appeal to my better angels if you pretend that you do not? Let me save you the trouble. I have none."

If he expected her to wilt, he was in for disappointment. If anything, she sat straighter, managing to look somehow regal. He supposed it was another form of armor.

Cenzo intended to strip it away. Every bit of it.

"I'm not attempting to make any kind of appeal," she said, sounding cool and unbothered. But he could see the way her eyes flashed and knew better. "All I'm trying to do is figure out what it is you believe will occur between us over the next month. I don't need an agenda, but I am interested in the specifics. So far, all of it is very vague. It will all be terrible. I will be ruined. My father will be torn asunder, blah blah blah."

"I like this," Cenzo said, amused. "Show me your fangs, little one. They are adorable."

She stood up then, abruptly. He thought she might

storm off into the castle, but as ever, she surprised him. Josselyn moved instead to the rail, gripped it, and stared out toward the sea.

"If you're thinking of jumping," he said with great indolence, "I would advise against it. It's not a straight shot, you see. You would likely live, in some or other reduced capacity. Not quite the dramatic gesture I imagine you're going for."

"I have no intention of jumping."

She turned back, and he had the interesting notion that this was perhaps the first time they had truly gazed at each other. No artifice, no shock. No manners.

And unsmiling, she was actually even more beautiful. There was nothing to take away from the simple, stunning architecture of her face. And that beauty mark that directed attention straight to that mouth of hers. He intended to taste her and take his time with it.

Soon.

Because of his plan, he assured himself. All of this was in service to the plan.

"There is no agenda," he told her, eventually, when she was beginning to look agitated. "I assume you have studied up on me, as I have you." He did not wait for her to confirm it. And besides, he was Cenzo Falcone. There was only so much study required. "Then you know that when I set myself to a task, I achieve it."

"I was under the impression that wasn't an issue of character, in your case," she said, her tone as even as her gaze was dark. "So much as unlimited funds to back any decision you might choose to make."

"Does it make a difference? I have spent the past two years studying your weaknesses so that I might use them against you. Your devotion to your father, check. Your martyr complex, check."

"If I had a martyr complex," she retorted, "I would be halfway into a swan dive even now."

"That is not how a martyr complex works, I think. It's the heat of the pyre that matters and the audience to behold it, not the actual immolation. But it is of no matter. Now that it is only the two of us, stranded here for weeks, there will be nothing to do all day, every day, but find buttons. And then push them."

"I admire your confidence that you will be the one pushing those buttons," she said softly. "As if I will be doing nothing at all but sitting idly by, waiting to see what you might use against me next."

"But you see, I cannot be pushed," he told her, almost apologetically. When inside, the dragon in him shot fire. "At the end of the day, *cara*, there is someone you will wish to protect. That leaves you weak. I have no such weaknesses."

"You do not wish to protect your own mother?"

"Françoise Falcone requires no protection," Cenzo assured her. "And even if she did, there is no possibility that you could ever leverage her against me. For whatever I might think of your family, her opinion is worse. Much worse."

Josselyn frowned. "Is that why she didn't attend the wedding?"

"She understands why I am doing this but felt she could not accord it her blessing." He inclined his head in a gesture that he knew looked like contrition on others. Not so much on him. "You understand."

"How odd." Josselyn let out a half-laugh. "My father thought it was because she was embarrassed."

The very idea had him laughing out loud. A real laugh, even.

"I have seen my mother in many moods, but I have never seen her embarrassed." He shook his head. "Though it is true that she feels that any American, by virtue of the newness and greenness of your connections, must be beneath not only the Falcone line but her own family, who trace their blood to the House of Bourbon."

"You misunderstand me," Josselyn said, a curious expression on her face. It made him wonder if he'd misjudged her—but no. That was impossible. Cenzo did not make mistakes. "I don't think bloodlines have anything to do with it. My father assumed your mother did not wish to show her face after she'd made such a play for him. And was, of course, denied."

"I beg your pardon?"

His wife did not seem to recognize her danger. She was leaning back against the rail now, suddenly looking entirely at her ease. A whisper of something washed over him, though he did not immediately recognize what it was.

It took him another moment to realize that it was apprehension.

But surely that was not possible either. He held all the cards in this. She had never been anything but a lamb to the slaughter.

And more, she thought the man he knew was to blame for the grief in him that never dissipated was *good*.

He held on to that outrage.

"I was only ten when my mother died, as you've already established," Josselyn said, sounding easier with every syllable. "My father used to tell me stories at bedtime, and he didn't read to me from books. He told me stories about my mother and my brother. About how funny and bright and brave Jack was, and how now he could act as my big brother no matter where I was. And about how he and my mother met, and fell in love, and built a life together. This became our tradition."

There was absolutely no reason, Cenzo assured himself, that he should feel a trickle of foreboding move down the back of his neck.

She was still speaking. "When I outgrew needing to be tucked into bed, every night we were together my father would still tell me stories about the past. I think it helped him as much as me, if I'm honest. And one of the stories he liked to tell was how he thought that perhaps he had fallen in love with my mother from afar. For how else could he explain that when his engagement was announced, a woman who he considered his best friend's, who he had always admired, propositioned him. But he turned her down for a woman he hardly knew."

Cenzo felt everything in him still. "Your father is a liar. Better you should know it now and stop spreading his poison."

Josselyn looked unmoved. "I don't think your parents had been married long. They all knew each other well, didn't they? The stories Papa tells of their youth seem like something out of a Hemingway book. A movable feast with the three of them all over Europe, your mother the woman that half the men they knew were in love with."

"My mother would no more lower herself to an American—" Cenzo began in a fury.

"Well, you're quite right, but only because my father didn't accept her offer."

"I feel certain that my mother is, even now, somehow aware of this slander and has suddenly come over horrified in her villa in Taormina." Cenzo shook his head. "Wherever could you have come by such a notion?"

"She wrote him letters, Cenzo," Josselyn said softly. "So even if I was tempted to think that my father had forgotten what actually happened, or had embellished it, I'm afraid there are the letters to tell a different story."

"You are wrong." Cenzo's voice was flat. "You have obviously never met my mother, for if you did you would know that she is not romantic. She comes from an ancient French line and was raised to concern herself only with how best she could carry forth that legacy."

And more, she had been devoted to his father. She was still devoted to his father.

"If you say so." This wife he'd been so sure he could crush beneath his shoe with little effort gazed back at him as if she knew she'd set off a seismic reaction inside him. She even shrugged as if this was all nothing to her. "But also, for a time, it seems that she was willing to throw it all away for an upstart American all the same."

Cenzo found himself standing and had no idea when he'd decided to move. Temper and something else flooded through him, making him feel a heady mix of lit up and darkly intense, and all of it was focused on the slender woman who stood before him, the Sicilian sun in her hair and the Sicilian sky on her finger.

And while he watched, she slowly smiled at him.

"Tell me again how it is that you have no buttons to push." She dared him. *She* dared *him.* "And I will tell you more stories about your mother, because believe me, there are many. After our engagement, I went through all my father's correspondence. It was fascinating. Illuminating, even."

Cenzo slashed his hand through the air. And though everything in him urged him to move forward—to put his hands on her, to handle this with his mouth on hers, his hands all over her skin—he held himself back.

Because he hadn't expected this, and that was a problem. He hadn't anticipated that she would turn the tables on him—it hadn't crossed his mind that she *could*—and that would take some thought. Some different plans, perhaps.

Some getting used to, certainly.

And he could not allow himself to lose, in the heat of the moment, what had taken him years of fury and focus to put into motion.

"I see you are a liar much like your own father," he gritted out. "How proud he must be."

But the meek, obedient virgin he had expected to easily break apart only smiled wider.

"That's a nice try," Josselyn said. "But the difference is, I know my father. I know him well. I haven't set him up on any kind of pedestal, and, in fact, have been his employee as well as his daughter, so I can truly say I know more than one side of him. Trust me when I tell you that I am deeply conversant on my father's flaws. He is not a liar. Neither am I." She studied him, still smiling. "But I'm beginning to suspect that your mother is."

Cenzo felt a seething kind of rage build inside him, and the hint of that deep, wild grief behind it, and it was not contained to the usual places. Here, with her, it pooled in his sex and made his skin feel two sizes too small, stretched over his bones.

"I will admit that you surprised me, Josselyn," he managed to say as if he was in full command of himself, as he should have been. "I did not expect you to traffic in such falsehoods. But do not worry. It will change nothing. I simply know better, now, who you really are."

He picked up the plates from the table, taking them, and himself, back inside.

And he was all too aware that she followed him, maneuvering herself so that she once more stood on the other side of the wide, long kitchen island and regarded him in that same steady way.

As if she thought she was in control of this.

"I wouldn't want you to get the wrong impression," she told him, and she was no longer smiling at him, all sharp challenge. "Papa was flattered by your mother's interest in him. The story wasn't told at your mother's expense, ever. He thought too highly of her. It was to highlight that even then, when he could have had a woman who he had long considered the finest of them all, he stuck with my mother instead. When he barely knew her. And before, in fact, they had gone ahead and fallen for each other. You can take that as an insult if you must. But it doesn't come from my father."

"You asked for an agenda." For the first time, possibly ever, Cenzo was not sure that he could keep his voice steady. Until he managed it, somehow. "For today, I suggest you acquaint yourself with this island. Explore it at will. Learn its nooks and crannies, take note of the ruins and the cliffs, and better still, note that there is nowhere to go. The quicker you accept that, the better."

"That was almost a lovely invitation. And then you ruined it."

"I will expect you to dine with me in the evenings," he continued in the same stern way, as if she hadn't spoken. "If you do not present yourself, I will come find you. You will not like that."

"More threats, naturally," she said, almost sunnily. "I see you've recovered from the shock of hearing that your mother is a person, as complicated as anyone else."

Cenzo refused to spend one single moment dignifying her lies—not even with a stray thought about his mother or his parents' often chilly, remote marriage. Not one.

He would blame her father for that, too.

"I intend to sleep in our bed every night," he told her in the same implacable way. "I will not force you to do the same, but you will have noticed, I think, that I meant it when I said there were no other beds here. I would not encourage you to come up with a makeshift one, either. I will not allow it. You may sleep in the marital bed next to your husband, or you may be uncomfortable. The choice is yours."

"You are all heart."

"It is my intention, *cara*, to take the virginity we both know you still possess. And soon. But do not worry unduly. I will not force myself upon you."

"What is an *undue* amount of worry in this situation, Cenzo?"

He only gazed back at her and did nothing to hide

the ruthlessness in him. The power of his will. Or his certainty that she would not only bend, but crumble.

"Let me guess," Josselyn said after a moment. "You believe that I will beg you for the pleasure."

"I know you will."

He felt like himself again as she stood there before him, clearly trembling in some kind of outrage, though she fought to conceal it. But he could see it all over her, making her attempt to stand there—straight and tall and drenched in serenity—fall slightly flat.

And he knew she wouldn't believe it, but he could still see her innocence all over her. He could read her too clearly. Her color was heightened once again. Her dark eyes were faintly glassy. And Cenzo had no doubt that if he were to reach over and touch her, her skin would be hot.

Just as he knew that if he reached between her legs, she would be wet.

But these were all discoveries he would force her to make. And then he would use them against her, one after the next.

"I tried to tell you this before," she said, enunciating her words in a manner that he supposed was meant to cut him to ribbons. "But I find you repulsive. Horrific. The only thing I will ever beg you for is a divorce."

She turned at that and marched herself out of the kitchen.

And really, he should have let her go. This was only the first day of a long siege.

But the dragon in him had woken again, and it liked the scent of her. His sex was thick and heavy, and he hungered for a real taste of that mouth of hers. Particularly now that he'd discovered that she truly did have fangs, and more, could use them.

He wanted her naked. He wanted her beneath him, astride him, on her hands and knees before him, the better to take his thrusts.

And all of these things would be his, he knew. All he need do was wait. And play this game he could already tell he would win. And handsomely.

But first, there was today, and he didn't like the fact that she thought she had the upper hand.

Without questioning himself, Cenzo followed her from the kitchen. He heard her boots against the flagstones, then each step as she started up the stairs into the tower. More, he could hear her temper in every crash of her feet against the old stones.

It was easy enough to catch her, then whirl her around, there in the narrow stairwell.

"But you said—" she began, her eyes wide as she gazed up at him. "You promised—"

"I wish only to kiss my wife," Cenzo growled. "On this, the first day of the rest of our life together."

"You don't want to kiss me," she threw at him, and he thought the way she trembled now was her temper taking hold. The most convenient of the passions, but he would take any. "You want to make one of your grim little points. You want to start what you think will be my downward spiral, until all I can do is fling myself prostrate before you and cringe about at your feet. Guess what? I would rather die."

"Let us test that theory," he suggested, and kissed her.

And this time, it had nothing at all to do with punishment. Though it was no less a claiming.

This time, it was a seduction.

Pleasure and dark promise.

He took her face in his hands, and he tasted her as he wanted at last. He teased her lips until she sighed, melting against him, and opened to let him in.

Then he angled his head and set them both on fire.

He kissed her and he kissed her, until all that fury, all that need, hummed there between them. He kissed her, losing himself in the sheer wonder of her taste and the way that sweet sea scent of hers teased at him, as if she was bewitching him despite his best efforts to seize control.

Cenzo kissed her like a man drowning and she met each thrust of his tongue, then moved closer as if she was as greedy as he was.

As if she knew how much he wanted her and wanted him, too, with that very same intensity.

And there were so many things he wanted to do with her. But kissing her felt like a gift, like sheer magic, and for once in his life, Cenzo lost track of his own ulterior motives. His own grand plan.

There was only her taste. Her heat.

Her hair that he gripped in his hands, and the way she pressed against him.

There was only Josselyn. His wife.

He kissed her again and again, and then he shifted, meaning to lift her in his arms—

But she pushed away from him, enough to brace herself against his chest. He found his hands on her upper arms.

"I agreed to marry you," she managed to pant out at him, her lips faintly swollen and her brown eyes wild.

"Not to take part in whatever sick revenge fantasy this is. I refuse to be a pawn in your game."

"You can be any piece on the board that you like," he replied, trying to gather himself. "But it will still be my board, Josselyn."

And he watched something wash over her, intense and deep, and realized that he was holding on to her as if he wished to keep her with him—even if she did not want to stay.

Which defeated the purpose of all of this, didn't it?

And more, made him the monster her father was.

He let her go, lifting up his hands theatrically. "By all means, little wife. Run and hide if that makes you feel more powerful."

And he really thought, in that moment, that Josselyn might take a swing at him. He had no doubt that if she did, the blow would land. It might even sting a little.

He kept his hands in the air, his mock surrender, and laughed at her as he stepped back.

Because he'd forgotten, entirely, that they stood on those narrow stairs.

She had kissed him silly.

It was his own mocking laughter that stayed with him as he fell, a seeming slow-motion slide backward when his foot encountered only air. He saw her face as the world fell out from beneath him.

Nothing but her lovely face.

And then there was nothing.

CHAPTER SIX

JOSSELYN WATCHED HIM FALL, everything in her seeming to fall with him. Her stomach plummeted to her feet. She flung out her arms as if she could catch him, but missed, doing nothing but rapping her knuckles against the wall.

He twisted in the air, then hit the floor of the next landing with his arms thrust out in front of him, before finally coming to a stop with a sickening thud.

Then he was still.

And this was Cenzo Falcone, so she expected him to leap to his feet again. To rise as if it had been nothing but a trick, so he could laugh at her mockingly all the more. So he could kiss her the way he'd just done, all that wildfire and shocking heat, and make her forget her name all over again—

But though she gripped the stone wall beside her, her eyes fixed on him as he lay there, he did not move.

The only sound was her own heartbeat, a mad racket in her ears, her breath sawing in and out of her as one horrible moment bled into another.

Josselyn threw herself forward, scrabbling down the stairs and dropping to her knees beside him on the lower landing. What if he was dead? What if—?

She couldn't think it.

A sharp pang bloomed in her chest, feeling too much like grief, but she ignored it. She reached out to touch Cenzo, happier than she wanted to admit that he was warm to the touch and that she could see no distressing, unnatural angles. Her fingers were shaking as she pressed them into his neck, but she was instantly relieved to feel his pulse there. Strong and steady.

"Okay," she said out loud, shocked at her own breathlessness, and that sharpness within. "Okay, he's not dead. Good."

But still he didn't move. She tried to think of any first aid dos and don'ts she might have picked up on over the years. He had fallen backward, but he'd twisted himself around and had somehow landed on his side. As she stared at him, wishing she'd done something useful with her life so she could handle this well, she could see a large, red bruise forming on his forehead.

She didn't think he'd suffered a spinal injury, but a head injury probably wasn't much better.

Josselyn reached for her phone, then stopped in the act of pulling it from her back pocket, swearing under her breath as she remembered. No cell phone service. No Wi-Fi. No possible means of contacting the outside world. She remembered that he'd said something about a radio. But she had no idea where one might be, or even how she would explain where they were or what had happened.

Could she take the time to look? Did she dare leave him? What if he lapsed off and died while she was scrabbling around the old castle for a radio that, for all she knew, he might have lied about having in the first place?

He murmured something then, his voice sounding thick and unused. She didn't think that he was speaking in English. Or even Italian, for that matter. Josselyn was relieved that he was speaking at all.

And she made a command decision, there and then.

"Come on," she said briskly, trying to put her arm around his back, thinking that might help him figure out how to get to his feet, since she certainly couldn't lift him. "Cenzo. You have to get up."

And to her surprise, he moved. First onto his knees, looking woozy, before pulling himself to his feet. She expected him to blink away the wooziness and then light into her, but he didn't. He only stared at her as if he couldn't place her, and then looked as if he might slump there against the wall and topple on the rest of the stairs.

"We have to move," she told him.

She didn't question that decision as she helped him down the stairs, sometimes shouldering his weight when he faltered, until they reached the main floor of the renovated bit of the castle.

But she didn't stop there, either. Because Cenzo moved with her when she encouraged him, clearly in a daze, and that was how she managed to get him all the way down to that rocky little landing on what passed for the beach. One step at a time, while the Sicilian afternoon grew deep gold and a richer blue around them.

The dinghy looked safer for a man of his size, but she led him toward the small sailboat instead, because there was no way she was going to row across the sea.

She thought they were just as likely to end up in Greece when her arms gave out and the current took over.

But one thing Josselyn knew how to do was sail.

She raised the sail and was pleasantly surprised to find it intact. Then she managed to get Cenzo into the boat as she pushed off, still not quite thinking through what it was she was doing. There was no medical attention for him on this island. That had to be the priority. For all she knew, if she hadn't wrestled him down all those stairs, she would still be searching all over the castle for the radio that—best case scenario—he'd probably hidden away to keep her from finding it.

And maybe that was all rationalization so she wouldn't have to think about things like kissing him until she felt inside out, despite everything he'd said to her this day, much less that grief at the sight of him fallen—but by the time she accepted that she was tacking out of the tiny, rocky cove and heading toward the mainland.

Across from her, Cenzo had slumped down against the gunwale. And no matter how she tried to rouse him with her foot against his leg as well as her voice, he didn't move.

If she wasn't mistaken, he was unconscious.

That couldn't be good.

Josselyn did the only thing she could. She gripped the tiller and kept sailing, letting the wind do the work and hoping that she'd made the right decision.

It had taken her a long time to get Cenzo down those stairs, so she was chasing daylight across the water. As she neared land, she was grateful to see some lights go on ahead of her to show her the way. Because otherwise, who knew where she would have ended up?

She found her way to a tiny harbor and was happy that she could tie the boat up at an actual dock rather than trying to haul it ashore with Cenzo still seemingly unconscious. And then, having done it, she had a moment's worry as she considered her situation. Should she leave him here? Or try to rouse him again and see if she could make him stumble his way toward whatever kind of village this was? He lay there, slumped against the side of the boat, and even so, there was no mistaking who he was. His power was evident even in repose. But with his eyes closed, it was easier to get lost in the perfectly sculpted lines of his face. To wonder about those stern yet sensual lips of his that she now knew far more intimately—

But there was no time for that, she told herself as the same heat that had overtaken her in that tower stairwell walloped her again. And so inappropriately. The man was hurt, and no matter her feelings about him, she was certainly not going to leave him to die while she dithered about his *lips*.

That thought spurred her into action. She vaulted out of the sailboat onto the dock, then charged her way up into the village. She slipped the Sicilian Sky off her finger as she walked, tucking it into her pocket, and told herself it was only smart not to brandish such a valuable piece of jewelry about in a strange place where she was more or less on her own.

Once in the tiny medieval village, she used her rusty Italian and got directions, not to a hospital, but to the local doctor.

"A retired doctor, *capisci*," said the kindly older man as he and the woman Josselyn had taken for his nurse, but who was likely his wife, rushed with her back down to the docks. "This is a small village. For a hospital it is necessary to go all the way to Taormina, but here I take care of what I can."

"It's very kind of you," Josselyn managed to pant out as they hurried along.

And it took the three of them, working together, to get Cenzo out of the boat. Then to move him along into the town, and to the doctor's small, makeshift office. Once again, he seemed half-roused but something like drunk as he shambled along, then seemed to pass out when he was lying on the exam table.

"He tripped and fell," Josselyn told the doctor as he checked Cenzo's vitals. The older man frowned as he examined that growing bruise on Cenzo's forehead. "I'm afraid he fell hard, and onto stone."

"You can wait outside while I check him out, *per favore*," the doctor said, in his careful English. "It is better."

Josselyn agreed that it was. She let herself out of the small medical office that must once have been the house's front room. Outside, the dark had fallen. She sat down on the step and looked around without seeing much of anything, possibly breathing fully for the first time since Cenzo had kissed her.

Since Cenzo had walked into the cottage in Maine.

She shifted, realizing her phone was still in her back pocket, and pulled it out so she could be more comfortable. But then it was in her hand, so she switched it back on and the screen lit up, reality returning in a rush with each incoming text, email, and message.

He had taken her to the castle to isolate her. But now he was out of commission, or at least slowed down.

Josselyn looked back at the door to the doctor's office, where Cenzo was now receiving appropriate medical attention. Then back at her phone, which represented freedom. Or at least, the means to put some distance between her and this man who wanted to maroon her on an island until she became an oversexed Stepford wife.

She swiped through to find a map, so she could see where she was. And there was something about that little dot, blinking at her. Telling her that she was right here, in a coastal village only a bit of a drive up the coast from an airport. Here, not imprisoned on a rock in the sea, firmly entrenched in Cenzo's clutches.

You are here, the dot seemed to say. *And you are* you, *still, despite his best efforts.*

Josselyn hooked her free hand over the nape of her neck, squeezing as if that might do something for the tension there. Then she took a few breaths, trying to reset herself. She could still see him falling backward. And that look on his face—not fear or panic, because he was still Cenzo. If anything, he had looked thunderstruck that gravity dared to assert itself upon him.

She almost found that funny now.

Josselyn wanted to call her father to assure him that she was all right, but it occurred to her as she swiped through to her contacts that she had more pressing things to worry about now. First, her father would assume that she was all right, so calling to tell him she was would necessitate telling him what had transpired. And she couldn't bring herself to break his heart over the phone. Second, and more pressing, Cenzo was likely to wake up fully at any moment, shake himself off, and come after her.

She had absolutely no doubt about that.

And so she had to question why she was sitting there on an old step in this tiny village, wasting precious moments, when what she could be doing was putting space between her and him.

No matter how he tasted. Or how that magical fire seemed to dance in her still.

Focus, she ordered herself.

Over the next half hour or so, out there in an ancient street, she made arrangements as swiftly as possible. At any moment she expected the door behind her to fly open, and the doctor and his nurse to come out, exclaiming the name Falcone to the night sky. It was inevitable, and that meant, ring in her pocket or not, Josselyn needed an escape route.

But when the door opened, it was only the doctor's wife, and she was smiling. A very soothing, professional sort of smile that was not remotely tainted with the sort of awe and reverence the name Cenzo Falcone generally inspired.

Josselyn smiled back, and hoped she looked… Well, whatever would be appropriate if she hadn't just put into motion an escape plan while her husband of less than a day lay in an exam room nearby with a head injury.

"He's looking much better," the woman said, more in Italian than English, but she spoke slowly enough that Josselyn could pick it up well enough. "But he is, how you say, he does not…" She pointed at herself, moving her finger over her face. "He cannot say who he is."

Josselyn nodded, trying to look serious. When secretly, she was perhaps slightly relieved that it sounded like he'd hurt his jaw in the fall. Which would save her his scathing remarks.

"You could take him to hospital," the woman continued. "In Taormina."

"He really can't speak?"

"Confused," the woman said, then shrugged, indicating with some pantomime that Josselyn should follow her inside.

Josselyn responded with even more pantomime that she would follow in a moment, pointing at her phone. She considered her options when the door closed, leaving her outside again, and as she did an SUV pulled up before her. And behind it, another vehicle, but this one with rental hire information on its side.

"You made it here so quickly," she said to the driver of the SUV. "I'm very impressed."

"Grazie," the man said, smiling broadly. "It was nothing."

Because it turned out that when offered an incredible gratuity on top of an already expensive request for speed, people were only too happy to oblige.

"Hold on one moment," she told him, calculating possibilities as quickly as she could. "I might have another job for you. Is that okay?"

The driver assured her that it was more than okay, so Josselyn turned and went back inside the doctor's office.

She braced herself for a round of questions and accusations about what it was she was doing with a man as easily recognizable as Cenzo Falcone, but when she pushed her way into the exam room, the doctor only smiled and asked her to step back out so they could discuss his condition.

Josselyn took a moment, looking past the doctor to where Cenzo stared back at her, his eyes open and an expression she could not possibly begin to categorize in those ancient eyes of his.

She shivered as she followed the doctor into the next room.

"He is awake now, this is good," the older man told her. "It is my opinion that if you watch him tonight and make sure there is no concussion and no more unconsciousness, maybe no hospital is necessary. Where did this happen? On your little sailboat?"

"Oh," she said airily, not sure why something in her cautioned her against telling the truth. "We made a day out of it. A pretty sail, stopping along the way to climb on rocks and things."

She expected the doctor to question her further on that, but he only nodded. "The concern is that he slipped in and out of consciousness a few times. Maybe this could happen again. At the hospital, they will be able to monitor him, make sure that all he suffers is this bruise, you understand."

"I thought he was confused, too?"

"He didn't want to tell us his name." But the doctor shrugged. "There are many people who react like this when they wake up to find themselves somewhere strange. Maybe this is nothing."

What it sounded like to Josselyn was that the mighty Cenzo Falcone did not wish it to be known that he had been laid low in this fashion. No doubt his ego wouldn't allow it. She nodded sagely. "My car is outside, so it will be easy enough to transport him. I really can't thank you enough for your help. What do I owe you?"

The older doctor looked as if he couldn't decide whether to be insulted or amused. "This is not necessary. We are in Italia, *sì*? He is okay, this is the important thing."

Josselyn thanked him, and then there was nothing to do—especially as the doctor and his wife gazed at her so expectantly—but step back into the exam room.

And face Cenzo at last.

He was sitting up on the side of the bed, that livid, darkening bruise doing nothing to dim the ferocity of his gaze. He looked rumpled and impatient and alarmingly sexy, and it was that last part that she was going to have to come to terms with, Josselyn knew. But not here. Not now. Not until she handled the details of this as any decent person would, and then made good her escape.

"There's a car for you outside," she told him in as steady a voice as she could manage. "It will take you to the hospital. Or wherever you want to go, if the standard of care at the Taormina hospital is not to your liking."

Cenzo continued to stare at her, looking more and more thunderous by the moment. He swallowed, as if his throat was dry. Then his head tilted slightly to one side, and she could tell by how gingerly he did it that even that little movement hurt him.

Josselyn supposed she was a great fool, because she didn't like to think of him hurting. It made her stomach go hollow again. Even when she knew that his entire aim where she was concerned was to make sure she hurt. And, through her, to hurt her father too.

Well, she told herself tartly, *you might not get applause for being the bigger person, but that doesn't mean you shouldn't do it anyway.*

And maybe, she thought then, he hadn't been as off base with his comments about her martyr complex as she'd wanted to imagine.

He was continuing to stare at her in that same way, as if he couldn't make sense of her, and it made her uneasy. Or anyway, that was how she chose to interpret the spike of heat and sensation low in her belly.

"It's encouraging that you're sitting up," she said brightly. "I thought for a moment there that you'd suffered something truly terrible, like a spinal injury. But that doesn't seem to be the case, thank goodness."

Cenzo's head tilted again, slightly more. Just slightly.

"I have no idea who you are." And his tone was accusing, as if it was clear to him that she'd done something to him. He shook his head slightly, then winced. "But perhaps this is of no matter, because I do not seem to know who I am, either."

Josselyn could not have heard that correctly. "What do you mean? Exactly?"

He made an expression of distaste, and the impatience she'd seen in his expression intensified. "What I said. You are looking at me and speaking to me as if you know me, but I am certain I have never seen you before. And when the doctor asked me my name, I opened my mouth to tell him but nothing came to mind. Can you explain this?"

And wasn't that the Cenzo Falcone experience in a nutshell, Josselyn thought as she tried to take that in. The man had woken up to find himself in a medical facility with no memory, and his first reaction was not fear or concern. Perish the thought! He instead demanded that others provide him with explanations.

"All right," she said as calmly as she could. "That's a curveball, certainly. What do you remember?"

He considered, then slowly shook his head—wincing once again, as if he'd forgotten he was hurt. "It is as if it is on the tip of my tongue, yet nothing comes. As if I need to concentrate, but when I do, there is nothing. A blankness."

"Nothing at all?" Her pulse picked up and ran. "Not even a shred of something?"

"I know I am speaking English to you, though I spoke Italian to the doctor," he said, his tone withering. Apparently that much was innate. He gestured at his own torso. "I know that I am fit and in excellent health. The doctor told me we were sailing and I can picture sailboats, the sea, beaches and tides..." He lifted a shoulder. "But none of it is specific. None of it is mine."

Josselyn's heart was beating much too fast. Of all the things she'd worried might happen, this hadn't rated so much as a stray thought. Because it was madness. So mad she almost thought he had to be faking it to see what she would do...

Except she couldn't imagine any scenario in which Cenzo Falcone would pretend for even one moment to be anything less than what he was. To appear in any way impaired, or seemingly helpless—not that he was acting as if he was either of those things.

On the contrary, he was lounging there on a hospital bed as if he believed that if he simply made enough demands of her, he would remember himself.

"Clearly you know more than I do," he said then, again with that note of accusation and a banked fury in his old coin gaze. "Perhaps you would do me the favor of telling me something. Like my name."

Only this man would wake with amnesia and fail to find the experience even remotely humbling. Josselyn almost wanted to laugh.

"Your name is Cenzo," she told him, and she expected to see a light bulb go off in him. She expected to see the centuries of Falcone arrogance slam back into place. She watched those eyes of his, waiting for them to change from simply cool and watchful to that full-on predator's stare that made her shiver just thinking about it.

"Cenzo," he repeated, as if trying out the name. "I assume that is short for Vincenzo? I do not feel as if I am a man with a nickname, if I am honest. It seems… Beneath me."

Of course it does, Josselyn thought. And managed, somehow, to keep from rolling her eyes.

"I have no idea if it's a nickname or not," she told him. He had a great many names, after all. Who was to say that Cenzo wasn't one of them? She hadn't been paying close attention during that part of their wedding ceremony. She had been far too busy ordering herself to stand still and look graceful, rather than turning on her heel and bolting back down the aisle to get away from him.

"The doctor made it sound as if you were my wife," Cenzo said, a heavy kind of disapproval all over him. Because along with the accusation and arrogance, he had apparently remained judgmental, too. "Can this be so if you know so little about your own husband?"

And Josselyn's heart beat even faster. She felt herself

grow warm, but this time, not because of anything he was doing. But because of her own audacity.

Because she couldn't seem to stave off the truly insane idea that had come to her. And no matter how she tried to push it aside, it seemed to grow larger and wider inside her.

Until it was all she could think about.

Because if ever there was a man on this earth who deserved a little bit of humbling, it was this one.

She stared back at him, her mind racing. She would have to rent an actual motorboat, or buy one, whatever. That way, she could monitor him herself and if there was trouble, get him back to land more quickly. That was the main thing.

Are you really debating doing this? a voice inside her asked. *You know it's wrong.*

She did. But maybe there were degrees of wrong. Because she had not signed up to be the object of his unhinged revenge conspiracies. And yet he had carried her off to that ruin of a rock, mocked and threatened her, and had been very explicit about what he planned to do to her while she was there.

And she believed that if he hadn't fallen, he would have set about doing exactly what he'd promised. He had already been doing it, she thought, remembering that kiss.

So really, what was the harm in turning the tables?

Unlike him, she had no intention of actually hurting anyone. Unlike him, she had no ulterior motive. This was an opportunity for the great Cenzo Falcone to see the world a little bit differently, for a change. That was all.

Maybe, she told herself piously, it might even make him a better person. In the end.

She couldn't deny that beyond all of that, she would certainly enjoy watching her powerful, overwhelming husband cut down to palatable size.

"Well?" he demanded. "Have you anything to say for yourself?"

And that sealed it, really. Because even now, when he had no idea who she was, what the relationship was, or even who *he* was, that was how he spoke to her. As if she owed him her instant obedience.

Oh, yes, she was definitely going to enjoy this.

And she would worry, later, about how it made her a terrible person.

She would worry later—when their month on that rock was up, no real harm was done, and maybe, just maybe, the vainglorious Cenzo Falcone had learned a lesson.

"I'm afraid the doctor put ideas in your head," she said, and smiled. "And because you've been banged up today, I will forgive it. But you do not normally speak to me in this manner, Cenzo."

She already enjoyed it. That was the truth of it. She already wanted to laugh out loud, she enjoyed it so much.

Instead, Josselyn held his gaze. "You're my servant."

CHAPTER SEVEN

TRY AS HE WOULD, Cenzo could not seem to access the great and abiding joy his employer told him he had once possessed in his job. In his life, which apparently demanded total immersion in that job.

"I have never met a happier servant," the *signora* had told him merrily while his head had still been pounding in that doctor's office. "You have often told me that you could not think of a single thing you would prefer to do. And, sure enough, your joy infused every moment of your day, every task you completed, everything you said and did."

A week later, Cenzo could not imagine how that could ever have been so. He felt a great many things as he sank back into his role, but none of them were joy.

Or even adjacent to joy, by his reckoning.

They had not gone to the hospital in Taormina. His employer had waved a breezy hand and told him that she would be happy to monitor him herself, unless, of course, he had a driving need to seek hospital attention, in which case she would have him transported down the coast at once. And Cenzo did not have to dig particularly deeply to feel that he did not have any such need.

His head had hurt that first day. There'd been a ringing in his ears, that pounding, and a headache every time he so much as drew breath, it seemed. When they'd left the doctor's office, she'd encouraged him to get into the back seat of the SUV that waited for her and had left him there a moment while she conferred with the driver. No doubt he should have listened to the conversation. He should have tried to glean any information he could about the bewildering state he found himself in.

But instead, he'd simply…sat there. And had the distinct sensation that allowing another to cater to him while he remained in the dark was new to him, in some way.

Which would make sense as a servant, he supposed.

They'd driven down to the water, where the *signora* had a boat waiting. A boat she piloted, only waving him off when he suggested that perhaps he ought to do the honors. For surely that was his role.

"Who knows if you remember how to operate a boat?" she'd asked in her merry way. "I'd rather not discover that you don't remember a thing while we're in the open water, if you don't mind."

He had felt as if he ought to argue about that, but hadn't.

And then she'd taken him across the water to a desolate slab of rock topped with ruins, where, she claimed, they would remain for a month.

He had helped as best he could—happy that the painkillers the doctor had given him had kicked in—while she brought the boat into the rocky, unwelcoming shore, then moved it back out again while towing the waiting rowboat. She'd thrown down an anchor and then had made as if to row them to shore.

Cenzo had drawn the line at that. He might have been wounded. And a joyful servant. But he was still a man.

He had done the rowing.

But it was when she started to lead him up the stairs that seemed to march on into forever, and rather steeply, that he was so dubious he'd had no choice but to share it. As perhaps servants did not usually do.

"This is a place you choose to come?" he had asked. "Deliberately?"

The *signora* had gazed at him serenely from two narrow steps above, putting her just below his eye level. "Oh, indeed. It has been in my husband's family for many generations. It's an excellent place to..." She had smiled widely. "Rediscover oneself."

Perhaps that made this the perfect place, Cenzo had thought, for a man as adrift as he was then. Though he could not pretend that anything about it *felt* perfect. Particularly not when the place was nothing but the remains of something better.

But his was not to reason why, he had tried to remind himself as they had climbed. His was to...*serve*, apparently.

He had tried to allow the notion of service to sink into him like the sun. To warm inside him and become...well, palatable, anyway.

When they made it up flight after flight of winding old stairs that wound around and around the isolated rock, he had found he liked the newer part of the castle much better. The ruins made him uneasy. It was as if they whispered secrets of other forgotten lives, draw-

ing comparisons he did not wish to entertain. Cenzo
vastly preferred the sleek lines of the renovated part.
He would not have said that it felt like a *homecoming*,
exactly, but for the first time since he'd woken up in
that exam room, he had breathed easier.

That had made him feel as if he was moving in the
right direction, no matter what else might have been
happening. It had felt like progress.

"You must have a splitting headache," the *signora*
had said as they stood in the grand foyer, all clean lines
interrupted with a bold wall here, a commanding piece
of art there. "Why don't you head to the kitchen and
get something to drink? I'm sure I have some headache
tablets that I can give you."

She had pointed in the correct direction, and Cenzo
had obediently taken himself off to a kitchen he was
pleased to find was as sleek and welcoming as the rest.
He had still found it difficult to imagine himself *serving* in any capacity, but he took it as a good sign that
the kitchen felt like his. The whole renovated part of
the castle did, come to that. But then, he was sure he
had read once—back behind that wall in his head that
he couldn't penetrate—that good servants felt that kind
of ownership over the places where they served. He had
the dim impression of a film featuring stately British
homes and some kind of saturnine-faced butler.

He had found all the glasses in precisely the place
he imagined they ought to be, for his convenience, and
that, too, seemed to indicate that he had indeed spent
time in this place.

It seemed to take the *signora* a great long while to
locate her medicine. When she'd come back, she had

seemed faintly flushed. As if she'd exerted herself in the search for paracetamol. He had opened his mouth to inquire, but had closed it again.

Surely servants did not last long in their positions if they asked such personal questions of their employers. Maybe he'd picked that up in the film, too.

She had slid the bottle over to him, smiling again. And he had admitted, then, that despite the racket in his head, he liked the way she smiled. Too much, perhaps.

"Why don't you take the rest of the night off?" she had asked. "And tomorrow as well. If you like, we can set you up in the master bedroom, because I really don't like to think of you sleeping as you usually do when you're trying to recover from something as traumatic as this has been."

He had tossed back a couple of tablets and swallowed them down without water. "How is it that I usually sleep?"

Again, she had smiled. Angelically, he had thought.

"You prefer a pallet on the floor. That seems austere to me, but you've always claimed that you feel better that way. You don't like to coddle yourself. Strength of body and strength of mind breeds strength of character, you always say."

Cenzo had thought he sounded like a bit of an ass, but kept that to himself.

"I will remain in my usual place, I think," he had said, more forbiddingly than he should have, given that she was his employer. He had tried to look…servile. "And hope it encourages my memory to return more quickly."

And he had thought she looked almost guilty then,

but he'd supposed that was his headache, obscuring everything.

When she had led him upstairs, the room that was designated as his looked like it might once have been a sitting room of some kind, though it featured only chairs and a table. No sofa. Not even a settee. There were suitcases stacked neatly in one corner and on the floor beneath the windows, a single pillow and a pile of nicely folded blankets.

Austere, indeed.

"Don't hesitate to call for me if you need something," she had said.

"I will, *signora*," he had replied.

Though he had privately thought that he would rather die than do any such thing.

He had lain down and pulled the blankets over him, then had waited for his body to relax into what it surely knew, no matter what he remembered. And instead had seemed able to think only of how hard the stones were beneath him.

But as the days passed, he became used to them. And to his little pallet beneath the window.

What he did not get used to in any hurry was his job. Or, as the *signora* told it, his *calling.* More than a career. More than simply something he did for money— assuming he had money out there somewhere.

But no matter how he searched within himself, Cenzo couldn't seem to find anything that resonated with that.

Still, he performed the duties expected of him. He found that he enjoyed cooking in that kitchen where he felt most like himself, whoever that was. He appreciated the excellent ingredients available to him and the greatest pleasure, he found as he compiled ingredients, was serving what he made to the *signora*.

Cleaning, on the other hand, he found distasteful in the extreme. And worse than that, simply tedious. Cenzo could not reconcile the joy he'd been told he'd once felt in performing these tasks with the boredom he felt while doing them now.

Sometimes it felt more like rage than boredom, but he did it all the same.

"Why don't you join me?" the *signora* asked one evening after he'd brought her the small feast he'd prepared. She nodded when he looked at her in surprise. "It seems silly for you to sit in the kitchen, eating by yourself when it is only the two of us here. You might as well enjoy this view too, especially since we are both eating at the same time."

Something in him had turned over at that, though he could not have said what it was.

But when he retrieved a place setting and his own meal, then sat down with her, it felt as if something in him...settled.

Had they eaten in this manner before? Was it a habit? Or was it more of an employer's whim, that she could carry out or not as she saw fit?

He thought he probably had his answer with that last one.

"Your ring is very beautiful," he said, because she was holding her wineglass before her and the ring caught the setting sun, sending it dancing all around them in shards of light. She looked startled, looking down at the enormous ring as if she didn't know how it had gotten on her finger. "Your husband is very generous."

"I suppose he is," she agreed. "But he is…complicated."

"All men are complicated," Cenzo replied. "Men like to claim they are simple, but it is a mask. Where it counts, they are always layered."

She seemed to take a long time to look up at him again. "Are you remembering?"

He laughed at that, then wondered if servants weren't meant to laugh when she seemed to react to the sound. Cenzo cleared his throat. "I remember nothing. But I feel certain, nonetheless."

The *signora* looked back at her ring, giant and blue, like a pool she wore on her hand. He was surprised he hadn't noticed it that first night in the doctor's office, because he'd certainly noticed it every day since.

"I think it is people who are complicated," she was saying. "And never more complicated than in the ways they interact with each other."

He thought it ought to have made him feel any number of things that he could not remember his own relationships. He felt certain, yet again, that he'd had them—even if he couldn't remember any details. In the next moment he knew that was true, because he remembered having sex. Not specifically. Not attached to any particular woman's face, but he knew. He remembered that much.

As did his sex, he discovered the next moment, when the *signora* lifted her face to look at him again and the setting sun made her gleam like honey.

Josselyn. The name bloomed inside him as if he had always known it. *Her given name is Josselyn.*

He grew harder, and understood exactly what the ache in him was, then. "Perhaps complication is a compliment," he said when he could speak without all that *wanting* in his voice. Or he hoped he could. "If relationships were simple, they would be boring, would they not?"

Josselyn seemed to have shadows on her face, or maybe it was the night drawing close at last, after another stunning blue Mediterranean day. "We wouldn't want that. Anything but boredom."

In his pallet, later, after she'd gone up to her room at the top of the tower, Cenzo found himself thinking far too much about this woman he lived with. And served. And had broken bread with tonight.

And wanted terribly, like a fever in his blood.

She was the most beautiful woman he had ever seen. He laughed as he thought that, because he couldn't remember any others, but even so, he was sure that if he could personally remember the faces of every woman he'd ever encountered she would still blow them all away.

The sun moved all over her the way he wanted to do. Cenzo found himself jealous of the *sun*.

Josselyn, he thought, her name like a song in him.

As the days passed, he found he focused on her more and more. Some days he thought he could almost taste her. Some nights he dreamed of kissing her, and there was something about those dreams that made him wake, panting. Hard as a spike. Desperate, which he sensed was not his typical state.

He often toyed with the heavy ring on his finger in the dark, finding it hard to believe that he had ever made the vow of celibacy Josselyn had told him he had.

"I find that doubtful," he had said when she shared this amazing revelation with him. When it had finally occurred to him that if it were a wedding ring, there must have been a wedding. And must therefore be a wife…out there somewhere. A notion that had not sat well with him. "Extremely doubtful, *signora*."

"You truly are a Renaissance man, Cenzo," she had replied, sitting in the little library room in the tower with a book open before her. And surely something was wrong with him that he'd begun to associate that particularly serene smile of hers with information about himself he was not going to like. "You wear that ring as a celebration of yourself. The commitment you made to *you*."

Josselyn looked as if she thought that was beautiful. Cenzo thought he'd like to punch himself in the face. That was a commitment that he could make to himself. It rather sounded like he needed it.

"How extraordinary," he had said. "I do not feel at all like a monk."

"Do any monks actually *feel* like monks?" she'd asked airily. "It seems to me that's the whole point of becoming one. If the vow was easy to make, would it be worth making?"

Cenzo had not shared his personal opinion, which was that some vows were deeply stupid.

Still other nights he lay awake and lectured himself. He told himself that he ought to be grateful. Because it wasn't as if he remembered any part of the job he'd done here before. Josselyn was constantly reminding him. She was unfailingly nice about it, always kind and patient as she told him he usually did things like gather fresh flowers and festoon them about, or scrub the floors with his own hands as he felt that made them gleam brighter. He knew he should have been far more thankful for her willingness to not simply…have him replaced.

But it turned out he was the sort of monk who struggled mightily with anything like gratitude.

And no matter what, no matter how he tried to trick himself into remembering something that might make sense of these choices he'd made, he always came up against that same wall.

His bruises faded quickly, and that almost made it worse. Because then he simply looked like a normal man, but one who'd been born at the beginning of the month. Fully formed, completely useless, and doomed to be a mystery to himself.

Cenzo felt, strongly, that he was not accustomed to finding himself a cipher.

It was better when he focused on Josselyn rather than himself. And the bonus was, he liked doing exactly that.

Perhaps it was the only thing he enjoyed. And perhaps that was the answer to the puzzle of his identity right there.

"What does your husband do when you take month-long trips to a place like this?" he asked one evening as they sat together in one of the rooms off the kitchen, because the wind had picked up too much to eat outside. She usually came to sit with him in the kitchen as he prepared their dinner each night, and, in turn, he had taken to eating with her all of the time now. It seemed simpler.

And though she hadn't reissued her invitation, she hadn't rescinded it, either.

Once again, Cenzo questioned how it was he had ever taken joy in servitude when he took far too much pleasure in pushing boundaries he shouldn't have.

Perhaps it is precisely the pushing of these boundaries, with her, that you took pleasure in, a voice in him countered.

Cenzo had no trouble believing that.

"I believe my husband has an endless capacity for entertaining himself with his own bank balance," Josselyn replied in a darker tone than usual. "Some men are like that. It is about what can be bought and sold, always. That's the pleasure they take in things, if they take any pleasure in anything. And it isn't about money, because believe me, they already have enough."

"Men are hunters." Cenzo shrugged. "What they cannot stalk for their dinner, they must hunt in other ways."

She looked at him curiously. "What do you hunt? Can you remember?"

"I cannot," he said. Yet for once it did not bother him. "But I feel certain that whatever it was, I was very good at it."

He liked the way she laughed then, as if delighted, even though he was baffled by it. For he had come to realize that no matter what, no matter that there was that wall preventing him from remembering the details about his life, he felt very sure about who he was.

Supremely certain.

And as he sat there, thinking about that certainty while Josselyn's laughter made music between them, Cenzo could suddenly triangulate a life that made sense.

Finally.

There was that ring on his finger that Josselyn told

him was a vow he had made. There was what she claimed was his commitment to his role here—his service to and for her. And the third point of that triangle, the most important point, was Josselyn herself. His *signora*. The beautiful woman whose laugh was brighter than the sun, and who sometimes smiled at him and made his chest feel too tight.

He could see the purpose in that life. And the beauty in it, too.

And perhaps that was the recipe for joy—maybe even that joy she had told him he had always felt in his work.

Maybe the work was incidental and the point was her.

He felt something in him roar at that, like a dragon, and knew it was the truth.

"It's a good thing that even getting knocked on the head hasn't taken away your sense of yourself," Josselyn said, though she did not sound as if she thought it was all that good.

"Surely losing one's memory should be clarifying." He found himself lounging back in his chair, his gaze on her. "Surely I should become more of who I am, not less."

Her dark eyes seemed particularly mysterious to him then. "That's the internal debate, isn't it? Some think a person is made of certain immutable characteristics, set in stone at birth. Others are sure it's our experiences that make us who we are. It's the nature versus nurture debate, and I'm not sure either side has ever won it."

"I cannot speak to your philosophy," he replied. "But while I may not recall the details about my life, I find that knowing myself does not appear to pose a challenge."

"You are a man with a singular sense of himself,

Cenzo." Her voice was quiet, and she seemed to cling tighter to her wineglass than she usually did. "You always have been."

"And your husband?" he asked. Because it was difficult to recall that she had one, he could admit. He didn't like that she was married. And there seemed no point in pretending that his acceptance of that unworthy thought wasn't also the acceptance of another, even darker truth. He wanted her regardless of her marital status. That was the beginning and the end of it, because she already felt like his. Cenzo could only hope that the things he wanted weren't stamped all over him as he gazed at her. "Surely you must have married him for his own collection of…singular characteristics."

She blinked then, an expression he couldn't read flashing over her face. He thought she looked almost… uneasy. Even upset. But she lowered her lashes and when she lifted them again, the expression was gone as if he'd made it up.

"My husband and I are separated," she told him, her voice sounding odd to his ears. "He is…focused on other things at this time."

"Is that why you are spending a month here?" With him instead of the man she'd married. The one who had a greater claim to her than he did, a notion he did not care for at all. "To find your own focus?"

But she stood then, and he knew that meant she was cutting off this conversation. And right when it had gotten interesting. Sure enough, she smiled in that way he already knew meant she did not intend to continue. Ever.

"I don't know why I mentioned that. It's irrelevant."

She cleared her throat, but that smile of hers seemed far less serene than usual. "Good night, Cenzo."

"Good night, *signora*," he replied, because that was the appropriate thing to call her.

Her name was a treasure he hoarded and kept to himself.

Josselyn headed up into the tower, but he lingered in the kitchen long after he'd cleaned away the remnants of their dinner.

It was as he had told her. He couldn't remember the details of his life, but the things he did know were bedrock certainties.

Like this one: Her husband was a fool, but he was not.

And if her husband was not man enough to claim the wife he had, Cenzo saw no reason why *he* should respect such foolishness.

Because he was the one who was here, making Josselyn laugh.

He was the one who tended to her, feeding her and caring for her, day in and day out.

As far as Cenzo was concerned, he was the only husband she needed.

CHAPTER EIGHT

JOSSELYN COULD NO longer pretend that she was anything but a terrible person.

Some days that weighed heavily on her. Other days, she rationalized that having made the choices she already had, there was no going back without causing even more trouble.

She had felt guilty immediately. The very moment the words were out of her mouth and Cenzo had blinked, clearly trying to imagine himself *a servant*. Josselyn hadn't been able to imagine it herself, really, but she'd said it. There was no taking it back. Surely that would confuse him even more.

That first night, she hadn't slept, because… Had she really told the man to go sleep on the floor with a head injury? Yes, she'd offered him the master bedroom, but she couldn't pretend she hadn't known full well he would refuse. That was why she'd rushed into the tower and moved his things. And surely that level of manipulativeness made her evil. Rotten to the bone, just as he'd believed her father was.

The way she'd told him his mother was, little though

he'd wanted to believe her in those last moments he was still himself.

Josselyn thought about that all the time—the poison his mother had fed him that had led him to think his only reasonable course was revenge.

What do you imagine his reaction will be to this *act?* her conscience liked to ask her daily. *He might well prefer a dose of poison to scrubbing floors.*

She'd tried to assuage her conscience by surreptitiously checking on him every hour on the hour throughout that first night, and the next few nights as well, just to make sure that her questionable desire to get her own back with him didn't result in any actual health issues on his part.

But he seemed in perfect health save for his lack of memory.

A few days into it, after she'd waved a hand and told him that he liked to clean the castle's many windows every Tuesday, she'd taken the hired boat out again. The helpful driver of the SUV that night in the village had arranged the whole thing for her, only too happy to do what he could after she'd demonstrated that she had unlimited funds at her disposal.

It was even a nice boat, she'd thought that first night, and then again when she took it out once more. Fast enough that she could make it back across the water to Sicily in less than half the time it had taken her to sail. That was good to know. It made her feel much better about choosing not to take Cenzo to the hospital. Once she'd determined that she could get to Taormina fairly quickly if she had to, she'd taken the opportunity to call her father. Just to check in. And to assure all her friends that she was alive and well in her archaic arranged marriage, despite all their proclamations of doom.

When she'd calmed all the nerves she could, she'd spent some time downloading articles on head injuries from the internet so she could make sure that she wasn't irreparably harming the man. And could spot any signs that his health was taking a dive.

As the days passed, Cenzo not only exhibited no signs of decline, he seemed to thrive. More and more by the day. And Josselyn was fascinated that even though he couldn't remember a thing, he was in no way less himself.

Arrogant. Commanding. Steeped in the whole of his glorious history. And quite obviously mystified by the notion that anyone would ever choose to be a servant, which she couldn't help but find entertaining.

Because you're an awful person, she would tell herself again and again.

But then she remembered what his plan had been for their time in this place. The revenge he planned to take on her, thanks to the lies his mother had told him. She knew they were lies. She'd read the woman's letters. And surely even this terrible charade she was inflicting on him was better than *that*. Because *she* wasn't trying to make *him* a slavering addict, so that she would somehow break her own father's heart for more of a taste.

She wasn't trying to *break* him. That was the difference, she assured herself.

Though her conscience wasn't so sure.

"You look distressed," Cenzo said one evening as

they sat out on the balcony, though the air was cool. Even here summer waned, however mildly. He indicated the first course that he'd only just brought out, a rich stew of eggplant, pine nuts, and plump, sweet raisins. "I hope it is not the *caponata*."

"Of course not," she replied. "How could it be? Your cooking is marvelous and you know it."

He inclined his head, regally. And despite herself, Josselyn wanted to laugh. Because for all they might have talked about nature versus nurture in their time here, it seemed that Cenzo's sense of himself was truly innate. He simply was that arrogant.

Even as a servant, he behaved like a king.

"And yet you do not look happy, *signora*."

"Is that important to you?"

And then, instantly, she hated herself for asking. Why was she torturing herself? Asking questions that had no answer, because this intent man who cared for her in his own imposing way was not her husband. She was all too keenly aware of that. This was a version of him, but she knew perfectly well that one day Cenzo would remember his true self—or they would leave here and someone would tell him the truth—and he would hate her. The way he had already hated her when he'd married her.

It made her stomach hurt to contemplate.

"It is quite clear that you are the focus of my existence," he said dryly. "How can you doubt it? You are all I remember."

"We'll see how you are in a few weeks." Josselyn tried to sound severe, because she wanted to laugh again and that felt perilous. It felt intimate. She wanted to bask in this version of Cenzo, who looked at her so intensely but clearly without any desire to harm her.

It made her imagine she could see things in those old coin eyes that she knew were never there.

Or wouldn't be there if he was himself again.

She was a terrible person for this. Josselyn knew she was. But the longer it went on, the less she seemed able to help herself. She would lie awake at night in that wide bed, high in the tower, and decide that tomorrow she would pack him up in the boat, take him to a real hospital where they would recognize him at once, and face the truth about what she'd done.

The truth and what would follow it. His condemnation. Possibly his loathing.

But every morning she would wake up and find herself in the alternate reality she'd created. Where beautiful, impossible Cenzo smiled when he saw her. Where he saw to her comfort, inquired about her needs, and more than that, talked to her as if she was a person instead of a tool to wield.

And in that alternate reality, it was far too easy to get caught up in how astonishingly attractive he was, especially when he wasn't seething with buried rage and revenge. How egregiously gorgeous. Especially because this Cenzo seemed to have no notion of how to dress like the richest man in the world. She supposed it was her fault, because she'd never corrected him when he'd appeared in little more than casual trousers and a T-shirt on the first day. She hadn't insisted that he dress like a butler because she'd been far too busy excoriating herself for her lies.

As the days wore on, she almost wished she'd in-

sisted on the formality. Because maybe if she had,
she would be able to think of him differently. Instead
of catching her breath every time she looked up and
saw him studying her. All that intensity and focus of
his, and all of it sharply focused on…tending to her
happiness.

Ruthlessly.

So implacably that it made her burn and burn.

Josselyn could not say that she was actually happy
in this situation. She was far too aware of the game she
was playing. And how temporary it all was, whether
she was burned alive or not.

Their time here was running out. Their days were
numbered.

And because it was temporary—or so she told herself—
she permitted herself to enjoy it.

Because this version of her husband was a delight.

He talked to her. He listened to her. He seemed genuinely interested in what she thought, what she said, what
she felt about anything and everything.

She knew better, but he made her heart beat funnily
when he smiled at her. He plied her with food. He insisted on running her baths. His eyes followed her everywhere. The heat in him found the fire in her, and
they both grew hotter by the day.

And even though she knew that he was just a version of Cenzo that she'd created, Josselyn found that
she was susceptible all the same.

Because it turned out that the Cenzo who existed
without a thirst for revenge was, more or less, pretty
much the perfect man.

A man who asked after her family and when she

told him of the tragedy that had taken her mother and brother so long ago, had reached over and placed his hand on her arm. A simple expression of solidarity in grief. In loss.

Even though she knew he could not recall his own loss, his own grieving.

It had moved her far more than any words might have.

This version of Cenzo was the man she'd dreamed he might be when she'd allowed herself to hope that she might have what her parents had.

Knowing he would hate that he had fallen so far was like an ache in her, because she knew that if she could, she would keep him this way forever. No matter what that made her. She couldn't unknow such a thing about herself.

"I have been considering the matter closely," he said one day, as they explored the ruins down near the waterline. It had been Josselyn's idea. Because she thought she needed to actually *do something* with all the strange nervous energy inside of her. Before it burst out of her in inappropriate ways. "But I cannot decide if I am a good man or not."

She looked out through a hole in what had once been an outer wall. She saw the sea before her, that impossible blue. And yet more knowable than the man behind her.

"Surely if you question such things, that already makes you better than some."

"Can a man be good if his thoughts are...unworthy?" he asked.

Josselyn wanted to ask him why he paused over that

last word. She glanced back at him, but as usual, his intense focus made her uncomfortable.

Uncomfortable is not the right word and you know it, she scolded herself internally. Because what she felt was too hot. Too interested. Too aware that there was no one on this hunk of rock but the two of them, that he was her husband, and that if she wasn't mistaken, the way he looked at her during these lost days of too many lies was lit up with all the same heat and need she felt herself.

Hotter than the Sicilian sun.

"Thoughts are just thoughts," she managed to say, trying to sound philosophical. "It's what you do that matters."

Indeed it is, she thought, and didn't quite manage to keep from wincing.

"It's what you do that is judged," Cenzo countered. "But it must begin within, is that not so?"

"I don't know why you're asking me if you already have an answer."

Her trouble was that all of this felt far too cozy. Too revealing. The searching conversations they kept having, too deeply personal even if he couldn't remember why he would never have had them with her before, felt like intimacy.

It felt like she was getting to know him. The *real* him.

She was all too aware how dangerous that line of thinking was.

Because the real Cenzo would loathe this. He would hate her for allowing him to expose himself. Josselyn knew that.

Yet she also knew that the real Cenzo would have taken great pleasure in doing the same thing to her.

So who was she to lecture him on how to be good?

"Maybe you can't remember the details of who you are," she said after a moment, turning her back to the watchful sea. "But maybe you don't need them. Do you have a sense of right and wrong? Do you know how you feel about things? I think the clues to who we are must be wrapped up in that."

"I believe I am a good man," Cenzo said with his typical conviction. But then he paused, studying her, the sun pouring over him like it wanted to hurt her. "Or I would like to be one. But I do not know if every man thinks these things. Perhaps it is no more than a convenient and flattering way to think of oneself."

"I believe that if you want to be a good man, then you can make sure that you are one." Josselyn's chest ached. "No matter what the provocation. No matter your past. No matter what lies have been told."

His copper and gold gaze seemed brighter, then. "Tell me what that entails."

And somehow, without her noticing, he had drawn close. She found her back against that half wall and then there was Cenzo above her, blocking out the sky.

She felt her breath change. She felt everything inside her pull tight, then seem to shimmer.

"It's not a recipe that you can follow," she whispered. "It's life. It's each and every choice you make over time."

Like the choices she was making now. Or not making.

"Maybe it is not that I truly desire to be a good man."

His voice was low. His gaze moved over her face, seeming to catch on her lips. On that mark just beside them. "Maybe it is that I wish only to be good for you."

"Cenzo..." she began.

"Let me in, *signora*," he urged her, his voice a dark thread that seemed to wrap all around her, then tug.

Again and again, pulling her to him. Making her want things she shouldn't.

Why shouldn't you? something in her asked. *This version of Cenzo would not hurt you. This version would hurt himself first.*

"Let me in," he said again, and his hands were on the wall beside her head. His face was lowered, hovering there just above hers. It would take so very little to surge onto her toes, lift herself up, place her lips on his.

Again. At last.

Some part of her thought she'd earned it. That she deserved a little pleasure here, before reality ruined them all over again.

"Josselyn," he said, and it made a new sort of heat prickle at the back of her eyes, because oh, how she loved to hear her name in his mouth. His perfect mouth. "You must know that all I wish to do is serve you."

And that almost broke her, but it was a gift.

Because it reminded her who they were.

The real Cenzo Falcone had no wish to serve anyone, least of all her.

Even so much as kissing him now would make her no better than he was. The way he'd claimed a kiss on the boat that first morning, the way he'd branded her with it, had told her in no uncertain terms who he was. But that didn't mean she needed to be like him.

She ducked away, out from beneath his arm, her heart pounding so loudly that it echoed back off the ruins. She wouldn't have been surprised if they could hear it all the way across the water in Taormina.

"Is that a bad thing?" he asked, turning so his eyes could follow her, though he stayed where he was. "I would have thought rather the opposite. Who does not wish to be served? In any and all capacities?"

Josselyn wished she could breathe regularly. She wished she couldn't feel that wildfire slickness between her legs. She wished it didn't seem like he was in control of her body even though he was no longer *this close* to touching her. And hadn't touched her.

And, because he believed himself her servant, might not touch her at all unless she granted him permission.

She couldn't tell anymore which part of that made her shudder, sending all those goose bumps prickling up and down her spine.

"The trouble is that you don't know what you really want," she managed to say. She even sounded vaguely in control of herself. "How could you? You don't know who you really are."

"You have told me who I am." He shrugged, and he looked dangerous and beautiful. Ancient and untouchable, standing here in these ruins where his ancestors had fought and died, lived and loved. She was sure she could feel their ghosts all around them, judging her as harshly as he would. "And I might not know any number of things, *signora*, but I do know that the things I want are not a mystery to me."

"I told you I was married," she said, expecting that to be a dose of cold water on this situation.

But Cenzo only shrugged, the corner of his mouth crooking up. "So you say. You have run away from this husband of yours and isolated yourself here, where no one can reach you. And you took me with you. I cannot say I see this husband of yours as a barrier."

She laughed at that, helplessly, because what else was there to do?

"You may not consider him a barrier," she said, her voice cracking a little. "But believe me, he is a force. When you feel that force, you will think quite differently about all of this."

His smile widened. "I like my chances."

The absurdity was almost too much for her. "Cenzo. This is not something that's going to happen. It wouldn't be right." She rubbed her hands over her face, not the least bit surprised to discover she was shaking. "Weren't you the one who was worried about how to be a good man?"

"I am not so concerned, it turns out." And though the day was blue and clear, Josselyn was sure she could hear thunderstorms brewing in the distance. "Whether you want to admit it or not, *la mia bella signora*, there is a fire between us."

"There may be," she said, because she thought denying it would make him more resolute. And because it might also actually, physically wound her to deny it. "But that doesn't mean we have to let it burn us alive."

"Maybe, Josselyn, I wish to burn."

"I don't."

It was not the first or even the worst of the lies she had told him, but this one stung. Horribly. Wounding her, just as she'd feared.

And because she was holding on to the faintest shred of virtue here in the middle of this mess she'd made, she made herself turn and walk away.

Before she found she couldn't.

CHAPTER NINE

As THEIR MONTH on the island wound down, Cenzo discovered, if not quite a joy in his menial tasks, a sense of satisfaction in completing them.

And could not help but feel it as a kind of victory.

He found he liked the simplicity of their days on this rock. He woke on his pallet, which he had come to appreciate. It was always still dark when he rose, and he liked the faint hints of dawn on the other side of the windows as well as the cold stone beneath his bare feet as he moved through the castle. Up and down the many stairs. He liked to run all the steps, twice, before making his way to the kitchen to begin preparing the *signora*'s breakfast.

He brewed strong coffee every morning, then threw together some batter to make the morning buns he knew Josselyn preferred. Particularly as a counterpoint to his rich, bitter coffee.

Of all the tasks he completed in the course of a day, he thought he liked none so much as when Josselyn wandered into the kitchen, her lovely, soft eyes still shaded with sleep. She always looked so grateful for the coffee he pressed into her hands and the sweet roll he'd made for her that was usually still warm. So grateful that it made him wonder about her. About the life she'd led on the other side of this strange month. About the things he couldn't recall. That such a small thing could bring her such obvious joy seemed to him like some kind of miracle.

He took it as daily evidence of her husband's unsuitability.

A topic he liked to think about a great deal, especially when Josselyn set off for her morning ramble about the ruins. Cenzo spent the mornings cleaning. He started at the top of the tower and worked his way down, and while that was one more area of this life of his that he would not describe as joyful, per se, he had come to find a certain fulfillment in the completion of his daily chores. And he liked that as he did them he could see Josselyn down below, frowning out at the sea as she took her morning constitutional, moving in and around the ancient stones.

He liked to think that what she worried over, as she stared out toward the horizon, was him.

Just as he liked to think that her nights were sleepless as his were, because the fire could be denied but that didn't make the flames any less bright.

"This is our last day here," she told him that morning, a tautness in the way she held herself that he disliked. "Men will come tomorrow to take us back. When they do, things will change."

"What will change?"

Today she had taken her coffee and her bun out to the terrace. It was another warm morning, the sun and the sea in seeming concert, as if the whole world was that same gleaming blue. Just like the blue stone she wore on her hand.

Something in him shifted uneasily as he stared at that stone today. The ring was always commanding, but it seemed to him almost to echo inside him this morning. But he couldn't quite catch hold of it. Like a melody he knew he recognized, though he'd forgotten all the words.

Cenzo concentrated on Josselyn instead.

He had grown to consider himself something of an expert on her expressions. On every stray feeling he could read in those lovely brown eyes of hers or the color in her cheeks. They seemed grave to him today.

"Everything will change," she warned him. "You must prepare for that. Things have been very simple here, but this is not the real world."

"You must tell me what my position is like in the real world, then," he said, not liking the dire way she was speaking—but also not particularly concerned. Let things change. He would remain the same. He was certain of it. "I'm not sure I know what the position of personal manservant typically entails."

Her smile seemed dry, and in any case, went nowhere in her eyes. "I don't think that's a title you're going to embrace."

"Come now, *signora.*" And he threw caution to the wind, then. "If you wish to release me from my position, say so. If that is the change you mean. Or I will be forced to think you are running away. That will not make your marriage any better. You must know this."

She swallowed, visibly, but she did not drop her gaze.

"I had hoped that your memory would come back

while we were here," she said, evenly enough. And he might have thought that his words had not affected her at all were it not for the pulse he could see beating out a mad rhythm in her neck. He liked that. He took some pride in it. "I hoped that you would not have to face reality without knowing who you really are."

"You are more concerned with who I really am than I have ever been." He could have sat with her at the little table, but he felt too…restless. That near-melody in his head was driving him a little bit mad. He leaned against the rail instead. "To be perfectly honest with you, I do not care at all what or if I remember. I know what I need to know."

"I think that's easy for you to say that now," she replied, sounding…cautious. "Because you don't know."

"This is what I know about myself, *signora*." He had started calling her that because it had seemed appropriate. It was a reasonable way to address the lady of the house. Or the castle, in her case. But he had come to like the way it tasted on his tongue. And better still the way that each time he said it, she always reacted. A widening of her eyes, a darkening of all that brown. A sucked-in breath, or her lower lip suddenly pulled between her teeth. Oh, yes, he liked it. "I am strong. I sleep upon stones and rise refreshed. At first it seemed to me that a life of servitude must be demeaning, but I have not found it so. There can be no shame in it. Everything I do here, I do well. What have I to fear from a reality that can only offer me more opportunities to excel?"

Josselyn laughed the way she did sometimes, as if she couldn't quite believe the things he said. As if she couldn't quite believe *him*, though that didn't make any sense.

"What's remarkable is that I know you believe this. You might even be right. Still, I know things that you don't know. And, Cenzo, there's no telling what kind of reaction you'll have when you learn them."

She looked so serious that he almost wanted to ask her more questions. To find out what she meant.

But he dismissed the urge almost at once. Because what did he care? He couldn't remember it anyway. He had vague impressions of what the world out there contained. When Josselyn had told him they were off the coast of Sicily, he had known not only what Sicily itself was, but other things about it too. That it sat off the coast of Italy. That it was a part of the Mediterranean region. Over the course of this month, with the help of some of the books in that small library, he'd assured himself that while he might not know himself, he knew the world.

He did not know how to tell her that he was not so concerned with what the world might show him. He was far more convinced that he would be the reckoning upon the world. But saying such things could only sound arrogant, coming as they did from a manservant.

Her manservant.

Josselyn had told him all along that what he did mattered far more than what he thought. That was how he decided, there and then, in the glare of their final morning and her dark predictions about what waited for them when they left this island, that he might as well do what he had wanted to do all along.

"Enjoy your morning," he told her. "And let me

worry about the things I will learn tomorrow. There can be no need to ruin our last day on the island, can there?"

She looked torn. She even opened her mouth as if she was about to tell him something important, but stopped herself.

He waited. Because, for her, he would always wait.

"Cenzo..." she began again, but when he only raised a brow, she shook her head.

Then left him there, going off on her morning walk.

It was a longer one today, but that gave him more time to prepare her lunch. And his plans. When she walked back up he met her in the courtyard, carrying a large basket with a thick blanket over one arm.

"What's that?" she asked.

"I thought we should have a picnic."

Josselyn moved her sunglasses to her head, anchoring back her thick, glossy hair. She was wearing one of her dresses today, a short-sleeved, pretty punch of color that ended far enough above her knees to make him feel the fire of her, everywhere.

But the look she trained on him was questioning. "Is that a joke?"

"Am I a man who makes jokes?" His voice was dry. "I cannot remember, but I rather think not."

She smiled. "No, indeed. You are many things, but I've never known you to be a comedian."

"Then perhaps you should accept that I have packed a small feast and intend to feed it to you in the open air, complete with a lovely view of the sea."

And it occurred to him after he set off, taking the stairs that wound not toward the ruins, but toward the back of the rocky island, that he was once again acting as if he was the one in charge rather than her.

He could admit that it felt more natural to him.

Cenzo felt that strange echo again, but shook it off.

And besides, Josselyn followed him. That told him she couldn't be too concerned that he had ideas above his station.

The spot he had in mind was a rocky outcropping, nestled slightly below where the first castle must have stood. It was accessible only by the stairs he took to reach it, carved into a smooth fall of rock with a sheer drop to the sea below.

"I don't ever come this way," she said from behind him. "Probably because it's terrifying."

"You will live, *cara mia*, I promise."

It was not until he'd walked a bit more, with only her shocked silence behind him, that Cenzo realized he had used an endearment. That it had just…slipped out. And it was certainly not the way a manservant addressed his mistress.

But he could hear her feet against the stones. She was still following him. He might have breached the rules of proper etiquette, but it hadn't turned her away.

The trouble was that every time Josselyn failed to put him in his place, he only felt bolder.

It was as well that this was their last day here, then. Better they should sort out what was between them alone, here, before the world intervened.

Before there were external reminders of the difference in their stations.

The outcropping had a thick wall behind it where flowers had grown over time, spilling down from above like a curtain of bougainvillea. And there were stones marking the cliff's edge, making it less dangerous than it might have been otherwise.

"What do you think this was used for?" Josselyn asked as she stopped in the middle of the wide ledge, her gaze out on the ocean before them.

"A lookout station, I imagine," he replied without thinking about it. It was only when she turned to look at him that he realized he'd said that with perfect authority. As if he knew.

He took a moment to examine himself, and it was true. He knew it. "Does that qualify as a memory? I feel certain I am right about this place. It feels like a fact."

"Why don't we call it a fact, then."

And she smiled at him.

That damned smile. It was the ruin of a man, though Cenzo felt nothing like ruined. She smiled at him and his heart danced in his chest. She smiled and the sea and sky seemed to tangle around each other, changing places and he hardly cared.

She smiled and the world stopped dead. And he had to believe that even once they left this place, it would be the same.

And what could he care about the world when he had her?

Because there were whole worlds in this woman, and he wanted to know each and every one of them.

Cenzo spread out the blanket he'd brought, then set about unpacking the lunch he'd made them.

"This isn't a lunch," she said admiringly, coming over to drop down to her knees on the edge of the blanket. "It truly is a feast."

"Mangia," he murmured.

He threw himself down on the blanket, stretching out on his side. And he watched as Josselyn helped herself to the food he'd prepared for her. Cured meats and hard cheeses, piled high, *arancini*, fried balls of creamy risotto, *busiate al pesto Trapanese*, the Sicilian version of pesto with a favorite local pasta shaped like a coil. And a tower of his handmade *cannoli* to finish.

Cenzo liked watching her as she filled her plate, and then, better still, while she ate. Josselyn was not missish, or overly delicate. She wasn't afraid to eat with her fingers, or lick them, or sigh lustily when the flavors overtook her.

He found all of it almost unbearably erotic.

"Why aren't you eating?" she asked. "I hope you don't think that will keep me hanging back politely. It's all too good. Must be the sea air."

"Must be," he agreed.

And he would have eaten, but he wasn't hungry. Or not for the food he had prepared, anyway.

"When is the last time you went on a picnic?" he asked. "It appears to make you giddy."

Josselyn frowned as if she meant to argue, but then the frown melted into a smile. "I don't know that I've ever been on a picnic. This might actually be my first time."

"Then you should be celebrated." Cenzo sat up and pulled out the bottle of wine he had brought, bubbly and sweet, much like she was today.

"Oh, I couldn't possibly," she began, already frowning.

But she went quiet, her cheeks flushed red, when he handed her a glass.

Cenzo lifted his glass in a toast, and the clink of the glasses together shot through him like yet another echo of the song he surely should have known by now.

But that was one more thing he could not bring himself to care about, not when his *signora*, his Josselyn, was sitting there before him, her bare legs kicked out in front of her and her shoes tossed off to one side. The breeze played with her hair the way he wanted to, lifting strands here and there and making her beauty seem all the more impossible.

"You will forgive me," he began, though at that moment he didn't care if she did. Even if he knew she would object, Cenzo needed to say it. "But you are the most beautiful woman I have ever seen."

She laughed, but her cheeks got brighter. "I am the only woman you've ever seen, as far as you know."

"Not true," he argued. "There was another woman. At the doctor's."

"Fair enough." Josselyn rolled her eyes. "I will accept that of the two women you remember seeing, you find me more beautiful than the one old enough to be your mother."

"I dream about you," he told her, keeping his eyes fixed on her face. And ignoring the tightness in his chest. "Then I wake to you each morning and the waking is better than what I dream at night."

Josselyn made a soft, sighing sound, and set her glass down on the blanket between them. "You shouldn't say these things. You can't mean them. You have no context."

"You keep telling me what I *might* feel. What I *might* know. Sometime in the future, perhaps. But I can tell you what I know now." Cenzo felt that echo in him again, but it felt like her. As if she was inside of him. "You, Josselyn. Everything in me is filled with you."

He thought she looked anguished. He watched, everything in him hectic, as she got to her feet. He liked the way she moved even now, lithe and easy. She moved to the rocks at the cliff's edge and he took a moment to appreciate the picture she made there, her hair blown back, her dress moving over her body, as she stared out into eternity.

Only then did he follow her. He came to stand behind her, close enough that her hair danced over him at last.

"I may not know who I was two months ago, but I know you," he said, his mouth at her ear. "I know you want me, Josselyn. It is written all over you. Every time you look at me. Every time you smile, or laugh. I don't need to remember anything when you are before me. I can see all the things I want as if they are emblazoned upon you."

"Wanting something doesn't mean you should have it," she said, though her voice was low. And he could feel the tremors that went through her, one after the next.

"Why shouldn't you have it?" he demanded. Then his hands were on her, taking her by the shoulders and turning her to face him. There was a kind of misery in her gaze, and he couldn't stand it. He couldn't bear it. "I do not wish to be cruel, but if this upset is for your husband, you must forget him. What kind of man allows his wife to go off with another man and live like this for a month?"

Josselyn was shaking her head. "Even if I told you everything that I know about you, don't you see? It would only be a story you were told. It would mean nothing."

"Let us write our own story," he said.

And then he could wait no longer.

Cenzo lowered his mouth to hers, and finally—*finally*—took her lips.

And kissed her as if his life depended on it.

It did, somehow. He was sure of it.

And it was a marvel of sensation. He felt exhilarated. As if he'd come home at last.

Better still, that fire between them ignited.

He thought she might pull away and run from him once more, but instead, she melted against him. And then, when he angled his head so he could taste her deeper, wilder, she surged against him, wrapped her arms around his neck, and threw gas straight into the flames.

Cenzo kissed her again and again, then had the presence of mind to scoop her up into his arms and carry her back over to the blanket. He lay her down in the middle, like she was one more dessert. A sweet banquet for him to enjoy.

He came down with her, every part of his body tight with need and wonder, because she was finally in his arms. *Finally.*

"I shouldn't let this happen," she whispered, though she made no move to get up.

"I want you," he told her, though it was more than that.

His heart was involved, and every bone in his body,

and every last part of him—from his dreams at night to his every waking thought. But he worried that if he called it what it was, she would balk.

"I want you," he said again, as if it was a vow. "And I cannot imagine there is any knowledge on this earth that could change that."

Then he set his mouth to hers again before she could argue, kissing her until she was pliant and soft. And for a lifetime or two they were tangled together like that in the open air, as if they were a part of the sea and the sky at last.

And it was true that he couldn't quite remember other women, but that didn't mean Cenzo didn't know precisely what to do. He pressed openmouthed kisses down the length of her neck, so he could set his mouth to that pulse that always betrayed her.

His hands skimmed down the front of her body, finding her curves and then making his way to the hem of that flirty little dress so he could do the whole of it in reverse. But this time with his palm touching her warm flesh and exulting in it.

He found her hip, then her breasts, and he could bear that only for a moment before he pulled back from her, stripping the dress up and over her head and tossing it aside. She wore a lacy little half bra that lifted her breasts to him as if on platters.

This banquet, he could not deny. Cenzo bent his head to taste her, to devour her.

To worship her.

And the first time she shattered, it was like that, her back arched and her nipple in his mouth while he played with the other, using her body like it was an instrument.

His instrument, playing his tune, at last.

Her moans licked all over him, spurring him on. He found the shallow dent of her navel, then moved even farther down to bite gently at one hip and to grip the other, his fingers wrapping around to test her plump behind. He spread her out before him, using his shoulders to keep her legs apart.

And he liked that she wore another little scrap of lace there, just covering her sex.

He followed suit, covering her mound with his open mouth, sucking gently on the lace until her cries changed pitch.

Cenzo stripped the panties off her hips and down her legs, then settled himself back into place. He drew her perfectly formed legs over his shoulders, lifting her up on the shelf of his hands and licking his way into all her soft heat.

She tasted even better than he could have imagined— and he had done little but imagine it this whole month. He found the center of her need and played with it, taking his time to find what made her jolt, what made her cry out. He filed away every buck of her hips, every arch of her back.

He learned her. All of her.

Cenzo brought her to the edge, then receded. Over and over, until she was sobbing out his name, throwing it out into the sky above them, the sea beyond.

And only when her fingers were sunk as deep into his hair as they could get and her hips seemed to rise of their own accord, did he finally take her over.

He held her there, still shattering and shattering

around him, until he thought that his own greedy hardness might undo him.

Only then did he sit back, looking down at this bounty before him. She was astonishing. Her taste was in his mouth, tart and sweet, and she sprawled out before him like a dream. He felt her beauty like a physical blow, as if Josselyn was shattering him simply by lying there.

And she was. He could feel it—everything inside of him turned to glass, then cracked into shards—as if he was defenseless.

As if he was hers.

It took him a mere moment to strip off his clothes and then he was coming down to her again, gathering her to him, so that at last they were naked together.

At last.

Cenzo knew that it had only been a month, but it felt to him like a lifetime. And even though he knew she was right, that he couldn't remember and lacked all context, he still had the bedrock certainty that he would feel the same no matter what he remembered.

Whatever his life might turn out to be, he needed her at its center.

It was nonnegotiable.

And he would prove it to her.

He positioned himself above her. Her eyes, dazed now, found his. His hardness moved through her slick heat, and he felt himself very nearly roar with the gut-punching pleasure of it.

"Cenzo," she managed to breathe out. "Cenzo, there's something I must tell you—"

"You can tell me anything you wish, *la mia amata,*"

he told her, his gaze locked to hers. His beloved. "Anything at all."

Josselyn blew out a breath. Her hands were pressed against his chest, but not, he thought, as if she wished to push him away so much as pull him close.

"I'm a virgin," she said.

He tried to take that in. He tried to make sense of it. But he couldn't. It was like a tidal wave, and there was nothing to do but swim.

"I told you, did I not?" Cenzo looked down at her as the wave hit him. Because there was only one truth. Only one conclusion. "You were always meant to be mine."

She shuddered, but he wasted no further time concerning himself with a foolish husband and a pointless marriage he did not pretend to understand.

Nor did he care. Not when there was this. *Her.* He worked the hardest part of him into the mouth of her sex until he felt the resistance in all that slippery heat.

Mine, something roared inside him. *Always and forever mine.*

Then, heeding an instinct he could not have named, Cenzo drove himself inside her.

And as he did, something burst inside him, an interior explosion of light and echo, like an endless cascade.

It went on and on, even as below him, around him, Josselyn shattered anew.

Cenzo was lodged deep inside her. Her heat seemed to scald him as she cried out and the rocks bounced the sound of her pleasure back to him, like a symphony.

And he knew.

He knew.

After far too long stumbling about on the wrong side of that wall, Cenzo Falcone knew exactly who he was. And what this wife of his had dared to do to him.

CHAPTER TEN

IT FELT AS good as it hurt.

That was Josselyn's last and only thought before
the power of it swept through her, leaving her shaking,
gasping, and little more than a mess of too much sensation and need.

She had thought him big and strong as he'd stood
beside her on the altar. But his strength seemed new
to her now, braced above her on a soft blanket with a
curtain of bougainvillea behind them and the Sicilian
blue all around.

New, too, because he was *in* her.

He was inside her, and the thought made her clench
down on that rampantly male part of him so deep within
her own body. Josselyn shuddered, and she was pleased
when she heard him hiss as if he felt that same rush of
pain melting into pleasure.

When she found his gaze again, he looked…different.

His predator's eyes were focused on her, intent in a
different way.

A familiar way—

But then, before she could work out what that might
mean, Cenzo began to move.

And all the things that had come before, each new sensation that had wrecked her and remade her, was like nothing compared to this.

The heat of him. That thick, impossible steel. The way he moved, each deep, drugging stroke teaching her that she knew nothing at all about her body, about the things she could feel, about what she'd been put on this earth to do.

For surely it was this. Two bodies become one, and in the becoming, this bliss. This joy, hot like fire and so sweet that it, too, hurt.

Josselyn wanted to hurt like this forever.

She wanted to keep her eyes on his, searching for something she couldn't have named if her life had depended on it. But instead, it was as if her eyelids were too heavy. They drifted shut, leaving her simply lost in the glory of this.

The rhythm of it. The advance and retreat.

As if they were no more and no less than the waves, the tide, the sea itself.

The sensation inside her sharpened, the glory of it expanded, and then everything broke apart—

And this time, as Josselyn spun out into nothing, she heard Cenzo let out a roaring sound, then fly away with her.

She had no idea how long it was they lay like that, his face buried in the crook of her neck, his weight too heavy and yet perfect. It was exactly what she most needed, just then. To be held and contained when she thought bits and pieces of her must have scattered from one end of the Mediterranean to the other.

And she felt as if she might cry when he finally

stirred, pulling out of her body and shifting to one side. Though he pulled her with him, rolling her so she was braced there on his chest, and that was new. Different.

It was all so new and different, Josselyn could hardly make sense of it.

Her breasts felt huge and oversensitive and every time she breathed, they seemed to drag against his wonder of a chest to send new heat spiraling through her. His legs were strong and hair-roughened and the slide of her soft skin against them made her...quiver.

Josselyn suspected she was a mess, yet she couldn't seem to make herself care the way she usually would. Because she knew she shouldn't have let this happen, but she had to fight with herself to remember why. All she wanted was to do it again.

And again.

She wanted to go back in time and spend their whole month like this. Why had she spent these days playing such stupid games when she could have been learning all these mysteries that started and ended where his body and hers came together?

Cenzo smoothed her hair back. It took her a moment to really focus on him, this gorgeous man who knew her now as no other ever had. *Or ever would*, something in her whispered.

His gaze moved over her face and she could feel it like another touch. Her beauty mark, her lips. Each cheek, as if he was committing her to memory.

When she had long since done the same with him and those aquiline features, brutal and beautiful, that could have been stamped in steel, bronze or gold.

When his gaze met hers again, it seemed to punch through her, stealing her breath.

He lifted his head, and kissed her gently, sweetly, on her mouth.

Then regarded her steadily, that mouth of his unsmiling while his mythic eyes blazed.

"Cenzo?" she asked, something cold spinning inside her.

"Little wife," he replied, an edge to his voice she hadn't heard before. *Not in a month*, she corrected herself. And her face must have changed as the import of his words finally hit her—as that not quite endearment slapped at her—because he smiled. "Your tragedy, Josselyn, is that I remember everything."

Her heart stopped. Or maybe she only wished it did, because when it kicked into gear again, it made her whole body shudder.

She tried to push away from him, but for a long moment he held her fast—a quiet, unnecessary display of his superior strength.

Then he finally let her go, but the message was clear.

Josselyn hardly knew what to do with herself. She expected him to rage at her. Something dizzy inside her wheeled around and around and she wondered if he might simply toss her off the cliff, here where she doubted very much she would live through it the way he'd claimed she would before.

You coward, a voice inside her chimed in then, harshly. *It would be remarkably convenient if he did such a thing, wouldn't it? Then you would never need to face what you've done.*

Her hands were shaking as she struggled to pull her

panties back on, then somehow fasten her bra with fingers like ice. She felt sheer relief when she finally pulled her dress back into place, and then stood, keeping her eyes on Cenzo.

Waiting for what must surely come next.

As she had always known it would, sooner or later.

He was standing now, dressing far more slowly than she had. Lazily, even. Josselyn wished that she could read his mind. That he would share his thoughts as he had this last month, but instead he only looked at the remains of their picnic there on the blanket.

"A servant," he said in wonderment, though there was that sharp, dark edge beneath it. "You made me a *servant*."

All of her justifications and rationalizations tasted like ash on her tongue, but she was a different woman now than the one who had married him, so filled with foolish hope. For one thing, she was no longer quite so naive. She had seen what she was capable of, how petty she could be, and there was no unknowing that.

But she was also terribly afraid that she had fallen in love with a man who did not exist.

A man she was married to, for good or ill.

"It is what you wanted to do to me," she reminded him, fighting to keep her voice level, and not quite succeeding. "Why is it so different?"

"My ancestors built this castle," he said, still in that same tone. "And you had me sleep on the stones they lay with their own bare hands. For a month."

"Wasn't that what was on offer to me?" Josselyn countered. "Either in a bed with you, the man who announced he wished to ruin me, or wherever I was most uncomfortable—isn't that what you said?"

He stared at her for a long moment, and it was as if she could see two men before her, one superimposed over the other. The ruthless man she had married, cruel and unconcerned with her feelings. And then the Cenzo who had lived with her here this past month, who had cared for her, worried over her, and made love to her.

One had made her a wife. The other had made her a woman.

And her heart felt firmly broken between the two.

He did not say another word, and that felt like a deeper indictment. Instead, he turned on his heel and started back up those stairs that had led them here.

Josselyn stayed behind, letting the adrenaline and all that leftover sensation wash through her, not surprised when she felt faintly sick. Rather than give into it, she busied herself with packing away their picnic and folding up the blanket. She did not look at the edge of the cliff again, for fear that strange near-joy that she'd felt at the rail far above one night would take her over again.

Because if it did she would never know if she wished to fly—or if she was taking the most expedient exit route away from this shamble of a marriage. And her own shameful part in it.

Cenzo had only threatened her, after all. She was the one who had actually gone through with it.

Eventually she started back up the stairs herself, one hand on the wall beside her. She concentrated only on the steps themselves, not the steep drop-off to one side, because looking at the water far below made her feel dizzy.

She made it back up to the gate, if slowly, and when she pushed her way through it, she braced herself for Cenzo. Would he be waiting? Would he be even more furious? Was it anxiety that charged through her…or anticipation?

But he wasn't there. She heard only her own footsteps echoing as she walked across the courtyard to let herself in the wooden door of this place she had been tempted to consider a kind of home of late. More fool her. It had only ever been a home of lies.

Inside, Josselyn walked carefully through the pretty rooms that flowed in and out of each other on the first level, her eyes moving this way and that to see if she could find him. For she had no doubt that she had not heard the last on the subject of her treachery.

But the more she thought about it, the more her own temper seemed to wake up inside her, blowing away the shame that had bloomed first.

Because he had planned to do these things to her. He'd been only too delighted to tell her all about it. She needed to remember that.

Not that two wrongs made a right, but it was important to remember that there *were* two wrongs. Not one. Not only hers.

She slid the picnic hamper onto the island in the kitchen, the blanket folded on top, and acknowledged that she'd expected to find him here. But the kitchen was ominously empty. Josselyn thought a moment, then set out to look for him. But it wasn't until she took the stairs down to an odd little gallery that ran along the side of the castle that she finally found him.

A place she had only ever visited once before, back when she'd arrived here.

Cenzo was standing, arms crossed and an unreadable expression on his beautiful face as he stared at a series of paintings on one wall. Across from him were three stained-glass windows, all sending a mad, giddy light dancing over him, tempting her to imagine that he was something other than dangerous.

When she knew better.

"Cenzo," she began.

But his hand moved, slashing through the air in a universal demand for silence, and the peremptory gesture made her jump slightly. And had its intended effect, because whatever words she thought she might say, they disappeared into the sudden constriction in her throat.

He did not look at her, keeping his gaze on the painting in front of him.

"Falcones do not divorce," he told her, his voice dark and low. "And that should not bring you comfort, little wife. It should terrify you unto your very bones. Because that means that I will never release you. I will never set you free. I will spend the rest of our lives making certain you understand exactly what it is that you did to me here. And paying for it. Again and again and again."

Her pulse picked up, but her temper came with it. "It's threats like those that lead a newly wedded wife to tell her husband, stricken though he is with sudden amnesia, that he's a servant. And threats like those that make it difficult to feel as badly about that as I should."

He turned to face her, his gaze a terrible fire. "Do not

worry, Josselyn. I will make certain you feel as bad as you should. I will dedicate myself to the task."

She believed him. And she could see their life together, rolling out before her, dire and upsetting forever. It made her stomach knot.

"If I had it to do over again," she said, because it was true and she thought she owed him the truth, if nothing else, "I wouldn't tell you that you were my servant. Though I do not think it has done you any particular harm to spend a month imagining that, for once, you were something less than the center of the universe."

"I will thank you not to imagine you can decide whether or not I have been harmed."

"Cleaning a toilet does not actually harm a person, you know," she shot back at him. "Any suggestion it does is, at best, melodramatic."

He only lifted a cruel brow, and she missed the other version of him so much it stole her breath.

"Is that so, *cara*? Because you have spent so much time in your pampered life scrubbing toilet bowls?"

And she could see it then, the true force of his temper. She could see the blaze in his eyes easily enough. But more than that, she could see the way he held himself so still, so carefully, as if the slightest thread that held him together might snap at any moment—and he might, too.

Josselyn should have been terrified by that, but what she felt instead was something closer to exhilaration.

It didn't make sense. Then again, none of this made sense. She had been raised to be meek. To obey her father, because they both knew that no matter her feelings on the subject, he truly did have her best interests

.at heart. She'd gone along with this marriage because she'd trusted her father—and, she could admit now, because Cenzo was more work of art than man and she'd had foolish, girlish hopes.

But this past month had taught her that when push came to shove, she was not meek at all.

And maybe, in another scenario, that might have made her a monster.

Yet she rather thought that here, on this remote island where Cenzo had intended to enslave her with sex and isolation, it made her a contender.

At the very least it made her his equal.

"You can be as angry as you like," she told him, lifting her chin as if that could take the brunt of his glare. "But I think we both know that given the opportunity, you would have happily done the same."

His jaw was so tight that she could see a muscle flexing there. And his eyes were little more than a blaze.

"This is a portrait of my father," he told her, indicating the portrait beside him. "I looked at this portrait every day for a month and had no idea who I was looking at. I cannot forgive it."

"I understand." She meant to bite her tongue, but it was as if it had a mind of its own. "But I feel I should point out that you couldn't remember anything. You wouldn't have recognized him no matter what I told you."

Cenzo's gaze blazed hotter, and surely it should have scalded her. "He is the one who renovated this castle. Before his time, there was nothing to do here but camp out in ruins, think about our ancestors, and pray for deliverance. But he made it a home. He used to come here every summer and spend at least four weeks alone. He said he liked the conversation between himself, the sea, and the sky." He dragged in a breath. "One year he came back from his retreat, got into the car that waited for him, and instead of driving back to the Falcone villa Taormina, he drove himself halfway up Mount Etna. Then over the side of a cliff."

"I read about his accident," Josselyn said quietly. "I'm sorry."

And it was as if he erupted, though he still stood still. She hardly knew how she remained standing.

"Don't you dare apologize to me," he growled at her. "Don't you dare, not with your wicked father's blood in your veins. Making you a monster like him."

That was a little too close to what she'd been thinking herself—and harder to dismiss when he said it. She focused on the part that wasn't her.

"Maybe now you can tell me what it is you think my father did to yours," Josselyn managed to get out.

"When I can tell you that to his mind, your father was a friend. His best friend, who he misses to this day."

Cenzo looked as if he might explode, but he didn't. He took a moment to breathe instead, while every hair on the back of her neck stood up.

"My father made one phone call when he came back from the island that night," Cenzo said after a few moments had passed. "He called Archibald Christie, his old roommate and supposed friend. They spoke for ten minutes and then he drove off to kill himself. Your father has never divulged the content of that call, but my mother has a theory. She maintains that the phone call was the last step in a campaign of envy your father had been waging against mine for decades. And that night, he won."

"My father never envied yours," Josselyn said, her voice shaking from all the emotions she dared not show. Not here. "He considered him a brother."

"My mother tells a different tale," Cenzo shot back. "Of how your father always wanted her, and how he could not handle the fact that she did not want him in return. How he worked subtly to undermine his supposed best friend, always pretending he might support him and then instead disappearing. Sometimes for years and years. What kind of friend is that?"

"Which years?" Josselyn demanded. "Was it when my mother died? Along with my brother? My father became a widower as well as a single father overnight. What kind of friend was your father not to understand this?"

"He had a darkness in him," Cenzo told her, as if the words hurt him. As if he would have given anything not to say them. "It grew worse the older he got and your father preyed upon it. Instead of soothing my father's fears, he inflamed them. He pushed him, because he bitterly resented that the man you think he considered a brother had not suffered as he had. He made sure that he did."

"That's crazy," Josselyn breathed. "And entirely false. If I were you, I would ask yourself why your mother would tell you such a story."

"Because it is true," Cenzo thundered at her, the stained-glass bathing him in color. "Your father was a poison to mine and he knew it. He took pleasure in it. I know he convinced you that his only aim in arranging a marriage between you and me was your safety, but that is not so. He wanted to make sure that he still had access to my mother and that he could still work his poison—this time, on me."

She wanted to laugh, but nothing was funny. And worse, she could see that Cenzo believed every word he said.

"Where is he, then?" Josselyn asked, her voice soft, but shaking. "I spoke to him when I last took the boat out. He did not demand to know where we were, so that he could race to my side and attempt to influence you. Nor did he attempt anything like that in the past two years—I know because I made his travel arrangements. He must be a terribly ineffectual villain."

"He plays a long game," Cenzo growled. "He is so good at it that you don't even know he's doing it."

"Cenzo, this is madness."

Josselyn tried to find even a hint of the man she knew in his stark features, but there was no hint of him. She had fallen in love with a man who didn't exist. When she'd known better. But she couldn't help wanting to somehow reach this version of Cenzo, too.

She tried again. "Whatever you may think of my father, however manipulative you might think he is, he loves his daughter. I am his only remaining child. If you believe nothing else about him, believe that."

"Yes, such love," Cenzo threw back at her. He prowled toward her, but she didn't back down. She didn't cringe away from him, or so much as step back an inch. Instead, she glared as if he didn't make her shake. Even when he wrapped his hands around her shoulders not hard, but with enough intention to make her quiver, down deep inside. "Such love indeed, that he would sell you to the highest bidder."

"It was an auction of one, as you are well aware."

"Such love, if you are to be believed, that he would deliver you to a man you hardly knew and wash his hands of you, that easily."

"I have already told you that his own arranged marriage turned into something beautiful. He thought he picked the best candidate for what he assumed would be a repeat."

He shook his head, his old coin gaze glittering. "You are delusional."

And she thought he meant that, too.

Josselyn didn't bother to argue the point. She doubted he would hear her. Instead, she held his gaze—and did not back down. "You are well and truly poisoned, Cenzo, but not by my father. He was happy enough to look you in the eye and shake your hand on the day he delivered his only daughter into your tender care. Yet your mother chose to hide. Why is that? If she is so certain that my father is the villain, why wouldn't she use the opportunity of her son's wedding to her enemy's daughter to set the record straight?"

"Because your family has done enough, damn you," Cenzo threw at her.

And then he was kissing her as if his life depended on it.

So she kissed him back in the same way, because she knew hers might. That was how wildly her heart thundered within her.

He swept her into his arms and carried her through the castle, up those winding stairs toward the top of the tower, and he did not spare so much as a glance for the landing where he had fallen a month ago.

Once in the sprawling master bedroom he threw her into the center of that wide bed where she had slept so many nights by herself, then followed her down.

This time they tore each other's clothes off. This time it was less a beautiful dance and more a different kind of combat. Wild and slick.

Hot and edgy.

"Do you think this will solve anything?" she demanded as he thrust inside her.

"It will solve one thing," he growled at her ear, as if his words were torn from him. "It will make this need less sharp."

But to Josselyn, every touch was sharper than knives.

And her curse was that she loved every cut.

Even if, when she woke the next morning, she was alone.

For a moment she was confused, especially because she could hear a sound she hadn't heard in some time—the motor of the large fishing boat that had brought her here.

She leaped from the bed and grabbed her wrapper as she ran, throwing it around her and somehow managing not to trip and kill herself on the stone stairs.

Josselyn raced down to the kitchen, where she had found Cenzo every morning since she'd come here, but it was empty again.

Save the note in bold, slashing handwriting on the island where her coffee and breakfast usually waited.

Find your own way home, little wife. And take heed—I will come for you when it's time.

She crumpled it in her hand, a terrible sob building inside her as she ran through the castle and out through the great wooden door. Then across the courtyard to the old gate.

When she pushed her way through and stood out on the wide steps, she could see the boat pulling away.

And the single, solitary figure standing out on the deck at the stern, his face tilted up toward the castle's heights as if he'd summoned her deliberately.

Just for the pleasure of leaving her behind.

CHAPTER ELEVEN

THE FALCONE VILLA had stood in some or other form for centuries. Each generation made sweeping announcements about all the changes they would make to the historic structure, yet none ever managed to leave so much as a fingerprint.

That was the trouble with a bloodline like his, Cenzo knew. Nothing it touched was ever truly its own.

He remembered his childhood here, mostly spent in the company of nannies and other staff, because his father was always too busy managing the vast Falcone empire.

And his mother was always too busy.

Cenzo felt that same swell of bitterness in him as he found his way through the marble halls he knew so well. The same acrid rush that he'd been fighting since he'd left the Castello dei Sospiri.

It had been another long month.

And Cenzo had been avoiding this meeting.

First, he had indulged his rage. His fury. He had flown to his property in Paris and had availed himself of civilization. The finest restaurants, the most diverting shows. He had told himself he could not possibly miss his flirtation with servitude. He could not possibly find his bed too soft and his waking hours invaded by worries over the happiness of a woman who had betrayed him.

But Josselyn was all he thought about.

And it wasn't as if that faded as the weeks went by. It was only that the longing for her became so commonplace that other things found their way in, too. Like the things Josselyn had suggested about his mother.

Cenzo had dismissed them all, of course—but that didn't keep him from going over them again and again. Especially as he was neither the man who had married Josselyn, bent on revenge, nor the man who had served her. He was both of them, and neither, and nothing looked as it had.

Not his own reflection. Not the world he did not live in, but only inhabited, without her.

And not his mother, either.

He found Françoise where she always was at midday, lolling about in her dressing room and tending to her toilette. Because she did not rise before noon, no matter what. She insisted that her chocolate be placed at her bedside so she might sip it slowly as she considered the day before her. She had always been very particular. And so quick to share her opinions on all things that he had been certain she could not have a single one he hadn't heard.

In this past month, he hadn't been able to stop wondering what he'd missed.

Françoise saw him in the mirror of her vanity table and waved her staff away.

"I hope you've come to tell me of your success," she

said when they'd gone. She sat in her favorite chair, there before her glass, critically examining her face. Ruthlessly looking for signs of age, he knew. He had once thought she was insecure, though he knew better now. "That you have reduced the girl to rubble and made it clear to her father exactly how you plan to treat her. Like the disposable whore she is."

Cenzo could remember, with perfect clarity, the man he'd been when he married Josselyn. He remembered all his plans in detail. He remembered the triumph he'd felt that she had fallen so easily into his clutches and how pleased he'd been that there was an attraction between them, because it would make his inevitable victory all the sweeter.

He could remember all of that, but the driving need to take revenge had deserted him. It had gotten tangled up in the way he'd served Josselyn for weeks, too deeply invested in her happiness to be able to swing that pendulum back to where it had been.

And savoring her innocence had not helped.

Because of those things, it was as if he saw the world in a different way. As if there were new colors and the old ones no longer made sense.

Not just the world in general, but *his* world. And his mother most of all.

"Your absence from the wedding was noted," he told her.

Cenzo would normally move farther into the room, but today he remained in the doorway.

"I should hope that my absence was noted." She let out an affronted little laugh. "I wanted to send a clear message."

And no matter how he had come at this problem, he always ended up in the same place. "I think you may have succeeded on that level, Maman. But I do not think it is the message you intended."

Françoise made a production of swiveling around in her chair so she could stare at him, her only son. Her only son and her only defender.

The sinking feeling inside him, his constant companion this last month, only got worse.

Because he had been heedless in his support of his mother, always. Heedless, reckless, desperate. She demanded no less.

And he, who had thought himself such an independent man, beholden to no one, had always, always done as she'd asked.

You are well and truly poisoned, Cenzo, but not by my father, Josselyn had said.

He hadn't believed that when she'd said it. But as time passed, it had seemed as if her words had grown barbed and weighted. And uncovered poison in him he never would have believed was there.

He still didn't want to believe it.

But he had spent a month of his life living without the driving need for revenge his mother had put in him. He remembered it too well.

That and the ghosts. The memories he'd never wanted to face.

Looking at her today, he felt empty.

"It is as I feared," his mother said, bristling. "You have fallen victim to the Christie girl. Yet another man felled by a taste of a common—"

"Careful, please," Cenzo said with a soft menace he

did nothing to hide. "You are referring to my wife. The future mother of the heir to the Falcone legacy."

His mother gasped, but he could see her clearly now. He could see the calculation in her gaze—and he had to wonder if it had always been there. He feared it must have been. How had he missed it?

"I had every intention of crushing Josselyn beneath my heel," Cenzo told her, still trying to see what he must have seen before. Still trying to find some softness, some real emotion. But there was only her armored beauty and that narrow glare.

Cenzo could remember too many things now, and they were things he should have remembered before he hit his head. But it was as if having amnesia had only awakened him to all the ways in which he'd forgotten the most important parts of his own life. He'd been weaned on tales of the Falcone legacy as if it was the only thing that could possibly matter. And after his father had died, he had been reeling about in despair—and his mother had filled his head with enemies and blame.

It had seemed a natural progression. Grief was for lesser men, surely.

But now he remembered all the rest of it. The strain that had always hung between his parents. His father's increasing isolation and his mother's brittle refusal to curb her social engagements, no matter how many times the society pages printed those photographs of her with other men that made his father ill.

Françoise had spun that, too. *Your father can be jealous, but I persevere,* she would tell him as a boy, as if she was the hero of the tale. Or, *Your father is protec-*

tive, that is all, for he alone knows the many wrongs that have been perpetrated against us both.

Cenzo understood now that he had believed he had enemies long before he knew what that word meant.

But now he knew that his greatest enemy had always been the lies his mother told.

"I am not my father. I will not give you an infinite number of chances. I will ask you once. Did you proposition Archibald Christie?" And Cenzo smiled coldly while she sputtered. "And before you answer, you should know that he kept your letters."

Because he hadn't seen those letters, but he believed Josselyn.

He believed her.

Once he'd understood that, he'd come straight here. For he believed her, even now. Even after she had made him think he was a lowly servant.

Françoise held his gaze, but said nothing.

And as that silence drew out, Cenzo faced perhaps the most shameful truth yet.

That even now, even when he knew better, he had expected an explanation. Something to exonerate her.

"I applaud you for not lying," he managed to say. He let out a hollow laugh. "It shames me to admit I almost wish you would."

Josselyn had torn the scales from his eyes, and he couldn't close them again. He couldn't go back to his willful blindness.

He couldn't pretend.

"You told me he killed himself in despair," Cenzo said, every syllable that he uttered its own condemnation. "After a conversation with Archibald Christie."

"He spoke to Archibald after he left the island and was dead soon after," Françoise replied haughtily. "What other conclusion can be drawn?"

"When did you last speak to him?" Cenzo asked softly. Because he'd spent hours and hours trying to get the facts to make sense with what Josselyn had showed him.

And her silence now confirmed his suspicions.

"He radioed you, didn't he?" he asked. "He couldn't call you from the island, but he often radioed in that year. You would lock yourself in his office and talk to him each night. And I always wondered why, when you told me he was depressed, it always sounded as if you were the one defending yourself. What was he accusing you of, Maman? I'm betting it was all those men you betrayed him with, over the years. And I bet that when he left the island, he called the man whose betrayal had hurt him the most, and first, only to discover the truth."

Her face only twisted. "You are wrong. He was a sad, ill man."

"He was a good man," Cenzo said, his voice thicker than he would have liked. "And he was a Falcone. He never would have killed himself. He drove halfway up Mount Etna so he would not come here in a temper, didn't he? You should never have let me believe otherwise."

And he faced the fact that even then, there was a part of him that wanted her to deny it. To explain all the little things he'd taken much too long to put together. To shine a different light on events that made them all make sense—and allowed him to revere her as he always had.

But she didn't.

Because there was no getting past the letters, was there? She'd written letters, Josselyn had read them, and he would rather have acted the servant for years than have to face what that meant.

"Cenzo," his mother said then, reaching out to him—no doubt reading the resolve on his face. "Cenzo, my son, this girl has confused you."

"On the contrary." He straightened from the doorway. And when he looked at his mother, he finally saw her. He finally, fully, saw her for who she was. Sheer poison, as Josselyn had known when he had not. He supposed that was one more thing he would have to live with. "Remember, please, that everything you consider yours is mine. Do not try to play your games with my wife. Or her father. You may stay here in this villa and rot—but if you test me, Maman, I promise you I will throw you out on the street. With my own hands."

She gaped at him. "You would not dare."

"I would advise you not to try me," Cenzo bit out.

That was how he left her, sputtering still. He had no intention of returning.

And now the weight of her lies was gone, only one thing remained.

The most important thing.

CHAPTER TWELVE

CENZO PRESENTED HIMSELF at the Christie estate in Pennsylvania the next morning. He had expected the door to be opened by staff, but instead it was Archibald himself who peered out into the November early morning gloom.

And did not smile.

"It appears you have already made my daughter unhappy," the older man said, though he still stepped back and beckoned Cenzo within.

"I intend to make it up to Josselyn," Cenzo said stiffly, "but I must also apologize—"

Archibald stopped him, there in the grand foyer where Cenzo had given Josselyn the Sicilian Sky long ago. "You forget that I chose you for my daughter. And I'm well aware that you thought me a fool. But I'm not one. You remind me of your father."

Cenzo's chest was too tight. His throat felt thick. What would have happened if he'd allowed this man to speak with him the way he'd wished to do before the wedding? Instead of steering the conversation away from his father every time? "Thank you."

"I have never known a finer man," Archibald said.

His dark eyes gleamed with compassion, and something else. "It's not only Josselyn that I wish to see happy in this marriage, son. I know that your father would expect me to do this. To make sure, as he could not, that you find the peace he never could."

Two months ago, Cenzo would not have recognized the sensation that washed through him, then. But he knew it now.

"You humble me," he managed to say. And then, "I will not let you down again."

And old Archibald Christie smiled, cannily. "See that you don't, son. See that you don't."

He led Cenzo through the house, in and out of rooms gleaming with the kind of quiet elegance he associated with his wife. Then out into the back, where a covered walkway led to a fogged-up greenhouse.

Archibald inclined his head, then left Cenzo to it.

He pushed his way inside, the humidity enveloping him instantly. There was music playing, a female singer crooning something heartbreakingly wry. He moved between the rows of plants, then stopped dead when he saw her.

His Josselyn. At last.

She had piled her hair up on the top of her head and was wearing a kind of smock over her usual uniform. Jeans and a T-shirt, both simple and sophisticated at once. Like her.

The very sight of her walloped him. She hadn't even turned around to note his presence, and still, he felt as if she'd sucker punched him.

And again, his memories did him no favors. Because all he could remember now was her. Not his plans before he hit his head. Not his certainty in himself after. All of that and then none of it, because all there was in the center, holding up the world, was Josselyn.

She glanced over her shoulder, then froze, taking her time to turn around and meet his gaze.

He didn't know what he'd expected. But it wasn't the grave way she regarded him now.

"You told me you would come. In your note."

He had forgotten he'd written a note. "I did."

"I thought it would be a while. Years, perhaps." She studied him. "I assumed public humiliations would play a part."

He thought of the way she'd sobbed in his arms as she'd taken her pleasure, again and again. The look on her face when he had told her he lost his memory. Cenzo had spent this whole month since he'd last seen her replaying every single thing that had ever happened between them. Over and over again.

And he did not want her gravity.

"You told me you wanted this marriage to work, Josselyn." He lifted a brow. "That you thought we were lucky because we did not start off muddled by romantic notions."

She looked away for a moment, and when she looked back at him she looked more sad than grave. It was not an improvement.

"You don't have to mock me," she said with quiet dignity. "If there was something I could do to take back what happened, I would do it. But I can't."

His jaw felt like granite. "Which part of what happened?"

Josselyn took a visible breath, as if gathering herself. "Making you my servant. It was petty. I regretted it almost immediately, but I couldn't take it back. I apologize."

Cenzo hadn't anticipated an apology. Not *to* him.

"You regretted it, yet you had me cleaning windows and scrubbing floors," he said dryly. "It seems to me that you owe me."

And then he had to bite back a smile. Because he had become adept at reading each and every one of her expressions while serving her. He knew that flush on her cheeks. He knew that particular shine in her eyes.

He was Cenzo Falcone, as close to a king as a man could be without a crown. And once a humble man-servant.

In both lives, he had always gotten what he wanted.

He did not intend for that to change now that he was both men. Now that he had learned both lessons.

"Cenzo," Josselyn said then, sounding…breathless. "Can we just…start over?"

And he moved closer to her, so he was directly in front of her. Close enough that he could have swept her into his arms. He could have kissed her silly, as every part of him longed to do.

But instead, he held her gaze.

And then, heeding the urge of the man he hoped he would become, not the versions he'd been, he dropped to one knee before her.

"I don't want to start over," he told her, every truth he'd discovered along the way in his voice. His gaze. "I don't want to forget a single moment, Josselyn. I want to remember them all. From the moment you came into that room in a cottage in Maine and upended everything. I took you to a ruined castle and thought that I would turn you into rubble, but you are the one who leveled me."

Her beautiful eyes widened. "Cenzo…" she whispered.

But he kept on. "How can I condemn you for the trick you played on me when what I planned to do to you was worse? Some would call it karma. But I call it a miracle." He reached over and took her hands in his, that stone that had cursed so many before him reminding him of what mattered. The sea and the sky and the place they were one. And this woman, who made all of them shine. "Because whether I remembered myself or not, there was you. And I am not too proud to use the debt you feel to keep you with me. To prove to you that despite everything I have done to you, and wanted to do to you, you are the one who won after all."

She looked fierce, even as that shine in her eyes spilled over into tears. "I don't want to win. I don't want either one of us to win, because that means someone has to lose. And what kind of life is that?"

"Josselyn—" he began.

But she silenced him by tugging her hands free and pressing her palms to his cheeks. Bringing her face to his as he still knelt there before her.

"I lost my mother and my brother in an instant. An afternoon storm and that was it. They were gone." Her voice was urgent and low. Her gaze was intense. "Life is so fleeting, Cenzo, and it can end so quickly. You could have died in that fall. And if all you think about is winning and losing, taking revenge and plotting against your enemies, don't you see? You're going to miss the whole thing."

He did see. He saw her, and nothing else had made sense since. Not until he'd found his way back to her.

"I have been two men for you," he told her then. "And I have spent this last month desperately trying to pretend that at least one of them was a lie, but I keep coming back to a single, inescapable truth. I wanted to bind you to me. I wanted to make you unfit for anything at all but my bed. And instead it is I who might as well be rubble beneath your shoe, Josselyn. You humbled me, and yet I think you saved me. Because had you not, I would never know." He lifted a hand and held hers, there where it still lay against his cheek. "Had you not toppled me from the height of my arrogance, I could never have known how much I loved you. How much I will always love you. And whether this life is long or short, none of it will matter at all unless I keep on loving you. Forever."

She whispered his name as if it was a prayer. "Do you know, all the while I was making you clean and cook and serve me, all I really wanted was you. Not the you I'd already met and married, but the one you showed me every night. Not twisted, but real. Fascinating and beautiful, commanding and breathtaking, and that was when you thought you were a humble man with a humble life. I wanted you then." Josselyn blew out a shaky breath. "And if I'm honest, I wanted you before. My father wanted me to marry a man of his choosing, it's true. But if it hadn't been you, there's no way I would have gone through with it. It was always you, Cenzo. Whatever version of you. It was still you."

"I love you," Cenzo told her, gazing up at her. "I want you to marry me, again. Just you and me, the sky and the sea, and who knows what we can do?"

"I will," she whispered. "I will marry you, again. I love you too. Because I have seen both sides of you, dark and light. Cruel and caring. And I have loved them both."

"I cannot promise that I won't revert to form." He took the hand that wore his ring and pressed his fingers to the blue stone that proclaimed her a Falcone. And forever his. "I can only promise that going forward, it will not take a knock on the head to put me right again. All it will take is you, my beautiful wife. My only love. Believe in me and I promise, I will be the man you deserve."

"And I will be the wife that you need," she promised him. "No pettiness or poison, Cenzo. Only this. Only us."

Tears still slid down her cheeks as she bent to him and kissed him at last. First a sweet seal on these vows they'd made today, but then the roar of his dragon rose up, becoming part of that fire that burned between them.

Passion, not poison.

Bright, hot, and theirs, forever.

And then she was in his arms, or perhaps he was in hers, and everything was that heat, that need, that impossible, glorious greed—and all of that was love. Every touch, every whisper, every sigh.

All of it was love, and he knew, then, that it would be like that forever.

They rolled this way and that, there in all that humidity, the air thick and perfumed with growing things.

It felt like a new beginning. It felt like spring, here in a dark November.

Because Josselyn's eyes were bright and her smile was beautiful, and she looked at him as if all she saw was the man he vowed, there and then, he would always be for her.

Always.

She settled herself astride him, still smiling as she looked down at him. His hands found her waist, and they both sighed a little, fully clothed as they still were, as the hardest part of him found that soft sweetness that was only his. Only and ever his.

"I love you," he told her, in every language he knew.

But her eyes lit up in the same way they had when she'd told him he was a servant.

"I promise you this, husband," Josselyn said, mischief in her voice and forever in her eyes. "You will never know a moment's peace. Your life with me will be a delicious agony. I will make you an addict for my touch, my gaze, the barest possibility of my approval."

His own words said back to him were electrifying. They made his heart pound. They made him hunger to taste her again. He wondered if they'd had the same effect on her, back then.

Josselyn leaned closer. "You will live for it. For me."

"This does not sound like a threat, my little wife."

She placed her fingers over his mouth and he nipped at them, making her laugh. "And I will do the same. We will be riotously happy. We will make each other feel safe, you and I. We will not be junkies, Cenzo, because we will know joy. We will raise our children swathed in it. And we will live, as long as we can, loving each other more. And more. And always still more."

"More," he agreed.

Because he was Cenzo Falcone. He would see to it.

And then he started as he meant to go on, there on the floor of her father's greenhouse, making both of them laugh, then groan.

Until, at last, they made each other whole.

And kept right on doing it for the rest of their lives.

* * * * *

COMING SOON!

We really hope you enjoyed reading this book.
If you're looking for more romance, be sure to
head to the shops when new books are
available on

Thursday 16th September

To see which titles are coming soon, please visit
millsandboon.co.uk/nextmonth

MILLS & BOON

MILLS & BOON

THE HEART OF ROMANCE

A ROMANCE FOR EVERY READER

MODERN

Prepare to be swept off your feet by sophisticated, sexy and seductive heroes, in some of the world's most glamourous and romantic locations, where power and passion collide.

HISTORICAL

Escape with historical heroes from time gone by. Whether your passion is for wicked Regency Rakes, muscled Vikings or rugged Highlanders, awaken the romance of the past.

MEDICAL

Set your pulse racing with dedicated, delectable doctors in the high-pressure world of medicine, where emotions run high and passion, comfort and love are the best medicine.

True Love

Celebrate true love with tender stories of heartfelt romance, from the rush of falling in love to the joy a new baby can bring, and a focus on the emotional heart of a relationship.

Desire

Indulge in secrets and scandal, intense drama and plenty of sizzling hot action with powerful and passionate heroes who have it all: wealth, status, good looks…everything but the right woman.

HEROES

Experience all the excitement of a gripping thriller, with an intense romance at its heart. Resourceful, true-to-life women and strong, fearless men face danger and desire - a killer combination!

To see which titles are coming soon, please visit

millsandboon.co.uk/nextmonth

MILLS & BOON

Coming next month

REDEEMED BY HIS NEW YORK CINDERELLA
Jadesola James

"I'll speak plainly." The way he should have in the beginning, before she had him ruminating.

"All right."

"I'm close to signing the man you met. Giles Mueller. He's the owner of the Mueller Racetrack."

She nodded.

"You know it?"

"It's out on Long Island. I attended an event close to it once."

He grunted. "The woman you filled in for on Friday is— *was*—my set date for several events over the next month. Since Giles already thinks you're her, I'd like you to step in. In exchange, I'll make a handsome donation to your charity—"

"Foundation."

"Whatever you like."

There was silence between them for a moment, and Katherine looked at him again. It made him uncomfortable at once. He knew she couldn't see into his mind, but there was something very perceptive about that look. She said nothing, and he continued talking to cover the silence.

"You see, Katherine, I owe you a debt." Laurence's voice was dry. "You saved my life, and in turn I'll save your business."

She snorted. "What makes you think my business needs saving?"

Laurence laughed incredulously. "You're a one-person operation. You don't even have an *office*. Your website is one of those ghastly pay-by-month templates, you live in a boarding house—"

"I don't need an office," Katherine said proudly. "I meet

clients in restaurants and coffee shops. An office is an old-fashioned and frankly completely unneeded expense. I'm not looking to make money off this, Laurence. I want to help people. Not everyone is like you."

Laurence chose not to pursue the insult; what mattered was getting Katherine to sign. "As you like," he said dismissively, then reached for his phone. "My driver has the paperwork waiting in the car. I'll have him bring it round now—"

"No."

It took a moment for the word to register. "Excuse me?"

Katherine did not repeat herself, but she did shake her head. "It's a kind offer, Laurence," she said firmly, "but the thought of playing your girlfriend is at least as absurd as your lie was."

Laurence realized after several seconds had passed that he was gaping, and he closed his mouth rapidly. He'd anticipated many different counteroffers—all that had been provided for in the partnership proposal that was ready for her to sign—but a refusal was something he was wholly unprepared for.

"You're saying no?" he said, to clarify.

She nodded.

"Why the hell would you say no?" The question came out far more harshly than he would have liked, but he was genuinely shocked. "You have everything to gain."

She tucked a lock of dark hair behind her ear, and he was momentarily distracted by the smooth slide of it over her skin. The change in her was truly remarkable. In her element, she was an entirely different person than the frightened teenager he remembered, and she carried herself with a quiet dignity that was very attractive.

Continue reading
REDEEMED BY HIS NEW YORK CINDERELLA
Jadesola James

Available next month
www.millsandboon.co.uk

Copyright ©2021 by Jadesola James

We Love Romance
with MILLS & BOON

Available at
weloveromance.com

LET'S TALK

Romance

For exclusive extracts, competitions
and special offers, find us online:

 facebook.com/millsandboon

 @MillsandBoon

 @MillsandBoonUK

Get in touch on 01413 063232

For all the latest titles coming soon, visit

millsandboon.co.uk/nextmonth

MILLS & BOON
A ROMANCE FOR EVERY READER

- **FREE** delivery direct to your door

- **EXCLUSIVE** offers every month

- **SAVE** up to 25% on pre-paid subscriptions

SUBSCRIBE AND SAVE

millsandboon.co.uk/Subscribe

WANT EVEN MORE
ROMANCE?
SUBSCRIBE AND SAVE TODAY!

'Mills & Boon books, the perfect way to escape for an hour or so.'

MISS W. DYER

'Excellent service, promptly delivered and very good subscription choices.'

MISS A. PEARSON

'You get fantastic special offers and the chance to get books before they hit the shops.'

MRS V. HALL

Visit millsandboon.co.uk/Subscribe
and save on brand new books.

JOIN THE
MILLS & BOON
BOOKCLUB

* **FREE** delivery direct to your door

* **EXCLUSIVE** offers every month

* **EXCITING** rewards programme

50% OFF
YOUR FIRST
PARCEL

Join today at
millsandboon.co.uk/subscribe

JOIN US ON SOCIAL MEDIA!

Stay up to date with our latest releases, author news and gossip, special offers and discounts, and all the behind-the-scenes action from Mills & Boon...

 millsandboon

 millsandboonuk

 millsandboon

It might just be true love...

GET YOUR ROMANCE FIX!

MILLS & BOON
— *blog* —

Get the latest romance news, exclusive author interviews, story extracts and much more!

blog.millsandboon.co.uk

MILLS & BOON

Desire

Indulge in secrets and scandal, intense drama and plenty of sizzling hot action with powerful and passionate heroes who have it all: wealth, status, good looks…everything but the right woman.

Four Desire stories published every month, find them all at:

millsandboon.co.uk